CW01175571

RANGER

DR. REBECCA SHARP

Ranger (Reynolds Protective, Book 4)
Published by Dr. Rebecca Sharp
Copyright © 2023 Dr. Rebecca Sharp

All rights reserved. No part of this book may be reproduced, distributed, or transmitted in any form or by any electronic or mechanical means, including information storage and retrieval systems, photocopying, or recording, without permission in writing from the publisher, except by reviewers, who may quote brief passages in a review and certain other noncommercial uses permitted by copyright law.

This is a work of fiction. Resemblance to actual persons, things, living or dead, locales or events is entirely coincidental.

Cover Design:
Sarah Hansen, Okay Creations

Editing:
Ellie McLove, My Brother's Editor

Printed in the United States of America.
Visit www.drrebeccasharp.com

To Dr. Spencer Reid,

Criminal Minds did you dirty, Pretty Boy.
You deserved a happy ending, so this one's for you.

RANGER

CHAPTER 1

Sydney

It was me—my fault. *I was the problem.* Taylor Swift played rent-free in my head for the last four weeks as what was left of my life imploded.

I'd become *that* author.

You know the one. Hated. Loathed. Scorned.

All because I'd killed off a beloved character.

The number in the little red bubble for my inbox ticked higher, taking my blood pressure along with it. *All. Your. Fault.* I stared blankly at the rows of emails appearing one after another, the subjects coming through in shouty caps. I shouldn't be looking. Gina had already taken away my social media access after *#cancelSydneyWard* started to trend—*thank God I didn't have TikTok*—but she hadn't commandeered my email yet. *Yet* being the key word. My agent and friend was nothing if not dictatorial in her methods of protecting me, and I loved her for it. But this was bad; even she was getting threats now, and it was all my fault.

I'd killed off the hero in a book series because he'd been inspired by my ex.

Hello, Anti-hero? Sydney Ward, here. Hold my beer.

I pulled my mug to my lips, sipping slowly on the hot coffee without care as it singed the very tip of my tongue.

I'd set up everything this morning to dive back into my writing cave for the first time in a month. The lemon candle on my desk oozed sweetness into the air in my New York City apartment. The fresh coffee dripped focus into my veins. The heating pad around my shoulders kept them loose.

I was determined to disappear into my next story and distance myself from the PR train wreck that was my life. Some people called it avoidance. I called it therapy.

"Just keep writing," I murmured to the beat of Dory's "Just keep swimming."

My inner critic whispered back, *just keep running*.

But instead of sticking to the plan, I'd clicked on my email, the unread messages pricking at me like needles to my balloon of creativity.

Emails from readers used to be the highlight of my day. Sure, every once in a while, someone felt obligated to tell me that they hated my books. Or even better, someone felt obligated to warn me that I was going straight to hell for writing spicy romance novels… conveniently forgetting there's an erotic poem included in the Bible. *See? Even God knows sex is good.*

Those kinds of emails were rare, and most of them Gina filtered out before I even opened my inbox. Not only did she filter out the bad, but she'd also created a special folder for the really good ones—the ones I could go back to when I was having a rough day; she'd labeled it "Good Vibes." Gina might have the mouth of a sailor, but she had the heart of a saint.

Which was more than I could say for the readers emailing me.

Subject: WORST AUTHOR EVER!

Subject: I hate you!!! I hope you die!

Death threats. Awesome.

New level of hate mail. Achieved. And Gina was too busy dealing with the fallout of my live television interview with Drew

Barrymore yesterday to have wiped my inbox… or banned me from it.

She was my one-woman trauma response team, except it wasn't looking good for my career. Barely breathing. Weak pulse. Every minute, I just waited for the beep of the flatline.

Subject: How could u do this!!! U ruined everything!

Me? How could I do this? Vince was the one who'd cheated on me—the one who'd slept his way through an army of Hollywood wannabe actresses. *My actor fiancé.* With his dashing smile and rich mahogany hair and perfectly chiseled chin… if he wasn't the makings of my very own book boyfriend… that was the problem.

The dashing actor and the demure romance novelist.

I'd been so stupidly enamored with my own fairy tale that I'd transformed Vince into a book boyfriend. *Literally.* Vince Bauer had become Vance Bower in my bestselling *Undercover Love* series. Vance was the hero to my private investigator heroine, Jenny, who mirrored my long brown hair and brown eyes, my quiet tenacity, and my love for Nutella. Readers had followed their relationship as it paralleled my own. Three years. Three books. A proposal.

And then I found out Vince had cheated. Was cheating. *And he wasn't sorry about it.*

"This is what actors do, Syd. It's part of the persona. Part of the job."

The old "*I had to sleep my way to the top*" excuse. My stomach turned, the memory of that night rose up like bile in my throat. Maybe he was right. Maybe it was the norm in Hollywood, and maybe it was the reason he'd been getting bigger and bigger roles in several Netflix series. Not a leading role yet, but who knew what could happen with one more well-placed screw?

I pressed my fingers to the bridge of my nose. "Dammit."

When I looked back at my computer, what greeted me wasn't any less painful.

Subject: How could you kill him? You should kill yourself!

I killed him. I'd killed the hero in a series that was supposed to have one more installment. Betrayed my readers' trust because Vince had betrayed mine.

But I couldn't keep him. I'd modeled Vance off Vince to a T. If I kept him, I'd never be able to write the last book. So, I killed him… and now, I was being canceled because of it.

Thirty-five novels. Twenty-one *New York Times* bestsellers, fifteen landing at number one, with a combined hundred and forty-two weeks on the list. Two books optioned for films. I was no Nora Roberts, but my rising fame had taken a drastic turn toward infamy.

Subject: You deserve to die! I'll never read your books again!

I couldn't blame them for being shocked and angry and upset. I couldn't even blame the lady who'd jumped up from the audience during my interview with Drew and started screaming at me, hurling insults like she was trying out for the Olympic Hate Speech team. By the time security escorted her from the set, the clips were already going viral on the internet.

My interview wasn't a six-part Netflix series or tell-all biography explaining why I'd done what I'd done, but it had been my moment to share my side… and it was the moment I realized no one cared. Halfway through my brokenhearted confession on live television, I'd paused to collect myself, and that was the moment this woman chose to unleash her hatred *at my very public, very painful lowest*. And that was it. They'd removed her, and I walked off stage.

What was the point? Why open myself up to people who didn't want to listen?

The worst part was that my readers had cared when I'd told them I'd called off my engagement to Vince because I realized he'd been unfaithful. They'd cared then; he'd been the target of their anger then. But they didn't care enough to understand how it changed the course of my book because it changed me.

My phone buzzed on my desk and I jumped, my heart leaping into my throat. I wasn't sleeping. Or really eating. The hate… the threats… the way I'd disappointed people I cared about, it was eating me up inside, and I didn't know what to do. I couldn't go back. But suddenly, it seemed like I couldn't go forward either.

I'd been staring at the same blank page for months, wondering if my own story was as bleak as the one I was trying to create.

"Hey," I answered Gina's call, wincing at just how worn my voice sounded.

"Did you sleep?"

"I closed my eyes. Does that count?"

"No. You need to sleep, Syd." Every day, her worried tone turned up a notch, but today, it was up three; the interview had been a disaster. "Sleep and stay inside."

My heart thudded in my throat. The press had been waiting outside my building from the moment I got home yesterday. Cameras ready, mics waiting like savages ready to pounce on a story.

'What happened on the show today, Sydney?'

'Was that woman a plant for attention? For sympathy?'

'Your ex-fiancé said you'd do anything for a good story.'

I wanted to throw up all over again. It didn't help that Vince took every chance he got to bash me to the press, capitalizing on my fame even though he was the cheater. *No such thing as bad press and all that…*

"And whatever you do, don't open your email. I haven't had a chance—"

"Too late," I interrupted her hoarsely.

Her string of curses made me blush. "Just close it. Right now. Don't read anything. Don't open anything. Just let me handle it."

She'd handled almost everything for me over the last six months. After I ended things with Vince, time passed in a fog. I'd finished writing *Broken Promises* in a betrayed blur, pushing my deadline back twice in the process because I'd agonized over killing off Vance.

Then the book released last month, and it had been a catharsis of sorts—like the last tie Vince had to my life was gone. Except now, what I'd done to protect my mental health was being used against me.

"Don't worry, G. They're not all death threats. Look, I just got to one from Darren that says, 'I've always loved you and I know why you had to do this. I'll be waiting whenever you're ready,'" I told her with a sad laugh. It was one positive email out of the first hundred. "At least someone is waiting for the final installment of the series."

"Syd..."

I knew that tone, and it wasn't good.

"What?" I asked with a strained voice. What else could possibly take me down any lower?

"I spoke with Anna this morning—"

"I have no update," I said without waiting for the question I knew was coming. "I haven't slept, G. What makes her think I've written any words on the final novel? If they want to push the release date, that's up to them, but right now, I can't promise anything."

"Syd..."

Her tone made me stop. "What is it?"

"I don't want to add to your plate, but you have to know... they aren't even sure they want to publish *Broken Bonds*."

My breath rushed from my lungs. "What?"

"After the fallout, they're weighing all their options... including calling it quits on this series."

And calling it quits on me. That was what it felt like—the already gaping wound in my chest being ripped even wider.

"I told her that quitting on the series would be the dumbest fucking thing they could do. Even angry fans are engaged fans, and no matter what they say, almost all of them are going to keep reading to find out what happens to Jenny. *Grey's Anatomy* survived multiple favorite character deaths. Plus, just look at Harry—"

"If you bring up Harry and Megan one more time," I warned, appreciating how she tried to draw parallels to make me feel better, but they were royals—or ex-royals, and I was just a romance author.

"Well, it's the truth. The people who hate them buy into

everything they put out just as much as the people who love them. Anna needs to get her Botoxed brain out of her Brazilian Butt Lift ass and realize that a majority of the readers who are angry will still buy the fourth book, even if it is just to rip you a new one. Again."

"Great." My head dropped, my forehead resting on my palm. "At this point, I don't even know that there will be a fourth book, so all this is moot."

"No. Absolutely fucking not. You're not running from your calling, Syd. You just need a break."

"What?" I couldn't have heard her right.

"A break. And not like a page break or section break. You need to get away. Leave the city. Relax. Soul search," she rattled off as I looked over the top of my laptop at the city skyline stretching along the horizon.

I'd picked this room for my office because I'd felt like a puppeteer from up here—the creative master of my fictional world. Until it all unraveled.

"Get away from what? My life?" I choked out a laugh.

Everything I had was here. My family had been when they'd been alive; I was an only child to a single mother. Mom's relatives were few, and all of them had died before her. My friends... a small circle, I'd admit, because I lived in front of my computer screen, writing à la Nora—eight hours a day, seven days a week.

"I think you should give this situation some time to cool off and give yourself some time to heal. See if the words start flowing again."

"Where would I go?" Why was I even asking this? Was I really considering just up and leaving?

"Out west, for sure. Like Wyoming. There's space and nature and... bison."

"Wyoming..." It triggered my memory, and I opened up the Good Vibes folder in my email, scrolling through the slew of names, many of them repeated, for the one I was looking for.

Wendy. Erin. Jane. Darren. Cora. Jake. Jane, again. Jer—JERRY.

A good chunk of the emails in this folder were from a man

named Jerry, including one he'd sent right after my breakup, inviting me out to Wyoming. I scanned his heartfelt message of support until I reached the town he'd mentioned.

Wisdom.

"It doesn't have to be Wyoming. You know, just somewhere where there's like… nature. And maybe a hot cowboy or two you could take for a ride—"

I interrupted her with a groan. The only men I wanted to think about were fictional ones.

"Okay, no cowboys. Forget the cowboys for now," she retracted. "This whole fucking drama is turning into a pressure cooker, and I think you need to get out of it."

It had to be the lack of sleep that had me closing my email and opening a new browser.

Wisdom, Wyoming.

Time to see if Google was on my side.

A second later, images of the quaint, small town that was a stone's throw from Jackson Hole popped up.

"Wyoming," I murmured, testing the word—the whole idea on my tongue.

"I want you to give yourself some space to decide what you want—if you even want to continue writing this series. Don't worry about Anna. I told her she shouldn't make any decisions on canceling the last book until I've read the first thirty thousand words."

"That's all you need to know if I'm broken?" I teased, pulling up a new search for rentals in Wisdom like I was actually going to go through with this.

"We've been doing this for seven years, Syd. I'll know if your heart isn't in the story anymore."

The invisible band around my chest tightened. *That was what I was afraid of.* If my heart had given up on the story, there was a good chance it had called it quits on me, too.

"And if it's not?"

"Then we'll navigate that plot twist just like we've done all the others, okay?" Gina encouraged. "But first, you need to get out of here. Forget about Vince. Forget about *Broken Promises*. Just get away from everything and take some time for yourself. You've needed it for a long time."

She wasn't wrong. The last vacation I'd taken was the three-day weekend to Vermont when Vince had proposed a year and a half ago. A belated Valentine's Day celebration. *Because he'd spent the real Valentine's Day weekend filming in Miami and probably hooking up with half of South Beach before coming home.*

I quickly blinked away the tears from my eyes, focusing on the sparse apartment rentals on my screen.

Yeah, this wasn't going to work. There was nothing—

I stopped scrolling when a listing caught my eye.

One-bedroom garage apartment. If that was the epitome of my downfall—leaving a New York City penthouse overlooking Central Park for a garage apartment in Wisdom, Wyoming—I didn't know what was.

"Syd? You still there?"

"Yeah." My spine straightened with a jolt of determination. "I was looking at rentals in Wyoming."

"And?"

"I'm booking one," I told her, clicking the reserve button without a second for second-guessing.

"Seriously?"

"Wisdom, Wyoming. Here I come."

CHAPTER 2

Sydney

I wished I could sleep on a plane. The young girl in the seat next to me had dozed off before we even taxied back from the gate. Meanwhile, I'd worn my comfiest leggings and a soft, oversized sweater, but even the double dose of sleep deprivation and a gin and tonic couldn't knock me out for the five-hour flight to Jackson Hole.

The silver lining was that I'd been wide-eyed as the plane descended through the Grand Teton mountains and surrounding lakes and landed in the middle of the national park.

The single terminal was new but tiny—so tiny compared to JFK. Of course, the second I stepped off the plane, I felt like I could sleep for days, so I grabbed a coffee while I waited for my luggage to come out on the carousel and then called an Uber.

"Welcome to Wyoming, dearie. You must be Sydney."

I did a double take when an older woman stepped in front of me as I waited at the curb. *Really? This was my Uber driver?* She had to be at least in her late sixties or early seventies. Her hair was permed to perfection, and her smile beamed as she approached me with an uneven gait.

I double-checked the license plate, but it was right.

"I am—"

"I'm Cindy. Here let me get that." She snatched my suitcase from my hand before I could stop her.

"Oh, it's—okay…" There was no point. She was already popping the trunk to her decade-old white Subaru and hefting my overweight bag into the car like she was a closet strongman.

"This is how I keep my arms toned," she declared, shutting the trunk and giving me a flex of her biceps. I couldn't help but smile. "Now hop in. We've got to get you to Wisdom."

The inside of her car was what I called "grandma clean"—the kind of clean that only existed at grandma's house, complete with that unmistakable scent of potpourri. And sure enough, as I buckled, I saw one of the cup holders was filled with the stuff.

My grammy was obsessed with the stuff. Mom and I had cleaned out so many boxes of it from her house after she'd died.

"All buckled in?" Cindy looked over her shoulder.

"Yeah."

Her smile widened, and then she hunched forward close to the steering wheel and pulled out… with pep… *a lot of pep.* I grabbed for the handle on the door, hoping she didn't notice.

"So, what brings you to Wyoming?" She probed as soon as we pulled out of the airport.

"A break," I answered, staring out the window at the massive mountain range to my right.

"You look like you need one, dearie."

I turned and met her gaze in the rearview. If this were New York, her comment would be an insult, but I'd had far worse things said to me in the last month than the truth. *I looked like shit.*

My hair was pulled up in a knotted mess on my head. There was a coffee stain on my comfy sweater. Every neuron in my brain felt fried. And the bags under my eyes were so big, I was surprised United didn't make me check them at the gate.

But here… I didn't feel any barb. In addition to her Grammy-clean car, Cindy also only had Grammy-concern in her eyes.

"How long have you been driving for Uber?" I changed topics

because if she was any more like my grammy, she'd be prying into my under-eye baggage for all my personal and professional woes before I could blink.

"Two years. I've lived in Jackson my whole life, so I know the whole area like the back of my hand. It's a funny story, actually." She chuckled. "I was at senior trivia night, and a question about Uber came up, and I had to ask the young man on my team what they were talking about because I'd never heard of such a thing before."

Senior trivia night? Did Cindy even have her license?

Of course she did. Uber had rules, I reminded myself.

"Anyway, he ended up showing me on his phone, and then I said how it sounded like so much fun, meeting all new people." She batted her eyes and sighed. "You know, you don't get to meet a whole lot of new people at my age, and if you do, they're new *old* people. And old people, well, they just… up and die… and it's terribly inconvenient."

My laughter surprised no one more than me, and from the way she kept looking back at me, it made her happy to make me laugh.

"I have a calendar to maintain. Book club. Trivia night. *Bingo*. Can't have too many social vacancies." Her eyes twinkled. "So, I got set up on Uber with a little technical help. Now, I get to meet so many new people."

We passed the *Welcome to Wisdom* sign and my breath caught.

The small town sprawled in front of the dash like the scene from an old Western movie. Flat building facades climbed up from the street. Worn but well-crafted to stand the test of time. Ornate but nothing over the top.

People walked along the sidewalk strewn with fall-colored leaves. They were all bundled up for the crisp November day, but no one was in a rush. We passed a couple leisurely window-shopping. A family coming out of an adorable coffee shop. The little boy trying to eat a croissant that was the size of his face.

No one in New York wasn't in a rush to go somewhere. To achieve something. To be someone.

Yeah, I needed some no-rush time.

Cindy rolled through a stop sign because there wasn't another car in sight. Ahead of us, only two stoplights broke up the main drag as far as I could see—which was as far as the mountain range in the distance, the snow-capped peaks stretching up to pierce the cerulean-blue sky.

My jaw went slack, watching the beauty of the mountains drift closer and the town pass by.

"How long are you in town for, dearie?"

I pulled my hair up into a knot on the top of my head. "Two months." Maybe longer, depending on how things went. I couldn't hide from reality—from my real life forever. But I'd stay here until the new year. Hopefully, by then, the press would have new prey to torment; they'd still been camped outside my apartment building this morning when Gina smuggled me into her car to take me to the airport.

"Well, you're just going to love it here. If you ever want a tour, just give me a holler. Happy to take you around." We turned off the main drag, and Cindy slowed the car.

"Thank you." I smiled as she pulled up to the curb.

"And you picked a great spot. Ranger did such a good job with the space. He worked so hard on it," she gushed.

"Ranger?"

Her head tipped. "The young man who owns the apartment you're renting."

"Oh." I swallowed. "Right."

The listing hadn't shown his first name, only Mr. Reynolds.

"He's quite a looker. All the brothers are, and just perfect gentlemen to boot, but Ranger... well, he's one of a kind," she said with a little chortle and shut off the engine.

"Shoot." I scrambled to grab my tote and jacket, some of my things had spilled from my bag from Cindy's *peppy* driving, but I'd been too distracted by the scenery to notice. Arm workout or not—I didn't want the older woman lifting my suitcase from the trunk again.

And I wasn't the only one.

When I made it to the trunk, Cindy wasn't alone.

"You're such a dear, Ranger. I don't know what I'd do without you." Cindy batted her eyelashes at the man lifting my bag from her trunk. I made the mistake of catching her gaze because she winked at me and then mouthed, *"Isn't he handsome?"* In the least discreet way possible.

My cheeks were already flushed by the time Ranger—my new landlord—straightened and faced me.

Handsome, she'd called him, and the word triggered every description of a hero I'd ever written. Tall, broad and muscular with hair that fell perfectly on his head and jeans that molded to his fine figure... *Yeah, Ranger was none of those things.*

My chin lifted to take in all of him.

Okay, maybe he was kind of tall, but it was the lanky kind of tall. He didn't have bulging biceps or a muscular chest under his button-down shirt and... *sweater-vest. Yup, that's right. A sweater-vest.* To be fair, he was strong enough to lift my suitcase without struggling, but that was the most I could determine about his strength.

My eyes greedily traced the lines of his face, always absorbing the little details that could bloom into inspiration later. Nowadays, there was only one phrase for what I saw; Ranger was a *pretty boy*. And the reason for it was because he was classically beautiful.

Handsome was handsome, varying in all its degrees and the eye of the beholder, but masculine *beauty* was a golden ratio layout of facial features inherently pleasing to the human eye. Length of the face. Placement of the lips. Hairline to eyelids. Length of the ears. And when they all came close to one point six, the brain registered that like an orgasm of symmetry—beautiful whether I wanted him to be or not.

Ranger was a sweater-vest-wearing version of Michelangelo's David... except a little more disheveled. His hair... *was a mop*. That was the only word for it. A mop of wavy, warm-brown hair that made him look adorably boyish.

A messy Michelangelo masterpiece.

How young was he? *He couldn't be twenty-five if that.* He looked like he could pass for a college student with his innocent eyes and tossed hair, though he dressed like an old man.

"Of course, Cindy. I'm happy to help." Ranger's voice was smooth and sweet like caramel, and almost immediately, he ducked his head, a lock of unruly hair crossing the boundary of his forehead.

"Sydney, this is Ranger Reynolds." Cindy patted his arm warmly. "Ranger, this lovely young lady is Sydney. I was just raving about the apartment to her. She really lucked out."

My jaw went slack. *Had I ever seen a grown man blush?* I didn't get the chance to think about it before he did this thing that dropped my attention to his mouth... his full lips gently pursed together and then sprung into a smile. A dimpled smile.

Now those dimples... those were the kind of dimples I'd give to a hero. The perfectly lickable kind of dimples.

"Thank you, Cindy," he murmured, embarrassed by the compliment and the attention for a moment before Cindy's loud gasp drew our attention.

"Oh my lordy—I've got another ride. Alright, kids. I've got to jet!" Cindy waved over her head and rushed back to the driver's door. "See you later!"

The door slammed and she pulled away from the curb *with pep.* And left the two of us standing there on the sidewalk.

Ranger looked back at me. "Welcome to Wisdom, Ms. Ward, and welcome to the Reynolds Retreat." His shy smile dipped his dimples a little deeper before it retreated... but not before warmth trickled down my spine.

Was I... attracted to him?

No. It had to be the gin I'd had... six hours ago. And the flying. And sleep deprivation. And the mind-numbing levels of stress. That was why my body was going haywire, mistaking intrigue for attraction.

Perfectly proportioned or not, I'd always been drawn to the

kinds of men I wrote about, the impressively muscular, confident Casanovas. Not beautiful men with dimpled smiles who dressed like the old man from *Up!*

"Sydney, please," I insisted with a soft laugh, adjusting my bag on my shoulder and extending my hand. "It's a pleasure to meet you, Ranger."

His smile fell and he stood frozen while I waited with my hand extended. Seconds passed like I was waiting for a watched pot to boil.

Well, this was awkward.

He stared at my hand like I'd just wiped my nose with it. Or my ass.

God, I needed to sleep.

"I'm... sorry." I dropped my head and my hand, feeling foolish as I rubbed my palm along my thigh. "If you just want to show me—"

"Did you know studies show more pathogens are exchanged by shaking hands than a ten-second kiss?"

My head snapped up, my wide gaze sinking into his mossy-green eyes. *Had he... Had I heard that right?* I blinked once... and then twice. *He had just said that.* I hadn't imagined it. And I didn't even think before replying.

"I'm sorry... was that supposed to be a pickup line?" If it was, it had the poorest delivery in the history of pickup lines.

Ranger's eyes bulged, and he visibly flinched as though I was the inappropriate one.

"What? No." He bundled his arms over his chest. "I apologize. I just mean... I only meant that research has shown that handshakes spread about a hundred and twenty-four million bacterial cells, whereas a ten-second kiss only transfers about eighty million."

My teeth sank into my bottom lip as he spoke. He was so... awkward, and I couldn't help but find it adorable. Any other man would've answered my question with something like *"Do you want it to be?"* and inserted their best smoldering look. But Ranger

Reynolds... tripped and tumbled down a rabbit hole of information, and I was mesmerized.

"That's... a lot of germs."

There were almost four billion men in the world, and I was confident I'd just met the only one who'd use that fact with only the purest, most sanitary intentions.

"Not just germs. Diseases. The common cold. The flu. Gastroenteritis. Hepatitis *A*. Norovirus..." He rattled off the information so effortlessly and without any flicker of guile, plucking it out of his brain as easily as pulling petals from a flower, and I realized in an instant that Ranger Reynolds was smart... the kind of smart that was, well, *well* above average. The kind of smart that put you grades ahead of your age-group and was sometimes accompanied by a neurodivergent personality.

"I had no idea they were so unsanitary," I replied, letting my gaze swim in his. His eyes were so soft and clear, like they'd never hidden a thought or feeling in his entire life—*like they couldn't.*

"Oh, yes. It's quite astounding when you think about it that handshakes are still so commonly used for greeting." His chin dipped, sending a lock of hair in front of his eyes that he haphazardly shoved back.

Another rush of heat burst free low in my stomach. How was it possible to be both adorable and sexy? *And to do it not only without trying... but without even noticing.*

"Yeah, it seems kind of crazy when you put it like that. Maybe we should start just making out with everyone instead," I replied casually—*jokingly*—but Ranger didn't laugh.

He gave me a horrified stare. Oh god, he thought I was serious.

"Well, there are a variety of other greetings, like fist bumps or elbow bumps, that are more hygienic—"

"Ranger," I broke in softly, a smile teasing one corner of my mouth. "I was just kidding."

"Oh." He flushed and his Adam's apple bobbed. "Of course."

And then he did this thing... I didn't even know how to

describe it. His tongue slid out, but it didn't just wet his lips; it pulled his full lips back between his teeth… almost like his tongue was corralling his mouth into quiet.

My jaw went slack, the heat in my stomach knotting itself into a steady ache.

Ranger Reynolds was unexpectedly sexy, and that might just be the most dangerous thing about him.

"Let me show you the apartment. Here, I can take your bag."

I could've handled it from there, but he had that look on his face—the same one that was there when he told me about hand germs; he was carrying my bag for me… *and it was a fact.* There was no demanding or possessive undertone. Just something as inarguable as the number of bacteria transferred during a handshake.

"Thank you," I said, but he was already several paces in front of me, my heavy duffel bouncing against his side.

The garage was a two-bay structure separate from the house, the second level lined with windows though the curtains were drawn at the moment.

He unlocked the door on the left of the garage bays, entering first but holding it open. Inside, there was a flight of stairs up to the apartment and a second door to enter into the garage so that you didn't have to go back outside.

"Here are your keys. The blue is for this door and then the red is for the apartment door." He held out the key ring, practically dropping it into my hand as soon as my palm opened.

He shuffled around, bumping his shoulder and then my bag in order to open the door to the garage.

"I'll show you the laundry room while we're down here." He led me over to a small alcove in the well-lit garage where there was a new washer and dryer and a small countertop for sorting. "If you have any questions, I left the instruction manual on the table and tabbed the most important parts."

Of course he did. I bit into my cheek to hold back my smile, but it didn't matter because he was already leading the way upstairs to the apartment.

It was exactly like the photos online. *A relief because I'd heard horror stories.* The front half of the apartment was an open space shared between the kitchen, dining room, and living room. The apartment was small, so it only fit a love seat, a round dining table with four chairs, and a closet-sized kitchen. *But what more did I need?*

On the other side was the bedroom, separated from the front by a faux brick wall that didn't quite reach the ceiling and the bathroom tucked into the far corner. That was the only part of the apartment that was fully enclosed.

Ranger faced the bedroom, then turned a one-eighty to the living room, and then back again to the bedroom. "Where would you like your bag?"

"Oh, anywhere is fine." I set my tote bag on the edge of the couch, running my fingers along the soft-blue linen.

When I looked up, I could practically see Ranger's brain working overtime trying to decide where specifically to set my bag in the bedroom. On the floor? Next to the dresser? He finally settled on the small bench at the base of the bed.

"Would you like a tour?" He shoved his hands into the front pockets of his khaki pants.

I sighed, suddenly feeling weeks' worth of exhaustion flooding my body. "I think I'll be okay. It's been a long day of travel."

Being here, away from the disaster my life had turned into… it was a relief. I needed to text Gina that I was all checked in, safe and sound, and then I was going to climb into that bed and forget about everything, *including any kind of alarm.*

"Oh, of course." Another thread of his fingers through his hair, like it was sifting through his mass of thoughts to try and find what he wanted to say next. "There are instructions for all the appliances on the table. If you have any questions or need help with anything, my phone number is on the contact sheet, but I live right next door."

"Thank you, Ranger."

More dimples before he dropped his gaze and headed for the door, which was directly behind me. I took a step to the side to move out of his way, but he stepped in the same direction. Then we quickly both shifted to the opposite side.

"Sorry—"

"Go ahead." This time, I pivoted.

He walked quickly by me, careful not to bump me but close enough that I felt the heat of him waft by. Goose bumps trickled over my skin, and I miraculously stifled a groan.

I was losing my mind. But hey, I'd lost so much else, so why the heck not?

Sure, Ranger was interesting and adorable, and I would admit, his dimples were perfection. But I couldn't be attracted to him... not really, not beyond an appreciative recognition for how good-looking he was. My type had been Vince. Charming, well-built, smooth-spoken.

And look at how well that turned out for you.

I shoved the annoying thought from my mind and closed the door. At this point in my life, there was only one type of man I was allowed to be attracted to, *fictional*.

I didn't care where clothes ended up as I fished for my toiletry bag and headed for the bathroom. I'd never been one to linger in the shower, no matter how good the heat felt. I was toweling dry in minutes and heading directly for the queen bed, the crisp white sheets just begging me to slumber.

This was going to be good. I sank into the pillow with a sigh. No ex-fiancés. No angry fans. No intrusive paparazzi. No book boyfriends. Just my little apartment and my awkward landlord.

Ranger Reynolds was as far from a typical romance hero as one could get... maybe that was how he managed to slip past all my defenses and invade my dreams as soon as I shut my eyes.

CHAPTER 3

Ranger

"Is there anything you need from the store, Mom?"

Eggs. Milk. Almond flour. Unsalted butter. Chocolate chips. Peanut butter. The mental list matched the ingredients I was missing for the chocolate peanut butter bar recipe.

"I'm good, honey." Mom walked through the kitchen and peered over my shoulder at the recipe I'd printed out. "What are you making?"

"Chocolate peanut butter bars for trivia night."

I didn't need the recipe; I'd had it memorized the first time I'd read it over. However, if I changed the recipe at all, I liked to note it on the paper before bringing copies with me to trivia night.

"Isn't that at the end of the month?" Mom moved to the fridge.

"I'm going to make the recipe ahead of time to make sure they come out correctly. Gunner said he would try them tomorrow and tell me how they are."

The seniors at trivia night weren't the only ones with a sweet tooth. My next oldest brother loved a good dessert and didn't care about being my culinary guinea pig. Gunner had always been the most reckless out of the five of us, though that had changed notably since learning he was going to become a father. Thankfully, not enough to refuse to test out my snacks.

"I bet he will." Mom chuckled, pulling out one baking dish after another and setting them on the counter. "I'm making stuffed peppers for dinner, and I prepped some for your brothers, too. Can you take them with you to the office?"

Mom might be responsible for the entire town as the mayor of Wisdom, but that didn't stop her from taking care of her children even though we were all grown.

And her stuffed peppers were incredible. She tried to show me how to make them once, but she didn't use a recipe. I tried to measure out the ingredients as she added them, but she told me I couldn't do that... that I had to feel it out. That didn't seem like a good idea; I wasn't good at feeling, so I stuck to baking.

"Sure." I nodded and opened one of my reusable shopping bags.

I worked with my three older brothers at our private security firm, Reynolds Protective. Most of our clients were wealthy locals and businessmen from the greater Jackson area who needed additional private security. Well, that was the part my brothers handled. I dealt mostly with information and risk assessment from my office at our building.

The three of them—Archer, Hunter, and Gunner—all lived on the hundred-acre parcel of property with their families. Meanwhile, I lived at home. In the basement, technically. And our youngest sibling and only sister, Gwen, was the only one who didn't live in town; she'd moved all over working as a nurse before finally settling in Carmel Cove, California, with her husband.

"I saw the light on above the garage yesterday," she said, packing her tuna salad sandwich for lunch next. "Is your new guest all settled in?"

Sydney.

I blinked twice. "I assume so. She didn't want a tour."

She really should've had a tour, but I'd struggled to insist on it. Sydney Ward made me... unsettled. I was still in the process of elucidating what my reaction to my new tenant was. She was very pretty, that was for certain. Big brown eyes. Long, chestnut hair. I knew what she looked like before meeting her because the rental website made everyone upload their driver's licenses for verification, but I also ran an additional background check on everyone who rented my apartment.

Sydney was the first one who didn't look like her photo. Well, she did because it was *her* photo... but she didn't. Something happened when I saw her in person... like I was seeing her for the first time.

There were little bits of gold in her irises that the photo didn't capture. Strands of hair that were more red than brown. There were details I wasn't prepared for, and I was always prepared.

It was very frustrating, and that was why I'd let the handshaking facts slip. I knew from previous experience when I'd explained the same fact to Archer's wife, Keira, that it could be misinterpreted, but I was flustered and it didn't make sense why I was flustered. And when that happened, facts just started coming out because those made sense, those I understood.

Chemically... biologically... my body found Sydney attractive. I'd spent a good portion of that night researching and reviewing all the anatomical and biochemical processes involved in my reaction to her. I wanted facts. I wanted to understand what happened. And I got them.

But what I didn't find was a reason why when she'd teased about making out instead of shaking hands, I hadn't simply mistaken her for serious; I'd wanted her to be.

I'd wanted to kiss my new guest, and there wasn't a single logical reason for it.

I'd never wanted something that was illogical, never experienced my body being out of sync with my brain. And that unsettled me. *A lot.* So, either I was going to figure out what happened to me—what caused my brain to malfunction—or I was simply going to have to avoid Sydney at all costs.

It was logical to avoid things that caused uncontrollable and potentially hazardous reactions. I already had a list of those. Shellfish. Cocaine. Explosives. *And now, Sydney Ward.*

It shouldn't be a problem. I hadn't had much interaction with my previous guests. I was only a contact in case of questions or emergencies during her stay.

"I'm sure she was tired from a long day of traveling." Mom poured coffee from the fresh pot I'd brewed into her thermos.

"That's what she said." My lips pulled tight, and I gathered my things. "Are you sure you don't need anything?"

"You know I like to do my own shopping." She looked at me in a way I didn't understand.

If there was something she was thinking, she should just say it. It didn't make sense why people held back or said things that were supposed to mean something else.

"Is that it?" I didn't like having to ask.

"You know you don't have to stay here for me, right, honey? I do manage to run a whole town by myself."

I blinked. What did being mayor of Wisdom have to do with me living in the basement?

"I know both those things, Mom. What do they have to do with each other?"

She walked over and reached up, cupping her hand to my face. "I just want you to know that you don't have to live here just to help me."

My jaw clenched. This was what I meant. Why couldn't people just give me the facts?

"I know that." Did she not want me here? Was that what she was trying to say? "That's not why I live here."

This was my home. What reason did I have to leave? I had my own apartment in the basement with a separate entrance. I contributed toward the mortgage and utilities. I didn't need space to have people over because there wasn't anyone to have over. I didn't have many friends aside from my brothers and their wives, and they were always welcome here.

I was… different. Weird. Awkward. I wasn't good at making friends like Gunner and Gwen, and I wasn't good at reading people like Archer and Hunter. I appreciated the irony of being able to read twenty thousand words per minute but being unable to read a person.

The only other people I felt comfortable around were children and seniors, and that was because neither group had a filter. I didn't have to read them; they told it like it was.

One day, I'd discover why humans were born with the ability to be honest about their thoughts, only to lose that ability until approximately seventy percent of their lifetimes had passed.

"Okay." She hugged me. "I just like to make sure you know."

"I'll be back later."

"Oh, do you want to take my car?" She offered when I reached for the door.

My car was having new tires put on and yearly maintenance done at Decker's shop. Decker Conolly was a family friend and mechanic who had an automotive shop just outside of Wisdom. He'd helped me find a good, used Volvo to purchase almost a year ago.

"Gunner said he'd pick me up."

Like getting my own apartment or house, having my own car hadn't really been necessary because my brothers could always pick me up and bring me to the office with them. But then they all started getting married and having kids, and logistically, it didn't make sense for me to ask them to continue.

"Okay." Mom went with me to the side door and watched me walk down the steps like she used to do when I was younger, waiting there until the school bus picked us up.

I looked over my shoulder, in the middle of giving her a wave, when I saw movement at the garage.

Sydney appeared in the doorway just as Gunner's Mustang rumbled loudly at the curb. Today, she had on jeans, a big sweater underneath her jacket, and the same sneakers she was wearing yesterday.

She looked up, and our eyes collided.

Dopamine. Norepinephrine. Serotonin. I flipped through the chemical Rolodex of what was releasing in my body to create the surge of attraction, but none of them adequately described the sensation of ungrounded electricity running through my body at the sight of her. The heat. The powerful current. It wasn't logical—*rational*.

I held my hand up in an abrupt wave and then spun, heading quickly for my brother's car. It would be better if we didn't have another conversation. Not until I understood what was happening to me and how to make it stop.

Still, that didn't stop my thoughts from wondering where she was going. *Had she seen the list of local recommendations I'd left on the table*? I gritted my teeth; this was why I should've given her a tour.

"Is that your new tenant?" Gunner asked as soon as I slid into the passenger seat.

"Sydney." I buckled. "Thanks for the ride."

Gunner hummed.

"Is everything okay?" I held my messenger bag on my lap.

Normally, he'd be flooring it down Mom's street by now, but instead, he watched Sydney until she turned the corner and then looked at me.

The slow smile that spread over his face was the one Mom always called trouble, but it was rarely aimed at me.

"Perfectly fine, Baby Brains." My nickname was a misnomer.

Technically, Gwen was the youngest, so I wasn't the baby of the family. However, Gunner claimed I was the youngest boy, so that was where "baby" came from. He'd first called me the name when he got an *A* on the English paper on Oliver Twist I'd written for him freshman year of high school; I'd only been in eighth grade at the time.

Gunner was sixteen months older than me. Hunter, another two years older than that, and Archer, another year older than Hunter.

"How's Della doing?"

Gunner's girlfriend was seven months pregnant and managed the Worth Hotel in downtown Wisdom. Even though she came from money and didn't need to work, she was at the hotel every day, updating and improving and guiding the business. I'd always been unsure if there was a woman who'd be able to make Gunner change his promiscuous ways, but Della was the solution, even if their relationship had an... unexpected start.

I'd tied with Gwen for being the second person to learn that Gunner was going to be a father; he'd called to tell her about the unplanned pregnancy and hadn't realized I was standing in the doorway.

While Archer was defined by his duty, and Hunter, a model of responsibility, Gunner was the most easygoing out of all of us, yet I couldn't recall a time when I'd ever seen him so shocked.

I'd tried explaining that even though the package says condoms are ninety-eight percent effective, real-world effectiveness shows them to work only eighty-seven percent of the time; surprisingly, that didn't seem to offer him any comfort. I wasn't sure why. I always felt better when I understood things.

Either way, after a few months, everything had worked out for the best, and now, I was the only one of my siblings who hadn't found love.

That was okay.

I was used to being the odd man out.

"Good. Lots of lower back pain, but still working."

"As the uterus grows, it can press on the sciatic nerve and cause sciatica pain in the lower back and legs."

Gunner's easy smile filled his face, but I didn't understand why he laughed; it wasn't funny.

"Planning on adding a fourth doctorate to your degrees?"

"No." My brows pulled together. "Why?"

The first two had been mathematics and physics. Then I added engineering. If we hadn't decided to open Reynolds Protective

Group in order to get Archer to move home from Boston, I estimated I'd have another three degrees by now. If it weren't for my brothers, there was a high probability I would've ended up locked in a lab somewhere, probably doing something really cool and world-changing but definitely doing it alone.

Even though it was hard for me, it was better when I wasn't alone. I was grateful they realized that.

"I'm teasing you, Baby Brains." Gunner playfully punched my arm and then slowed the car, turning onto the private drive that led to our business.

Even though we'd collectively purchased almost a hundred acres of property, the office building didn't sit very far from the road—zero-point-four-two miles, to be exact. I'd been responsible for all the engineering and building plans. The rest of the land was broken up into parcels for each of us. Archer had built his home within a year of moving back to Wyoming. Hunter had followed after meeting his wife, Zoey. And Gunner's house had gone up in record time; the construction weeks from being completed so that they could move before the baby was born; right now, they were living in one of the suites at the hotel.

I had no plans for my parcel. My savings were better used in other investments, like the garage apartment that I'd been renting out for almost a year now. Based on my current projections, I'd recoup my investment in the next eight months.

"Oh. Right." My lips pinched and then released to mirror his smile. "With Keira and then Zoey and now Della being pregnant, I thought it would be prudent for me to research the process so I'm prepared."

Gunner swung into a spot in front of the building fast enough that I clutched my bag so it didn't fall. Gunner's driving was my least favorite out of all my brothers. No matter how many times I explained that driving faster wouldn't result in statistically significant time savings, he still drove well over the speed limit.

Gunner shut off the car, but instead of getting out, he turned and reached for my shoulder. "You know what's even bigger than your brain?"

I blinked. "Well, lots of things. A human brain is only, on average, three pounds and the size of ten tennis balls. So even something like a watermelon—"

"Your heart," he interrupted me. "I was speaking figuratively, Baby Brains, that no matter how much you inflate that noggin with facts, it doesn't come close to how much you care about everyone around you."

"Oh." I dropped my gaze, embarrassed.

Gunner chuckled. "C'mon. Before Archie gives me shit for making us late."

We got out of his car and headed inside.

I'd designed our office building with function and longevity in mind. It ended up having a modern rustic feel with lots of big wooden beams paired with large windows and a steel framework.

There was a small lobby with a stairwell that led to the second floor where Archer, Hunter, and Zoey had offices. Gunner and I worked from rooms on the main floor, where there was also a break room with a fridge, and in the basement was our gym and server room.

Gunner led the way to Archer's office at the end of the second-floor hall. Our oldest brother sat at his desk, the Grand Teton mountains stretching across the windows behind him, and Hunter took one of the chairs in front of him, both waiting for us to join them.

"It's my fault we're late," Gunner remarked and sank onto the couch.

"We know," Archer grunted.

I took the remaining chair, holding my bag in my lap.

"Alright, let's get right to it. Hunt and I have that tech retreat in Jackson at the end of the week." Archer gave a quick nod to Hunter and then looked at the couch. "Gunner, you're handling your future father-in-law's real estate summit at the Worth."

"On it."

"Ranger, I have a bunch of new client applications that came in over the weekend. If you could go through and do your normal dive, I'll check back in with you on Friday once I'm back from Jackson."

"Okay." My chin bobbed.

"Pretty low-key this week. Anything else we need to discuss?" Archer surveyed the room.

"Mom made stuffed peppers for all of you. I'll leave the trays in the fridge."

"Great."

"I have something to discuss," Gunner chimed in behind me, and I turned just in time to see that "trouble" smile appear again. "I'd like to discuss Baby Brains's new tenant."

"Why?" Blood rushed to my cheeks.

"Oh boy..." Hunter grumbled.

"Because you have a crush on her."

"What?" My bag fell off my lap, and I scrambled to pick it back up, my iPad, notebook, and the two books I was rereading spilling out from the open flap. "No, I don't, Gunner."

"Who's the tenant?" Hunter asked.

"You awkwardly waved at her this morning and then practically ran for the car; your cheeks were still red by the time you got in the seat. I don't need to be a doctor to diagnose that crush."

"I don't have a crush." I huffed and shoved my things back in my bag. "Maybe my face was red because I was rushing because you were late."

"Touché." Gunner sat back and folded his arms. "But then, what's the reason for your face being red now?"

"Gunner..." Archer warned him with a low voice.

"Just saying, I'm here for expert dating advice if you need it, Baby Brains."

Hunter snorted. "I wouldn't consider your advice expert."

"Oh, no?" Gunner sat forward, and I knew the two of them were about to butt heads. "What would you call it then—"

"I don't need any advice because I don't have a crush," I declared and stood from the chair. "I think that means the meeting is done for the day."

I exited the room without looking at any of them as they argued behind me. I wasn't even at my desk for five minutes before Gunner knocked and let himself into my office.

"You know I'm just teasing you, bud."

"You're teasing me like I'm a child, Gunner, and I'm not." I leveled my stare at his.

If there was one person I never shied away from, it was Gunner. Maybe because he was the closest to me in age. Maybe because when Dad died, I remembered Gunner being there with me. Playing with me. Making me laugh. I was the closest to him out of all my siblings, and that was why it irked me so much when he treated me like a child.

I was thirty-two. I had more degrees than all of them combined. I excelled at my job. I had more money in the bank than the business made in a year and investments that were profiting by leaps and bounds. I might be the youngest and still live at home, but I was smart and more financially sound than most people who were twice my age. Yet, no one seemed to care about those facts.

The only facts people got stuck on were that I still lived at home with Mom and had a nonexistent social life. *Because those things somehow negated all of my achievements and success.*

"You're right, and I'm sorry." His smile fell and he nodded. "I struggle to talk about serious things without making jokes about them, so I'm sorry. I'm working on it, I promise. I just want to see you happy… to see you with someone to share your life. That big heart of yours deserves to be loved."

My lips firmed together, and then I exhaled deeply. "It's okay."

"So…" His eyes flicked side to side. "Are you going to talk to your… Sydney?"

My jaw tensed. "She's my tenant, not my Sydney. And, of course, I will talk to her if she needs something."

I set to organizing the files that Zoey had left on my desk, preparing to sift through the stack of potential clients.

"Or you could just talk to her to get to know her."

I stared at him. "Why would I do that?"

He stared back. "To get to know her… because you like her."

"I just met her."

"That's right, and I believe a certain someone once mentioned some study in some smarty-pants journal that said people decide on their attraction to someone within seconds—"

"Minutes," I corrected, unable to let him completely bungle the fact. "The Journal of Social and Personal Relationships found that people generally make accurate predictions on their romantic interest in someone within four minutes of meeting them."

"Aha!" He pointed at me. "I knew it."

"I can't believe you remember that." I wrinkled my nose, annoyed that he *chose* this thing I'd told him two years ago at a Fourth of July BBQ to remember.

"I'll try not to be insulted and remind you that you're not the only one with a memory, Baby Brains." He chuckled and shook his head. "You don't have to admit to liking her. It's fine. You could just talk to her. She's out here by herself. Maybe she'd like a friend?"

I should've stayed silent, but my brain brought up the image of her eyes. All the gold flecks. And her smile. It was unusual how even the memory evoked the same reaction in my body.

"Talk to her how?" I asked and sat in my chair.

Gunner shrugged. "Like small talk."

"I'm incapable of small talk."

"Oh, bullshit," he charged. "You're perfectly capable, I know you are."

I exhaled slowly. "She's my tenant, Gunner."

With a sigh, he lifted his hands in surrender. "Fine, but just know I fully support you if you change your mind."

"Okay," I said, even though I wouldn't. It didn't make sense to change my mind even if I had felt something… different… when I met Sydney.

She was my tenant and lived in New York. Even if I was as smooth and confident as my brother, it was still statistically unlikely that a relationship would work out; those chances exponentially slimmed when I replaced his sexual prowess with my social awkwardness.

But it made him happy to think I might try, so I let it go.

"Oh, Gunner." I stopped him before he shut the door. "If Della starts getting numbness in her legs or feet, she should see her doctor."

He smiled. "I'll let her know that Uncle Brains is looking out for her."

I smiled. Uncle Brains.

I liked being an uncle. I liked kids. They didn't filter what they said either, so I was never left wondering if I'd interpreted something wrong.

Sometimes, I thought about if I'd ever have kids of my own… but that would mean having someone to have them with, and once again, I was back to the part I wasn't good at. Smart people knew their weaknesses; brilliant people avoided them at all costs.

Gunner seemed to think differently, but objectively speaking, he was the least smart out of all of us, so it would be foolish for me to hope for a statistical long shot. I'd never had a girlfriend. Never been on a date. The odds of me developing a relationship with someone to the point of having children weren't in my favor.

Especially if the first woman I felt any kind of attraction to was only my temporary tenant until the new year.

CHAPTER 4

Sydney

"Cheers." Gina held her massive wineglass up to her screen and I did the same with mine before we both drank.

It was our weekly WineTime check-in: Friday night, nine p.m. sharp. Well, for her, it was midnight, but Gina was the night owl to my morning person. With the time difference and the hours she was putting in, Gina insisted on a FaceTime every Friday so she could actually *see* me.

Proof of life and all that.

"You are looking so much better, Syd."

"A little," I admitted and took another sip of the pinot noir.

At least I got hungry out here. Back in New York, the stress had completely obliterated my appetite. In the last three weeks, I'd gained back seven of the fifteen pounds I'd lost following the backlash of *Broken Promises*. Now, my clothes looked stylishly loose rather than ill-fitting.

"How was your week? Are you relaxing?"

They were the same two questions she'd asked the last two weekends when we'd video chatted. After all this, she was on track for the Momager of the Year award. *Look out, Kris.*

"I send you photographic proof of relaxation every day." Even though we kept our calls to the weekend, texts and photographs flew back and forth constantly. *Who else did I have to talk to?*

"Right, but those could be photoshopped." She took another gulp from her large wineglass; it was oversized because of me.

Because of the fallout.

Guilt unsettled my stomach. While I was out here, losing myself in the wild nature of Wyoming and the small-town charm of Wisdom, Gina was back in the city dealing with demanding publishers, canceled events, and angry readers. My only consolation was that while I fractured under that kind of pressure, Gina thrived, even if it did necessitate several large glasses of wine.

"I sent you selfies, G. But yes, I'm feeling better. You were right. I needed… to get out of there—away from everything." I swirled the liquid in my glass.

New York had been a pressure cooker, memories of Vince's betrayal compounded by the backlash from readers. My apartment had my bestselling book covers framed on the wall in the hallway. I didn't realize until I was here… until I wasn't walking by them every day… just how much seeing them made my heart break. Reminders that the career I loved had been grounded on a man I'd lost. Losing Vince's cheap love was one thing… losing the love of so many readers was another. *Maybe I had neither to begin with.*

"Of course, I was right. That's what agents are for," she quipped.

When she'd dropped me off at the airport, Gina had staunchly forbidden me from accessing any kind of social media or logging into my email. *You need to heal, Syd. Nothing else matters.* At first, it felt like everything else still mattered. The books. The contracts. The fervor. The anger. I wanted to make it all better. I wrote happy endings, for crying out loud. Did they honestly think I *wanted* to kill off Vance? He was no longer a hero. What was I supposed to do? Pretend?

No one deserved a false love, even if it was easy. Not even a fictional character.

"Was that a bike in the picture you sent me the other day? Did you get a bike?" she probed. "And shouldn't it be snowing out there?"

I chuckled. "Not yet."

I'd spent most of my first two weeks exploring Wisdom on foot. The sight of people strolling through town on that drive from the airport had stuck with me and turned into daily walks down and back along Main Street.

I made a point to stop at the quaint coffee shop, Brilliant Brews, on my way back. It had been one of Ranger's recommendations, and it hadn't disappointed. The eclectic decor and extraordinary espresso were the highlights of my mornings.

"I overheard some ranchers talking at the coffee shop this morning that we're going to be in for some big storms. Apparently, any time winter starts mild like this, it ends up packing a punch."

It was only November, so there was still time. In the meantime, I was going to take advantage of the only moderately cold weather to spend time outside, since sitting in front of my computer wasn't an option.

"Ranchers?" She hummed and I waited for a cowboy comment that never came. "You didn't answer my question."

"About the snow?" My brow creased, and I brought my glass to my lips.

"About the bike," she countered, arching an eyebrow. "Where'd you get it?"

I licked my lips. "I saw it in the garage last week," I said with a shrug, trying to seem as casual as possible. "It was really nice on Monday, so I asked my landlord if I could borrow it, and he said sure."

"Well, of course you were welcome to borrow it, Syd." Gina snorted. "You flashed him your tits. Bet he'd let you borrow some other things to ride if you asked him nicely—"

"Gina," I hissed and broke into something between a laugh and a groan. "I told you we weren't going to discuss what happened *or* my landlord again."

I picked up my phone from where it was propped up against a candle on the table and carried her with me to search for a snack.

"Literally, you made the entire trip out there worth it within the first week." She cackled.

Without work or being online, the days really started to blend together, but that day I remembered. *That day I wouldn't soon forget.*

It was the fifth day I was here. I was in the shower. And all of a sudden, the world started to end.

Or so I thought.

The whole building started to shake violently, and I... well, I didn't know what I thought. Earthquake? Nuclear bomb? All I knew was that one minute, I was enjoying a perfect hot shower, and the next, I was sprinting to the front of the apartment to see what was going on.

Who cared about a towel when the world was ending?

Sure enough, the rest of the world sat perfectly stable. It was only my building that was shaking because the old garage door was opening for the first time during my stay.

It would've been great if running naked to check the false alarm earthquake was the most memorable part of what happened. *Unfortunately, it wasn't.*

Cleared from world-ending destruction, I stared at the Volvo hatchback below. As a romance author, my first thought upon recognizing the car model was that there was a glittering vampire in the front seat. *Wrong again.* Instead, it was my beautiful, genius landlord with his long, messy hair and crystal-green eyes staring up at me from the driver's seat.

I shivered, my nipples pebbling at the memory.

See, there were two kinds of people in the world. The first were people who pulled into a garage as the door was going up. *I was one of those impatient ones who tempted fate.* The second was those who waited until the door was *completely* elevated before entering.

Ranger was that second kind of person. A waiter.

And that meant when I rushed to the window with my boobs

bouncing freely into the apocalypse, he sat right below, patiently waiting for that damn door to go *all* the way up... and getting a full view of my naked chest in the process.

Our eyes connected like the snap of two magnets before his dropped to my chest and went wide. Breasts. Nipples. The whole shebang. Thankfully, the windows didn't go low enough to expose anything else because the instant rush of heat over my skin didn't stop at my chest. It didn't stop until it burrowed between my thighs.

Just like that moment when he'd thought I was serious about making out. It stoked a fire inside me that I thought for sure had gone out. And that was why I hesitated to step back for just an additional second.

I wanted to see his reaction. I wanted to find any indication he felt the same because I'd thought about him and his facts and awkwardness a ridiculous number of times since my arrival. Meanwhile, it felt like he was avoiding me.

"It's literally been the highlight of my week, rehashing your encounter. Please don't take this from me," Gina begged.

"You're crazy." Or maybe I was crazy... crushing on my landlord.

I opened the cabinet where I'd stocked up on boxed goods and snacks the day after I'd arrived and stared at the empty shelves. *Great*.

"Not crazy, just practical. You left Vince six months ago, and we both know you haven't gotten laid since. You're already out there in the middle of nowhere with no one to answer to. Why not seduce the sexy Einstein and see what happens? Maybe it will be... *enlightening.*"

I closed the cupboard with a sigh. I needed to go to the grocery store tomorrow for more snacks.

"Seriously? Sexy Einstein?" Maybe I'd overshared about my unexpectedly good-looking landlord, but how was I not supposed to share the "making out is cleaner than handshakes" conversation? *Who would keep that to themselves?*

"Well, you told me I couldn't refer to him as Nerdy Michelangelo."

Right, only I was allowed to do that... in my head.

"How about you just refer to him as my landlord?"

"So much less fun." She drained what was left in her glass. "Oh! How about a compromise?"

I propped my phone back up against the tall candle in the center of the kitchen table and sank into a chair. "How do you compromise on seducing someone?"

Gina grinned. "By having Jenny do it."

My eyebrows lifted. "You want me to turn my landlord into Jenny's new love interest?"

There was no way. I needed a miracle to make this last book happen. Magic Mike himself would have to step out of the pages of each physical copy, give the reader a lap dance, and *maybe* then they'd consider forgiving and forgetting about Vance.

"He's not the typical kind of hero I write—"

Except for those dimples... Ranger's dimples were on point.

"Exactly." Gina pointed at me. "If you give them anything close to Vance's character, you'll lose readers to the comparison. So, give them something completely different—give yourself something completely different. Maybe then the words will come."

I locked my lip between my teeth, rolling it through my bite several times while I considered it. "I don't know."

I hadn't even opened my computer since I'd arrived. There was no point. I didn't have writer's block. That would imply I'd actually sat down and tried to write; I hadn't. I knew I'd only be staring at a blank page, so I avoided it.

"Well, I do, and I think it would be perfect." I watched her down the rest of her wine.

I'd come out here to focus on myself, but along with that came figuring out if I was going to continue to write or if my hiatus would be permanent, figuring out if I could find my way back to happy endings when my own story wasn't writing so well.

Gina would never mention my deadlines. God bless her soul. She'd keep her lips sealed shut about the crap I was sure Anne was giving her because she cared about me. But not speaking about them wouldn't make Anne's demands go away.

My contract was for one more book in this series, and every day I didn't write was one day closer to my deadline—one that couldn't be pushed back again.

I'd caught the email from Anne just before Gina had picked me up to go to the airport. Because of the backlash, she was demanding the final book either on schedule or not at all. A delay would only worsen the negative press.

"You do the big reveal about Vance being a villain all along, and then Smarty McHotpants joins the case, Jenny lets her guard down, or maybe accidentally flashes her tits, and boom, nuclear-level chemistry."

I snorted. "Smarty McHotpants?"

"Chemical Casanova. G-spot Genius. The Nerdy Nutter."

I let out a small shriek of laughter and doubled over. I didn't know if it was all of her ridiculous nicknames or the wine that was hitting me hard, but I kept laughing until tears rolled down my cheeks.

It was probably the first time in a year I wasn't crying from sadness or anger, or betrayal.

"Sounds like you have it all figured out." I gasped in air and wiped my cheeks.

"Easy peasy. You can thank me later with my end-of-year bonus." Gina pretended to examine her nails, but her smug smile showed she was clearly satisfied with herself.

My laughter died with a little shake of my head. If only it were that easy. But maybe… maybe it would be *easier* to use Ranger for inspiration. My dreams certainly had no trouble doing exactly that.

"Well, I'll think about it."

"You're going to write him. I can see it," she charged. "Have you talked to him at all?"

"No." I spun my empty glass in my fingers. "Not since I asked to borrow the bike."

And his response to that had been polite, professional, and abbreviated. The only time we'd texted before that was the day after I'd arrived, when he'd messaged to see if I'd settled in okay and if there was anything I needed; there wasn't.

It was no surprise this place had so many great reviews; it had taken less than a day to realize just how much thought and care Ranger had put into the apartment. From the drawer organizers in the kitchen to the heated mattress pad on the bed and even to the spare toiletries underneath the sink in the bathroom, grouped together for each week I'd be staying here… every detail went the extra mile.

And I couldn't forget the binder of restaurant recommendations grouped by cuisine, sightseeing recommendations grouped by season and then color coded by fitness level, and the instruction manuals carefully annotated at the back.

"Have you seen him recently?"

"No." I firmed my lips so they wouldn't spill that I thought he was avoiding me. Maybe seeing my boobs had the complete opposite effect than I'd expected.

"You should text him. Ask him to show you around. Or get drinks." Her eyes twinkled. "See if he enjoyed the show."

I groaned. "How about a compromise? I make a solid attempt to write this final book on time and you leave my landlord out of it."

The last thing I needed was a guy in my life right now, regardless of what my body wanted.

Gina harrumphed. "Yeah, yeah. Text me tomorrow."

"I will. But G—"

"No." She wagged her finger at me. "I know what you're going to ask, and the answer is no. I'm not telling you what's going on or what people are saying about your sudden vacation; it doesn't matter."

"At least tell me if they are still harassing you?"

She couldn't completely hide her shuttered reaction. "It's just the news cycle, Syd. This is how it goes."

"Gina..." I locked my hands in my lap. "You don't have to give me the gory details, but I need to know the truth. How bad is it?"

She sighed. "They're no longer outside your apartment."

"Well, that's good."

"I thought so, too, until I realized it's because they went looking for Vince."

I grimaced and shook my head. "He's in California."

After I ended our engagement, he'd packed his things and said he was moving to LA. Apparently, he'd accepted a new role in an upcoming series he hadn't even told me about that was filming out there. But that was how he always did things—by thinking of himself first and then gaslighting me for not being supportive if I had any concerns.

"Nope." Her lips popped on the *p*. "Apparently, he's in Brooklyn."

"Really?" My eyebrows lifted. "Wow."

"Yeah. Guess his plans changed."

"Who knows. Who cares," I muttered. He was probably lying about the TV role he got in the first place because he was so pissed I was breaking off the engagement.

"Well, I wouldn't, except for the fact that he's been more than willing to talk to the paps and drag your name and your books through the mud."

"Seriously?" I pressed my fingers to my temple, hating the way my throat started to tighten up. "I'll write a letter and have Don send it."

It would be better if all of my communication with Vince went through my lawyer—including a firmly worded letter informing him that I would take legal action if he continued to lie about me for attention. Because that was all it was.

"I can do—"

"No, G, you're doing enough. I'll call Don on Monday and have him handle it."

She groused for a minute and then conceded. "Fine."

"I need you for more important things."

"Like making up names for your hot landlord?"

At this point, I was willing to concede on that. "Yeah. Sure. Fine."

"Fine." Her eyebrows popped up and a slow smile spread over her cheeks. "That's it! That's the one."

"What?"

"Your landlord is the real Albert *Fine*instein."

My head dropped back and I groaned. "I can't."

"Yes, you can," she insisted glibly.

"I think I hear a blank page screaming my name." I waved at the phone screen. "I'll talk to you later. Bye."

I ended the call to her laughing and then pushed my phone to the side, eyeing my laptop like it was a bull about to charge. But for the first time in months, I felt the urge to write... because I couldn't get Gina's suggestion out of my head.

Give yourself something different.

A boyishly handsome genius hero. Part awkward. Part adorable. *And wholly attractive.*

I rolled my bottom lip through my teeth, allowing myself to go back through all the little details I'd collected about Ranger in the last three weeks.

It was amazing the kinds of things you could learn about someone just from watching them when they thought no one was. Not that I was a stalker or anything, but I loved people-watching. Being an author involved a lot of creating but also a lot of observing. Observing places and events, people and interactions, all for inspiration.

Almost every spot in the apartment that wasn't the bathroom or in the bed afforded a panoramic view of the short driveway to the road and the front of the house, so I could see anything that happened out front.

I caught the blue Mustang that picked Ranger up in the morning as I sipped my cup of coffee and the Jeep or sometimes the Range Rover that dropped him off at night. That was until he got his car back and now the whole building shook to announce his departure and arrival.

Sometimes, I saw the men who gave him rides home, too. They'd get out of their cars and go inside for a couple of minutes before leaving. *Brothers,* if I remembered Cindy's comment correctly. *They're all lookers.* She was right.

Thank God I'd left out that Ranger had hot, hunky brothers, or Gina would be on the first flight out here. She'd also take me straight to the emergency room if I told her I was surprisingly… not attracted to them. Maybe it was the altitude that turned everything upside down—that left me dreaming every night about *Mr. Fineinstein.*

I groaned and grabbed a match from the kitchen to light the lemon candle on the table. I'd picked it up from one of the local shops during one of my walks through town earlier this week. Maybe it was a sign that my brain was warming up to the idea of writing again… I always wrote with a candle burning.

A candle and soft jazz in the background.

I opened my laptop and created a new document. White space, like a plot of open land that would be built on and seeded, nourished and landscaped until an entire story was constructed on it.

On him.

The first week—after the boob incident—I'd walked to the window after feeling the garage door open and close. Ranger was backing down the drive when an elderly woman dropped her bag on the sidewalk; she wasn't in his way, so he could've easily ignored it. Instead, he stopped. Parking and shutting off his car completely before getting out to help the woman collect her things and escort her across the driveway to make sure she was okay.

On his return to his car, he'd noticed me in the window and our eyes locked again.

Was it possible to get to know someone without talking to them? Because every time I saw him, that was what it felt like was happening.

I'd catch him walking out to meet the elderly mailman, talking with him for long minutes before collecting his mail and returning inside.

And then there was Thanksgiving…

I opened up my computer, allowing my newest memory from yesterday to flood my mind.

Ranger's whole family had come over for the holiday, their familiar cars filling up the street out front. I'd planned to spend the night binge-watching *Bridgerton* and avoiding how I was spending the holiday alone, eating a turkey sandwich, but the tiny squeals from the driveway interrupted my plans.

Ranger was out there, chasing around two toddlers with another baby in his arms. He made them laugh and giggle with zero shame for the ridiculous faces and sounds he used to do it, and I couldn't look away.

His wide, white smile wasn't measured before it burst over his face, those dimples coming out like the sun over the horizon. I wondered just how warm they'd feel if he were smiling at me.

Ranger had chased his niece and nephew until they couldn't run anymore, and when he led his little charges back to the house, his gaze tilted up to the apartment just before going inside. Maybe I'd feel bad for watching him if he didn't always look to the window like he hoped I was there.

Or maybe that was my unspent imagination spilling into real life.

Give him to Jenny. Be satisfied with that happy ending.

Before I knew it, my fingers were moving over the keyboard. The soft click of the keys adding its own melody to the jazz that pervaded the room. It got darker. The candle burned lower, but that page filled up with words. And then the next. And the next.

The unassuming genius medical examiner came to life as he interacted with my brokenhearted heroine. Slowly but surely, the hesitant fingers of the story start to pull me deeper.

The candle I'd lit burned lower and lower. But for the first time in months, the urge to write was there and I wasn't going to let that go. Minutes turned into hours. The words on the screen started to blur until, at some point, I rested my head on the table and the story I was writing became the dream I was dreaming, the hero the same in both.

CHAPTER 5

Sydney

"Sydney?"

The call of my name was followed by a firm knock on the door.

I jolted awake, gasping as my knee banged on the underside of the table.

"Sydney? It's Ranger."

My heart thudded wildly as I quickly pieced together where I was and what had happened. *Candle. Music. Computer.*

I'd fallen asleep working. *How long...* I groaned when I saw the clock on the oven. *It was almost midnight.* My candle was almost completely burned down, *and Ranger was at the door.*

"Sydney? Are you okay?"

"Yes. Coming!" I blew out the candle and rushed to the door, hitting the lights as I opened it. "Hi, sorry. I'm okay."

Ranger waited on the other side, his hands in his pockets and his expression stern. My heart squeezed at the sight of him. *God, I'd forgotten how strikingly beautiful he was up close.*

Meanwhile, I was braless in a tee and pajama pants. And I could practically hear Gina telling me not to worry about it because it wasn't like Ranger hadn't seen me in less...

I swallowed over the lump in my throat as his soft-green stare carefully trekked over me. Not to see what I was wearing. Not because my nipples poked obnoxiously against the fabric of my shirt. No, he looked me over like he was checking off boxes of a health questionnaire form in his head. Color. Coherency. Cognitive awareness. Overall physical health.

I pulled my bottom lip between my teeth. That would make this better, right? If he wasn't interested in me at all?

Just when I almost had myself convinced that might be the case, his stare stumbled as it moved back over my chest, unfiltered appreciation in his eyes.

I shivered. He was definitely interested.

Ranger shifted his weight and looked over my shoulder—looked anywhere but back at me. "I saw the light flickering, and I worried there was a fire since your lights are usually off by now. I didn't realize it was a candle."

Usually off by now? My pulse thrummed. Maybe I wasn't the only hyperaware one…

"Oh, yeah." I nodded, flattening my hand on the door and nodding to the table. "I lit it while I was working and then dozed off. I'm sorry. I didn't mean to worry you. Thanks for checking in." As I spoke, I took a second glance over him, realizing not only was he dressed like he normally was, jeans, button-down shirt—*vest included,* but there was white powder all over it… all over him. "Were you baking?"

He looked down and then began brushing vigorously at the spots to erase them. "Chocolate peanut butter bars." His brow furrowed, realizing just how much of a mess he was. "I was mixing up the last batch when I noticed the light—did you know that a house fire happens every eighty-seven seconds?"

My jaw went slack. "No." I swallowed. "I didn't know that."

"But only two percent are caused by candles." Satisfied by his quick cleanup, he shoved his hands in his pockets and nodded. "Forty-nine percent are caused by cooking."

"Right..." I murmured.

Ranger's instantaneous knowledge base was fascinating but not as mesmerizing as the way he spoke. The confidence of his lips. I wished I could be as sure as he was about... everything.

Then I noticed the smudge of flour just above the corner of his mouth. Without thinking, I brought my thumb to my lips, wetting it with my tongue and then reached for him.

He didn't move, and I didn't stop. Not until my finger touched the soft warmth of his cheek. I wasn't sure what I expected. Maybe that he would be as hard as his facts. Or as cold. But he was neither. He was warm temptation—sweet fruit from an expansive tree of knowledge.

Like the swing of a pendulum, his breath released just as my lungs inhaled. Back and forth, we traded on the momentum, neither willing to put a stop to the moment as I swiped the flour away.

"There was a spot of flour..." I offered quietly, my thumb lingering even after all the traces were gone.

"Thanks." The trace of husk in his voice surprised me, and I quickly drew my hand away.

He immediately reached up to where my finger had been, brushing over his cheek like it was suddenly foreign to him.

"Sorry," I murmured, unsure what kind of midnight insanity prompted me to lick my landlord clean, but it was no excuse.

"I'm a messy baker. Even with an apron, I'm not quite sure how it happens." He scratched his head, looking adorably sheepish as our eyes connected once more.

"Do you always bake at midnight?" I folded my arms, catching the unfiltered drop of his gaze to my breasts.

Every time his focus broke and he looked at me like this, it felt like warm goose bumps covered my insides, the sensation even more electrifying than when they erupted over my skin.

"Usually," he said with an audible strain in his voice. "I don't want to be in Mom's way, so I use the kitchen once she's in bed. I don't mind it, actually. It's nice to work in the..."

"Quiet," I finished for him, recognizing the look of someone searching for the right word.

"The quiet." His chin dipped.

"Sometimes, I write at night for the quiet. There's just something different about being awake when everyone else is asleep. Something intimate." The word slipped out before I could stop it, and Ranger's eyes widened. "Anyway, I haven't been able to write for a while, and then I just got going tonight and lost track of time and obviously how exhausted I was."

It was the perfect cue for Ranger to say good night and leave, but he didn't take it. *No.* He didn't even recognize it.

"What are you writing?" he asked instead.

My lips parted. "A romance novel."

I didn't expect him to know who I was or what I wrote. Men weren't typically part of my target audience, not to mention I envisioned Ranger to be a nonfiction kind of guy.

"Your thirty-second book, I believe?" he asked without missing a beat.

I swayed against the door, not expecting him to know who I was, let alone any details of my career. Then again, cancel culture was the kind of thing that spread like wildfire, so who knew? Maybe Sydney Ward's infamous fall from fame had made it all the way to Wisdom.

"Yeah..." My brow pulled together. "How did you know that?"

Dumb question because now I was pretty convinced that Ranger Reynolds knew everything. If *Who Wants to Be a Millionaire?* were still on, he would be my "phone a friend" every single time.

"I looked you up before accepting your application. Thirty-two books. Twenty-five *New York Times* bestsellers..." His head bobbed as he rattled off my accolades like there was a Rolodex built into his head, some of the numbers and statistics I wasn't even aware of.

"Oh."

"My brother loves your books."

"Really?"

"And his wife." He nodded enthusiastically, draping a lock of hair onto his forehead though it went entirely unnoticed by him as he continued, "It's sort of how they met. Through your books. Well, technically, at a book club, but they were there because of your books."

"Wow." My voice caught. It was stories like this that I tucked away for the hard times.

"Don't worry, I didn't tell him you were staying here. I wouldn't share a tenant's information."

"Oh, I didn't think—thank you." A small smile lifted my lips.

"Of course." And then came the lip pull—the flat of his tongue drawing his lips back between his teeth.

I shivered, our eyes locking for another long beat of silence. Once more, it was a moment carved out for a goodbye. For a *"Glad you didn't set my apartment on fire, Sydney. Have a good night."* But it never came.

Ranger Reynolds was an enigma. He could be wearing a button-down shirt and vest, yet covered in flour. Wearing a tie, but his hair was tossed like churning waves. And he could be smart… impossibly smart… but so unaware of social cues.

I could've ended the conversation and sent him on his way—*should've*, probably—but I didn't.

"Have you read my books, too?"

I had never asked that question before. It felt awkward and intrusive… presumptuous. But I couldn't help myself. He'd said his brother and sister-in-law had. There was a selfish part of me that wanted to know if he had, too.

A selfish part that wanted to imagine Ranger reading a romance novel.

I wanted to know what would go on in that brain of his. Would he pick it apart for inconsistencies? Would he read the sex scenes? Would they turn him on, or would he get lost in anatomical and positional facts? *Would they make him blush?*

Heat pooled between my legs, imagining that blush.

"No. Hunter said he was going to loan me one last year, but he never did. He probably forgot." He thought for a moment. "Do you have a copy I can borrow?"

My jaw went slack.

"I'm sorry. Of course, you wouldn't. You're on vacation. I'll ask Hunter when I see him next. Actually, I think Mom has some in her office," he rambled on. "Do you have a recommendation on where I should start?

"Actually, I have a copy you can borrow..." I trailed off, leaving the door ajar as I went to the couch and pulled out a worn copy of *Twisted Fate* from my bag. "It's the original version, so the cover is different if you look it up now," I warned him, extending my copy with its frayed cover and worn pages.

"You brought this out here?" He rubbed his hand vigorously on the side of his pants before taking the book, and I bit back a smile. A little bit of flour wouldn't be the worst thing this book had seen. But his thoughtfulness was endearing.

"It's silly, but it's like my security blanket while I'm working." I always had my first book close by while I was writing, a reminder of why I started.

Normally, I wouldn't recommend *Twisted Fate* to a new reader. Every author who ever existed was self-conscious about their first novel—a debut was like a toddler's first steps. An unstable and uncertain charge into a new world. Yet, at the same time, those steps were precious and full of promise. Those steps existed without the knowledge of failure, falling or bruises. They existed at a moment when you didn't care who was watching or the stress of their expectation, a moment where it was just one step after another. Exciting, invigorating, and filled with endless possibilities.

And for some reason, that was the author I wanted Ranger to meet. The uncertain yet fearless one who'd started this journey, not the one who'd honed and tempered her passion into a best-selling craft. Not the one who'd fallen and wasn't sure if she had the strength to stand again.

"It's not silly to keep close things that bring you comfort." He stared at me, and for a brief, soothing moment, it felt like he was peering directly into my soul. And then his gaze dropped back to the book. "I'm excited to read it."

"Thanks." I watched his eyes move so fast over the blurb he couldn't have actually read it. Maybe skimmed. It prompted me to ask, "Have you read romance before?"

"No."

I tried to ignore the pang in my chest. Maybe this was a bad idea.

"But I think I'd enjoy them. Hunter and Mom certainly do."

"What do you normally read?"

"Any genre, really, though I'm not particularly fond of horror." His tongue slid out and wet his lips. "Reading is good for the brain. It increases knowledge, expands vocabulary, strengthens cognitive skills—did you know that reading can reduce stress by up to sixty-eight percent? It works faster than listening to music or drinking a cup of hot tea."

Listening to him was like watching Da Vinci paint the Mona Lisa or hearing Mozart compose a symphony, or being taught the law of gravity by Isaac Newton himself. I couldn't help but stand in awe.

When I didn't respond, Ranger looked up, blinked, and added, "It was a 2009 study at the University of Sussex."

"I… believe you." I'd just wanted to see what else he had to say. "Books are the best kind of escape."

He nodded in agreement. "Are you sure I can borrow this?" He inspected the book again thoroughly. "It looks like it's a very personal copy."

"Yes. A fair trade for letting me borrow your bike." The words were out before I could stop them, and his eyes whipped up.

We were both recalling the flashing incident. There was no question. Heat prickled like it was barbed wire wrapped around each molecule of oxygen, latching to the inside of my lungs to be carried through my veins.

And it was ridiculous. I couldn't be attracted to someone I'd barely spoken to. But then, what was attraction, if not the ache to know more?

And Ranger… he made me want to know more about him without even trying.

"Well, I'll let you get back to your chocolate peanut butter bars. They sound delicious," I murmured, hearing the husk loaded into my voice.

His mouth pulled tight, realizing he should've left minutes ago. "Right. Of course." His head bobbed, and he clasped the book in front of his groin.

And I looked. I couldn't stop myself. I stared at the stretch of his pants that peeked out from the edges of my novel for a single, unmistakable second before my gaze snapped back to his face, the color in his cheeks deepening.

Perfect, now I could add cock ogling to my landlord's list of grievances against me.

"Let me know what you think of the book." I winced. Really, Syd? What if he hates it? He clearly won't be able to lie about it.

"Thank you, again. Good night." He turned and sped for the door.

"Good night, Ranger," I called, but he was already halfway down the stairs, moving like there was an actual fire in the apartment.

For some reason, I stood there, waiting until he'd exited the garage before I closed the door.

What was I thinking? I buried my face in my hands. First, I'd flashed the man. Now, I'd just given him a raunchy romance novel. If I wasn't trying to seduce him, I certainly wasn't being very convincing about it.

I shut off the lights, leaving only the dull glow that oozed in front of the windows. Instead of heading straight for bed, I found myself padding over to the glass and peering down to the two first-floor windows on this side of the house.

Sure enough, Ranger moved through the kitchen, appearing in one window and then the next. I smiled, watching more flour end up on his vest as he mixed the batter before he disappeared from view; I presumed to put the baking tray in the oven. Another minute later, he stepped into the other window, and I saw him reach for my book that he'd set on the island.

He turned, and I swore I stepped away in time. He hadn't caught me watching. I'd been quick enough. *Plus, he couldn't see me standing in the dark...* I almost had myself convinced by the time I climbed into bed and buried myself under the covers.

I needed to stop distracting myself with Ranger Reynolds. No matter how he looked at me or the way my body reacted, he was my landlord. An acquaintance.

A perfectly handsome prodigy but an acquaintance nonetheless.

Maybe that was why the words had come so easily tonight... because what I wanted couldn't happen in reality. The only space in my life for any kind of relationship existed in the blank pages of my next book, safely between the covers where my heart couldn't be broken again.

CHAPTER 6

Sydney

I shouldn't take it personally. The first lesson of being an author was learning that not everyone was going to like your books, and that was okay. Not everyone liked pineapple on pizza or ketchup on their eggs, and let's not even venture into the love-hate relationship people had with anchovies...

People had preferences, and my books weren't his. But for some reason, the knowledge still stung.

I sucked in a deep breath of cold, crisp air and pedaled harder, trying to work off my disappointment.

I'd opened my door yesterday morning to find my tattered copy of *Twisted Fate* waiting on the other side; my heart sank like a stone into my stomach. Sure, it was resting on top of a saver full of chocolate peanut butter bars that were to die for, but what were they except a peace offering?

Sorry, your book sucks. Here's some chocolate.

I mean, it definitely wasn't the worst way someone had told me they didn't like my stories.

My legs burned as I pushed around the next turn. *Why did I even care what he thought?* Why did it bother me that he'd left the book and treats outside my door and then disappeared *all* day? *Was it that bad?*

He'd come home at quarter after eleven last night. Not that I was watching the clock, but of course, the garage door had woken me up. He hadn't been out that late in the three weeks I'd been living above his garage, and I hated that the only logical explanation was me. *That he was avoiding me.*

"Dammit," I muttered, picking up speed on the bike path that paralleled the road that led to Jackson and beyond it into Grand Teton National Park.

I shouldn't have gone for a ride today. The temperatures had finally dropped into distinctly snow-ready territory, but I couldn't stay in the apartment any longer. Not only was I hung up on Ranger returning my book within hours of me loaning it to him, but the only thing I had to distract me from that was the two-hour conversation with my lawyer, Don, and drafting a cease and desist letter to Vince.

What a trade... the man I couldn't stop thinking about for the man I never wanted to think about again.

I huffed, my hot breath clouding the air.

I never should've offered Ranger the book. Sure, he'd asked for the copy—said he thought he'd like it—but he was probably just being polite. Maybe I should've been less distracted by his delicious dimples and unending knowledge.

I pedaled until my legs burned, pure fire flooding the muscles. *Just a little farther...*

Pop! The tension in the wheels instantly disappeared as the chain popped off the gear.

"Shit." I used the handle brakes and brought the bike to a wobbly stop.

My legs protested as I steadied myself and the bike, doing nothing more for a good minute while my thrumming pulse and racing heartbeat slowed. Lowering the kickstand, I swung my leg over the bike and crouched to fix the problem.

Didn't have to worry about popped chains on my Peloton.

"Shit," I muttered, examining the chain in my quickly freezing fingers. It hadn't just popped… it was broken. I let out a deep exhale. There was no putting that back on.

Straightening, I planted my hands on my hips and looked one way and then the other along the road. I hadn't biked that far, so maybe I could walk it. I took a single, shaking step and then grabbed for the seat of the bike. *Double shit.* There was no way I was walking anywhere with my legs like Jell-O.

And that left me with only one solution.

Ranger.

I slid my phone from the zipped pocket of my jacket and found his number.

"Hello?"

"Hi, Ranger? It's Sydney." Why was my stomach in a knot?

"I know. I have your number saved in my phone."

"Right." I winced. "I'm really sorry to bother you, but I was out for a bike ride, and I thought the chain popped but it actually broke. I was wondering—"

"I'll come get you. Just share your location to our message thread."

"Okay, one second." I put him on speaker while I did what he said. "Sent."

"I'll be right there."

"Oh—" The call ended. "Okay then."

I shoved my phone back in my pocket and then redid my ponytail. *Great.* Not only did he not like my book, but the first time I had to face him after his abrupt book return was when I was sweaty and gross and wearing only yoga pants and a sports bra.

I'd just started to stretch to pass the time when Ranger's Volvo pulled into the turnout I'd passed when I'd heard the pop. *Wow, he got here fast.* Maybe I hadn't biked as far as I thought.

I pulled my bottom lip between my teeth, watching as he parked and shut off the car. My stomach did a little flip as he tucked his hair behind his ears and headed toward me.

What was it about him? Sure, the internet had the power to turn "dad bods" into a thing, but had I missed the memo on sweater-vests? Was that a super sexy secret weapon I hadn't been aware of? *That was what it felt like.*

Ignoring the increasing thump of my heart, I grabbed the bike, lifted the kickstand and wheeled it toward him.

"Are you okay?" he asked, meeting me on the path.

One look from him was all it took to simultaneously warm me and make me shiver.

"Yeah, it just snapped while I was riding." I folded my arms.

"Here, let me take it." He grabbed the handlebar and took charge of maneuvering it to his car. "The chain is old. I should've changed it when I stopped riding it to work."

"It's not your fault." I hoped he didn't think that it was.

The hatch lifted. He put the seats down and effortlessly loaded the bike into the trunk. I sagged with relief as soon as he started the engine and heat blasted from the vents.

"I'll get a new chain and have it fixed by tomorrow for you." Ranger definitely sounded like he was blaming himself.

"You don't have to do that." I buckled, watching him do the same from the corner of my eyes. "I probably won't go out anymore if the weather stays like this."

"Well, I don't want to leave it broken," he said, like doing anything else was complete blasphemy.

The conversation faded into silence as he examined every number and dial on the dash as though it were the cockpit of a plane and we were about to take off.

"Thank you for picking me up."

"It's not a problem." Ranger looked both ways and then pulled back onto the highway toward Wisdom. "I just have to stop back at my office, if that's okay. I left my bag when you called."

It sounded like it annoyed him more than it did me. "Yeah, of course." I wondered how infrequent it was for him to forget something.

We hadn't been on the highway for more than a minute before his blinker clicked and we turned off down a wood-lined drive.

"Where do you work?" I wondered as we rounded the corner and a building came into view.

Wood ballasts and steel beams framed wide glass panels in a design that was both functional and sophisticated.

"Reynolds Protective Group. It's a private security firm that my brothers and I own."

"Private security..." I stared at the building that loomed in front of us, noting the security cameras tucked discreetly into various corners.

"We do mostly personal security for wealthy clientele or celebrities that are in town." He parked out front and turned off the car. "I'll only be a minute."

I tried to imagine Ranger as a bodyguard. Maybe it should've been hard, but it wasn't. Security wasn't just about size, it was about smarts. It was about risk assessment and tactical advantage. And to be skilled while also remaining unassuming... well, that was the whole premise of Clark Kent, wasn't it?

Movement on the other side of the glass caught my eye. The door opened again, and Ranger appeared followed by another man. *One of his brothers.* His hair was slightly darker, and up close, he was definitely *private security sized*, but the resemblance between the two, mostly in their eyes, was unmistakable.

He said something to Ranger, glanced at the car, and then did a double take when he saw me.

I wasn't an expert at lipreading, but I'd recognize that look anywhere. *A fan.* This was the brother—Hunter—who'd read my books.

I reached for the handle; the least I could do was say hello after everything Ranger had done for me.

"Hunter, please—" Ranger protested as I got out of the car.

"Hi, I'm Sydney." I extended my hand.

"I know who you are, Ms. Ward. I'm a huge fan. My wife and I both." Hunter clasped my hand and shook it. "It's so great to meet you."

"Thank you." I smiled and snuck a glance at Ranger, who stood with his hands shoved in his pockets, watching our interaction. "Ranger mentioned you enjoy my books. I really appreciate your support."

"Enjoy them? I'm sure you get a lot of orders, but I actually purchased a personalized copy of one of your books to propose to my wife."

"Zoey." I sucked in a breath, the memory hitting me full force. I'd never forget writing that inscription, knowing I needed to use the scenario in a future book because it was so romantic.

And I'd never forget the fleeting thought that Vince never would've done something like that for me. Of course, I'd brushed it off because he did other things. Fancy dinners. Expensive gifts. Bottomless... Meaningless compliments. I'd been the idiot, wanting a fairy tale so badly that I'd been duped into a farce.

"You remember?" Hunter's eyes went wide.

"I never forget a big romantic gesture like that... or the honor it was to play a role in it." I shoved the twinge of pain aside and forced my smile higher. "I might have to use it in a book someday."

"Use it... holy shit." Hunter wiped his hand over his mouth. "That would be amazing."

"Sydney, we should get going—"

"Did Ranger tell you we have a monthly book club in town?" Hunter cut him off. "It's more or less a Sydney Ward fan club for how frequently we pick your books as our monthly read."

"Hunter..."

Heat rose to my cheeks. "No, he didn't."

"I know you've... got a lot going on right now with the book and everything..." And there it was, the pinprick in the happy bubble, reminding me that my time to breathe untainted air would eventually dwindle. Hunter cleared his throat. "But if you're going to be around... available... we'd love to have you—"

"Hunter," Ranger interrupted his brother firmly and took a step forward, asserting himself into the conversation. "She's a guest here. It's not appropriate to interrupt her time—"

"It's fine, Ranger," I said and put my hand on his arm without even thinking.

Heat prickled my skin, but it wasn't half as intense as the way he looked at me and then immediately backed down.

"No, my brother's right," Hunter admitted with a nod, looking at Ranger like he admired but also didn't recognize him—a look that Ranger was completely oblivious to. "I shouldn't be taking advantage of you renting Ranger's place. My excitement got the best of me. I apologize."

"Don't apologize," I assured him with a smile. I should've released Ranger's arm at that point, but for some reason, it felt like my touch was reassuring him that I was okay. "I can't make any promises because I'm on a deadline... but when is your book club?"

I had no reason to give him hope. The thought of going to a book club made me feel like an imposter. A fake. Someone who thought they had love all figured out but couldn't have been more wrong in my supposed area of expertise.

How could I go and talk about love when I clearly knew nothing about it?

"It's two Saturdays from now. Right before Christmas."

I held my smile steady. "I'll see what I can do."

"Awesome." Hunter tried to contain it, but he looked as though I'd just told him I was going to name a character after him. "And I'll drop off that extra bike chain I have tomorrow morning," he tacked on, addressing Ranger this time.

"Thank you."

We said our goodbyes, Hunter returning inside as Ranger and I headed back to the Volvo.

"I apologize. He shouldn't have done that." He pulled out of the lot and drove back toward the highway.

"I was the one who got out of the car, Ranger. After what you told me, I wanted to meet him. I'm always happy to meet fans." *Or at least I was eager to meet the one Reynolds brother who was a fan of my books.* Though I wished the boost of confidence had done more. "I didn't realize he was your brother—I mean that the proposal book I signed was for your brother."

"Yeah." He smiled. "He'd do anything for Zoey."

I hummed, feeling the pit in my stomach deepen as my inner Jennifer Lopez reminded me, *Those who can't do, teach. Those who can't find a decent man write book boyfriends.*

"I thought you might have told him about me." Hunter was more of a fan than Ranger had let on. He didn't just enjoy my books; he'd used one to propose to his now wife. I wouldn't be surprised or blame Ranger for letting it slip that I was renting his apartment.

Ranger's eyes flicked to me and then back to the road.

"I said I wouldn't," he said it so matter of fact that it made my breath catch.

Of course, I remembered that, but he could've easily told his brother and instructed him not to say anything. He could've shown him my book. Taken photos of it. Done a million things to make his brother happy at my expense, but he hadn't. He'd respected me—a stranger—above it all.

"I know." I blinked rapidly and swallowed over the lump in my throat. I'd been hurt by so many people who'd claimed to love me and have my back. It was no wonder I had trouble trusting my handsome landlord, even though he'd given me no reason not to. "Thanks, also, for the chocolate peanut butter bars," I said, changing topics. "They were really good."

He smiled. "I'm glad you liked them. They were a hit at trivia night." *Not as much of a hit as those dimples were with my lady parts.* "And thank you for loaning me your book."

The warmth inside me shriveled up, and I turned my head to the window. *No need to make it awkward.*

"Romance novels aren't for everyone, but it was nice of you to give it a shot with an open mind," I murmured.

"A shot?" His head tipped, brows pulling tight. "I don't understand."

Don't go down this path. Don't prompt explanations you might not like.

But he looked so confused—frustratingly confused, that I couldn't stop myself. "Well, you returned it yesterday morning."

"I did." He blinked, clearly not catching on.

Great, he was going to make me spell this out.

I inhaled deeply and then blurted out, "You only kept it overnight, so I'm assuming you didn't get very far before you realized it wasn't for you. Which is really fine. I'm not offended at all, and we don't need to talk about it."

He stared at me like I'd just insisted that two plus two equaled five. "I read the whole book, Sydney."

My jaw dropped. "What?" I laughed nervously. "The whole… Did you… stay up all night or something?"

Sure, I had die-hard fans do that before—wait up on the eve of release day for my book to hit their Kindles and then read until the sun rose. But Ranger wasn't that, was he? Or had I just assumed the worst rather than thinking he'd loved my book so much he couldn't put it down?

"No, I didn't stay up all night." *Well, there was my answer.* "It didn't take me very long because I can read twenty thousand words per minute."

It was a good thing I was already sitting—no, it was a good thing I wasn't driving the car because it was one of those slam-on-the-brakes, what-did-you-just-say moments.

"Twenty… thousand." *How fast did normal people read? And how long did it take them to finish a book?* I folded my arms, unable to process the number fast enough. "So, it took you…"

"Less than ten minutes to finish your novel. I think I read a little slower than normal because I've never read a romance novel before." His lips pursed like the thought annoyed him. "But I can recite it back to you if you don't believe me."

"Recite…you're joking." My laughter fell flat when he began speaking again.

"'She opened her eyes to a room she didn't remember. Her head pounded and blood was splattered all over her clothes. She'd been compromised. Her cover blown. And now, the man she'd been hunting had gone from prey to predator. 'I know you're there,' she called—'"

"Stop! I believe you," I cried out, desperate to stop what would've become a full-blown recitation of my entire novel. "I just…" I gave my head a little shake, trying to process it. "You read my book in ten minutes…"

"Less than ten—"

"And you can narrate it back in its entirety… perfectly… from memory. So, you can read a billion words per minute—"

"Twenty-thou—"

"And have a photographic memory," I concluded in awe.

"Twenty thousand and an eidetic memory, not a photographic one," he corrected. "A lot of people get those things confused because they're similar, but having a true photographic memory has never been scientifically proven to exist. Having an eidetic memory means being able to recall high levels of details about an object or experience after only seeing it once."

Everything. He could remember everything he'd ever read. I almost had to laugh because, after thirty books, I sometimes forgot passages or scenes that I'd *written,* let alone read.

"That's… you're incredible," I said before I could stop myself.

Now the color really pressed into his cheeks, my compliment embarrassing him.

"It's not really my choice, it's just how I am."

"Still…" I trailed off with a soft chuckle. "Half the time, I can't even remember the names of side characters or main characters' children in my books. I can't imagine being able to recall… everything. It's… mind-blowing."

He shrugged. "It's how my brain works."

It was incredible to me, but it was normal for him. To know— to remember literally everything.

All I could think about was the character, the Receiver of Memories, from *The Giver,* the older man who remembered the entirety of their civilization's memories. And how the blessing of near-perfect recall was married to the burden of carrying every pain with every pleasure.

I bit my lip. "Isn't that… overwhelming?"

The change in him was so subtle I almost missed it but so stark it made me catch my breath. I couldn't imagine what it was like to remember everything perfectly. Every high and every low. What a weight he must carry.

"Sometimes," he rasped quietly.

I swallowed and searched for something else to say. I didn't want the conversation to continue down this path; I selfishly wanted those dimples back.

"So, are you like the fastest reader in the world?"

"Oh, no." He laughed and my stomach fluttered. "Howard Berg holds that title and the highest rate of twenty-five thousand words per minute. He did that back in 1990. Although I haven't timed myself recently to see if I'm getting closer. I almost hit twenty-one thousand when I was working on my PhD, but then we decided to open Reynolds Protective Group, and I haven't checked my pace since."

"You have a PhD?" I shouldn't be surprised—*I wasn't surprised; I was fascinated.*

"I have three."

"Three…" I choked.

"Mathematics. Engineering. And physics."

"Wow," I murmured, forcing my gaze to the window so I wouldn't keep staring at him like a fool. What other words were there? None. *Here lay Sydney Ward, prolific author, dead from lack of words. Rest In Peace.* "I guess why not when you can remember everything you read…"

"I enjoy reading. Hunter just got me a new Kindle for Christmas last year, so that's good for keeping physical copies to a minimum."

"I bet," I murmured. "Soon, the Library of Congress is going to have to start borrowing books from you."

"Well, the Library of Congress has around fifty-one million

books in its catalog, so even if I averaged thirty books a day, every day for a year, it would still take three thousand—"

"Ranger." I reached over and placed my hand on his arm, wrecking his train of thought. Again, heat trickled through my fingertips like a steady stream of lava. "I was kidding."

His eyes met mine and then lowered to where I touched him. Slowly, I pulled my hand back.

"Oh." He blinked and then his tongue slid out, pulling his lips between his teeth before he declared, "Right."

All those books... and I'd given him a romance novel.

Don't get me wrong, I was damn proud of my books, but to a man who'd consumed more books than most of the people on this planet... combined... I was realistic that my novel probably wasn't in his top ten literary masterpieces.

"I did enjoy your book though," he insisted, and my heart skipped. "It was very informative."

Informative.

My head tipped to the side, all of my thoughts shifting off-kilter.

Informative wasn't normally a word used to describe my books... or romance novels in general. *He said he liked it though, so it had to be a compliment, right?*

"Thank you." *I think.*

I bit into my tongue, tempted to ask what he meant by informative. *About the genre? About explicit content? That one wasn't even one of my spiciest...* But I was far more interested in him at the moment than I was in what he thought about my books.

"So, three doctorates... how old are you?"

"Thirty-two. I'll be thirty-three on March ninth."

Thirty-two. Older than I thought... but still two years younger than me.

"And you went from math and engineering and physics... to a bodyguard?"

"Well, not exactly." Color tinted his cheeks. "I don't work in the field. I prepare all of the information and data analysis for our clients, handle all the research and data collection, and then provide any technological assistance from the office."

That made more sense, for sure. Except there was just this look on his face that made me wonder… that made me ask…

"Do you want to work in the field?" I could tell instantly that my question surprised him.

Ranger opened and closed his mouth several times. He wasn't used to not having an answer to a question, and for some reason, that made me feel good; that even though he knew everything, I could still surprise him.

"I'm the best at what I do, so it makes sense for me to work behind the scenes. I can collect and process information so much faster than my brothers," he said without an ounce of hubris.

That wasn't what I asked, but before I could probe, we were back at the house and pulling into the driveway.

This time, I was front row and center as Ranger waited for the garage door to rise completely before pulling inside. My eyes drifted up, seeing clearly through the window into the apartment and confirming my suspicions that he'd *definitely* seen my naked boobs that first week.

And now I knew that thanks to his *eidetic* memory, he'd remember my breasts in vivid detail until the end of his days. *Wonderful.* I swallowed a groan.

"Thank you for the ride."

"Of course. I'm sorry about the bike. I'll have the chain fixed tomorrow if you change your mind about riding," he said as we got out of the car.

We met at the back of the Volvo, him pausing to allow me to walk by.

"Thank you," I repeated, and we stood for a second in silence. "I'm going to go—"

"Of course." He took a half step back even though I didn't need the room. I'd just passed by him when he called, "Oh, and Sydney."

"Yeah?" I spun on the balls of my feet, feeling something in my right calf pinch uncomfortably.

"Please don't feel obligated to go to Hunter's book club if you really can't. He'll be okay," he assured, and I couldn't help my small smile.

"I know, but I'm still going to think about it." I swore I didn't say it for the dimples, but the flutter in my stomach called me a liar.

He ducked his head. "Have a good afternoon."

I headed for the door to the stairs.

"You, too—ahh—" My leg cramped hard, and I started to go down.

My hands shot out, prepared for a cement landing when an arm hooked around my waist and hauled me back so forcefully both my feet lifted off the ground.

Even though lanky was the first word that came to mind, Ranger was surprisingly strong. *Unexpectedly.* He'd picked me up and steadied me like I weighed no more than a doll.

"Are you alright, Sydney?" Ranger panted, his warm, heavy breaths brushing my ear. "What's wrong?"

"Sorry, my leg just cramped really bad," I explained, my adrenaline morphing into something that was as equally hot as it thrummed through my veins. "I'm sorry. I'm fine." I tried to put some weight on my right leg, and as soon as I did, another sear of pain made me gasp and sag.

He pulled me tighter, his arm wrapped around my middle, the whole of his front pressed to my back... my ass.

"You're not fine," he insisted with a low voice that inched dangerously close to a growl.

Neither was he.

His breaths were labored, warmly caressing my cheek. I swore I could feel the heavy beat of his chest as it rose and fell in rapid time with my own. And lower... lower I felt the swell of his erection and my core responded with a warm knot of ache.

"Ranger…" I turned my head, putting my face within inches of his.

Our eyes connected, curiosity and want growing from his deep-green depths, and then those eyes lowered to my mouth. My lips peeled apart like a seam split by heat, and for a moment, the pain evaporated—everything evaporated except for him.

And then he shuddered, re-collecting himself and what he should be doing.

"Let me help you upstairs," he said matter-of-factly, turning and lifting me into his arms.

I hung on to his neck, keeping my face close to his chest where he couldn't see my embarrassment.

"I was biking really fast when the chain broke—" I winced when my foot bumped the wall as he climbed the narrow stairs, the cramp in my calf worsening. "It must've tightened up from stopping so quickly and then not stretching." I exhaled through another wave of pain.

Ranger opened the door and set me down at the edge of the couch.

"Thank you—" I stopped short when he lowered to his knees, reaching for my right foot and propping it on his thigh.

"Can I remove your shoe?" He looked at me, blinking innocently.

My head bobbed, the pressure in my leg worsening. "Sure," I squeaked.

"Stretching and massage are the best for a leg cramp. So, I'm just going to remove your shoe," he said as my sneaker came off and hit the floor. "And stretch out your calf."

"Ahh," I whimpered and shivered as he carefully flexed my ankle forward and back. It hurt, but it was the good kind of hurt; it was the hurt that was helping.

Back and forth, he coaxed my locked muscles to release their hold.

"Deep breaths," he encouraged and I closed my eyes, focusing on his instructions. "You're so tight. Just breathe through it."

My inhale hitched on its way down into my lungs.

Did he just say that?

My core clenched. Oh my god. What was wrong with me?

I squeezed my eyes tighter, forcing myself to focus on my leg, not fantasize about my landlord.

"Okay, I'm going to work my fingers along your muscles. Just keep breathing." His voice had a slight husk to it now as his fingers inched up my ankle to my calf.

I bit into my cheek, but not before a small whimper escaped. Now, my leg wasn't the only thing that was cramping.

"Does that feel good?" He pushed harder.

"Mmm." I nodded quickly, trying to rein in my racing pulse.

This was horrible. And sad. Did I really need to get laid so badly that I was getting turned on by a calf massage?

"That's it. Just relax for me a little more. Almost there."

I peeled my eyes open and stared at him. This wasn't healing, it was torture.

Torture to hear him. Torture to watch him. Torture to see his attention so focused on his hands, on the way his fingers stroked and rubbed the entire length of my calf. He was so focused on me in a way that no one had... ever... focused on me before. I wondered what he was thinking... *wondered if he knew what I was thinking...*

"Do you want me to go deeper?"

Nope, he definitely didn't know what I was thinking, or he wouldn't have said that.

There was no inflection. No insinuation. No flicker of the eyes or tease of his fingers. Nothing except the slight purse of his lips. Ranger asked with the purest of intentions, but it didn't matter because, apparently, my rational brain was cramping, handicapping me into hearing sexual undertones in everything he said.

What would it feel like if that attention—that intensity of his was focused on other parts of me? Want and ache like I'd never felt before coiled at the bottom of my stomach, a different kind of pressure craving for release.

And that couldn't happen.

"No!" I said a little too forcefully, bolting upright and yanking my leg back. "It's good. I'm good." I rose and almost tripped in my haste to step away from him and the couch. "Much better now, thank you."

The cramp had subsided, but the price I'd paid for relief was far more painful.

"Oh, good." He was still a little concerned. "You should take a hot shower to keep the muscles relaxed."

"Yup." I nodded enthusiastically and thumbed awkwardly in the direction of the bathroom. "I'm just going to go do that. Thank you. Again." I backpedaled, lopsided, because I still had one shoe on. "For everything."

I reached the other side of the apartment, waved like an idiot, and then closed myself in the bathroom.

My chest heaved in deep breaths as I turned on the water *to cold*. The last thing my body needed was more heat.

What was I doing? I buried my face in my hands and stifled a groan. I came out here to get away from everything... to heal... to figure out if I could even write again. Not to hook up with my sexy, nerdy landlord. I might not have an eidetic memory, but I remembered that much about my plans.

The cold shower was brutal and useless. When I was done, I threw on a shirt and grabbed my laptop. My last resort to coax the ache from my system. I wrote and wrote, stacking every layer of my frustration out on the page because that was as far as it could go. And when I'd left Jenny just as knotted up about her hero as I was about Ranger, I climbed into bed, ready to sleep off the rest of my fantasies.

I lasted ten whole minutes of tossing and turning before I muttered a low curse and reached for the small pink vibrator I'd brought with me.

Goddamn you, Mr. Fineinstein.

CHAPTER 7

Ranger

I hadn't been thinking.
    Breathe in.
    That was the only conclusion.
Breathe out.
    But I'd never… not thought before. Never not analyzed and considered and processed. It hadn't seemed possible. *Cogito, ergo sum. I think, therefore, I am.* It wasn't just a philosophy, it was a fact.
    Breathe in.
    But the second I touched Sydney—held her—the neural highways of my mind came to a crashing halt. I understood the chemical reaction. I'd read every textbook and journal I could find on the body's reaction to attraction in the last week and a half. A rush of dopamine, norepinephrine, and serotonin flooded into my system, but nowhere could I find why my brain stopped working.
    Breathe—
    "Ranger?" A loud knock followed by Gunner's voice inside my office popped my eyes open.
    I stood and pushed open the closet doors. "Yes—"
    "Jesus—" My brother jumped back, his hand reaching for his waist even though his weapon wasn't on him. I guess I'd really

surprised him. "What… what the hell are you doing in the closet, Baby Brains?"

His brow furrowed. I'd seen that face enough to understand it meant he was worried about something.

"Meditating." I shut the doors behind me and straightened my vest.

"In the closet?" He folded his arms.

He didn't remember the closet, but I did.

"Meditation is best practiced in a space devoid of distractions so that the attention can stay focused inward. Doing that in the closet removes sound and activity and light from my senses."

Gunner's head tipped, watching me sit down at my desk. "Alright, I'll bite. Since when do you meditate?"

My chin dropped. "Since last week."

"Why?"

I blinked twice. "Meditation is a great tool to reduce stress and anxiety, to improve focus and self-awareness—"

"I wasn't asking for the textbook, Baby Brains. I want to know what happened to you last week that made you feel like you needed to meditate."

My lips pulled together firmly, disliking the answer I had to give. "I stopped thinking."

"What?" His eyebrows reached for his hairline. "When? Why?"

"Yes, it's very concerning. It just happened. One minute, I was talking to Sydney in the garage. The next, her leg cramped, so I caught her to steady her, and then everything just went blank." I felt it again, the tense vibration in my body that appeared when I recalled the memory. "There are a variety of explanations for why the thought process can completely stop. Stroke, seizure, a handful of mental health illnesses—"

"Wait, wait, wait," he interrupted. "Rewind. You're telling me your brain stopped working as soon as you held her? How do you know?"

"Because all the thoughts were gone, Gunner." I huffed and

drummed my fingers on my desk. *Was he not listening?* "One minute, my thoughts are all there like a million-lane highway where I was just switching from one lane to the next. From driving to saying goodbye to Sydney to cataloging the steps to replace the broken bike chain… and then the highway was gone. And it was like I was in a field. Except I wasn't, I was in the garage. But I felt warmth like I was in the sun. There were goose bumps on my skin like from a breeze."

"Ranger…" Gunner was smiling at me.

"This has never happened before, Gunner. It could be serious." I stopped because Gunner made a noise, and that was when I noticed he was chuckling. "Why are you laughing? What if this is a symptom of a transient ischemic—a ministroke? Do I have brain damage?"

Gunner's loud hoot startled me as he threw his head back in uncontrolled laughter.

"I don't understand why you're laughing," I told him bluntly. "I'm telling you I lost my ability to think, and I can't find a medical explanation for it."

He laughed harder.

"I think I need to see a neurologist," I tried to emphasize the severity of this issue, but for some reason, my brother doubled over and started wheezing. "You're not very helpful," I grumbled.

Gunner held up a hand, waving it at me as he gasped for air, reeling his amusement in. "You don't need… a neurologist," he said between heaving breaths.

"I disagree."

"Baby Brains, you didn't stop thinking. You were just thinking with a different part of your body," he informed me, but he was making no sense.

"That's not possible, Gunner. No other part of your body has the capability to think. Your brain is what controls—"

"You can argue with me, Ranger, but for once—for maybe the very first time ever—you're wrong," he declared, and I shifted in my seat. He was wrong. I was never wrong. "You weren't thinking because you were feeling… because you've got the hots for your romance novelist renter."

I wasn't surprised that Hunter had told the rest of our brothers about Sydney; he was far too excited to keep that to himself.

"I understand how attraction works, Gunner. I have an IQ of one hundred and eighty-six. I know the chain reaction of dopamine—"

"You understand how it works, Baby Brains, but that's not the same as feeling it." He approached the desk and pointed at the surface. "Put your hand out."

I hesitated and then slid my hand forward.

He pulled something from his pocket and the next thing I knew, he'd snapped a rubber band on the back of my hand.

I tugged my hand back. "Ow—what—"

"You understand the process of what just happened, right? Probably how fast the rubber band was going when it hit your skin. What happened to your skin and nerves when it did"—I opened my mouth to respond, but he kept going— "but understanding doesn't mean you didn't feel the pain. It doesn't mean you didn't respond by pulling your hand away and rubbing the skin. So, you can understand all about the chemical reaction of desire, but that doesn't change what happens when you experience it."

I wrinkled my nose. I didn't like his explanation, but the lingering sting on my skin from the rubber band made it hard to refute.

"Okay." I wrinkled my nose. "How do I make it stop?"

He chuckled low again. "Give me your hand again and then tell me how you're going to make the rubber band not sting." When my brow creased, he continued, "You can't turn it off, Baby Brains."

I didn't like that answer either.

My mouth opened and shut. I'd been more at a loss for answers since I'd met Sydney than I'd ever been before in my entire life. It was disturbing. *Unsettling*. It was the kind of thing I would expect would make me want to avoid her presence… except it didn't. That was the most concerning part of all.

All these things I didn't understand were happening to me because of her, but I still found myself thinking about her all the time. Wondering how her day was going. Wondering how her calf was feeling. Wondering how her book was coming along. Wondering if I would stop thinking if I touched her again.

A disproportionate amount of my days… and the whole of my nights… passed thinking about her.

Normally, I wouldn't be able to claim something like that as fact since dreams occurred during the REM cycle of sleep, which was only about twenty percent of the entire night; to remember the dream, I'd have to wake up during that cycle each time. Statistically, the odds of that happening every night for almost two weeks were slim. However, I'd woken up all those mornings aroused. So even though I couldn't recall the dream, it was clear what… and who… it had been about.

"You have a crush on Sydney Ward, and I would just like to take a moment to say to you, for the first time ever, *I told you so*," he declared again with a triumphant smile. "You should ask her out."

"No." I opened up my computer and locked my eyes on the screen.

"Why not?"

"We've already had this conversation. She's renting my apartment and that would make things inappropriate."

It was already inappropriate that I'd just picked her up and then massaged her leg without even asking. But I'd just… reacted. Her cry of pain… watching her about to go down. There was no sense that I was doing the *wrong* thing except in hindsight when I recalled how she'd bolted off the couch and ran to the bathroom.

Guilt made my stomach uneasy. What I needed to do was apologize, not make things any worse by asking her on a date.

"Was it inappropriate for me to knock up a client's daughter?" He pressed.

I felt blood rush to my cheeks. "That's different."

"Because it's me?"

"Because this is me, Gunner... and I don't ask women out." I shifted in my seat.

"No, Baby Brains. You *haven't* asked a woman out. There's a difference—and not only a grammatical one," he said pointedly and then sighed. "I'm always the one who tells you that you're going to find someone... that you're going to find love just like the rest of us. So, you can protest all you want, but all I'm saying is that I've never seen you crush on someone before... Never heard you admit to not being able to think before. If being around Sydney makes that happen, that sounds to me like the kind of thing you explore."

I pulled my lips into a firm line. I'd thought I'd wanted what my brothers had. Love. Children. A family. But this couldn't be how it happened. I was too rational for that—too rational to fall for someone who was from the other side of the country.

"I'll think about it."

Gunner's mouth tipped up on one side. "Oh, I'm sure you'll overthink it, Baby Brains... but I hope you get to the same conclusion as me."

"What did you come in here for?" I asked before he could walk out.

"Oh, right." He patted his hand on the doorframe. "I just wanted to let you know I sent over some details for a new client who called this morning."

"Okay." My head bobbed and I opened up my email for the information and then looked back at him because he was still standing there.

"You could invite Sydney to your trivia night or go with her to Hunter's book club—"

"Gunner!"

"Alright, alright." He lifted his hands in surrender. "I'm going."

Once he left, I returned my attention to my work, but my focus wasn't wholly there. I still went through the motions, accessing information, public and private records for the social media influencer who was coming to Jackson Hole in January, potential threats, and the most secure places to stay. But that required only a fraction of the effort.

The rest of my thoughts revolved once more around Sydney. I couldn't ask her out. Not until I'd apologized… and not until I understood what she was thinking—what she thought about me. Because even though she'd practically run to the bathroom… that only happened after she'd let me take her shoe off.

I dragged my hand through my hair.

It didn't make sense. How was she okay with that, moaning as I massaged her calf one minute and panicked the next? I had to have done something—something I didn't realize. One of those things I didn't pick up on because it wasn't… because I wasn't… *smart enough.*

I gritted my teeth, barreling through the rest of my work for the day like I was out to prove there was nothing I couldn't figure out. Archer was going to check on me tomorrow morning when he saw that I'd completed every task in my inbox for the entire week… in one afternoon.

But there was nothing that drove me to madness more than not understanding.

No matter how smart I was, I wasn't smart enough to stop the effect Sydney Ward had on me… or to figure out if she felt the same.

"What's on the late-night menu tonight?" Mom came up behind me, yawning as she peered around my arm.

"Nutella brownies." I held on to the bowl tight, working the sticky batter into a seamless consistency.

"Ooh. Well, if you're taking them to someone else, you better make sure you hide them good because I've got a council meeting first thing in the morning, and those sound like the perfect sugar rush to get me through the commotion."

"On a Saturday again?" I asked, watching as she grabbed a cloth and absentmindedly began wiping up the counter, which was a complete mess.

I was a messy baker. Actually, I was a messy lot of things. Research showed messiness and clutter were common characteristics among people with higher IQs. My brothers thought it was comical how I never really noticed the mess until someone either remarked on it or went to clean it up; my mind was always busy in another lane of thought.

"Well, everyone's working during the week, so it's a little easier to meet first thing on a Saturday when everyone is fresh."

I couldn't think of anyone who was more dedicated to Wisdom's community than Mom. It was how she ended up having meetings on Saturdays. It was why she'd help out on the local ranches in the springtime when all the calves were being born and the ranchers could use a couple extra hands.

And it was all because that same community had stepped in to help her when Dad died. A single, grieving mother of five children couldn't do it alone, and she hadn't. Now she was giving back.

"So... how are you liking your guest's books?"

My head snapped up, watching as she casually licked the Nutella knife. "Did Hunter tell you?"

I was going to have to say something to him. Sydney had obviously come here to get away. If he was telling everyone that she was in town, it would ruin her vacation.

"Oh, Ranger," she tsked. "Your brother doesn't have to tell me a single thing that happens in my town, let alone on my property." She stuck the knife in the dishwasher. "I ran into her in the driveway the other day and recognized her instantly. You can't read romance novels and not recognize Sydney Ward—not if you're in Jerry's book club, at least."

Jerry owned the local hardware store; he and his wife, Trish, hosted the town's romance book club that Hunter had invited Sydney to.

"Oh." I set the bowl down and reached for my baking sheet.

"Don't worry. I'm sure I was cooler about it than Hunter."

I wasn't sure what that meant, but it didn't sound promising.

"So, have you finished all her books?"

"All the ones you have," I admitted.

After I'd read *Twisted Fate*, I immediately went to Mom's collection and read all of the ones on her shelves. I ordered the rest online, but they weren't scheduled to be delivered for a few days yet.

"I know. I'm woefully behind on her newer books, but they're all wonderful, aren't they?" She gushed. "And Sydney just seems like such a sweetheart. I just can't believe what happened to her. Such a shame. Jerry's still worked up over it, and it's been months."

I faced her, confused. "Something happened to her?"

Mom's eyes widened. "You didn't... Oh." She paused. "Sydney was in a relationship for a long time. Engaged. It was a big celebration among her readers. And then, it had to be maybe eight or nine months ago, she called off the engagement. She found out her fiancé was cheating on her."

I fumbled the spatula in my hand, sending it to the floor and sticky brown batter all over the tile.

Mess.

"Sorry," I mumbled.

"I'll get it." She ushered me away.

"I didn't... know that." I'd done a background check on Sydney when she'd requested the apartment, but I stuck to facts. *Did her license match her information? Did she have a criminal record?* Unlike for RPG clients, I didn't dig into social media or, worse, the regular media for any kind of information.

But this...

"I don't understand how someone could cheat on her," I said, hearing how my voice changed because I was suddenly angry for her. Angry because I couldn't understand how someone could be so idiotic.

Cheating on Sydney was the equivalent of dropping a lit match on the ground at a gas station. It was practically incomprehensible that someone could be so stupid.

She was beautiful and talented and passionate. And preceptive. The way she saw things... the way she saw me.

"That's because you have a good heart, Ranger." Mom smiled as she stood, giving my shoulder a pat when there was a knock at the front door.

"I'll get it." She left the kitchen and returned a minute later, a large box of roses in her arms. "As much as I wish these were for me..." I helped her set them on the counter. "I think... these are for your guest."

"I'll take them over."

Before she could reply, her phone blared with an incoming phone call.

"Thank you, honey. It's Amy." She held up her phone and backed out of the room. "I've got to go over the agenda for tomorrow. Have a good night..."

My plan was to apologize to Sydney in the morning. I'd run through several scenarios, everything from a text message to going up to the apartment as soon as I got home from work, but tomorrow morning felt most appropriate.

But these flowers threw a wrench in that plan. They were for her, and it didn't feel right to not deliver them tonight.

I wiped my hands on my pants, picked up the box, and left my brownie batter waiting on the counter.

I'd just give her the flowers and apologize for what happened last week. *I was sorry for carrying her. Sorry for rubbing her leg. Sorry if it was inappropriate for me—* Before I knew it, I was at her door.

There was commotion—*voices*—coming from inside. I'd been so lost in thought I hadn't even heard her talking.

"Yes, Don sent the letter."

My knuckles rapped twice. "Sydney? It's Ranger."

More commotion and footsteps.

"Gina, I have to—"

"It's him, isn't it? Mr. Fineinstein—"

"*Bye!*" Sydney was ending the call as she opened the door, phone in one hand and a wineglass in the other. "Hi. What's up?"

Her eyes scanned over me, and she shivered. Probably because she was only wearing shorts and a tank top. *And no bra.*

My dick stirred, blood rushing to the organ to make it thicken and pulse. *Why couldn't I control myself around her?* My lips pulled into a frustrated line.

I shouldn't be distracted by her chest. I shouldn't be recalling in *vivid detail* when she'd come to the front window topless. My body shouldn't be reacting because my brain knew it was inappropriate.

But when it came to Sydney Ward, there seemed to be no such phenomenon as *mind over matter* because the only thing that mattered was her.

"I'm sorry. I didn't mean to interrupt your call." I cleared my throat and shifted my weight, not used to having to hide a... physical reaction to someone.

"Oh, it's fine. It was just my friend slash agent, Gina." She folded her arms and then untucked one to brush her hair back from her face. "Were you baking?"

My gaze dropped. Cocoa powder dusted the sides of my khakis from where I'd wiped my hands. *Mess.*

"Nutella brownies," I said sheepishly, trying to brush away the dark marks for a second before I realized it was a bad idea to bring her attention below my waist.

"That looks—sounds amazing."

I looked up just in time to see how she rolled her bottom lip through her teeth; her stare definitely pointed directly at where my erection stretched the front of my pants.

Crap. I winced and shifted the box of flowers in front of me like a shield. This apology was as much of a mess as I was.

"Are those... for me?"

"Yes," I confirmed, and her eyes went wider. *She thought they were from me.* "No. I mean—I'm sorry." I shoved the box toward her. "They were delivered to the house for you, so I brought them over."

"Oh." She reached for them, her glass of wine tipping as she tried to take hold of the flowers.

"Actually, I can bring them in for you—" No. That was exactly the kind of inappropriate—

"That would be great." She stepped aside and took a healthy gulp of her red wine. "They're probably from Gina. Fridays are our Zoom sessions, and I've been struggling, so that's why there've been three glasses of wine involved."

I slid the box onto the table. I didn't know why but something prompted me to turn it and inspect the side.

To: Sydney

From: Your one true love.

"Ugh. Gina's ridiculous." Sydney rolled her eyes, chuckling from beside me at the inscription.

Time to apologize and leave, Ranger.

"Look, Sydney." I pulled my lips tight. "I wanted to apologize for the other day when your leg cramped, and I carried you. I don't think—I shouldn't have—"

"Helped me?" She stared at me like I was crazy.

"Well…" I dragged my hand through my hair. "I thought maybe I upset you."

She bit into her bottom lip, her gaze sliding up to mine. "Why would you think that?"

My mouth opened, but no words came out.

"You stopped me from face-planting in the garage and then made my leg feel like new…"

"I…" I gulped and raked my fingers through my hair. "You just ran into the bathroom, so I thought maybe I'd done something to upset you. I'm probably wrong. I'm not good at reading… people."

Her shoulders slumped and she gave her head a little shake. "No, that was all my fault. It… it wasn't you." She backed away from the table and finished off the wine in her glass.

"Oh." I buried my hands in my pockets, my eyes darting around the apartment.

I liked seeing the mark she left in the space. The unmade bed. Her laptop open on the couch. The candles on the table. I liked knowing she was here—that she was comfortable here.

"How is your leg feeling?"

"Fine. Sore, but fine." She sighed softly. "The least of my problems."

My brow creased. "What are you struggling with?"

Maybe I could help. I was good at fixing problems... finding answers. And maybe if I had a reason to think right now, those thoughts would drown out the steady thrum of other things—other feelings—from my system.

She looked at me and then gave me her back as she went to the sink to rinse her glass.

Or maybe it was none of my business. My lips pursed in annoyance. I never... thought about those things until it was too late.

"Struggling?"

"You said that your friend sent you the flowers because you're struggling."

Mom's revelation stayed on repeat in my mind. Was Sydney struggling because of her ex-fiancé? *Had something happened? Was she okay?* That was all I cared about.

"Oh, it's nothing." She dried her hands and began looking through the cabinets. "I'm fine."

Fine. Gunner said to never believe a woman when she said she was fine. I didn't want to call Sydney a liar, but... something inside me didn't believe she was okay. An instinct, I guess. A kind I'd never had before.

"Are you sure? If there's anything I can do to help..." I had no idea what that could be and felt like a fool for asking.

"Well, unless you can help me write this book, I think I'm on my own," she murmured, flashing a wry grin over her shoulder as she opened the cupboard next to the fridge. Her eyes scanned the shelves all the way to the top when she exclaimed, "Aha!"

My jaw went slack, watching her tiny shorts ride up as she reached for the vase. Inches of her thighs. Higher and higher. Until the bottom swell of her ass peeked out. Blood thudded wildly in my ears, and my jaw slackened.

I was so hard it was... startling. I'd had erections before, of course; they were a natural part of life... of being a man. But they'd never felt like this. I'd never been so painfully aroused it felt like I couldn't breathe. Thankfully, she faced away from me because I had to adjust myself.

With a low grunt, I rearranged my straining cock, desperate to alleviate the pressure.

Her small whimper drew my immediate attention, and I caught Sydney planting her hands on the countertop, about to climb on top of it.

"Wait, Sydney. Let me." I strode over like a bull in a china shop, practically shoving her into the fridge as I easily plucked the vase from the top shelf and handed it to her. "Here."

As soon as it was in her hands, I retreated to the other side of the table, using the back of one of the chairs as a shield.

"Thank you." She filled the vase with water and brought it to the table, arranging the flowers as she admitted, "I'm not good at asking for help."

"Why not?"

She paused and looked at me for a second like she'd never been asked that before.

"I only had myself to rely on for a long time. My mom was a single mom who was constantly trying to find her soul mate, most times at my expense. She was either working or dating, never really around to help me, so I never learned how to ask." She returned her attention to the roses with a shrug. "She died when I was nineteen, and I guess it's a hard habit to break, especially when people I try to trust end up letting me down."

Like her ex-fiancé.

"You can count on me." It was the truth. *A fact. I would never let her down.*

Sydney looked at me, her lips parting. "Ranger—"

"Maybe I could help you with your book." I folded my arms, determined to prove it to her. "I wrote all of my brother's English papers in high school. Plus, I've read almost all of your books, so if you need a reference—"

"All of them?" She squeaked.

"Well, Mrs. Basil really didn't like Gunner—"

"I meant all of my books."

"Oh." I ran my fingers through my hair. "Well, I read all the ones my mom had. Twenty-one of them. The Broken series and the newer books I had to order."

She stared, pulling her bottom lip between her teeth. When she did that, my body reacted like a flame responding to an accelerant. She described it in her books as heat flooding every cell. My brain knew it was vasodilation. The widening of the blood vessels to allow more blood flow which increases warmth.

But just like the snap of the rubber band, being able to explain the physical reaction wasn't the same as feeling it. *And all I could feel was the way I desired her.*

"Thank you, Ranger. But I'm fine—I'll be fine." *There was that fine again.* She spun and swayed a little. I stepped forward—another instinct to make sure she was stable—but she grabbed the edge of the counter and steadied herself before my help was needed.

"I'm happy to help…"

Her pulse fluttered against her neck; my heart wasn't the only one beating a little harder. A little nervous.

"Ranger, I'm trying to write the first kiss," she said, her voice suddenly breathless.

My body's reactions and reality crashed together. *First. Kiss.*

"Oh." I reached for my throat, my own voice sounding unstable.

"So, I'm sure you don't want to help with that." Her low laugh was husky—rueful—as she tucked a stray hair back behind her ear.

My mouth opened and then shut.

I should go. I didn't always catch on to the clues in time, but this time, I was certain it was time to leave. To say good night. Walk out. Return to the Nutella brownie batter. It was very clear anything else would cross the professional boundaries I was trying to keep in place.

Except she didn't say I couldn't help her or that she didn't need my help. She'd said that I wouldn't want to help, and that was factually incorrect.

I wanted to help. I wanted her to know she could count on me. And I wanted it more than anything.

I stepped forward, my head ducking down. A strand of hair tumbled onto my forehead, and I quickly reached up and brushed it back.

"Ranger…"

My gaze collided with hers. I recognized the emotion in her voice, questioning and hopeful. My heart pounded in my chest harder than I'd ever felt before.

And maybe I also wanted to know what a first kiss would be like in a perfect world—in one of her books. Then I'd know what to do when it came time for me to kiss someone in real life.

"If you want my help, Sydney, I'd like to stay."

CHAPTER 8

Ranger

Her full lips peeled apart, sucking in a quick breath that made her chest inflate.

Was that the wrong answer? Had I misinterpreted what she said... what she meant?

I stood paralyzed. Every silent second made me second-guess myself. I never second-guessed a response. Not once. I never responded unless I was certain the answer was right. But she'd had three glasses of wine. Maybe she'd meant she didn't want my help, and it came out wrong.

God, I was so bad at this.

Gunner—Archer—Hunter—any of them would know. But me... I knew everything else but this.

"Sorry—" I reached for the back of my neck and went to turn.

"Wait, Ranger." She rushed to the couch, digging out her computer from under a pile of blankets. "I'd like you to stay. I'd appreciate... the help." She blew strands of hair from her face and opened the screen. "I've been stuck at the same spot for almost a week, and I just can't..."

"Just tell me what to do. I'll do anything."

She peered up from underneath her eyelids. *Anything.* I'd meant anything to help her.... *Right?*

She set her laptop on the table and folded her arms, the movement pushing her breasts against her tank.

"Tell me how to write a first kiss."

She focused on her desperation. Three glasses of wine and writer's block were a heavy distraction. *But not for me.* My eyes were drawn to the outline of her nipples. They were pink. The shade of ripe raspberries, I recalled from those few seconds all those weeks ago. I wondered if I rubbed them, would it make her moan like she had while I massaged her leg?

I winced, my cock jamming against the waist of my pants.

"I can't—I don't—" I croaked and then cleared my throat. "Why don't you tell me a little about the story?"

"You said you haven't read the Broken series?"

"Not yet, no." My brow creased. "I can download a copy and read it now if you want. It will only take—"

"Ten minutes, I know." She waved her hands and popped her lip through her teeth again. "No, it's better if you don't... if you haven't read them."

My head tipped. Was this the feeling Archer had when he said there was more to a situation? More to an answer? I'd never understood how it was possible to feel that until now.

She stared at the screen, rolling her bottom lip between her teeth until the buzz in my blood returned. *Vasodilation. Heat. Want.*

"How about you tell me where you're stuck," I murmured.

"Well, my heroine, Jenny, is working with a medical examiner, Max, to solve a murder." She started to walk toward the window as she talked, the sway of her hips—her ass—fighting to steal my attention... and fighting dirty. "They've been working on this case and the tension is building." She stared outside, but it was late; there couldn't be much to see except the soft glow of streetlights. "The case has... revealed painful things about her previous relationship, and Max has really been there for her."

"What things?" I hadn't read the series, but it sounded like the story was rooted in more than fiction.

Her lips peeled apart. "Her ex wasn't the kind of person she thought he was."

Mom's words came back to me. *Like hers hadn't been?*

Sydney looked away and continued to pace. "Now, they're in Jenny's office, and Max just told her about some test results, and she's frustrated, and I know the moment is right for them to kiss… I just…" Her shoulders slumped. "I just keep hitting a wall."

My jaw clenched. I kept having to steer my thoughts back on track because every time she walked away from me, my focus was drawn to her shorts that were still hiked up from earlier; the bottom curve of her ass teased me from the edge with each step.

My dick throbbed against my pants. I was so attracted to her, I didn't… I didn't know what was happening to me, but I craved more of it.

It was like when Gunner took me out for my twenty-first birthday. Two hard seltzers were all it took for my words to slur and my balance to tip. This attraction was like getting drunk for the first time; I wanted to know what would happen as much as I was afraid of it.

I was still trying to pinpoint the reason I couldn't get her off my mind. Was it her beauty? I couldn't recall a woman more beautiful than Sydney. Was it because I'd seen her breasts? I'd never seen a woman's naked chest outside of a movie or TV show, even if this instance had only been an accident. *Was it because she made the thoughts stop? Because touching her made feelings make sense?*

"Ranger?" Her voice pulled me from the spiral of thoughts, and I looked up to see her walking slowly in my direction.

My muscles pulled tight in one cohesive motion when she came to a stop right in front of me. All of the ache concentrating on one thing: *her.*

"Well, if she's upset, then he would probably comfort her." I gulped, clutching the chair in front of me like it was an anchor to reality—to rationality. My heart pumped harder against my chest.

More blood. More heat. More cells, tingling with arousal. With every second, matter rose higher and higher over my mind. "That's what your heroes do in roughly sixty-four percent of your other novels."

Roughly because I hadn't read them all.

"You'd think, after all those books, I'd have this down to a science by now." Her resignation spurred me.

Science. Facts.

The proverbial light bulb went off in my head.

"Did you know philematology is the science of kissing?" I blurted out.

"What?" Her eyebrows lifted.

"The science of kissing. The study of the muscles, mostly the orbicularis oris." I lifted my hand, my finger poised to trace around her mouth to indicate where the muscle was, but I stopped. *I shouldn't touch her. I shouldn't—*

"Show me."

I sucked in a deep breath, burying oxygen along with her instruction in my chest. *I still shouldn't touch her.* Except my hand kept moving forward.

When we were little, Gunner would provoke Hunter. Poke him or pinch him, just to annoy him if he was bored, and when Mom would step in, Gunner would always claim, '*I didn't do it. My hand did.*' It was a foolish excuse, like his hand could act independently of his brain. And I never understood where he could come up with it.

Until now.

My finger drifted to the corner of her mouth with a mind entirely of its own, touching down on the soft skin without regard for rationality or restraint.

"Simple kisses use as few as two muscles and burn two to three calories." Facts fell from my mouth in a voice I didn't recognize, but my brain focused only on the path of my finger along the slope of her upper lip. "But passionate kisses can involve as many as twenty-three to thirty-four facial muscles. Those can consume between five and twenty-six calories per minute."

Her lips parted, and my finger settled lower on the full swell of her bottom lip. I tested the plump flesh. Pushing. Stroking. It was so soft—softer than I'd imagined. Like a silk pillow against my finger. No wonder she always bit it.

What if I was the one biting it?

My jaw locked, but the rumbling noise from my chest still slipped out. I felt the catch of her breath, but I couldn't pull away.

"Lips are a hundred times more sensitive than the tips of your fingers." A shiver ran through her. "In fact, lips are even more sensitive than—" *No.* I caught myself and jerked my hand back, but the rest of me remained rooted in place—locked under her stare.

"More sensitive than..."

I swallowed. "Than your genitals."

"Really?" She lifted her eyebrows, the orbs of her eyes flickering in the light.

In her books, she sometimes related the heroine's eyes to gemstones because of their color or the way they glittered. I stared hard, but there was no gemstone to match the warm brown of her eyes, nor did they glitter or glisten. But maybe that wasn't the point. Maybe the point was that her stare... when it was trained on me like this... was something precious. Something rare and valuable and indestructible. *Something I never wanted to let go of.*

"It's possible for a woman to orgasm from kissing," I said, my voice rough. "Not that I—I mean—from what I've read, it's possible."

I shouldn't keep talking, but I couldn't stop. Facts were my shield. My buffer. Usually, they came out to build up my walls, but with Sydney, each fact was like another brick tumbling to the ground.

Her lips quirked up ever so slightly, and then her tongue slid along the seam. "So, you're saying I should give my heroine an orgasm from this kiss?"

"What? No—I mean—That's not—" I flinched, caught even more off guard.

"Then how would you have this first kiss go, Ranger? If not straight to orgasm?"

My jaw went slack. *Danger.* She was too close—everything was too much… again. "I… don't—I'm not… sure."

"Then tell me about your first kiss." Her gaze lowered to my mouth. "Maybe that will inspire me."

Blood collected in my cheeks. More vasodilation. Increased blood pressure. Heart rate. Breathing.

Chemistry and anatomy, fact after fact, ignited in my brain… but they didn't stop. They caught fire and flamed until there was nothing left of them but ashes underneath the blaze of attraction.

"Oh. Well, I haven't…"

Her gaze traveled over my face, and my answer was given away without a single word needing to be spoken.

"You've never kissed someone?" Her eyes widened.

My jaw clamped shut, my tongue sliding out and drawing my lips in. I hesitated because I didn't want her to tell me to leave. I didn't want her to ask what made me offer to help when I had no clue about what I was helping with.

But I also didn't know how to respond with anything other than the truth.

"No."

Thirty-two and never been kissed. I wasn't ashamed of who I was and the things I had… or hadn't experienced, but I was used to the impression it gave people of me… an impression I didn't want Sydney to have.

"Why not?" Her brow creased, and I wanted nothing more than to reach up and smooth it. "Have you never wanted to?"

I couldn't stop myself from picking up on every detail, including how she asked, like it was my choice when most people would assume the opposite. That it was because I was awkward and not very social, I'd never had the opportunity to kiss someone.

"No, but it's not about wanting to. I want to make sure it's right. When I learn things, I study everything about them, read and research until I'm confident I won't make a mistake," I told her, unable to shake the rasp from my voice.

"You've never kissed someone because you haven't learned enough about it?"

I felt my heartbeat all the way in my throat. "I've learned a lot from your books about that. I've read all those perfect first kisses, so I think I have a good idea of what it takes to do it correctly when the time comes."

"So, I'm the one who taught you how to kiss?"

"Well, your books," I confirmed, allowing my chin to dip before I realized it brought my mouth closer to hers.

Our breaths tangled in the small space. Hot and unsteady. Panting more so than breathing. *She had to feel this heat too, right?* My body was reacting to her pheromones, so I wasn't the only one sensing that this was more than a conversation.

"And what did they teach you?" Her tongue dragged over her bottom lip, and my erection pulsed, leaking precum like water trickling from a dam about to burst.

I'd never been this aroused before—and neither had I ever needed to exercise such restraint.

"To angle the face," I croaked. "So the noses don't collide."

"Show me."

Touch her. That was really what she was asking.

I swallowed hard, watching my hands frame her cheeks and tilt her head to mine.

"What else did you learn?" she murmured, and I swore her eyes had changed color from their warm brown to a caramelized honey.

"The position of the lips." It was impossible to swallow. "To press soft at first and then add firmness." My blood pumped so loudly I could hardly hear myself speak. "How to coax the mouth open with my tongue."

All the things I'd felt before intensified as though they were put in a pressure cooker. Even the slightest change—the slightest hitch of her breath or brush of her chest into mine—created an exponential response in my body.

"How the tongues would interact. Where mine should stroke and explore," I went on, my voice completely hoarse. "The sounds you would make to indicate your pleasure."

A soft moan escaped her mouth, and a quake ran through my entire body.

Nuclear fission seemed less powerful than the way being around her made each and every one of my cells come apart. A chain reaction that released desire until my body was nothing more than a collection of atoms bound to her by the laws of attraction.

"All that?" She bit her bottom lip and then her hand reached up.

I didn't see it, only felt her palm flatten to my chest. Goose bumps cascaded over my skin at the first brush of her fingertips. I'd never been touched by a woman before. Not like this. Not… more than platonically. My heart clambered under her hand, running a marathon while I remained rooted in place.

"Your books were very instructional," I rasped, my thumb anchoring to her bottom lip and sliding over the full pink swell as her head tipped closer.

I'd never been this close to kissing a woman—never been this close to a woman, period. And I was on the verge of exploding, like I had no more control over my body than I did in high school. *Maybe even less.*

"Informative," she breathed out the word. "You said they were informative."

"Yes. Very." I exhaled roughly, my mouth drifting closer to hers.

"Then you know a kiss is more than technicalities. The only way to know if you got a first kiss right… is to do it."

Our eyes locked, and another deep groan quaked unmistakably from my chest. It wasn't possible—physically possible—for eyes to speak, but hers did. More than speak. They screamed, *"Kiss me."*

"Are you testing me?" I rasped.

Please say yes.

"Yes."

The invisible chain holding me back snapped. My mouth crushed hers, rough and sloppy at first in my eagerness, but I wanted her too much to worry about failing.

Desire surged through me. Her lips were even softer than they'd felt to my thumb. And her moan… I shuddered when she instantly sighed onto my lips. It had to mean she wanted this—*my kiss.*

Angle of the mouth. Tongue to stroke—no, slide along the seam—*Fuck it.* I couldn't think. She'd done that thing again where my thoughts fell to the ground like loose confetti, desire trampling over them with its irrational fervor.

My lips slanted over hers, and I felt both her hands grab hold of my vest and pull me closer.

God, she tasted so good. Sweet and tart and all Sydney. I slid my tongue out, wanting more—needing more—and dragged it along the entrance to her mouth. Her lips parted, and her tongue darted out to tangle with mine. Warm and soft and welcoming.

Jesus.

They never described it like this. Not my brothers. Not her books. They never described how blood became electricity surging and arcing through my veins. They never described this kind of heat that consumed but didn't burn.

Kissing her was nothing short of tasting fruit from the tree of knowledge, and I wanted to know everything.

I stroked along the sides of her tongue, tasting every inch of the soft heat before exploring the recesses of her mouth. Normally, there would be a million facts my brain processed about a situation, but for this, it only logged her reactions. It tracked every time her breath caught as I slid my tongue deep into the heat of her mouth. It marked each soft moan when I sucked on her tongue and then her bottom lip.

Was it always like this? Did all women taste this good? I groaned as her arms wound around my neck. Was it supposed to feel like I was losing my mind?

My dick pulsed painfully like it was about to erupt. I'd never needed to orgasm like this before—never felt an ache of this magnitude. I inched forward until she bumped into the table. I didn't know how to describe what I wanted—what I needed—except that it all involved more of her.

But somehow, she knew.

Holding on to me tight, she lifted herself onto the edge of the table. Her legs instantly drifted apart, and I stepped between them, drawn by some kind of magnetism.

"Sydney," I groaned, my eyes screwing tight as my hips collided with the heat between her thighs, sending a surge of desire so strong through me, my cock started to leak cum. The dam of my orgasm breaking in steady drops.

I panted heavily, sliding my hands down the column of her neck until they latched on to the racing thrum of her pulse.

I wanted more, though I knew I shouldn't. Only one kiss. *Only this test.*

"Sydney..." Gritting my teeth, I peeled my hands from her throat, but as soon as I did, she tore her mouth from mine.

"Please." She took my right wrist and brought my hand to her breast.

I didn't know who was the first to quake, me or her.

"Oh god," I groaned, my hand latching greedily over her flesh.

My heart was going to explode; it had never beat this fast in my entire life. *One eighty—one ninety—*I couldn't count. *I didn't care.* All I wanted was her. The soft swell of her breast filled my hand. The heat of her skin through the fabric. The bead of her nipple pressed into my palm.

I ground my teeth together, needing more—needing to know more, even if it killed me.

She continued to imprison my wrist as I tested the weight of her breast, rolling and kneading her flesh until I knew which ways made her moan—until she did nothing but moan and squirm against me.

"I saw your breasts that afternoon in the window," I said

raggedly, the confession bubbling up from where I'd locked it away, trying to pretend for her sake like it hadn't happened.

"Ranger..."

"You were right there... without even the towel..." I forced a breath through my lips as my fingers slowly closed in on the peak of her nipple.

"I was in the shower. I thought the garage door going up was an earthquake," she blurted out breathlessly.

"They're red with a little pink. Like raspberries," I ground out, circling my fingers around the edge of her nipple. I wanted to know what she'd do... what sounds she'd make... what I could make her feel if I touched it. "So perfect. I wanted..."

"Tell me."

"I wanted to touch them. Taste them." I panted, desire ravaging my system like I was overdosing on a drug on my very first attempt to get high.

She moaned and her head fell back. Like a ravenous beast, my lips descended on the curve of her jaw, needing to taste any part of her I could get my mouth on.

"I wanted... *fuck*—" I broke off with a choked gasp as her hips rocked forward, grinding right into my throbbing cock.

Stars exploded in my vision and my mouth dove for hers, kissing her with a violence I couldn't control as my hips rammed forward, their natural instinct to thrust toward her heat.

The table jerked and slid from the force, throwing me off balance. I reached out to stop myself from falling and knocked over the vase of flowers. That was when the moment crashed to a halt.

The vase thudded over onto the table, water sloshing everywhere. Sydney let out a small cry, scrambling off the table before she was soaked and grabbing the vase before it rolled completely off the table. In the distance, screeching tires pierced our little cocoon from outside. Horns blared and people yelled.

I stumbled back, dragging my hands through my hair and

gasping for air like the room was running out of it. It was all... too much. *Too overwhelming.*

By the time I looked at Sydney again, she'd righted the flowers and was toweling up the water on the table.

Our eyes locked over the mess. *My mess.*

"Ranger—" She pressed her fingers to her mouth, her lips swollen from my kiss.

Fuck. Another bolt of lust struck me, knowing the mark I'd left on her body. Imagining all the other marks I wanted to leave.

"I'm sorry. I didn't mean for this—" I stammered, locking my hands in front of my raging erection as though I could hide it.

"Don't be sorry. I shouldn't have—" Sydney stepped forward and reached for me.

"I need to go." I stumbled backward toward the door. "Good night. Good luck with the book."

I spun and let myself out of the apartment, bolting down the stairs but halting at the door. My eyes squeezed shut, my dick so damn hard it hurt.

"Shit," I muttered and pushed through the door into the garage instead, not stopping until I reached the back corner by the washer and dryer.

Adrenaline lashed through my veins, holding me hostage until I gave my body release. Within seconds, I had my belt and pants undone, panting as the pressure released on my swollen erection.

I grabbed for a freshly washed cloth with one hand while the other fisted the meat of my cock. I swayed forward, clutching the counter as the pleasure made me see stars. One firm grip and I was about to explode. Clenching my eyes shut, I put my special brain to use—my eidetic memory reconstructing every detail of the last half hour. Every touch and feel. Every scent and sound. Every taste and sensation of Sydney's perfect mouth.

Like my own personal porno, I played through the vivid details in slow motion while my fist jerked along my length. The tomb-like silence of the garage ate up the sounds of my rough breaths and the hard slaps of my hand along my swollen flesh.

"Fuck," I choked out the word, doubling over as my orgasm ripped through me without warning.

Cum jetted onto the counter before I caught the rest in the cloth, my cock soaking it with my release. I stayed like that, hunched over and gasping for breath, for several long minutes before I felt the steady fingers of reality slowly thread back into my mind.

I quickly cleaned the mess I'd made, righted my clothes, and let myself quietly out of the garage, but not before stealing one last glance to the top of the stairs.

Had she heard me?

Had she felt the same?

I went around the back of the house, entering the basement apartment through the separate door and heading straight for the shower.

Had I lost my mind?

Kissing Sydney had felt forbidden. Addictive. And I wanted to know more. *I wanted to know everything.* But I couldn't.

Somehow, I had to find a way to live with not knowing everything about her because she was my temporary neighbor and nothing more.

CHAPTER 9

Sydney

That first kiss was one for the books. *Literally.* Whoever sewed the stereotype that someone who'd never kissed before would automatically be bad at it deserved a special place in hell for how woefully unprepared I was to have my world turned upside down by Ranger's kiss.

Or maybe it was me; I should've known better.

Ranger had three PhDs. Three. He could read and memorize an entire novel with perfect recall within minutes. And I doubted his ability to learn how to kiss quickly?

Newsflash. There was a difference between inexperienced and incompetent. And I pitied myself—and anyone else—who foolishly equated the two.

I'd joked it was a test, but Ranger hadn't come unprepared. He'd studied facts. Fiction. And sure, there were a handful of seconds right at the beginning where everything was all over the place, but he'd adapted. He'd followed the structure from my novels like they were instructions I'd written specifically for him and then evolved.

When a certain stroke of his tongue made me moan, he did it again. When the firm bite of his teeth on my lip made me whimper, he made sure to repeat the torture.

Was there such a thing as a prodigy of pleasure? Because Ranger had the brain *and* he had the touch.

Someone should call Shania and let her know that Ranger Reynolds was ready and waiting to impress her much.

I chuckled and then winced when pain pulsed in my temple. I reached for my cup of coffee, downing a big gulp, and wishing the Advil would get rid of this post-wine headache faster, but that was about the only ache it would erase. The soreness of my lips. The sensitivity of my skin. The hum between my thighs. There was only one remedy for those—and based on the way he ran out of here last night, I didn't expect to see Ranger today.

It was probably for the best. My tongue dragged over my lips, savoring the tingle and the memory I wouldn't soon forget.

If I saw him, we'd either have to pretend that kiss hadn't happened—*impossible*—or talk about what happened now. And I didn't want to hash out the logistics of why getting involved in a fling with my vacation landlord was a bad idea. All I wanted was to bask in the warm buzz of an incredible kiss—to enjoy it for a little while, not think about what I had to *do* about it.

I tapped out a message to Gina; she was still probably sleeping even with the time change, but that was okay.

Me: You're never going to believe what happened last night.

I shook my head. She'd read that and think I'd slept with Ranger. *And she wouldn't be far off...* at least with what could've happened if fate hadn't intervened.

I pulled my lip between my teeth. What was I thinking, asking him to help me with the first kiss scene?

For sure, it was because of the wine. *That was a good excuse, right?* Better than just being a horny romance author turned on by her never-been-kissed landlord. *Yeah, definitely.*

I groaned and padded into the bathroom, flipping on the faucet and splashing some cold water on my face. My head was still pounding. Maybe a walk and some cold winter air would clear up my headache.

I pulled out a long-sleeve tee and a pair of leggings from my suitcase, changing quickly. Next were sneakers and my winter jacket. First, a walk. Then some breakfast. More coffee. And finally, all the words.

The silver lining of all the unresolved tension Ranger left me with was that I'd gotten it out in my manuscript. When I'd first started the series, I'd written my and Vince's first kiss straight into the story, memorializing it for Jenny and Vance. I wouldn't make that same mistake again.

Even if I wanted to, I couldn't.

When I thought about writing down the experience of Ranger's kiss and the emotions it evoked... words failed me. For the first time, words didn't seem like enough.

With Vince, I'd shared our first kiss with the world, and now I was paying the price. But Ranger... I couldn't share that kiss even if I wanted to. It would be like trying to catch a shooting star.

I jogged down the stairs and paused at the bottom.

I might be the only woman in the world who felt this way, but hearing Ranger jerk himself off after he left the apartment was one of the hottest experiences of my life.

I'd listened to his rough grunts echo up the staircase, the rhythmic slap of a fist on flesh like an erotic drumbeat before he came. But it was knowing that he couldn't even make it out of the building before relieving himself that really made my core strain with want—knowing that big amazing brain of his wasn't strong enough to stop how much he wanted me.

Heat seeped from my core.

"Great," I muttered and squeezed my thighs together. *I was hungover and horny.*

This frigid walk better work miracles.

I reached for the doorknob, and my fingers smashed into something in their way.

"Ow—" I pulled back and saw the slice in my finger lined with blood. *Awesome.* I grabbed the envelope, shoved into the doorjamb, and slid it free.

Sydney.

Only my name was written on the front in scratchy handwriting.

This better not be an apology, I thought as I tore open the envelope. Ranger didn't seem like the kind of guy to leave notes. He either steered clear or dove headfirst into conversation… but who knew how he'd respond after being kissed for the first time?

I opened the folded sheet, scanning over the words so quickly that it took a second to register their meaning and for my heart to stop.

How could you do this? How could you betray us like this? I swear you're going to pay for what you've done. I'm going to destroy you like you destroyed everything.

I stumbled back and sagged against the doorframe.

More threats. The words stretched and swelled on the paper as I struggled to focus.

Though I wasn't hardened to them by any means, I'd gotten enough variations on the same to not be completely surprised by the hatred leveled at me for killing off a fictional character. What frightened me though—*no, what absolutely petrified me*—was that there was no address on the envelope to or from.

Someone had hand-delivered this.

Someone not only knew where I was staying but had come here, *had trespassed,* in order to leave this note in the door.

My jaw went slack. I couldn't even feel the cold air, fear effectively numbing me from the inside out.

What was I supposed to do? Did I go to the police? What would they do?

I was thousands of miles from home—thousands of miles from anything familiar—and someone had not only found me but come here to threaten me. My hand holding the letter started to shake so badly I locked my arms over my chest to get it to stop. I felt like I was stranded in the middle of the ocean with a shark circling nearby. I had no idea who he was or where he was, or when he would strike. *All I knew was that he was out for blood.*

I started to gasp, air moving unevenly in and out of my lungs.

What did I do? I looked up and saw the house in front of me. *Ranger.* He would know what to do. He worked for a private security company. He knew everything. *And he promised I could count on him.*

I didn't even feel my feet move before I was at the side door, my knuckles rapping frantically on the glass, my eyes constantly straying over my shoulder.

"Hi, Sydney." Lydia answered the door with a wide, warm smile—so warm that on any other day, it would've felt like she was greeting one of her oldest friends. But not today. Today, not even the sun could melt the icy claw of fear from around my throat. "Why don't you come inside, dear?" she continued, quickly perceiving that I wasn't alright.

She ushered me into the kitchen, grabbing a stool and directing me onto it.

"Are you alright? Did something happen?" She asked, peering into my eyes as she pressed her hand to my forehead in a very motherly move.

"I'm… I'm sorry," I stumbled over my words. "Is Ranger…"

"Of course." She nodded quickly. "He just went next door to bring in Mrs. Jenkins's trash cans. Just stay right here and drink this."

A water bottle appeared in front of me, but I didn't trust my hands to crack open the cap without spilling it all over the floor.

"Sydney." Ranger charged into the room, and I did a double take; he had on sweatpants and a tee shirt. I'd never seen him dressed so casually before.

"Are you okay? You don't look okay." He came in front of me and took my shoulders, concern creasing his brow. "Is it… is this because of last night?" His hands dropped as though his touch made things worse.

"No." I shook my head, the motion loosening the hold I'd had on my tears. "No. I'm sorry. It's this." The paper fluttered in my unsteady grip. "I was going to go for a walk, and it was in the door, and—"

"Where's the envelope?"

I didn't even realize I still had the envelope clutched in my other hand.

"There's no address. No address."

"Sydney—"

"Someone put it there, in the door. They knew I was here. They found me—left it—" I broke off with a deep breath as Ranger's arms came around me—engulfed me in a tight hug.

"I'll figure out who sent this. I promise."

He promised.

Ranger promised.

And how could I not believe him? How could anyone not believe Ranger Reynolds?

He slowly drew back and cupped my cheeks, making sure I was focused only on him. "I'm going to have my brothers meet us at the office, alright?"

My head bobbed, my throat too tight to speak.

"We'll figure out what's going on and make sure you're safe." He sounded so sure I wished for the kind of confidence he had. "It's going to be okay."

A tear broke free and fled down my cheek. Instantly, his hand was there, his thumb catching the warm bead and wiping it away.

The inside of the Reynolds Protective building was just as impressive as the outside, and with all the security features, I breathed a little easier once the front door closed and locked behind us.

Ranger led me through the lobby and down the hallway to a

conference room on the left. It was a smaller room, but the landscape paintings hung on the walls gave it the serene austerity of a museum.

His brothers were already seated at the round table, two open chairs waiting for us. They rose when we entered.

Ranger began the introductions. "Sydney, these are my brothers. You know Hunter." The energy coming off Hunter was completely professional compared to the day we'd met. "This is Gunner and then Archer."

Details filled in my general sketch of Ranger's other siblings. I'd only caught them in passing and at a distance over the last month.

Archer extended his hand first, carrying with it the severity and responsibility of being the oldest sibling. He and Hunter had the most similar features. Same eyes. Square jaw. Similar hair color and cut. Gunner's features were a little more relaxed and his hairstyle a little looser; he was also the only one who smiled when he greeted me—a smile that looked like a replica of the one his mom gave me this morning.

But Ranger... looked like none of them. Well, he did, but he didn't. Lighter, longer hair. Softer features. Fuller lips. Cindy's words returned from that very first drive into Wisdom; *Ranger is one of a kind.*

"Ms. Ward—"

"Just Sydney. Please," I insisted and took a seat in the chair Ranger pulled out for me.

"This was left in the doorjamb to the garage apartment this morning." Ranger slid the note and envelope across the table so his brothers could take a look.

"There was no address on the envelope," I said even though it was obvious, fear turning my mind into a broken record.

Archer and Hunter examined the note first before handing it to Gunner. Meanwhile, Ranger pulled out an iPad from his bag and set it on the table.

"Security feeds?"

"I'm checking now. I have a camera angled toward the driveway but none on the garage, so I'm not sure how close of an angle I'll get."

My heart rose into my throat, watching the video appear. He scrubbed back through time. I watched myself walk backward from the kitchen door and into the garage as everything went in reverse. A couple seconds later, a man appeared in the frame and Ranger slowed it down.

The camera sat just above the entrance to the kitchen, so it only gave a profile view of the suspect at best.

"Does he look familiar?"

Pain seized in my chest. "No."

I wished I could answer differently, but he had on a black track jacket with a high neck and a blue-and-white baseball cap. Truthfully, it could've been any of the men sitting at the table right now, and I still wouldn't have recognized them from the angle and attire.

"The hat looks like it could have a logo on it." Ranger leaned forward and zoomed in on the footage. "I can try to sharpen the image and see if the hat might help us identify him."

"It's worth a shot, but all that could mean is that it was a delivery person, someone paid to just stick the envelope in the door, which would be the smart thing to do."

"I'll call up Chief Diehl and see if we can get traffic cams from Mom's street," Hunter chimed in. "If he drove there, maybe we can get a shot of him getting in a car. Maybe a license plate."

Archer nodded in agreement and then looked at me. "Do you have any idea who would send something like this? Any enemies that you know of?"

Hunter's gaze snapped to mine. *He knew.* Of course, he knew. Anyone who was a fan knew.

My jaw went slack, and I felt the warm vines of embarrassment creep into my cheeks.

"Lots of them. Unfortunately," I replied quietly, the knot in my stomach twisting tighter.

"You have lots of enemies?" Archer confirmed, looking from me to Ranger and then to his other brothers in shock.

And he wasn't the only one; Ranger stared at me with complete confusion.

I took a deep breath and swallowed. "Yeah."

"Sydney..." I heard the question in Ranger's voice—the question I knew needed to be answered.

I held on to those last seconds with childish desperation. I'd come out here to escape the havoc I'd created—to retreat and regroup. But there was no escaping reality; it had found me... with its fangs bared, ready to rip apart my sanity.

"It's okay," Hunter said with soft support, and I could've cried.

"I have a lot of people angry at me right now because I killed someone—"

"A character," Hunter was quickly to chime in.

I nodded. "I killed a character in one of my books, who was originally inspired by my ex-fiancé," I quickly clarified. "He was supposed to be the hero, and people are really upset about it."

Gunner's arm dropped onto the table. "So, people are coming for you because you killed a fake person?"

"Trust me, I wish I could tell you no," I murmured. "The release really... blew up, and not in a good way. I was getting a lot of hate mail back in New York, the press and paparazzi were relentless, so my agent suggested I get away from it all for a little while."

"So, you came out here..."

"Who else knew you were coming to Wisdom?" Archer asked.

"No one. I mean, just my agent." I shivered. "That's why..." My eyes dropped to the letter. I couldn't even say it; all I could manage was to nod at the piece of paper like it was a loaded gun.

"You said you were receiving messages before?" Archer probed, and I nodded. "Were any of them like this?"

"Honestly? I don't know. They definitely weren't hand-delivered notes." I locked my hands in my lap because they'd started to shake. "There was an incident on a talk show right before I left, and after that, my agent took over my email because she didn't want me seeing any of the messages anymore. I wasn't... coping well with the hatred."

"People are assholes," Hunter muttered and leaned back in his chair with a huff.

"Did anyone ever come to your apartment in New York? Or approach you at an event?" Ranger asked, his expression drawn so tight it was impossible for me to read.

"No. Not that I know of." I shook my head. "We hadn't even gotten that far in the release cycle, and I doubt we would have with how poorly the book was received."

I hated how my voice choked on the last. I hated to admit I'd failed at the one thing I was supposed to be good at in front of the man who never failed at anything.

"And what about your ex?"

"Vince?" I choked out and then shook my head. "No. This wouldn't be him. I broke off the engagement nine months ago when I found out he'd been unfaithful."

"Was he angry?"

"Well, yes." I shifted in my seat. "But not like this. Plus, why now? Why here? I've been living in our old apartment in New York, so he could've found me anytime."

"Would he be upset that you killed off his character?"

It was sad that the idea was so far out there I was able to laugh at it at a time like this. "No," I assured them, adding for good measure. "Vince never read any of my books."

I felt Ranger looking at me, and I was sure he was thinking the same thing I did every day. *How could I have stayed with Vince? How could I have been so fooled?*

Archer grunted, not quite convinced. "Alright, let's start with access to your emails. I'd like Ranger to go through them all and see if anything is similar in verbiage or tone to this."

"I—" I stopped myself, swallowing down my dumb protest. Someone was threatening my life. That was more important than worrying over what Ranger would think of me after he read every horrible thing that people felt they had a right to say. "Of course. Yes." I nodded. "Whatever you need."

"Your agent's information," Gunner chimed in and pushed a notepad in my direction. "I'll give her a call and see if there is anyone that comes to her mind or any communications she might've received since you've been out here."

"Of course." I went to reach for the pen, but my hand was shaking so badly that it slipped from my hold and clattered to the table.

"Here, let me." Ranger picked up the pen and slid the notepad in front of him. "You mentioned her name was Gina?"

I nodded, both beyond grateful and incredibly afraid, as I rattled off her number.

"So, what do I do now?" I knotted my fingers tightly together in my lap. "I'm supposed to go back to New York in three weeks. Should I just leave now—"

Archer opened his mouth, but it was Ranger who spoke first. "I don't think that's a good idea."

I watched the other three sets of eyes all shift to their youngest brother, varying degrees of surprise crossing their faces. I guessed that Ranger didn't typically assert himself like this on their cases. Based on what he told me, he seemed more involved behind the scenes of the business.

"If there are more angry fans, going back to New York, back to a massive city where more people know how to find you and there are more places to hide, is only going to make flushing out this stalker even harder."

"Ranger's right," Archer declared. "Staying here narrows the pool of suspects—"

"Stalker?" My attention hadn't gotten past the word.

He wasn't wrong. Of course, he wasn't wrong. But there was just something so much more… serious… when he said stalker compared to discussing an angry fan.

Ranger winced and then pursed his lips.

"Sydney, you said that no one except your agent knew you were coming out here. Unless this person coincidentally happens to live in Wisdom and somehow learned you were renting Ranger's apartment, it's, unfortunately, more likely that someone has been watching you… following you… trying to figure out where you went when you left New York," Hunter said calmly though his jaw ticced like there was something personal about this situation for him, too.

"Based on the situation as you've described, it's most likely he's what's known as a celebrity stalker, someone who fixated on you because of your books and fame," Ranger added, and I wished his facts were as comforting to me as they were to him. "He could've even been a superfan whose feelings shifted to revenge when he felt betrayed by your last book."

I almost wanted to laugh at how crazy this all was. *A stalker? Me?* It wasn't bad enough to just have angry fans; I had to have angry, psychotic ones who followed me across the country to threaten me for killing someone who didn't actually exist.

"And there's no chance the note is just a bluff? Just someone trying to punish me with fear for… writing a book they didn't like?"

"Are you willing to take that risk?" Archer countered.

My shoulders slumped.

"No," Ranger answered before I could.

My head swiveled, my eyes catching his before they quickly averted back to his brother.

"No, I'm not," I replied, too. "So, I stay…"

"Until we find out who sent this, yes." Archer's chin dipped. "Now, both doors into the garage and the apartment have keypad locks. Of course, after this morning—"

"I'll install another camera directly above the entrance in case he comes back," Ranger broke in. "I'm also going to put in wireless panic buttons in the apartment in case of an emergency."

"Good." Archer swiveled his head to me. "Now, as far as when you leave the apartment, you'll have one of us accompanying you at all times."

"I'll take morning shift, Archie," Gunner chimed in, cracking his knuckles.

"I can do afternoons—" Hunter began at almost the exact same time

"No," Ranger declared and closed his iPad with a thud.

Hunter's brow furrowed. "Do I have another commitment I'm unaware of?"

"No, I meant neither of you has to take shifts." His lips firmed. "If Sydney needs to go somewhere, I will go with her."

"Baby Brains—"

"My target precision and accuracy scores are just as good if not better than yours, Gunner. I've taken every self-defense class we've offered here, and I passed Hazard's level-two combative course at Armorous Tactical last year," Ranger insisted through locked teeth. "I'm more than capable of keeping Sydney safe if she needs to leave the apartment."

"I never said you weren't, Baby Brains. I just—"

"Gunner," Archer interrupted in warning, shooting his brother a "stand down" stare; Gunner listened.

"It makes the most logistic sense, too, since I live right there; I can be available at any time," Ranger insisted.

"I agree," Archer declared, bringing an end to the debate. "Gunner, I want you to contact her agent about any possible threats, and Hunter—"

"I'm checking with Diehl on traffic cams. Got it."

"Sydney, do you have any questions?"

Yes. Why this? Why me? Why now?

"No. No questions." None that had answers, anyway.

"Okay, Ranger will keep you updated with anything that we find. In the meantime, if you see anything suspicious, let him know. If you leave the apartment, let him know. If you're worried about anything—"

"Let him know." My head bobbed. "I understand."

"Alright. We'll touch base later today and see where we stand."

When I woke up this morning, I thought that making out with my hot nerdy landlord last night was my biggest problem. I guess the joke was on me.

Now, I not only had a stalker, but the man protecting me was the same gorgeous nerd I couldn't stop thinking about. How was I supposed to ignore my crush when I was relying on him twenty-four seven?

CHAPTER 10

Ranger

Sydney waited until the garage door was closed completely before getting out of the car.

She'd been silent the whole ride back to the apartment. Her arms folded, her vacant stare out the window. Normally, silence didn't bother me; I liked the quiet, but I didn't like this. She was upset, and she tried to hide it.

I wished I knew what to do—knew the right thing to say. Instead, I said anything—everything else to try and fill the void. *To make her feel safe.* I told her about the additional cameras I was going to install outside the garage and in the apartment. The models. The resolution. The angles and coverage. I rattled off all the specs, thinking it would comfort her.

Instead, the subtle slide of her tears reminded me that I was failing. That I didn't know enough. Knowledge was power, but in the face of her tears, I was powerless.

"I'll start outside and then install the one in the stairwell." My jaw clenched as I grabbed the first camera box from the back seat.

"Okay." The word was hardly a whisper; when I straightened, she was gone.

Failure. I ran a hand through my hair. *What was I supposed to do?* I peeled open the camera box, reaching for the instruction booklet.

I wished Sydney came with instructions. *How to care for. How to comfort.*

Was I supposed to take her hand? Pat her shoulder? Or should I keep my distance because she was now a client? *Because she was in danger?*

And because I'd kissed her.

I'd kissed her, and I couldn't stop thinking about it. The memory of her lips held me hostage. And now, I had to figure out how to do the one thing my brain was designed not to do. *Forget.*

Forget her taste. Forget her softness. Forget the way she wanted more—*wanted me.* Because I had to protect her.

I hauled a ladder from the garage outside, positioning it directly in front of the door. Within thirty minutes, I had the additional exterior camera secured and wired. It captured a wide angle of the driveway and the street—if anyone so much as walked along the sidewalk in front of the house—they wouldn't be able to hide from this camera.

The second camera was for the top of the staircase. I made sure my footsteps were noticeable as I climbed the stairs; I didn't want to startle her.

"Sydney?" I gently rapped on the door, which opened a moment later. Her glazed, red-rimmed eyes tightened the band around my chest. "I just need a chair. The ladder wouldn't fit on the landing."

"Yeah," she said quietly and stepped back, allowing me inside to take one of the chairs at the table.

I was glad she left the door open while I worked. Every few minutes, I checked on her as she sat at the table, staring blankly out the window like she was afraid to look away from it.

I worked quicker this time around, mounting and installing the camera, and was almost finished when her voice drew my attention.

"Hey, Gina." Sydney pinned her phone to her ear and pulled

the sleeve of her sweatshirt over her hand, quickly using it to wipe the tears that trickled down her cheeks.

I didn't want to eavesdrop, but the door was open. There was a prolonged silence before Sydney began recounting what had happened... and what we were doing about it.

"I know you already talked to Gunner, but have there been any threats? Like real ones? To my email or socials or you..." Sydney probed.

My skin prickled as I linked the wireless camera to the app on my phone.

Gunner had already messaged the both of us to say that Gina couldn't think of any angry fan who stuck out; he'd also confirmed that Gina hadn't told anyone that Sydney was out here.

He'd then followed up with a message only to me right as I finished the outside camera to say that there were hundreds of angry emails sent to Sydney since the release of her latest book, but no one who'd taken the next step to find her and personally confront her or someone who knew where she was.

"Yeah, I know." Sydney pulled her knees to her chest. She looked so small, curled up in her seat, and my jaw tensed, hating that I didn't know what to do except focus on facts.

"He's... umm... here right now, installing more security cameras."

My eyes connected with hers, and whatever her agent said in response made the pink in her cheeks deepen.

"Alright, I'll talk to you later. Love you." She ended the call and then angled her phone over the table in my direction, clearly taking a photo.

"Sydney?" I stepped down from the chair, and her eyes met mine.

"Sorry. I wanted to send her a picture of the flowers and thank her." She'd read my thoughts.

"Oh." *That made more sense than her taking a picture of me.* I picked up the chair and carried it back to its spot by the table. "All done."

"Thank you." She chewed on her bottom lip nervously.

Maybe I should leave—give her some space. Maybe she wanted privacy to talk to her friend. And if I stayed, there was a chance she'd bring up the kiss and... I didn't have answers, only questions. Why had I stayed? Why had I agreed to help when I had no practical knowledge of kissing?

Because I couldn't stay away. Because I'd wanted to know more about the way she made me feel. And when it was all said and done—when I'd spent all night thinking... analyzing... what had happened, only one fact remained: it wasn't that I didn't know how to kiss her—*it was that I didn't know how not to.*

"Do you..." Her voice cracked and she ducked her head.

"Do I what?" I couldn't leave now.

She took a deep breath and lifted her eyes to mine. "Do you think this person... wants to hurt me?"

Something stretched... strained... inside my chest. An urge to... reach for her. Hold her. But that wasn't appropriate. Not at a time like this.

"Only two percent of all stalking cases result in homicide, but most of those are instances where the stalker was a former intimate partner."

Speaking of... I needed to text Archer to make sure he'd follow up on Sydney's ex. Vince was still a likely suspect, no matter how sure she was of the contrary.

"Do you think... he would actually hurt me?"

I blinked twice. She had to know she was repeating her question, but why? I'd given her the best answer I had—the most current statistics based on the evidence—My thoughts stopped when a tear slid all the way down her cheek, catching on the swell of her lip.

And then that hand—the one with a mind of its own—cupped her cheek and wiped the tear away with the pad of my thumb.

She didn't want statistics; she wanted safety.

"I won't let him." It wasn't an answer; it was a promise.

"Ranger…" she murmured, her downcast eyes rose to mine just as her phone buzzed.

I let my hand fall so she could answer the message.

"Oh my god…" Sydney's hollowed voice stopped me cold, her face turning ashen right in front of my eyes.

"Sydney? What—"

"The flowers," she choked out and shoved her phone at me.

Gina: Syd… I didn't send those flowers.

Anger rippled through me. I looked up from the screen to see her grab the roses right from the vase and carry them to the trash, not caring about the leaves or the trail of water slopping across the floor in her haste to get rid of them.

"They're from him. He sent the flowers." She let out a small cry and shoved the flowers into the garbage like they were cursed, pushing them down like she could bury them six feet under rather than just to the bottom of the can. "He sent them and then the note. It was him."

She was spiraling.

"Sydney." I set her phone on the table and went to her, taking her shoulders and instructing, "Breathe."

"Twice." She trembled. "He was here twice."

"It's possible, but the note on the flowers was drastically different from the note in the door."

To me, the inconsistency was glaring. A double yellow line that couldn't be crossed. But Sydney couldn't see that, emotion overtaking logic.

"Who else could it be, Ranger? No one. No one else knows." Stems snapped and crunched as she wedged them deeper. "It has to be him."

"I'll call the local flower shop and get information on who sent them."

When I released her shoulders to grab my cell, she started to wrestle the trash bag from the can, bumping and banging it on the floor. It wasn't enough to put the flowers in the trash. She wanted the trash gone.

"Sydney—" I took her arm, helplessness clawing at my chest.

For a split second, all I could remember was Mom's agonizing wails from behind her bedroom door after Dad died. No one could go in except Archer. I tried to—I wanted to be with her. But they wouldn't let me. Instead, Hunter took Gunner and me and Gwen upstairs to our room and said aliens were invading and that we were only safe in the closet.

Neither Gunner nor Gwen remembered hiding in the closet; they didn't remember that walls and floors and doors weren't enough to dampen Mom's despair. But I did.

Everyone thought it was amazing to have a brain—a memory like mine. They didn't consider that an eidetic memory wasn't selective. It didn't pick only the happy or helpful moments to retain, it held on to all of them in perfect detail. Even the painful ones.

They didn't remember it like I did.

Had I known I'd remember every moment of that grief, I wouldn't have stayed in the closet. And because I did remember it, I swore I'd never give myself a reason to remember myself as helpless again, especially with Sydney.

"I don't want them here. Anywhere," she blurted out, wiping her cheek with her sleeve. "I want them—"

"Here. I'll take them." One day, she was going to get good at asking me for help. Until then, I was going to continue to prove that she could count on me.

I dislodged the bag from the can and tied it shut, immediately carrying it from the apartment. She wanted them gone; they would be gone.

I didn't stop at the big garbage can in the garage. Instead, I took the bag to the end of the block, across the street, and tossed it in the dumpster behind the Mountain Motel. On my way back, I called Archer and let him know about the flowers—that they'd been delivered from a local florist in town. I told him I was going to call—it was usually my job to check up on things like this—but he insisted on handling it.

"Your responsibility right now is Sydney, Ranger. Making sure she feels secure and comfortable. Now it's your turn to give us a chance to have your back."

I wanted to ask if he had any suggestions on how to do that—how to make her feel better, but I didn't. I had to figure it out on my own.

CHAPTER 11

Ranger

When I returned to the apartment, Sydney was kneeling on the floor, wiping up the trail of water. As I got closer, I noticed that no sooner did she dry a spot than more drops appeared in its place.

"Sydney." I knelt down, my heart starting to pound. Placing my hand on top of hers, I stopped her frantic movements.

She paused, and then her shoulders began quaking with uncontrolled sobs.

I didn't get a chance to think—or overthink—because there was only one right answer. I reached out and gently drew her to me. Instantly, her body caved against mine, almost like a balloon being deflated of air. Her shoulders shook, and her tears collected in the fabric of my shirt until they soaked right through it.

"It's going to be okay. I know this is scary, but no one is going to hurt you, I promise." I would stop at nothing to make sure of it. "It's going to be okay."

I repeated the words over and over until the phrase lost meaning and became nothing more than a series of sounds. *Semantic satiation.* But that didn't matter because it wasn't the words calming her, I realized; it was me. Maybe I knew what to do after all.

Eventually, her sobs settled, the shake of her shoulders slowing until she breathed deep and drew back from my chest.

"Here," I murmured, reaching in my pocket and handing her my handkerchief.

"You carry a handkerchief?" She sniffled and dabbed her eyes.

"They're very practical and environmentally friendly," I murmured, picking up where she'd left off drying the floor. "Tissues and paper towels make up seven point six billion pounds of waste each year, so by using a handkerchief, I can reduce my contribution by twenty-five pounds per year."

She let out a watery chuckle, catching the last of her tears and then folding up the square.

"I'm sorry." Her tongue slid over her lips, and my body tightened.

I gritted my teeth. My mind was the strongest thing about me for the last thirty-two years of my life. Until Sydney came into it.

Achilles had his heel. Samson had his hair. Superman had kryptonite. And I... I had Sydney.

"Don't apologize." I rose abruptly and extended my hand to help her up. When she took it, I saw her palm and fingers were cut up from the thorns on the stems. "I'll get some Band-Aids. Sit." I pulled out the chair and made sure she was in it before heading for the bathroom; there was a small first aid kit under the sink.

I reached for the cabinet when I stopped short. A bright-pink silicone wand rested on the edge of the sink.

My eyes widened, but inexperience didn't equal idiot; she had a vibrator.

She must've washed it and left it there to dry. But if she washed it, that meant she would've used it. *Had she used it last night? After my—our kiss?* My face heated and my dick started to stretch. *Had she needed relief like I had?*

I bit into the side of my cheek and quickly grabbed the entire kit and rushed back to the kitchen. Now wasn't the time to think about that.

"Here. Let me." I dragged the other chair close to hers.

I needed it close enough to take care of her cuts, but it wasn't until I sat down that I realized I hadn't left very much room for anything between us. She'd had her legs folded on the chair until I was seated, then they came down and interlocked with mine.

Vasodilation. Dopamine. *Lust.* It was pointless to continue to explain away a feeling that I couldn't avoid.

"Give me your hand," I instructed, tearing open an alcohol swab.

I inhaled sharply when the back of her hand came to rest, not on the table, but on my leg. My eyes snapped to her sliced-up palm, staring at it like it was as threatening as a grenade. *One wrong move and I could knock the pin loose.*

But I couldn't bring myself to move it.

"This might sting," I warned with a low husk to my voice, seeing that some of the cuts were fairly deep. *She'd been so upset she hadn't felt the pain.* My throat locked around itself and I struggled to swallow.

I took her hand in mine and ran the wipe over the longest cut. She hissed in pain.

"Sorry."

"It's okay." She pinned her bottom lip between her teeth, and my dick instantly swelled in my pants, recalling what that lip had felt like between my teeth.

I shifted in my seat, hoping to hide my body's reaction even as her fingers sat inches away from the straining evidence of my arousal.

I wondered what her hand would feel like wrapped around me. Squeezing. Stroking. The chair squeaked as my hips jerked. *Shit.*

"I didn't realize why you came out here… what happened with your book," I blurted out, scrambling for any kind of conversation to distract my brain.

Was this what happened to every man when he was attracted to someone? The urge… the ache… to have sex with her was…

consuming and irrational; she was upset and in danger, and all my body cared about, for lack of a better term, was fucking.

It was so… unlike me. But neither could I stop it.

"I thought I could get away from it all." She let out a sad laugh that turned into a groan. "I can't believe someone would go to these extremes to threaten me… and all over a book."

My brow creased, another question bubbling to the surface as I peeled off the backing of the Band-Aid. "Why didn't you keep his character?" She could've easily finished the series without killing off the hero.

"Because everything about him was Vince. Every detail and nuance. And because he cheated on me for years. How did I continue to paint someone as a hero when he'd hurt me in the worst way?" Her voice caught.

My jaw locked, and anger surged through my veins. Every time I thought about the man who'd hurt Sydney, I wanted to hit something. But I didn't. Instead, I forced myself to stay focused on my task. I'd watched my brothers reach that tipping point about so many things over the years, justifiably or not, but even though I recognized it, I never experienced it until now.

"I've had readers tell me they skipped a book of mine because the hero had a family member or their child's name, but I was supposed to write a whole novel with my cheating ex as the hero?" She let out a weak laugh and shook her head. "I'm not a machine. How was I supposed to write a happy ending I didn't believe in?"

My eyes snapped up. "You're not."

She laughed softly. "Gina hoped I'd find a way to have him drawn and quartered in the story. I can't imagine where we'd be if I'd made that happen."

"Or subjected him to the Judas cradle." The form of torture he deserved for betraying her trust.

"Excuse me?"

"The Judas cradle is one of the most painful ancient ways to die by torture," I offered. "Essentially a wooden pyramid where the tip is inserted into the anus and then weights are added—"

Her fingers closed on mine. "I think I get the picture."

"Oh." I pursed my lips and muttered, "Well, that's what I would've gone with."

A small smile lifted her lips. "Next time I'm in need of history's worst punishment, I'll be sure to check with you."

"Oh, that wouldn't be the worst."

"There's something more torturous than having a spike slowly driven up your ass?"

"Yes." I looked up at her and replied before I could think. *Everything with Sydney was always before I could think.* "Losing you."

Her lips parted, her inhale pulling softly at the oxygen between us.

My heart pumped hard into the front of my chest. I said it because it was just as much a fact as any other kind of torture, but somehow, it was more.

"Ranger..."

I cleared my throat and averted my gaze back to her hand, carefully wrapping the last bandage around the tip of her finger. "All done."

She took my hand before I could pull away, the memories of her taking my hand last night—dragging it down to her—"About last night..."

I drew my hand back and stood, clearing my throat. "It was for the story. We don't need to talk about it."

No matter what Gunner said or what my brothers had done, I was going to keep this professional.

Her gaze sank for a moment, examining her hands before she nodded. "Okay."

"I should get going—get to work reviewing those emails." I backed toward the door. Mostly, I needed some space to remember that this was now a case, and she was now a client, not just the tenant renting my apartment or the woman I'd kissed. "I'll let you know if we learn anything. In the meantime, you should try to relax—"

"Can you stay?" Her lip quivered as she rose, tucking her arms to her.

I tensed. "What?"

"Can you work through the emails from here?" She rolled her lip between her teeth. "I just… don't want to be alone."

"I…" I exhaled slowly. Facts bubbled to the tip of my tongue. She was safe here. Cameras. Alarms. And I was right next door.

"Please," she murmured.

But none of that mattered against the look in her eyes. No one had needed me before. Not like this. And I… the smartest decision would be for me to leave, but for the first time, the smartest decision and the right decision weren't the same.

"Okay, I'll stay."

"You can use my computer." She opened her laptop, keyed in her password, and handed it to me. "I'm just going to shower."

The image of her pink vibrator flashed in my mind.

"Don't worry, I won't come rushing out in a towel again," she joked, but if she thought to lighten the tension in the room, her idea backfired.

Now, I just pictured her breasts. Full and ripe. Their pink tips begging to be tasted. And the way she'd put my hand on them last night.

"I'll be on the couch," I declared and spun, beelining for the farthest corner of the small apartment and practically slamming her computer down on my dick to keep it under control.

My want would have to wait. Right now, she needed me.

She showered while I scanned through her emails. It was no wonder that Gina instructed her not to go through these… a lot were supportive, but the ones that weren't, their cruelty floored me. How people could say such horrible things… I sent copies of the messages that had a similar tone to the note to Hunter so he could help me research the senders.

Several minutes later, Sydney came out of the bathroom—fully dressed—and sat on the other end of the couch with her e-reader. She read while I worked, the quiet settling around us for hours.

I didn't even realize the sun had set until my phone rang. The buzzing stirred Sydney, where she'd drifted down on the couch next to me. I'd been about halfway through her emails when she'd dozed off next to me, curling deeper into the couch… and closer to me. I should've moved to give her more space, but then she curled her feet under my leg, wanting its warmth. So, I stayed. I tugged the blanket off the back of the couch and covered her while I continued to analyze her emails.

"It's my brother," I told her gently, hating that the first look she had when she woke was panic, and then I answered Hunter's call. "Hello?"

"Are you home?"

"Yes. No." I winced. "I mean, I'm at the apartment with Sydney. Did you find something?"

"Dinner."

"What?"

"Zoey and I got tacos from our favorite taco truck. We were going to swing by and bring them to you. Figured you probably haven't eaten much all day."

Now that he mentioned it, I was hungry, and I hadn't seen Sydney eat anything either.

"Oh, okay. Umm, hold on." I held my hand over the phone and asked Sydney, "Do you want tacos for dinner? Hunter and his wife are offering to bring some over."

Her eyes turned to saucers. "Is that even a question?"

My head tipped.

"Yes." She pushed herself up. "The answer to tacos is always yes."

"Oh, okay." I lifted my hand from the speaker. "Hunter?"

"Did you just ask her if she wanted tacos?"

"Well, I didn't want to accept if she didn't want—"

"Never ask a woman if she wants tacos. Tacos are life."

"I'm not sure what that means, but tacos sound great."

Hunter laughed. "Alright, we'll be there in five."

I closed up Sydney's laptop and put it on the charger while she straightened the small space. I met my brother and his wife at the entrance to the garage as soon as they pulled into the drive. Hunter handed me a full bag of food and carried another one himself.

"Hi, Sydney," Hunter greeted her again and then motioned to the dark-haired and kind-eyed woman by his side. "This is my wife, Zoey."

In spite of everything, Sydney's face lit up when Zoey could barely contain her excitement and pulled her in for a hug.

"It's so wonderful to meet you," Zoey gushed.

"You, too." Sydney beamed. "I told your husband I'd never forget his proposal request. I melted when I got that email."

Zoey blushed, sliding Hunter a glance. "He is pretty amazing."

"Well I'm glad I could play a small part in your story."

"Small part?" Zoey laughed. "Your books saved me."

"Saved you?" Sydney looked at me, but I wasn't sure what Zoey was talking about either.

"I... umm... I actually moved from Florida to Wisdom because I was being stalked," Zoey confessed.

"You were?" That had Sydney's attention.

"Yeah." Zoey nodded. "I came here and stayed at the Betty B&B, and Jerry, one of the owners, gave me one of your books to read. A lot of people say books are an escape, but for me, they are a refuge. A safe place to feel happiness and love and... everything that wasn't fear." She paused and brought her fingertips to her mouth, blinking rapidly. "Sorry, I told myself I wasn't going to cry," she said with a small laugh even as she wiped a tear away. "I didn't know you then, but your books were there for me—*you* were there for me, so now, even though you don't know me, I just want you to know I'm here for you."

I knew about Zoey's situation because we'd help catch the person threatening her, but I didn't know these details.

"Thank you." Sydney's soft words were almost impossible to hear right before she wrapped her arms around Zoey, hugging her like they'd been friends forever rather than acquaintances for five minutes.

"Ranger, why don't you help me unpack the food?"

I followed Hunter to the table and helped him unload the carryout containers, the rich aromas of Mexican food filling the apartment.

"She's okay, Ranger," my brother assured me, and I realized I kept losing track of what I was doing because I kept looking at Sydney. "I thought it might help Sydney to talk to someone who's gone through a similar situation."

Zoey's case had been a little different but I'd imagine the fear was similar. The sense of helplessness. And it looked like Hunter was right; Sydney relaxed and opened up to my sister-in-law within minutes.

"Alright, ladies. It's taco time."

When we sat down to eat, the conversation turned to anything and everything except books and stalkers. Zoey talked about their daughter, Charlie, who was next door with Mom. Hunter shared stories about our childhood while I corrected all of his flawed recollections. The time with them went almost as quickly as the food. Before they left, Zoey reminded Sydney about book club next weekend.

And then it was just the two of us again.

I loaded the paper bags full of garbage into the can. "I'll take this out on my way—"

"Can you stay a little longer?" Her soft voice cut through all my thoughts.

My feet rooted to the floor. *Stay.* I shouldn't—but I wanted to.

My eyes lifted and met hers, heat spreading through my body. "Sure."

"I was going to put on some reruns of *Friends*," she said, walking over to the couch.

My thoughts shifted gears, reminding me that it was nighttime. Reminding me that we were alone. *Reminding me of how sweet she tasted.*

"Okay." I pushed my hands into my pockets.

This was a bad idea, and it must've shown on my face because she dropped her head into her hands and then looked at me once more.

"I'm sorry, Ranger." Her shoulders slumped. "You probably have other things you want to do, and I've asked you to stay here all day. I'm fine. I know I'm safe. I'm just being—you can go."

"I'm staying, Sydney. There's nowhere else I'd rather be." It was the truth—inconvenient, maybe, but no less true. "I just want to run next door and shower and change. I'll be right back."

"Are you—"

"I'm sure."

I hurried next door, using the back entrance into the basement. After a quick shower and change, I swung through the kitchen and grabbed the container of Nutella brownies.

When I entered the apartment, Sydney stood by the window, and I was sure that she'd been watching the driveway the entire time I was gone, paranoid that whoever did this was waiting out there.

"I brought Nutella brownies."

"Seriously?" Her eyes widened as she took me in.

"I thought you might want a snack." I closed the door behind me.

"That's not..." She shook her head with a small laugh, approaching as I peeled off the lid. "I wasn't talking about the snacks." She hummed softly when she saw the brownies and picked one off the top. "Tacos, Nutella brownies, and gray sweatpants."

I looked down at the gray joggers I had on. I didn't understand how they were like the other two. "These are my favorite sweatpants. Gunner got me these for Christmas last year. Is there something wrong with them?"

"No. They're… great," she said and stuffed the brownie in her mouth.

We settled on the couch. I'd seen *Friends* before, so I remembered every episode. It was still entertaining but not as intriguing as the woman beside me. My gaze strayed more often to her, especially when the show made her laugh—which was only a handful of times because she fell asleep before the end of one episode.

I clicked the TV off, not wanting to wake her.

I should go, but I couldn't leave her on the couch. She should be sleeping in bed after a day like today.

Carry her to the bed. A simple, logical solution.

I crouched in front of her and worked my arms underneath her legs and shoulders. When I lifted her, she snuggled into my chest with a sigh.

My jaw went slack. *God, she was so warm and soft.* Did all women feel like this? Or was it just Sydney? They all certainly wouldn't fit like she did in my arms.

My jaw locked, the thrum of desire beating my body to life. I knew I should've… relieved myself… in the shower before coming back, but all I could think about was the look in her eyes when she asked me to stay. So, I rushed to get back.

Now, I was paying the price; my logical solution came with unintended and irrational consequences.

It was only a couple of steps to reach the side of the bed. I carefully laid Sydney down and inhaled deeply, my face close to her hair.

Logically, I knew the human nose could detect over one trillion scents, but with each breath, the only thing I smelled was her sweetness.

"Ranger," she murmured before I could release her.

"Yes?" I croaked.

Her eyes fluttered open to mine. "Don't go."

I tensed. She wanted me to stay?

"I don't want to be alone tonight," she added softly, the furrow in her brow returning—the one she'd had when she realized the flowers weren't from her friend.

She was afraid.

"Okay." I swallowed hard. "I'll stay on the couch if you want—"

Her fingers curled into my shirt, holding on tight. "I want you to hold me," she confessed. "I feel safe when you hold me."

My jaw went slack and my dick stirred.

Hold her.

I didn't—I'd never—

"Can you stay here and hold me for a little longer?"

My mouth went dry. My dick stretched and hardened to stone in my sweats. I definitely should say no. She wouldn't feel safe if she knew how my body responded to her suggestion. But I couldn't say no.

More than that... if she asked, I'd never let her go.

"Sure."

I slid her farther into the bed, pulled the covers over her, and then climbed on top of them. I'd never slept with a woman like this or... any other way. My brain knew it. And my body *definitely* knew it. But there was nothing I could do. I'd promised to keep her safe—promised she could count on me—and if that meant holding her all night long, I'd suffer the pain in my groin to make it happen.

She settled into the crook of my arm and immediately went back to sleep. Meanwhile, I stared wide-eyed at the ceiling and wondered what was happening to me. For the first time in my entire life, I had no explanation—no reasoning for what I was doing.

I was acting on feeling and even though I knew it, there was not a single thing I could do to stop it.

CHAPTER 12

Sydney

I couldn't bring myself to tell him he didn't have to stay.

For a whole week, Ranger and I spent almost all of our waking hours together in the apartment and many of our sleeping ones. Every night, it was the same routine… TV until I fell asleep and he carried me to bed, climbing on top of the covers and holding me for… I wasn't sure how long. All I knew was that when I woke up, he was stretched over the small couch, his long limbs hanging off the end.

His neck had to have a permanent crick in it by now, but still… I couldn't bring myself to tell him I was okay on my own. *Nor could I admit that maybe I didn't want to be.*

After six days, we had more information but no solid answers.

The flower shop had been a dead end. The delivery guy had been just that, and as for any receipts or records from the purchase… well, it was a flower shop in Wisdom, Wyoming, and the person who'd purchased them had paid in cash.

Gunner had reviewed the limited traffic camera footage from that night but had come up empty. In a town with only two stoplights, there wasn't much footage to review… or enough angles to

Lastly, Ranger had gone through my emails in record time, but the list of email addresses that had sent anything even remotely threatening wasn't insubstantial, so it was taking time for Ranger and Hunter to parse through each address and figure out who it belonged to, and if that person had visited Wyoming recently.

So far, they hadn't found any matches. Not only that but apparently, there were a surprising number of bogus emails. Addresses were created to send a single, hateful email and then inactivated. It seemed like it would be impossible to find who was behind those emails, but Ranger insisted he was going to try.

All of these things filtered in over days while Ranger and I fell into a routine that, by the time I was comfortable being alone in the apartment without him, I didn't want to be.

It was more than not wanting to be alone with my thoughts... my fears. I wanted to know more about Ranger, like he was a book I couldn't stop reading. Each page turned with new facts, new stories, new insights, and even after a week, all I wanted was more.

I wasn't quite sure I adequately understood what it was like to be attracted to someone's mind before I met Ranger, but now, I craved his conversation, his thoughts and his endearing facts just as much as I craved his touch. But that was the one thing I didn't get—the one thing that disappeared almost completely from his radar.

Our kiss wasn't spoken about again, as though what happened before the threat existed in an alternate universe. But our attraction hadn't gone anywhere—desire snaked through the foundation of our relationship like a weed, springing through the surface faster and faster as we tried to cut it back.

At first, it was little things that broke through. The way he looked at me when he thought I couldn't see. The way he blushed if we inadvertently bumped or brushed into each other. And I couldn't forget the gray sweatpants each night.

The second night he'd stayed, I'd woken a little when he went to carry me to bed, and I couldn't help but peek at the front of his gray sweatpants.

More than peek. I needed to more than peek in order to see all of him.

Let's just say that his IQ wasn't the most massive thing about him.

I'd written countless stories with virgin heroines and heroes that were turned on at the thought of being the first, but here, the roles were reversed, and I found myself fantasizing about what it would be like if I were his first.

From there, it was a downward spiral. Erotic dreams woke me on the brink of orgasm, only to find Ranger gone from the bed, the light on in the bathroom and the sink running. When I closed my eyes again, my ears picked up on another sound muffled by the water—*by design*. Ranger's low grunts echoed like an unmistakable base underneath the running water. My sex dreams had turned him on. So, I listened and savored every moment and then replayed them in my mind during my morning shower.

Over the course of the week, the bathroom turned into a masturbation station—*Gina's phrase, not mine*—between his nightly visits and my *extended* showers. She thought I should just go for it—make a move, but I couldn't. Ranger wasn't the kind of man who could be swayed from what he knew was the right thing to do, and in this case, the right thing to do was to keep things professional with me.

I was in danger. He was protecting me. I didn't even really live here. His whole life was in Wyoming. I was still recovering from a bad relationship. He'd never been involved with a woman before.

So, we clung to the veneer of friendship, both knowing it would be crazy to break it.

"Sydney."

I turned. Ranger had run to the grocery store for me, and I'd been so lost in my thoughts I hadn't noticed his return. I wished they had grocery delivery here, but they didn't. And the thought of going to the store—a public place where anyone… anything… I hugged my arms over my chest, ashamed by the rush of fear icing my veins.

"Are you okay?" Ranger carried the two large paper bags into the kitchen and set them on the counter.

"Yeah." My chin bobbed, and I went to help him unload the food. "Your mom's lights look great."

Christmas was in a week, and Lydia had been out each of the last three mornings, stringing up lights on the front of her house.

"It's her favorite thing to do for Christmas because the lights were Dad's favorite thing." He smiled, his dimples making me shiver.

He'd told me about his dad's tragic death, both of us sharing what it was like growing up without a father. In those moments, I could really see just how much his brothers meant to him—how they'd stepped in as role models and protectors for him and his younger sister; the two of them too young to remember anything about their dad.

"Do you usually help her?"

It was the first thought that crossed my mind when Archer showed up each morning to get on the ladder and hang the higher strands; he wouldn't have to be there if Ranger wasn't with me.

He shrugged, and when he didn't answer right away, I knew I was right. "We all pitch in."

"I'm sorry." The lump in my throat swelled.

I tried not to think about the holiday that was coming—tried not to think that I could neither ask Ranger to forgo his family to stay with me nor presume to invite myself. I'd spent Thanksgiving alone just fine... but in a matter of weeks, everything had changed.

I blinked and found Ranger standing in front of me. He'd stopped unloading the groceries and now reached for my shoulders.

"Don't apologize, Sydney," he ordered. "You're my priority."

My breath caught; need tying one more knot in the oxygen between us. I wanted him to pull me closer—wanted his kiss that made me forget everything else. I wanted to release all the pressure that kept building from these moments.

"Ranger..." My voice was husky, the ache between my legs growing.

I'd never had someone be there for me like he was—so dedicated to taking care of me that it stole my breath.

He released me and stepped back, trying to put distance between us like that would make this stop.

I wanted to tell him it wouldn't work—that it was like continually blowing air into an already-stretched balloon; at some point, no more air would fit. *At some point, all this pressure was going to burst.*

"I was thinking we could go to the book club." He returned to stocking the refrigerator.

"What?" My head snapped to him. *Was that day here already?*

"Unless you really don't want to."

"It's not that." I swallowed over the lump in my throat, trying to decipher my thoughts as Ranger came over to me.

"You just haven't left the apartment in a week, Sydney," he said slowly, a crease in his brow forming, and I knew he'd been mulling this over for some time. I'd refused several of his offers to even go for a walk, first around the block, but even when he'd suggested a walk on the Reynolds Protective property. "Our goal is to protect you... not imprison you. There haven't been any other notes or threats. We haven't found any indication that this person is still in town."

But also no indication that he's not.

"I know, but..." *But what? Was I really thinking I'd just hide in the eleven-hundred-square-foot apartment until they found him? Or forever, if they didn't?*

Maybe... if it meant I was hiding with Ranger.

"If you don't want to go to the book club, we can do something else, but I'm taking you out."

My eyes snapped to his. Only then did he realize what he had said.

"I mean, you need to get out of the apartment. Just for a little." He cleared his throat and returned to the bag of produce he'd been unloading.

I chewed on my bottom lip for a second and then sighed. "Okay."

I'd texted with Zoey a handful of times since they'd brought us dinner, and if there was one thing she was adamant about, it was not letting fear consume me. Part of this was fear. There was someone out there who had it out for me because I killed off a fictional character. Someone who didn't know me. Someone who'd tracked me to Wyoming just to threaten me. But the other part of this was him. *Ranger.*

If I left the apartment... if I started to think things could go back to the way they were—or even the way they were supposed to be, with him only escorting me if I needed to leave the apartment... then I wouldn't see him as much as I did now.

"And you're coming?" I asked, even though he'd said he was taking me.

He blinked, staring at me like there was no other option. "Of course."

I hummed and went to the window.

The sun was setting, and I loved the warm glow it set over the sleepy town. I never thought the bustle of the city bothered me. The lights and sounds and sirens at all hours of the day and night. But then I came out here and the peace... it settled an anxious hum in my blood I hadn't even known existed.

"Which book are they reading?"

I missed my readers. I'd always been so active on social media and signings, and the complete absence of those things for the last two months was taking its toll.

"*Covert Affair.*"

"Oh." That was one of my newer books; it was released a couple of months before *Broken Promises*, and it was one of my spiciest. "Do you want a synopsis?" I wondered aloud, recalling that he'd only read most of my older backlist; he'd mentioned ordering the others, but I hadn't seen him with any of them since he'd been staying at the apartment.

"I already read it."

"What?" My jaw dropped. "When?"

"After you fell asleep last night."

Ten minutes. Right.

"I didn't even realize you had the book."

"It came last week." He nodded. "I brought several of them over with my laptop the other day, so I've been reading them when I can't"—he paused, shifted his weight, and then finished—"once you're asleep."

Our eyes held one another, and warmth tingled through my veins. He read them after he was done taking care of himself in the bathroom every night. He wouldn't let himself come back to bed with me, so he settled for reading my books.

"If you don't want to go, Sydney, we don't have to—"

"No, I do." I looked at him and smiled.

He was right, *as always*. I needed to get out of the apartment. I needed to not sit here and let fear and uncertainty consume me. And after everything I'd heard about this book club, I had a feeling this was a good escape from my situation... not the least part of which was the way I wanted Ranger.

Ranger parked carefully in front of the Betty B&B right next to his brother's Jeep. I could already see the small gathering of people in the front bay window.

The old Victorian building rose up with a nostalgic air. The attention to detail and inviting entry were exactly what I would picture for a small bed-and-breakfast nestled in the Teton mountains. And with Christmas around the corner, twinkle lights kissed every seam of the building, with garland strung around every frame. The image belonged on a postcard or a storybook.

We climbed the front steps, and a cold rush of air made my teeth clack together. A flurry hit my nose, and I looked up at the sky, clouds shielding what would normally be an assortment of constellations. They were calling for snow tonight. Like everything else in my life, the winter weather had been locked up in a cloud for weeks, building up steam and pressure that was finally starting to slip out.

Ranger held the door, and I'd hardly stepped into the front hallway before I heard it.

"Jerry! She's here!"

I turned to the sitting room on my right just as a middle-aged man, his beard streaked with slices of gray, turned and saw me.

His jaw dropped and he reached for the woman at his side—I assumed his wife by the way she supported him.

"Sydney... Sydney Ward." He stared. "You're here."

"I heard this book club was something I couldn't miss," I said with a smile. "You must be Jerry."

I swore I thought he was going to cry as his head bobbed, glancing to his wife and whispering not so subtly, "She knows me—she knows my name."

He approached me in a daze, his hand trembling as he extended it in greeting.

I looked at it and grinned. "Someone once told me how many germs are exchanged in a handshake." I felt Ranger shift behind me. "So, I guess it's a good thing I've always been more of a hugger."

He went into shock as I embraced him but then hugged me back an instant later.

"We're so thrilled to have you," he said and drew back, reaching for his wife, who happily came to his side. "This is my wife, Trish. We're both huge, huge fans."

"Welcome to Wisdom, Ms. Ward," Trish beamed.

"Sydney, please," I told her and hugged her, too.

The group was small—almost everyone a familiar face. Aside from Trish and Jerry, Hunter and Zoey were there as well, along with Cindy and another woman who'd come with her. It was by far the most intimate book event I'd ever gone to.

Jerry took our jackets and Trish served us mugs of steaming

mulled wine, ushering us to the love seat. Ranger sat next to me but tried his best to stay as close to the side of the couch as possible. *More distance.* Again, the balloon inflated, and I felt the confines start to creak.

There were finger foods and homemade cookies on the table for everyone to share.

"Wait, are these…" I peered closer at the cookies.

"You bet they are," Trish winked. "It's tradition. I make the chocolate chip cookies from *Dangerous Desires* for every book club."

For several minutes, everyone just chatted and ate. Outside the window, flurries fell in a steady stream. There was a fire crackling in the hearth, but the only heat I felt was from the man next to me. He was quiet here. Observing. Perceptive.

To be—by far—the smartest person in the room and yet carry such an understated presence was almost… hypnotic. And the embodiment of Teddy Roosevelt's saying, *"Walk softly but carry a big stick."*

In more ways than one…

"Alright, gang. Welcome to this month's book club. As you all know, we have a very special guest with us tonight. Sydney Ward, the author of *Covert Affair.*"

Murmurs of welcome rumbled through the group.

"Thank you for having me. I'm really glad to be here tonight." I lifted my mug and took a sip.

Only Ranger knew how grateful I really was. As afraid as I was of leaving, getting out of the apartment had been, for lack of a better or less-overused phrase, the release of a breath I didn't realize I was holding.

"Well, we certainly don't want to put you on the spot, seeing as how you're on vacation in town. So just feel free to chime in if you want." Jerry's broad grin was permanently affixed to his cheeks, and I was fairly certain that if I chimed in with my grocery list, he'd still listen with rapt attention. "So, we'll start with our usual book club format by going around and talking about our favorite or most memorable part of *Covert Affair*."

"Oh! I'll go first," Trish exclaimed and chuckled. "When Sasha hit the kidnapper with the frying pan."

I grinned, warmth seeping through me as the whole room laughed with her.

"What a scene to open with."

The heroine, Sasha, had nailed the man who'd broken into her house to abduct her.

"It was one of my favorites to write," I offered. "Someone left *Tangled* on at my dentist while I was getting my teeth cleaned; it was so funny that I wanted to incorporate a frying pan somewhere in a book."

Everyone took their turns while I sat and absorbed the love this group had for my books. I wasn't one to bask in my own accomplishments. Normally, I kept my head down and wrote; even on release day, I didn't take a break from writing. And while I did some publicity events and signings, it was hard to feel connected to readers like this, and trying to do it online wasn't the same. After my latest release, I wasn't sure I'd ever be able to connect with them again. But this... being here and hearing their conversation... gave me hope.

Before I knew it, I heard myself speaking up again, telling them my inspiration behind the suspense. How I figured out how the villain was going to be. Confessing that I hadn't known what the plot twist was going to be until it happened. Minutes ticked by. Favorite scenes turned into deeper conversations about the characters and the plot. And one mug of mulled wine turned into three while the space between Ranger and me on the couch evaporated until his leg was resting along mine.

"How about you, Ranger? I didn't know you were a fan of Sydney's," Cindy exclaimed, eager to draw in the only one in the group who'd stayed silent.

Ranger blushed. "I just started reading her books recently."

"Ahh, a newbie! Well, go on and tell us what your favorite part was," Trish urged.

His brow creased. "I think it would be the hotel shower scene."

My heart tripped, and I almost choked on my mouthful of wine. Vince hadn't even read my books. Meanwhile, my landlord-slash-bodyguard had just up and declared a sex scene—*a shower sex scene*—as his favorite in front of a (small) crowd.

"You're picking a sex scene?" Hunter gaped.

Ranger blinked. "Am I not supposed to?"

"No—I mean—"

"You pick whatever scene you want, honey," Cindy chimed in over Hunter, shushing him with a wave of her hand. "I loved that one, too."

"Oh, it was so good." Trish fanned herself. "Definitely one of the spiciest you've ever written."

Because when I wrote the book, Vince was working a lot and even when he was in town, we rarely had sex; that was only a few months before learning he was cheating on me.

"Why'd you pick a sex scene?" Hunter probed, resting back in his chair, arms folded. "That's a Gunner move."

Ranger's blush deepened at the rumble of laughter through the room.

"Seriously, Ranger. No judgment. I want to know."

Ranger shifted on the couch, rubbing his leg along mine. I locked my teeth together, afraid to make a sound because all I wanted was to hear his answer.

"It was my favorite because it was the first time Sasha was vulnerable with Jason. She was covered in blood and called him, knowing how it could look. But she took a risk to trust him, and he proved to be there for her at her worst. He took care of her. Washed the blood from her…" His Adam's apple bobbed as he swallowed, clasping his hands tight in front of him. "The scene was both physical and emotional intimacy, and I found that very moving."

Silence settled in the room.

"I agree with Ranger," Zoey spoke up. "That's one of the things I love about your books, Sydney. You don't shy away from the importance sex can have in a relationship."

"And this is why Ranger wrote all my English papers in high school..." Hunter muttered, but not low enough that the whole room didn't hear him.

"Oh!" Trish clapped her hands together and then winked at Jerry. "How's this for fun—favorite Sydney Ward sex scene of all time?"

Now, I was really blushing.

"Restaurant bathroom scene in *Dangerous Liaisons*, and I will fight anyone who disagrees with me," Jerry claimed and reached for Trish's hand.

"Library in *Undercover Love*," Hunter said, adding, "And I'll be happy to fight you."

Cindy picked a pool scene from *Target Heart*.

"Any scene involving Dixon," Zoey chimed in with a grin.

"Seriously?" Hunter sat forward and stared.

"What? He's pierced!"

Hunter lifted a brow. "Say the word, and I'll bring Prince Harry into this marriage tomorrow."

"It's actually a Prince Albert," Ranger chimed in. "If you're referring to the genital piercing that passes through the urethra—"

Jerry hooted. Zoey shook her head, laughed, and pulled Hunter's face to hers for a kiss. I glanced at Ranger and wondered if it was possible for his face to turn any redder.

Hunter's phone buzzed and stole his attention. "Damn. It's already ten. We should head home."

"Ten?" Cindy fiddled to find her watch. "Oh, dear, we should get going, too." She and her friend rose along with Hunter and Zoey.

Within a matter of minutes, the rest of the small group bundled into their coats and said their goodbyes. I insisted on signing everyone's books before they left until, finally, it was only Ranger and I left in the entryway with the owners of the B&B.

"Oh, Sydney." Jerry came up to me, wringing his hands. "I have something for you. Just wait one minute."

He went behind the small check-in desk in the hallway and opened a drawer. Whatever he pulled out was small because when he returned, it was clasped completely in his fist.

"When we heard you might be coming to the book club, we wanted to give you something—a gift for joining us and for writing these stories that brought us all together." He shifted his weight. "I don't... I hate to bring this up, but I saw that last interview and I just need you to know that woman and all the others like her; they're a minority."

My throat swelled.

"For romance readers—the real ones—we know romance is love against all odds, even when those odds are pretty shocking and shitty. It's knowing that a happy ending is coming, even in the darkest moments. You've given me that—you've given all of us that, so we made you this to help you remember it's what's coming for you, too."

I blinked back tears as he opened his palm. A metal band lay in the center of it.

"Now, before you get any ideas, I have to confess that I own the local hardware store and this is just a nut that Trish modified," he continued and reached for my hand, testing the homemade ring on each finger until he found one that fit. "So, you don't forget that no matter what the page says, no matter what hardships and heartbreak this chapter brings, in the end, love wins."

Love wins.

The heavy metal slid down my vacant ring finger. *Of course.*

"Thank you," I said with a watery voice and pulled him in for another hug.

I hadn't needed a reminder that there were still readers who loved my books... I needed the reminder that, at my core, I was a romantic. A romance reader.

And romance readers didn't give up on their happy ending.

"Wow." My long exhale appeared as a white cloud in front of me when we stepped outside.

In the hours that we'd been in the B&B, the snow had layered a thin blanket over every surface. I could hear the plows in the distance, but they hadn't come to this end of Main Street yet, leaving the carpet of white untouched.

Everything was so... pristine. So beautiful.

It was probably the mulled wine that sent me traipsing out into the middle of the road, savoring the kiss of snowflakes on my cheeks.

Ranger called from behind me, but I didn't turn.

It was almost as though I'd stepped back in time. There were no cars. The old western facades of the buildings from a century or more prior rose up. With the streetlights low and the moon bright, it felt like I'd stepped into a snow globe time machine, the flakes catching the midnight light all around.

"Sydney?" Ranger stood at the edge of the sidewalk, his hands in his pockets.

"Come look." I waved my hand.

I had to bite back a chuckle when he looked both ways before stepping out into the street. There wasn't a car for miles.

"What are you doing?" There was no judgment or chastisement to his tone, just that pure wonder.

"Just... taking it all in." I stretched out my arms and then another crazy idea popped into my head. "Let's make snow angels."

"Oh, I don't think that's—"

I was on the ground before he could finish, flattening my back onto the snow-covered street.

"Come on. There's no one on the road." I extended my hand. "It's a snow angel moment."

"What's a snow angel moment?" He stepped off the curb.

"A moment you have to savor." I patted the snow next to me

and then looked down the still street. "A moment where everything kind of just stops to let you have it. Where even though it makes no sense to lie down in the cold, wet snow and flail about, you do it… because it's magic."

When I looked back, Ranger stood over me, watching me with an intensity I felt in my bones. And then he crouched down to join me on the ground.

My head rested in his direction, watching his hair tumbling over his forehead as he sat and lay back. Our eyes locked. And then I let my limbs swing first.

He should've lain farther away because our arms and legs collided as they slid through the snow. I didn't know why—*no, I did know why, lots of mulled wine*—but it made me laugh, and he smiled in return. Swipe after swipe, and neither of us moved, our hands brushing back and forth over each other like that was the real magic we were making.

After a minute, we stopped, our hands resting together between us. My fingers found his. Without gloves, I should've felt the cold of the snow, but there was only heat—only an ache I couldn't extinguish.

"They say the first snow angels were made by Medieval Jewish mystics," Ranger said quietly.

"Really?" I played along, not wanting to let go of him or this moment just yet.

"To purge themselves of evil spirits."

I hummed and stared up at the crystal stars that studded the black satin sky. "Maybe it will work for me, too." *Spirits… stalkers… Tomato… Tom-ah-to.*

"North Dakota holds the world record for most snow angels made simultaneously in one place. Eight thousand nine hundred and sixty-two."

"Wow. That's a lot of angels." A drift of cold air blew down the road and made me shiver. Ranger must've been watching me because he immediately rose.

"We should go. It's getting cold."

I lingered for a moment longer until he extended his hand to help me.

"Careful," Ranger instructed, but wine and snow and a handsome bodyguard were a very slippery combination.

I took hold of his hand, but my foot lost traction and sent me crashing straight into his chest. The dusting on the ground was as magical as it was treacherous.

I tipped my head up, my breath fogging the frozen air. "Sorry."

"Are you okay?" He made no move to release me.

No. My lips parted, my eyes roaming every line of his face. I was not okay—I was not okay for wanting him the way I did.

"Ranger..." I murmured huskily, my gaze centering on his lips. "You picked a sex scene, and I want to kiss you."

Maybe those two things were unrelated. Or maybe that moment inside the B&B had been his moment of vulnerability, of emotional intimacy, and I couldn't take the pressure—the distance anymore.

I wanted him. I wanted Ranger Reynolds, no matter the consequences.

"Sydney..." His head drifted down.

"Kiss me, Ranger." I curled my hands into his jacket and tipped my head to meet his descending mouth.

A heavenly moan spilled from my chest when his warm lips pressed to mine. Tender yet firm. Almost instantly, the warm swipe of his tongue slid along the seam of my mouth, entering it with confidence as soon as my lips parted.

He was a phenomenal kisser, not because of practice but because he learned quickly. If it took him ten minutes to read an entire steamy romance novel, it took him ten seconds of real-world application to learn exactly where to stroke and what pressure to apply.

My arms wound around his neck, locking me to him. The kiss deepened. Consumed. The soft sounds of the sleepy town faded into the background.

He kissed me like I was this giant unknown, and he wasn't going to stop until he'd uncovered every fact and facet of my desire.

Our tongues tangled in the heat of our mouths, tying invisible knots to prevent us from ever breaking apart. When his teeth bit gently into my bottom lip, I quaked in his arms, the sensation spiraling straight down to my core.

I'd never doubted any of his facts, but as my inner muscles clenched and released in time with the firm tug of his mouth on my lip, I believed he could make me orgasm from just a kiss.

I wanted him to.

My hips rocked harder against him, searching for the hard evidence of his arousal through all our clothes. I gave way to the surge of sensations—a growing avalanche of want inside me that turned the kiss ravenous.

We turned in the street, feet sliding in the snow as we devoured each other, a week's worth of want releasing like a torrent. I didn't know if it was seconds or minutes later when a loud honk reminded us that we weren't alone.

Ranger immediately drew back, panting. The car had given us sufficient warning to get out of the middle of the street, but still, Ranger ushered me in a hurry back to his Volvo in the parking lot and secured me in the passenger seat.

Warmth continued to fray the seams of my body as we drove slowly back to the apartment. The effects of the kiss surrounded us just as magically and treacherously as the snow, reality unable to clear the heavy layer of desire that blanketed our every interaction... our every breath.

Like a tightly bound rope coming undone inside me, I was tired of hiding how much I wanted him. Tired of him having to do the same. I knew things were complicated. I knew that acting on attraction wouldn't make them less so.

But this snow angel moment wasn't over yet.

CHAPTER 13

Ranger

I had yet to pinpoint the very first error in my judgment tonight, but I believed it was somewhere between picking a favorite sex scene and having lain down in the middle of the street to make snow angels.

It was well before I kissed her, I knew that much. The kiss was simply the product of a reaction I hadn't realized was occurring. Desire had been a smokeless, odorless chemical in the air, like methane as it displaced oxygen and logic from my brain until attraction asphyxiated my restraint. I kissed her like she was oxygen, and I should've known better because when methane is drowned in oxygen, it combusts. And I would have, too, if it hadn't been for that car.

I'd driven slowly back to the apartment, but the snow covering the road wasn't the most treacherous part of the journey. *This was.* Being back in the apartment with her. *Alone.* Our kiss hung between us as tangibly as a metal chain.

Sydney stood by the table. We'd left our coats, soaked from having lain in the snow, hanging in the garage. But her cheeks were still a pretty red, the color spilling onto her neck and chest. My eyes roamed over her curves with unabashed appreciation. Even through her shirt and bra, I could see the outline of her hard nipples, and my dick throbbed.

"Sydney…" I croaked, willing myself to say good night and leave, but nothing came out.

"Most people wouldn't admit to a sex scene as being their favorite." She reached back and gripped the edge of the table, leaning against it.

This would be easier if we didn't talk about the sex scene. Or sex in general. Especially when she dragged her tongue over her swollen lips.

"I'm not most people."

She pushed away from the table and came toward me. I firmed my lips and swallowed. This moment was my best chance to leave if I wanted to reduce my odds of needing to kiss her again.

Leave, Ranger. Say good night.

My brain instructed and then hollered its logic… and my body ignored it.

"Tell me what was memorable about the sex scene," she murmured once she was in front of me.

"The… emotions." I cleared my throat.

Sex could be emotionless. A physical transaction of pleasure without anything more. But it could be more, and because I knew it could be more, I'd never felt comfortable settling for anything less.

She held up her finger. "You told everyone about the emotional intimacy. I want to know what was memorable about the physical intimacy."

My cheeks warmed, and I pursed my lips. What was memorable was the way I'd imagined myself in the scene with her.

Sydney reached up and undid the top button at my collar. My breath exhaled in a whoosh as though it had been stopped up in my throat.

"I… don't know."

A second button gave way to her fingers, and I made no move to stop her.

"Was it the kiss?" Her eyes focused on my mouth. "Or how she sucked him off before they had sex? Or was it the sex?"

"The oral sex," I blurted out, my heartbeat drumming in my ears like an entire marching band. I'd read that part several times. I couldn't be sure what it was about the idea of having her mouth on my cock, but it made me so hard I couldn't see straight. "And the regular sex. All of it. Just… all of it." My throat bobbed, and I croaked out, "Very informational."

Her teeth snagged her bottom lip and my dick jolted in my pants.

"Ranger…" She was so close I could smell the sweet scent of mulled wine on her breath.

"Sydney." I gritted my teeth. "We shouldn't… We should … go to bed." *No.* "I mean, you should go to bed. I'll—"

"Disappear into the bathroom in the middle of the night to jerk off?"

My eyes shot wide. "You…" *Shit.*

"I hear you." Her hooded gaze met mine. "And I replay the sounds every morning when I take my shower." The pink tip of her tongue darted over her lips again. "I bring my vibrator in with me and get off on the memory of you getting off."

"Syd," I choked out and gripped her shoulders. For what? I had no idea. I had no idea what was happening to me other than that it was all desire's fault.

I gasped in air because I needed oxygen—needed it to survive. Except it was also the thing that started my combustion all over again. To breathe was to want her.

"Kiss me, Ranger."

She didn't need to ask twice. My mouth dropped back to hers with the powerful arc of a wrecking ball, smooth and unstoppable.

I thought I'd taste the spiced wine on her tongue again, but the only thing I could taste was her desire mixed with my own. All it took was one kiss for me to learn that stroking my tongue along the side of hers made her shudder. One kiss to learn that biting and then sucking on her bottom lip made her moan. One kiss to imprint in my memory everything that brought her pleasure.

And I was fully prepared to recall it with perfect clarity for the rest of my life.

I wasn't prepared for what would happen if I had the opportunity to use that knowledge again.

My hands found the sides of her face, cupping her cheeks and angling her head. Maybe it was instinct. Maybe it was a subconscious suggestion from all of her novels I'd read. But what it wasn't was thinking. My tongue and mouth moved only in search of her response. The heat of her sighs, the soft tremble of her moans.

Her want was intoxicating. It made me hot and hard and hungry—everything but hesitant.

I didn't even feel her grab the edge of my sweater-vest until she was dragging it over my head. Moving next to the buttons on my shirt. By the time that hit the floor, the only thing I could feel was every pulse of my cock straining against my pants. I'd never been so hard in my entire life—*and I would remember*. I'd never wanted anything as badly as I wanted her.

Her kiss. Her touch. Her mouth wrapped around my cock.

"I don't—I can't—" I broke off, panting and in search of words I couldn't find.

She made me speechless. Thoughtless. *Powerless*.

"Let me," she murmured huskily, her palm flattening to the bare skin of my chest. "You know everything, Ranger. Tonight, I want to know you."

My mouth parted as her fingers slid down my stomach, the last of the oxygen in my lungs evacuating along with the threadbare ties of my restraint.

Tomorrow, I'd figure out how to make sense of all this. I'd figure out how to rationalize my decision. But tonight, feeling overtook the mountains of facts. The untrained, inexperienced part of me took down the Goliath of my genius with a single stone.

I couldn't move as her fingers undid my belt and worked open the waist of my pants before shoving them to the floor.

"Off," she ordered, and I stepped out of my pants and kicked them to the side, standing in nothing more than my boxer briefs that tented out in front of me.

I knew my dick was about to explode, but the wet circle in the otherwise light-gray fabric advertised just how horny I was.

Hooking her fingers into the waist of the fabric, she drew my underwear down with her as she knelt in front of me.

"Sydney..." I ground out, reaching for the sides of her face and finding her gaze. I could still feel the wetness of the snowflakes on her cheek, in her hair.

God, she was so beautiful. *Too beautiful.* She shouldn't be on her knees in front of me—shouldn't be doing this. I groaned low. One lick of her tongue was going to send me over the edge.

"I want to taste you." She licked her lips and then dropped her eyes to my cock, more precum leaking out under her inspection.

My heart pounded against the front of my chest as her hands framed my hips. "Just breathe, Ranger. Tell me a fact."

A fact.

About fellatio.

"Until 1950, fellatio was still considered a felony in all forty-eight states." I hissed when her fingers closed around my girth, the flow of information in my brain crashing to a halt.

"A felony..." Her head tipped closer until I felt the heat of her breath on my throbbing flesh. "What else?"

I tried to swallow, but it was impossible. Her mouth was so close. The grip of her fingers was so firm.

"Blow jobs were made popular by the Mob—by a film—a porno they bankrolled in the seventies." I panted through the facts, but trying to pluck them from my mind was like trying to grab dandelion seeds after they'd been blown to the wind.

"The Mob movie?" Her eyes flicked to mine as her fist slowly stroked me—pulled my cock closer to her quirked mouth.

It was pure anticipation that reined my orgasm—the need to know the feel of her mouth on me was more important—more necessary to my survival than anything else I could think of.

"You've heard of it."

"Tell me." Her lips opened wide, her hand angling my cock to land inside their warmth, but her eyes stayed locked on mine.

"*Deep Throat*," I choked out. "Watergate named their source after the movie."

Her mouth closed over the tip of my cock. Pleasure and pain erupted like I'd never felt before. Her lips. Her tongue. The tightness. The velvet heat. It was like a bomb went off inside me.

"Oh fuck," I exclaimed, white spots bursting in my vision as pleasure seared through my veins with brutal force. I jerked my hips back, popping my dick from her lips. *Holy... shit.* I gasped and stepped back unsteadily.

"Are you okay?"

"I think... I think I need to sit."

She grinned. Rising, she pushed me back until my legs hit the bed, and I sank onto the edge of it.

"Better?"

I nodded. "I can see why someone would make that a felony," I said hoarsely. "It felt too good." *Too good to stay upright kind of good.*

"Tell me." She knelt between my legs, running her hands up my thighs.

My dick bobbed against my stomach, wanting the heat of her lips again.

I reached down and grabbed my length, a low hiss pushing through my lips. Her hands slid them toward my groin. My jaw locked, watching them converge on my dick and peel it from my hold.

Was this supposed to happen? Was my body supposed to feel like it was stretching to the very brink of its seams? Was my heart supposed to feel like it was about to beat itself straight out of my chest?

Was I supposed to be completely consumed with the thought of her mouth sliding down my dick?

"Tell me what you're thinking, Ranger." Her eyes glittered. "I want to know what's going on in that big brain of yours."

"I'm thinking about your mouth wrapped around my dick. I knew it would be wet and warm, but I wasn't prepared…" My teeth ground together. "It doesn't make sense how good it feels."

"Do you want me to do it again?" Her lips curved up ever so slightly before she slid her tongue out and licked along my crown.

"*God, yes.*" My hips bucked, my cock bumping against her lips. "Yes. Do it again," I begged, but I wasn't ashamed.

Her lips formed an *o* and sucked my tip through them.

A sound I didn't know I could make erupted from my chest as pleasure pressurized in the base of my spine. I searched for the facts—for the mechanics of what was happening to me, for all the different reactions and responses that came together to create an orgasm. But my mind was blissfully blank. Nothing but a white blaze of desire as her mouth slid down my length.

"God, that feels so good, Sydney." My hand tangled in her hair, holding on as she went lower and then I tried to hold her back when she was going too far. "Don't. You'll hurt—*fuck*—" My body revolted when my tip hit the back of her throat and she swallowed. My hips drove higher, my hand imprisoning her head. I didn't want to hurt her, but I couldn't help myself.

As soon as the wave of pleasure crested, her head moved up and her lips slid off my dick.

"Are you okay?" I scoured her face, swearing that, for once, I'd be able to see it in her expression if she wasn't. "I didn't mean—I couldn't help it."

"Don't be sorry, Ranger." She licked her swollen lips. "I did it on purpose."

"You did?" My brow furrowed. "Why? Your mouth can't fit all of me." It was an anatomical fact, not hubris.

Her husky chuckle made my body tingle.

Her chin dipped. "I know how strong your mind is," she said throatily. "I want to be the one who makes it lose control."

I didn't get a chance to respond before her mouth suctioned around my dick again, pulling herself down my length like a warm, wet vise. I tipped back onto my elbows. It couldn't be possible for something to feel this good—this powerful. But it did. And I was powerless to stop it.

My fingers tangled back in her hair, holding her head steady as my hips thrust into the downward motion of her mouth.

"You feel amazing. I don't... fuck..." I gasped as her teeth skated along my length. "I don't understand how it can feel this good."

I groaned each time she bottomed out, the sound of her sputtering around my dick making it swell even thicker. And every sound I made only seemed to push her to move faster... to go deeper.

My mind was already lost, I wanted to tell her, but I couldn't speak. Sweat beaded on my brow. It was a miracle I hadn't come already. The only reason had to be that I was addicted to the sight of her sucking my cock, and I wanted to make sure I had a damn good memory of that before this night ended.

I stared in a trance as her head bobbed up and down along my cock, red and glistening from the wetness of her mouth. There was nothing except her. Ache built like a hot pressure at the base of my spine. Pleasure eating up the oxygen from my lungs and driving me toward combustion.

"Syd..." I gurgled, but she didn't slow. "Sydney." I wanted to tell her—to warn her that I was going to orgasm. But my release was like an avalanche in my brain, barreling down over everything.

I tried to tug her head, but her hand reached up and grabbed my wrist, pinning it to the bed and interlocking her fingers with mine.

"I'm going to come," I panted and squeezed her hand. "Sydney..."

My hips rocked up from the bed, driving the tip of my cock against the back of her throat over and over again like I could defy anatomy and force those final fractions of an inch deeper inside her mouth. She moaned along my length and my balls tightened.

I fought the urge to close my eyes because I had to see this—needed to remember this. I needed to memorize the way my thick, pulsing dick disappeared into her pink lips. The way saliva leaked from the corners of her mouth as she pulled me deep.

I knew it was coming. *I knew I was coming.* I felt the slow contraction of her mouth and throat as she tried to swallow around me one last time, and it sent me hurdling over the edge.

I let out a rough shout as my orgasm rocked through me. My cock pumped into her mouth, and I felt the warmth of my cum fill up her cheeks and throat.

I didn't breathe—couldn't—for what felt like minutes as my body reeled from release. I'd never come like that before.

"I didn't…" I swallowed. "I didn't know it could be like that."

Slowly, her mouth slid up my length, releasing the weight and swallowing down my cum. Even spent, the sight made a fresh wave of desire tug at my senses.

"I know." Sydney sat back on her heels with a low hum. "I wanted to be the one to show you." She reached up and wiped the corner of her mouth with her thumb.

My heart was already pumping, but I felt my cheeks warm.

Should I have warned her better? Had I misinterpreted the way she'd grabbed my hand? What if she hadn't wanted my cum in her mouth?

"Did you know there are health benefits to swallowing semen?" I said quickly and reached for my boxer briefs, quickly tugging them up my legs. "Semen contains spermatozoa which contain cortisol, and cortisol increases oxytocin which elevates moods."

"Oh?" Her tongue dragged along the rim of her lips.

I stood and scanned for my sweatpants, keeping my hands clasped over my still semi-hard penis. "It also contains serotonin and melatonin—"

"Ranger."

I stopped and turned when she said my name.

She was standing now, her hand outstretched with my sweatpants in her grasp and a knowing smile on her face. "I wanted to swallow."

"Oh." My tongue slid out and I pulled my lips between my teeth. "Okay. Thanks," I murmured and took my sweats, almost falling as I tried to hastily pull the joggers on.

"But those facts are... good to know for the future," she said as I straightened, the color in her cheeks deepening as her stare drifted back down to my groin.

I'd never attempted to orgasm twice in a row. I'd never needed to. But the way she looked at me made my dick stir like it could go another round, even though the rest of me felt like I'd been pulled apart and stitched back together all wonky.

The loud, steady beeps of a snow plow coming down the road drew our attention to the outside world—one that still existed even if we had forgotten about it for a little while.

"I'm going to get ready for bed," she declared and headed for the bathroom, closing the door behind her.

I exhaled and speared my fingers through my hair.

Getting your dick sucked is life changing, Baby Brains. I could distinctly recall Gunner's words when he'd picked me up late from school after an SAT prep session. I remembered the smell of the girl's perfume that still clung to the fabric of the seats in his car. *One day you'll understand.*

That day had finally come.

I looked around the room, searching for my lost mind, when I saw the rest of my clothes strewn all over the floor. One after another, I snatched up my shirt, vest and jacket, my phone tumbling from my coat pocket and bouncing onto the floor.

"Damn." I picked it up and checked for cracks, seeing a message from Hunter on the screen.

Hunter: You make it home okay?

That was over an hour ago. I was surprised he didn't send out a search party.

I walked over to the couch and set my clothes on it, typing out a response.

Ranger: Yes.

Outside, the snow was still coming down. I stepped up to the window, surprised to see not only how much snow had fallen… but also the solitary person standing on the sidewalk directly in front of the driveway and staring up at the apartment. *At me.*

Was that him? Sydney's stalker?

I quickly opened my phone. There was no way I could get dressed and down there in time to confront him, but if I could just get a photo. I zoomed in on the dark-clothed figure as quickly as I could, but it wasn't fast enough. The only photos I got were of his profile and back as he walked away, though he was carrying a very large bag at his side.

What was in the bag? A weapon?

"Ranger?"

I quickly closed my phone and tucked it into my pocket, my heart drumming rapidly.

"In here," I said, picking up my vest and folding it. I did the same with my shirt and pants. There was no point in telling Sydney about the man now; the only thing that would do was make her worry. *Again.*

I'd just finished setting my folded pants on the couch when Sydney appeared at my side.

"Will you stay?"

I straightened and stared at her. It hadn't even been a thought in my mind to leave.

"Of course." I nodded.

Hearing that, she walked over and slid underneath the covers.

I took my turn in the bathroom, firing off a text to my brothers with the photos I'd taken of the man in the driveway. They were garbage; we'd never be able to pull a usable facial photo from the shots, but I had to tell them someone was still watching Sydney.

As soon as that was done, I stripped down again and got in the shower. The spray of warm water on my face hit me with another thought.

Should I have pleasured her?

I wiped my hands up my face and along the sides of my head. *Shit.* I was an idiot. I'd orgasmed, and she hadn't. *Double shit.* I refused to chalk it up to inexperience or the idea that I'd lost my mind. I'd made a mistake, and I was going to fix it.

I washed quickly, determined to even out the oral sex score, but when I came out of the bathroom, Sydney was nestled well underneath the covers with her eyes shut. *Damn.* I pressed my lips together. *Tomorrow.* Tomorrow I'd make it up to her.

I tiptoed through the room, not wanting to wake her, but when I reached the edge of the bed, her sleepy murmur stopped me.

"Will you hold me?"

I exhaled slowly, feeling a pressure in my chest that I couldn't ease.

"Of course."

I settled in next to her and pulled her against my chest, savoring the warm caress of her breath on my skin.

I didn't want this to end. I didn't want her to leave. Wyoming. Wisdom. Or my bed. The thoughts didn't make sense—not with the reality of our lives—but I couldn't control them. I didn't understand how I could… feel… for someone so quickly. So completely. So beyond logic. But it happened.

I couldn't think straight, but there was no stopping it now. She changed something in me. A chain reaction that couldn't be halted. The only thing left to do was wait and see what became of me when this was all done.

CHAPTER 14

Sydney

My phone blared like a gong next to my ear. *Why had I set an alarm?* My groan was halfway through my lips when my eyes shot open. *I hadn't set an alarm.* I scrambled from the bed, my phone vibrating on the nightstand.

"Sydney?" Ranger appeared from the kitchen, shirtless with the coffeepot in his hand. "Good morning."

A warm shiver coasted along my spine.

"Hi." My breath rushed out.

Time slowed for one delicious second, allowing me to absorb every inch of my intellectual Adonis. His tousled blond hair and bare chest. The way his gold-green gaze snagged on my mouth, he shifted his weight to try and hide his body's reaction, but I saw that, too. Everything from his dimples down to his d—

My phone went off again, interrupting my train of thought. "Sorry, it's my phone."

I fished through my jacket pockets until my hand crashed into something hard, the sound of metal hitting plastic making me wince. I pulled out my cell, missing the call but having my attention stolen by the silver band on my ring finger; more snapshots of last night came back to me. Book club. The gift from Trish and Jerry. The snow angels.

Ranger losing his mind over a blow job.

I shivered, suddenly flush with the memory.

"Everything okay?"

My head turned, and I nodded to him. "Gina was calling—is calling me." She was rarely this insistent. Then again, I was rarely a victim of a stalker.

"Hello?"

"Are you fucking kidding me?"

I jerked the phone away from my ear and turned down the volume.

"What? What's going on?"

The last time she'd talked like this was when I'd told her I'd found the DMs on Vince's phone from all the women he'd been sleeping with.

"How could you not tell me, Syd?" She groaned. "If you told me, I would've been prepared. I wouldn't be waking up at five a.m. to field this shitstorm—"

My heart leapt to the center of my throat. "What are you talking about? Tell you what?"

"About Ranger!"

"About—" I covered my mouth with my palm and winced. *How could she... She couldn't...* I'd been awake all of two minutes, and *I* was just now remembering all about Ranger.

I glanced over my shoulder, watching the man in question carefully measure out perfect scoops of coffee grounds for the coffee machine. *He wouldn't have...*

Giving him my back, I lowered my voice. "How do you know about Ranger?"

"Seriously?" she charged. "It's all over the internet. Gossip sites. Socials. Everywhere."

I covered my mouth with my hand, catching the choked gasp that rocketed from my chest in dismay. "What?"

This couldn't be happening. I forced down the swell of nausea, hearing Gina's voice on the other end of the call but unable to distinguish a word as I rushed over to the table and flipped open my laptop.

"Sydney—"

I felt Ranger's confused stare but ignored it as I opened a browser, my fingers shaking so badly I could hardly peck out my own name into the search bar.

"How? How would they know?" I bit out, my voice trembling. "It's literally been one night, Gina. One kiss and one night, how would someone—"

The seconds it took to load results felt like hours.

"One night? What are you talking about?" Gina balked. "Sydney, the internet is blowing up with the news that you're—"

"Married," I shrieked, my phone dropping from my fingers into my lap.

This couldn't be real. I scanned over the articles and posts and viral tweets, shock pummeling me in waves.

Married.

"Sydney, what's..." Even Ranger trailed off, his shock evident in his silence as he read the headlines.

They thought I was married. They thought Ranger and I were married.

Gina's voice yelled out from my crotch, but I couldn't listen to her right now. Not until I understood what was happening.

"I don't understand," I muttered, clicking on the first link for the *Daily Glass*, a popular tabloid that'd greedily milked every ounce of drama they could from my disastrous interview with Drew Barrymore.

They'd found me—followed me to Wyoming.

My heart clambered up into my throat, trying to escape the tightness in my chest as pieces of the story fell into place—no, more like toppled like dominos of disaster.

There were photos of us... everywhere. Ranger's garage and the apartment. Outside the B&B for book club last night. Photo after photo, distance shots of us in the sitting room at the Betty. And then after, in the street…

"They followed me." My voice was hollow, the words dry from my chest that burned with each breath.

As I scrolled, it got harder and harder to breathe. Every second of my precious memories from last night was plastered all over the internet like a comic strip.

When we'd lain in the middle of the street. Making snow angels. Our kiss. But the last photo was the reason for all of this—the image of me clutching Ranger, a zoomed-in shot of my left hand on the side of his head.

"Oh my god." I lifted my hand from the trackpad, staring in horror at my ring finger, the thick metal band glinting back at me.

It was no wonder the paparazzi thought I was married; I'd been wearing a ring on my left hand.

"Sydney." Ranger rested his hand on my shoulder.

I shook my head in disbelief, trying to breathe, though it felt like my head was under water. The press had assumed many things about me in the past but nothing like this.

And I only had myself to blame.

I shouldn't have worn the ring. I shouldn't have made snow angels. I shouldn't have wanted to hold on to that magical moment with him long enough for one more kiss.

"Here, let me," Ranger's soft voice peeled back my trance as he carefully reached right for my crotch—*What? Oh. Shit.*

"*Sydney!*" Gina's voice boomed as Ranger put the call on speaker.

"Hello, Gina? This is Ranger Reynolds," he answered so politely my heart ached. "I'm sorry, Sydney needed a minute…" he trailed off and I groaned, only imagining what she was asking—saying. "One moment, Gina."

He muted the call and crouched next to me, finding my gaze. "Are you alright?"

I whimpered. Even now, he was protecting me—protecting whatever space I needed to process this. *No.* Being attracted to my nerdy landlord was what got me into this mess in the first place.

"No. No, I'm not alright," I said with a strangled laugh. "I have a stalker. The press found me. And because of some well-timed photos, the world thinks we're married."

He crouched by my side and took my hand in his. I felt the weight of that damn ring pinned between us.

Married.

"We'll figure this out." He squeezed my fingers. So warm. So sure.

"How do you know?" I reached out with my other hand and pushed back some wayward curls from his face.

God. Had he gotten even more… beautiful… since last night?

His tongue slid between his lips, and then he said, "I have three PhDs. If I can't figure this out, no one can."

"Fair." I exhaled slowly.

He handed me my phone. "She wants to be put on speaker."

Hitting the button, I brought my friend into the conversation. "Gina? I'm here—I'm sorry."

"Thank God. Are you okay?"

"I've been better," I muttered wryly. I was a little far from okay, but that didn't matter. This situation wasn't just going to pause itself because I wasn't alright. "I can't believe this—"

"You can't believe this? Why didn't you tell me you're married?"

"Because I'm not—we're not married, G." My eyes flicked to Ranger's. It had to be the lingering shock that made my chest squeeze when I insisted on the contrary.

"Last night, we went to a local book club with some of Sydney's fans, and one of them gave her that ring," Ranger explained.

"It had fit best on my ring finger, and after three glasses of wine, what did I care? I didn't know I was being watched."

"Jesus, Syd."

"How did I not know—not see someone taking our photo?" I searched my memory from last night. Outside the B&B. In the middle of the road.

Cameras... flashes... anything...

Ranger. He was the only thing I could remember.

"It was probably only one of them. You know it only takes one to sell a story—"

Ranger stood abruptly and muttered something under his breath.

"What is it?"

His lips drew together tight. "There was a man outside last night."

"What?" My chair protested when I turned it too quickly.

"While you were in the bathroom, I was folding my clothes by the couch and saw him standing at the end of the driveway. I thought"—he broke off and scratched the back of his neck, a pained look overtaking his face; he'd thought it was the man stalking me. *In a way, he hadn't been wrong.* "He had a large bag and now that I think about it, he could've very well been a photographer. I took his photo, but he was far away, and it was dark and snowing."

So, I shouldn't get my hopes up.

"Paparazzi," I corrected, staring at the computer screen like I had laser vision that could wipe all the photographs and fake news from the internet. "Calling them photographers is like referring to a rowboat as a cruise ship."

"How the hell did they find you out there?" Gina broke in with the same thought plaguing me.

"I don't know," I croaked and then my head snapped up. "What if my stalker is a pap?"

My eyes met Ranger's, and I saw him pull out his phone; I presumed to message his brothers with the possibility.

"And what? Because you've been hiding in a garage for a week, he decided to blast your location to the world? Wouldn't that be counterintuitive?"

"Maybe. Unless he thought it would draw you out."

"Well, he couldn't be more wrong about that." At this point,

I was ready to dig a deep, deep hole if that was what it took to not have my personal life under a microscope. "What are we going to do—what am I going to do? Oh my god…" I pinched the bridge of my nose.

"Just stay calm, Syd—"

"Stay calm? The world thinks I'm married!" I covered my eyes with my hand, refusing to look at Ranger as I said it because I was afraid I couldn't hide the devious little thought that wondered what it would be like to be married to Ranger Reynolds.

And that was very bad.

"Right. So, about that—"

My hand slapped down on the table. "I have to put together a statement," I declared. "A blog post. Something on my website and socials to correct the story—to put the truth out there. I think if we get it up by tonight—"

"Whoa, whoa, whoa. Slow down there, tiger."

"Slow down where? They're crying wolf to the world, and I need to let everyone know they're lying."

"They're not crying wolf, Syd," Gina chided. "They saw smoke, and they called it a fire. It's going to be a pretty hard sell to convince them you're not married when they have photos of you with a ring on and your tongue so far down Ranger's throat you could rim his assho—"

"Gina!" My cheeks burned.

Ranger blushed and then stood. He walked over to the opposite end of the table, his brow creased with a permanent kind of concentration.

"Hey, some people are into—"

"I know," I cut her off. "But can we please focus? We have to correct this."

"Fine. You want focus? You want my opinion. I think it's a mistake to immediately refute the story," she declared flatly. "In fact, I think it's a mistake to refute it at all."

"What?" I almost fell off my chair.

"Syd, you had the sympathy of your entire fan base when your engagement to Vince ended, and then you wrote a book that—while I understand why you had to do it—doesn't change the fact that to some of your fans, it looked like you threw their sympathy back in their face by killing off one of their favorite heroes."

"I..." My mouth clamped shut for a second. "Okay..."

"Now, the story's out that you're in Wyoming because you went and got married. But have you looked at the responses? I mean, I'm watching your email tick up by the minute as we speak, and all of the subject lines are congratulatory."

"What are you saying? That I pretend to be married for some good press?"

"I'm asking you how you think it's going to be spun if you pull another one-eighty and tell them, *'Hey, guys, wearing a ring and kissing a mystery man, but I'm not married'*?"

"What does that matter if it's not the truth?" My brows pulled tight.

"You know why, Syd. You write romance, for Pete's sake. People don't want reality. They want fantasy. They want broody Jason Momoa with an eight-inch pierced dick, intimacy issues, and a heart of gold."

"Not all of them," I grumbled, more images from last night flashing through my mind.

Ranger propped back on the bed, the cords of his neck straining as I sucked his cock. The cut of his lean abdominal muscles pulled taut with pleasure. The pained concern he had when I choked myself on his length. *Lean but long.* And the way he looked when he came.

I'd never felt power like that before. Sure, I wrote about blow jobs all the time, and I'd given Vince head plenty. But I'd never seen someone so buttoned up... someone whose mind was so strong succumbing to something so mindless before. It was all I wanted. I hadn't even cared about my own pleasure—the ache between my legs was a distant thought, too weak to keep me awake once I was in bed. All I wanted was for Ranger to let go—for him to feel.

"You know what I'm saying. In the media, the truth doesn't

matter, only what sells. Right now, it's the hope. The happy ending." She let out a long exhale. "If you take that away and call them out, they will ruin you to your readers. They will claim you were just trying to get attention—to lure them out with a fake story and paint yourself the victim."

"No, they won't—"

"No? Let's play it out for argument's sake. So you send out a press release stating that you're not married, then what? You think they're going to apologize and leave you in peace?"

"Well…" I sighed. "No. They won't." They were sharks who'd been given the scent of blood. There was no point in pretending otherwise.

"So you're not married, but then why are you wearing a ring, Ms. Ward? And why on that finger? Oh, a fan gave it to you? Really? Who was that?" Gina blasted me with questions like a mock pap.

"Just let me think—"

"And who are you kissing? Is he your boyfriend? Your fiancé? Is he the reason you came out here? No, not your boyfriend? Then why are you kissing him? Why is he staying with you? What's going on?"

"Wait—"

But she didn't because she was making her point—a point I wished I couldn't see. "Is this just a fling? Is this to make your ex jealous because he's moved on? Oh, he works at a security firm? Are you in danger? Is this because of your last book? Are you trying to gain sympathy with readers—"

"Enough," Ranger's hard voice fired from across the table, finally getting her to stop.

"I'm sorry, Syd." Gina took a deep inhale and exhaled. "You know that would just be the beginning, and whatever your answers are, they will spin them. And if you don't answer, they'll find someone who will. They'll try to talk to Ranger—"

"I wouldn't talk to them." He grabbed the back of the chair, his knuckles white.

"And what about your brothers? Their families? Your mom?

Your friends in town?" Gina sighed. "You know they won't stop. It's the whole reason you went out there."

God, this was so messed up. The way the media spun stories rivaled the skills of Rumpelstiltskin, except instead of turning them into gold, they twisted them into garbage gossip.

"So, you're telling me to... do nothing?" My head was spinning. "To let them peddle their lies, so they'll leave me alone?"

"It's winter in Wyoming. Christmas is in a couple days. I'm not saying pretend forever—just give it a few days for the story to blow over—"

"And what if they look it up?" I started to shake my head. "They won't find a marriage license, and then they'll claim it's not the truth anyway, and I'll be right back on the hook for faking this publicity stunt."

"If this guy cared about the truth, he would've confirmed that before writing the story," Gina grumbled.

I looked at the ring, feeling its weight so much more than I had last night, and then up to Ranger, who'd stayed quiet with his thoughts almost the entire time. "Tell me you don't want the world to think you have a wife. Tell me this is insane," I begged.

"It is, but Gina's not wrong. This isn't Europe. There aren't any federal laws protecting against paparazzi. Plus..." The muscle in his jaw flexed like it was holding something back.

"What is it?" I asked, watching his tongue draw his lips back with hesitation. "Just tell me, please."

"It might... be safer to let the story stand."

"Safer?" I sat back and stared. *Now this was about safety?*

"I'm thinking about what this news will do to your stalker." Ranger buried his hands to his sides. "If he views a husband as a threat, it could deter him." He paused, and I knew there was more. "And if he views me as an obstacle, I'll be his target instead of you."

"No, Ranger..."

Ranger turned toward the window, something catching his eye.

His arms fell to his sides, and as soon as his expression darkened, I shot out of my chair; I couldn't take any more surprises.

"What? Is it him?" I strode to the window, and Ranger pivoted to block me from looking outside, but he wasn't fast enough. "Oh my god."

I cupped my hands over my mouth, a cry breaking free.

"What's going on?" Gina's voice echoed from my phone on the table. "Ranger? Sydney?"

"We need to move," Ranger clipped and then manhandled me in a bear hug away from the window—*away from the cameras.* "We're still here, Gina."

Thank God he responded because it felt like the room had started to spin, sweeping me up in a tornado of truth and lies where it didn't matter what was what because, in the end, it was going to destroy me.

"What happened?"

"It's not just one, Gina," I said hoarsely, swallowing hard and forcing myself not to cry. "There are paparazzi lining the street outside the apartment. Setting up camp."

Even with snow on the street, a biting frost in the air, and Christmas around the corner, there had to be ten, maybe more, paparazzi bundled up and prepared for battle, their cameras slung at their sides like weapons waiting to be shot. And they were prepared. There was no missing the folding chairs, huge thermoses, and coolers of food—enough supplies sufficient for a stakeout.

"Fucking bloodsuckers—"

"I'll handle them," Ranger said firmly, guiding me back to the chair. "I'll call my brothers and the chief; we'll make sure they know what will happen if they step onto private property or harass anyone."

I nodded, but that was only half the battle. Not even half.

"One of them is going to go looking." My voice cracked. "There are a dozen or more of them out there. One of them is going to realize we aren't really married. I should just tell them now."

I tugged on the metal band around my finger, needing to get it off—needing to get rid of the cursed thing. *Where was Frodo when you needed him?*

"And what happens when her stalker realizes it's not real?" Gina demanded, my heart plummeting.

"I don't know for certain," he clarified, his lips pulling tight. "But... given the tone of betrayal in his message, I'm worried he could see this as another sign of duplicity."

I shook my head with a frustrated cry. My finger turned red, but it refused to release the ring. "They're going to figure it out. Someone is going to find out the truth and accuse me of faking this, so I might as well—"

"Sydney." Ranger stopped me and framed my face, holding my focus on him. "They can't accuse you of faking a marriage if there's proof that it's real."

My movements stilled and my gaze lifted to Ranger's. His eyes were so clear—just like everything else about him. Nothing false. Nothing murky. Nothing uncertain.

But he couldn't be saying what I thought he was.

"Ranger..." My brows pulled together, watching as he reached for my hand.

He gently massaged my swollen finger, heat coiling tight in my stomach as he eased the ring back into its resting spot. His gaze rose to mine, his solution written clear as day in his eyes.

"We're going to get married."

I ended the call before Gina could say anything beyond her initial shriek—good, bad, or otherwise. Things had gone from crazy to downright insane in a matter of seconds, and matrimony wasn't the kind of decision that required a third party.

"If we get married, then the records will be there," he went on as though he were explaining simple arithmetic.

Me plus him equaled married.

I couldn't marry Ranger... *could I?*

"No, Ranger." I shook my head and stood, starting to pace the living room. "You can't—this isn't your problem."

I wasn't his problem.

"That doesn't mean I'm incapable of fixing it," he asserted, folding his arms, a thread of annoyance infiltrating his tone.

I'd heard it before. The day we'd gone to his office and met with his brothers. It was the same heightened frustration he had when he'd felt like they thought him incapable of protecting me.

"I know that, but..." I pressed my hand to my forehead, making sure this wasn't just all a fever dream.

Ranger stepped in front of me, his expression as determined as ever.

"I promised you could count on me," he insisted, his voice softer but still steady. "So, count on me, Sydney. Let me keep you safe."

My lips peeled apart. *Count on him.* My heart stumbled in my chest, though I wasn't sure if it was running away from this situation or running toward him.

If anyone had considered all the options and knew what to do, it was Ranger. I had to trust it was the right thing—I had to trust this marriage of convenience he proposed was the only way.

"And then we'll get a divorce?"

His chin dipped. "When the paparazzi leave, and we find whoever is behind the threats."

My life had been reduced to a romance trope... but at the end of the day, a trope was better than a train wreck. So, before I could think better of it, I nodded and agreed.

"Okay." I shivered. "I'll marry you."

CHAPTER 15

Ranger

"They're still out there."

I looked over to the window at my wife, with the low evening light creeping in and snagging on the sharp edges of concern, highlighting her profile.

My wife.

Sydney was my wife.

I found my thoughts steeped in the idea over the last day. *I was married.*

Marriage had always been a pragmatic concept for me. I'd watched my brothers fall in love, and for as many times as I wanted to... feel... like they did, I accepted that marriage was a possibility but not so much a probability for me. But as it turned out, marriage had ended up being a practicality.

It was the most logical solution to Sydney's situation. It was no skin off either of our backs to get married if it kept her safe from the rumors and the press, but mostly from the man stalking her. When compared with that, all the other benefits of this arrangement paled.

By and large, celebrity stalkers were deranged. I had no idea how this man would react to seeing the news that Sydney was married, or worse, how he'd respond if the marriage was a sham. And I wouldn't risk it; I wouldn't risk her.

Sydney stood at the very edge of the windows, trying her best to remain unseen, but the layout of the apartment made that impossible. A second later, the flashes coming from outside reflected on the window, and she took a quick step back, hitting her leg on the side of the couch with a wince.

They were like vultures out there, hungry at the first scent of blood. Or matrimony.

"It's only been a day, and this is a big story." Her eyes snapped to mine, and I cleared my throat. "I mean, relatively speaking."

"Relatively." She hummed. "Isn't there a Haley and Selena eyebrow feud to cover? Or more Easter eggs to uncover for Taylor Swift's upcoming tour?"

"Easter eggs?" My brow crinkled. Easter was months away.

"Never mind." She sighed and gave me a small smile. I didn't know what it was, but I missed something.

"I expect the paparazzi to last a little longer than a day, even with the holiday," I returned to our conversation. Christmas was in six days. It was likely that many of the paparazzi hounding the house would leave to be with their families.

"Maybe we'll get lucky and the snowstorm will drive them away."

"I don't believe in luck, but I do believe in probability, and it's unlikely they're prepared for the kind of weather we're expected to get."

She walked over to me, my body reacting with a familiar ripple of tension. "How are you so calm? There are people camped outside your house. You're stranded in a garage apartment with a stranger you married—"

"You're not a stranger. You're my wife." *Fact.* I folded my arms, hoping it would hide the increasing rate of my pulse.

She shivered, her gaze lowering to my mouth. "What's keeping you calm?"

Anything that kept my thoughts away from the memories of the other night and the feel of her lips wrapped around my cock.

"Statistics," I croaked, tore my eyes from her mouth and turned so she couldn't see the physical evidence of my arousal.

It couldn't be normal to think about a blow job this much, but that was a problem for another day; I was only a genius, I couldn't be expected to handle everything.

"Do you want to make Nutella brownies?" We both needed a distraction.

"I don't have Nutella."

I nodded. "I grabbed some from Mom's earlier."

I needed a few things from the house, not the least of which was to thank Mom again for yesterday.

As soon as Sydney said yes to my plan, I ducked out the back door of the garage and went over to the house to talk to Mom. First, because we needed to get to the courthouse and get married, and there was no better person to make that happen expeditiously than the mayor of Wisdom herself.

And second, because though it wasn't real, I had to tell her in person that I was getting married.

"Are you—of course, you're sure," was what she'd said. I knew she had opinions; it was a very bold decision to make for a woman I hadn't known for very long. *But I was sure.* So, she called up Judge McKinney.

Without all the fanfare, the actual ceremony took less than ten minutes.

Mom cried. I was sure this wasn't the kind of wedding she imagined for me. I'd never imagined it, but this way made sense. It was short and to the point. Questions. Answers. *I do. I do, too.* And a kiss.

I didn't know what a wedding was supposed to feel like or what a fake real wedding was supposed to feel like, but it didn't feel wrong to be there. It didn't feel uncomfortable, and I didn't feel uncertain.

It had to be because I was protecting her, but standing in the courthouse, marrying Sydney Ward, felt like exactly where I was supposed to be.

"Okay." She needed something to distract her from the paparazzi, and I needed something to distract me from her.

"We'll need eggs and butter from the fridge," I told her and went to the opposite cupboard to grab the dry ingredients and the jar of Nutella.

"Have you heard from your brothers?" She set the ingredients on the counter and then rested her hip against it.

"Not since this morning when Archer texted to check in." I pulled my mouth tight for a second.

After deciding to marry Sydney, the decision not to tell my brothers the truth about what we were going to do was the second-easiest decision of the morning.

I loved my brothers. Respected them. Admired them. Appreciated them and everything they'd done for me. I also remembered with acute clarity all the times they'd stepped in and inserted themselves into situations they didn't think I was capable of handling.

That meeting when Gunner thought it would be best for them to protect Sydney instead of me was just the tip of the iceberg.

I understood where they were coming from. I was far too smart to be oblivious to my weaknesses. However, they cared too much to be cognizant of all my strengths—of all the things I could handle if they gave me a chance. And without a doubt, this would be one of those situations. They'd go to the ends of the earth to help Sydney, but they'd never consider doing it at my expense… which is exactly what they'd see our marriage as. A personal price I shouldn't have to pay.

So, after we'd hung up with Gina, I reached out to Archer about the media.

My oldest brother listened as I explained the situation and made my case about why it was safer for Sydney to not correct the media's assumptions. *Never complain, never explain.* If it worked for the royal family, it would work for us.

After some thought and grumbling, he'd agreed. And once he was on board, I didn't have to worry about the others.

So, while Archer, Hunter, and the local police set some clear boundaries on what was private property and how seriously they'd consider any breach of it, Sydney, Mom, and I snuck out through the back of the house and took Mom's car to the courthouse.

"I can't believe there's nothing else they… anyone can do about the press."

It was shockingly disappointing how little protection there was for people who were the target of intense—intrusive media attention. But dwelling on it wasn't going to change anything.

"We need one cup of Nutella." I handed her a measuring cup—a distraction—while I opened the bag of flour.

"You got the big jar," she exclaimed, holding up the jumbo-sized container.

"I was making several batches," I explained. "Did you know the largest jar of Nutella ever made weighed over three-thousand pounds and was four feet tall?"

"Seriously?" She scooped out a cup and dumped it into the mixing bowl where I'd already added the flour and sugar.

I nodded and began mixing the Nutella and eggs in with the flour. "It's the second-most selling sweet spread after peanut butter."

"You know everything about Nutella, don't you?" She took the spatula from me with a smile.

"Not everything, but I read an article printed in the *New York Times* on February 7—World Nutella Day three years ago that had a lot of interesting information about it," I murmured, watching as she mixed the batter. I should've stepped away from her, but I couldn't.

Instead, I reached over the stove and turned on the oven, letting my arm brush against her.

"Did you know twenty-seven percent of Americans say they can eat an entire jar of Nutella in one sitting?"

"A whole jar?"

I grinned and grabbed a baking dish. "Yeah."

"Wow."

We worked in silence for a few minutes, adding in the rest of the ingredients and pouring the batter into the dish. I knew uncomfortable silence—awkward silence. I knew because oftentimes, I was the one responsible for it. But this silence was different. Peaceful even though we were surrounded by a media storm.

And then some commotion outside drew her attention, her shoulders slumping once more.

She went to peek out the window, but my hand on her arm stopped her.

"It doesn't matter." Whether there were one or a hundred of them out there, it didn't change that we were in here... where they couldn't touch us.

Sydney drew a deep inhale, holding my gaze and then angling her body away from the windows once more.

"I'm sorry."

"Don't." I reached for her chin, imprinting flour onto her skin as I lifted it. "It was my choice, and I stand by it." *I'd stand by her until she no longer needed me.*

"I bet getting married wasn't high on your statistical probability list for the year."

I should release her. Step away. Preserve space where there was already so little. But I couldn't, no matter how many times my brain told me it was the smart thing to do.

Apparently, when it came to my wife, I didn't want to be smart; I just wanted to be around her.

"No, it wasn't." I couldn't lie. "But life is unpredictable, and sometimes you just have to roll with the punches."

Her lips parted, drawing my hungry gaze to the fullness of her mouth. Like Pavlov's dogs, the sight of her lips made me hard. *Really* hard.

I grunted just as the oven dinged.

While I loaded in the brownies to bake, Sydney walked over to the table that we'd slid farther away from the window. She sat and rested her hand on her closed laptop. I knew as soon as she opened it, she'd start searching and reading any new stories that had been released in the last couple of hours.

And that was what they were—*stories*. Not news. News implied fact, and from what I'd read, there was more truth in Sydney's fictional romance novels than there was in the gossip being printed about her—*our* relationship.

"What made you decide to write romance novels?"

"My mom." She looked at me, her computer remaining closed. "She went through so many boyfriends. I just wanted to give her a happy ending."

"That's understandable." I went to the sink and started to watch the bowl and measuring cups we'd used. "We all want to make the people we love happy."

"Is that why you don't want to tell your brothers that we got married?"

I stopped and looked at her, wondering how a woman who'd known me for so little could also know me so well.

"No." *Not entirely.* "If I tell them, we will waste time arguing about how they think what we did was wrong, and it wasn't, and we shouldn't be spending time debating it."

And this was only for a couple of weeks—maybe months. Once the story died down, once we uncovered who'd sent the note, we'd get a divorce; that was the plan we'd outlined yesterday afternoon as though we were going over a grocery list.

Sydney said we could blame the distance or the publicity. Divorce rates in the US were estimated to be between forty and fifty percent, so statistically, we hadn't started out with great odds. Gina pointed out that by then, our marriage would've lasted longer than most of the Kardashians; I didn't know who that was, but Sydney seemed comforted by the reference.

If it all went smoothly—the press left on their own, the stalker was apprehended—I calculated there was a fifty-eight percent chance that my brothers never needed to know Sydney and I had legally married.

I turned back to the sink, rinsing the soap from my hands.

"If you don't give them a chance to see you differently, they never will." Her voice carried to me.

My chest tightened.

"I don't want to hurt them."

"Even if it means hurting yourself?"

I dried my hands. When I set the towel down, she was beside me, her upturned face at my shoulder.

"I'm sorry. I shouldn't be prying. I just… You're a good man, Ranger. Caring. Capable. Loving them doesn't mean you have to allow them to underestimate you."

She stared at me as though I were under a microscope, all my tiny fears and flaws and hopes normally hidden by the impressiveness of my intelligence visible to her. *My wife.*

"I'm not an expert on loving." My brothers didn't know the weight I carried, but to tell them would hurt them, and I loved them too much to do that.

She reached up and brushed her fingers on my vest as though there was a spot of flour on it, except there wasn't. I'd double-checked before washing my hands. So what was she doing except looking for a reason to touch me? Or was this proof that she'd seen one more of my hidden truths? *Did she know how badly I wanted to feel her touch again?*

"There are no experts on loving, Ranger. Just people brave enough to try." Her gaze slipped to my mouth; it lay in wait for my lips to come closer.

"Sydney…"

Aside from the chaste kiss we'd shared in front of the judge for the ceremony, I'd kept my hands—my everything to myself last night and the whole of today. I had to.

What happened after book club was an… anomaly. An

incredible anomaly. I didn't have a clue what happened after something like that. *Was it because she'd had the mulled wine? Was it a mistake? Was it a fluke or the beginning of something more? What would happen if we let it grow now that we were married?*

I wanted the answers, and they all seemed to lie on her lips—buried in the sweet heat of her mouth. Written on the warm strokes of her tongue.

I needed answers.

"Ranger..." she said my name with the promise that she had them.

My head moved lower, my hand halfway to her cheek, when the timer buzzed, making us both jump apart.

"I'm sorry," I murmured, grabbing oven mitts and pulling the tray of brownies from the oven, the heat hitting me just as harshly as how close I'd come to making a giant mistake. Forget telling my brothers I'd actually married Sydney. What would they say if they learned I still wanted a relationship with her?

I was a genius, but that level of complication was beyond my comprehension.

"While they cool, I'm going to hop in the shower." *A very cold shower.*

Until I figured out the right way to handle this situation, I was going to run from it.

I barely heard her reply as I grabbed a fresh set of clothes and disappeared into the bathroom, groaning with relief as soon as I freed the zipper on my pants.

The smartest thing I could do for our marriage was to keep my hands—and mouth—off my wife. But for the first time in thirty-two years, the smartest choice and the easiest choice weren't the same.

CHAPTER 16

Ranger

"I don't see them."

I flicked my eyes over to Sydney as she checked the side view and then looked over her shoulder through the back windshield of my car.

"I don't either," I agreed, my gaze roaming along her profile. Even under this stress, she was still the most beautiful woman I'd ever seen.

I drove slowly down Main Street; as predicted, it had snowed on and off for the last couple of days. We'd gotten several inches last night, so there was still a thick coating of slush on the ground.

"I can't believe they're still here."

Christmas was in two days, and the paparazzi camp hadn't dwindled yet. After leaving the apartment to get dinner on our wedding night, it took me fifteen minutes just to get out of the driveway. On my way back, I'd made the unilateral decision to not return my car to the garage. Instead, I parked it on a neighboring block and walked back to the apartment, cutting through the backyard to avoid the press.

And so far, my plan has worked. I'd gone out again for food several times and gas yesterday and wasn't followed. Today, though the heavier snow had dwindled the number waiting out front, we'd still snuck out the back door of the garage, trudging to my car on the neighboring street.

"I'm sorry," Sydney murmured for the thirty-eighth time since Monday.

"Don't apologize. It's—" I broke off, pumping the brake for a second as we approached the red light at the intersection. "It's okay," I finished when the brakes caught and the car slowed.

"What is it?"

"We must've caught a slick spot," I said, testing the brake pedal once more. It had felt squishy for a second when I'd first attempted to stop but seemed to be fine now.

Sydney bit into her bottom lip. If it were possible to put a permanent dent in her bottom lip, she would've done it by now. She was so worried about... everything. Especially everything I was doing to help her.

"Did you know the average person will spend six months of their entire life waiting for a red light to turn green?" I'd found these kinds of things were good at pulling her from the tangle of her thoughts.

Her breath released in a whoosh just as the light in front of us changed.

"It's probably double that if you live in New York," she murmured with a small smile as I continued to drive us toward the grocery store.

"Probably."

We reached the grocery store in a few short minutes, and I parked right next to the door in case we had to leave quickly. The store wasn't too busy for Christmas being days away, probably because of the snow we'd had last night.

Inside, I grabbed a cart and headed for the far end of the store. One of the wheels squeaked with each revolution.

"Do we need any frozen stuff?" Sydney folded her arms and walked beside me.

"I don't think so. Just some milk and cheese from the dairy wall, but I always go down each aisle in order to make sure I don't miss anything."

"You've got grocery shopping down to a science, too?"

I looked at her and realized she was teasing me.

"I was always responsible for the list when we went to the store with Mom. Archer would walk with Mom. Hunter stayed with me. And Gunner and Gwen would be off making friends."

All I needed was one look at the list to know everything on it; then Hunter and I would zip through each aisle, grabbing what was needed so that we didn't need to be there any longer than necessary; Mom struggled when people stopped to offer sympathy.

We rounded the corner into the dairy aisle, with Sydney tucked right by my side so that I was in front of her. A freezer door opened just as we entered the aisle, and Sydney jumped, her hand flying to her chest.

"What cheese do we need?" she asked, visibly shaken.

"Mozzarella, ricotta, and parmesan."

Her chin dipped. "I'll grab them."

She sped to the cheese section as the woman who'd been reaching in for a bag of frozen corn straightened.

"Hey, Ranger." The younger woman smiled, her brown hair pulled back underneath a *Brilliant Brews* beanie. "I hear congratulations are in order."

"Hi, Jess, and thanks." I smiled, recognizing the local coffee shop owner instantly. Sydney returned, her hands filled with cheese. "Sydney, this is Jess, one of the owners of Brilliant Brews."

"Hi, Sydney!" Jess greeted warmly. "I've seen you at Brews a couple of times. It's nice to meet you."

"Yes, I thought you looked familiar. Sorry, I'm new in town."

"Oh, don't apologize at all." Jess smiled. "Welcome to Wisdom. I'm sure we'll be seeing a lot more of you now."

I started to grimace and caught myself; they wouldn't be seeing a lot of Sydney... and not for long, either.

"Oh, Tara's calling. I've got to go. Nice meeting you, Sydney. Have a nice Christmas!" Jess exclaimed and then answered her phone.

"Tara is her business partner at the coffee shop," I told Sydney as soon as she returned to the cart, her eyes darting around to all the people in the aisle—all strangers to her. "We've known both of them for a long time. Zoey actually used to work there when she first moved to town."

"Oh." Her shoulders slumped. "I'm sorry. I don't know why I'm acting like they are going to jump out of the freezer or something."

"Don't be sorry. You don't know any of these people, but I do." I nodded to the couple in the corner by the ice cream. "That's Pete and Donna. Local ranchers." I then pointed out the man and woman by the milk. "And that is Angelo and his daughter, Angel. They own a dry-cleaning business. And the woman at the very end rounding the corner is Doris; she owns a housekeeping business."

"Thank you." Her head tipped, a strand of hair slipping free from the long braid down her back. Without thinking, I reached out and tucked it back behind her ear, warmth shooting along the nerves in my finger.

It was because it was out of place. Not because I missed touching her. Not because I still couldn't stop thinking about her mouth sucking off my cock. The memory hadn't left me for the last four days, my body in a state of constant hunger that I tried to hide.

It wasn't like there weren't plenty of distractions, but none of them were enough. I'd never had a thought I couldn't shake before, and it was unnerving.

I'd also never had a blow job or a wife before, so I tried to take that into consideration before deciding if I needed professional help.

"Of course."

I quickly dropped my hand to the handle of the shopping cart, returning the squeaky wheel to its rapid pace. As we went through each aisle, I pointed out each person and told her who they were.

By the time I pulled a can of black olives from the shelf, she'd become much more relaxed.

"Olives? In lasagna?"

I grinned. "Mom insists it's her secret ingredient."

I was going to attempt to make Mom's lasagna again. I'd recalculated the measurements for the recipe three times, and I was pretty confident it would turn out this time.

We made it through the entire store to the farthest aisle when familiar voices called to us from the other end.

"Ranger? Sydney?" Jerry and Trish headed toward us.

"Oh my gosh, I don't even know what to say." Trish immediately pulled Sydney in for a hug.

"Congratulations. You say congratulations," Jerry instructed with a shake of his head. "We had no idea—"

"Oh, don't fib." Trish swatted him. "We both were wondering if there was something going on when we saw the way the two of you looked at each other at book club—"

"I meant we had no idea it was on the brink of *marriage*." Jerry took his turn hugging Sydney.

"It was a... spur-of-the-moment decision," Sydney replied for the both of us.

"They don't call it *falling* in love for nothing." Trish embraced me. "Congratulations."

"Thank you," I murmured.

Jerry came next. "Your dad would be so proud," he said as he hugged me.

I hoped so. Dad was known in Wisdom for doing the right thing, and it was the right thing to do whatever it took to protect Sydney.

"So, when did this happen? Did you meet before coming out here, or was this just since you've been in Wisdom? We want to know the whole love story." Trish beamed with eagerness.

I looked at Sydney; we hadn't come up with a story because

we'd been keeping our heads down. But if anyone would come up with a convincing love story off the cuff, it was a romance novelist.

"It just happened... since I've been staying here. We bonded over baked goods and books," Sydney began hesitantly. "And then one night, I asked him to help me work through the first kiss scene in the book I'm writing and... that was it."

"One kiss and you knew," Trish said, and I blinked twice, imagining—hallucinating—for a moment as I saw her face turn into that heart-eyed emoji.

"Yes." I nodded to confirm.

Trish was about to probe further, but a second later, there was a commotion at the end of the aisle.

"Over here!"

Rapid shutter clicks followed the triumphant cry. *We'd been found.* Sydney stood frozen by my side. *Damn.* I stepped in front to shield her. Meanwhile, Trish and Jerry crowded together with their cart in front of them, almost like a blockade.

"Sydney, how did the two of you meet?"

"Was it love at first sight?"

"When was the wedding?"

"We need to go," I said with a low voice and put my arm around her, breaking her trance.

"This is one heck of a rebound after your breakup! Hot movie star to small-town nerd. What do you think your fans will say?"

I wasn't fazed by their words, but Sydney flinched, and that made me angry.

I hadn't even realized the growl-like sound had come from me until Jerry put his hand on my chest.

"Take her and go. We've got this," he said low and then winked.

Like a small-town comedic version of Bonnie and Clyde, Trish and Jerry shared a look before they started arguing—*loudly*—in the middle of the aisle. Hands waving. Arms flailing. They shoved their cart across the aisle like a blockade, knocking things off the shelf.

They made it impossible for anyone to get a good shot of Sydney and me as we rushed for the register.

We worked as a team, scanning and bagging at the self-checkout, so it took less than a minute before I scanned my phone to pay and grabbed the receipt. The last time I looked over my shoulder, I saw Trish throw her entire mug of coffee onto one of the paparazzi, proclaiming it was an accident and she'd been aiming at her husband.

I loaded the bags in the trunk while Sydney got in the passenger seat.

The first thing I noticed when I got in the car was the turmoil in her eyes. Emotions were a language I struggled to read, the grammar and syntax and conjugations varying from person to person, making it impossible—even for a genius—to decipher.

But Sydney… Sydney was like my own personal Rosetta Stone. She was both a question and the answer. The unknown and the tree of knowledge. A relative stranger… and my wife.

Maybe it was the time I'd spent with her over the last month. Maybe it was having a physical connection with a woman for the first time in my life—my first reason to feel. But when I looked at her, it wasn't just her emotions I'd begun to be able to translate… it was my own.

Desire. Protectiveness. I learned more about myself by being around her, and if that wasn't a good foundation for a marriage— even a temporary one—I didn't know what was.

"I'm sure they're just trying to get in a couple last shots before they leave for the holiday," I tried to reassure her.

With the snow and us staying holed up in the apartment, they hadn't gotten any new photographs in days; the stories all recycling the ones from the street that night. If they didn't get more fuel, their stories would run out of steam, and they would leave town even sooner.

"I know, but you haven't even been able to go see your niece."

Gunner's girlfriend, Della, had given birth the day after Sydney and I got married. Another reason added to the list of why I wasn't going to tell my brothers the truth right now; my whole family was celebrating baby Skye's arrival, and it didn't seem right to take away from that.

The press was the easier reason to avoid going to the hospital to visit them.

"Gunner said it's better anyway. They aren't allowing visitors in the NICU."

Skye's blood sugar wasn't regulating, so the doctor transferred Skye to the NICU for observation and testing until they could get it under control. I knew it wasn't something to be concerned about, but I kept that to myself. Out of all of them, my marriage would upset Gunner the most, and he had enough on his plate.

Skye's arrival was also the reason our family Christmas had been postponed. With Della and Gunner still in the hospital for another two days at minimum, Mom declared that our holiday dinner would wait until the new year when everything calmed down.

"Ranger... about what they said..."

"It doesn't bother me," I told her as we turned onto Main Street.

"I should've told them that a nerd is always preferable to a lying cheat."

"Did you know the term *nerd* was coined by Dr. Seuss in his book *If I Ran the Zoo*?" I changed the subject.

Again, that drew her smile, and I felt heat rush through me. With Sydney, my facts never seemed wasted or out of place.

"I'm sure it must feel like you're running a zoo right now with these animals who won't leave us alone," she grumbled, her smile dimming as she checked the mirrors once more.

"They're not behind us," I told her, hating the way her eyes went back to yo-yoing to the side-view mirror to see if the paps from the store were following us.

I was fairly confident the fact that they weren't was also Jerry and Trish's doing, most likely blocking in their cars so they couldn't leave.

Sydney's head straightened, but her eyes continued to stray to the side-view mirror.

"I bet running from the paparazzi wasn't what you envisioned for the third day of marriage."

"No, it wasn't," I said matter-of-factly. "But only because I never imagined myself married."

Ahead of us, the light turned red. I pressed on the brake. Once more, the pedal felt... soft and the car struggled to slow. I pushed harder as we were quickly approaching the light and busy cross traffic, and then it offered no resistance at all.

"What the—" I pumped the brake twice, but nothing happened. Shit.

"Ranger—" Sydney grabbed for the door, the car about to coast directly into traffic.

"Hold on!" I yanked the emergency brake. The car jerked but then started to slide on the snowy road. My arm swung out in front of Sydney's chest and I whipped the wheel, anything to get her as far from harm's way as possible.

Several horns blared.

Sydney screamed as the car spun a full one-eighty before coming to a stop. A truck swerved to avoid the back of the Volvo and then slid to a stop on the other side of us.

"Ranger?" Her wide stare found mine.

"Are you okay?" I gripped her shoulder.

She nodded, tears pooling in the corners of her eyes. "What happened?"

I shook my head. "I'm going to find out."

My heart clambered all the way in my throat. Something wasn't right. My brakes were fine. Decker just replaced the calipers and pads. And yet, they hadn't worked.

"Stay here," I ordered and put the hazard lights on, grabbed my cell phone, and got out of the car.

It was positioned backward and halfway through the intersection. If there had been another car in front of us, I would've hit it. If

I hadn't been driving slow because of the snow or if I'd waited any longer to brake, we would've gone right through the intersection and been hit from both sides.

"You alright, Ranger?" The familiar voice jarred me from all the calculations spiraling in my mind of how bad this could've been.

I looked over the roof of the car.

Bruce.

The driver of the truck was the most well-known bartender at the Wit and Wisdom bar at the Worth Hotel. As many people came for his well-spun tales of the town as they did for his expertly crafted cocktails.

Not that I drank them, but according to Gunner, they were the best in the greater Jackson area.

"Yeah," I told him as I walked around the back of the car.

"Just happened to have these in the bed from the hotel," he said, holding up a bright-orange cone before plopping it in the slush near the back of the car. He then proceeded to remain on the road and direct the slow-moving cars through the intersection around mine.

"Thank you."

"You hit a slick spot?"

"No. I don't think so." I pulled my lips tight.

"Congratulations, by the way, on getting hitched. I saw the papers." He grinned and scratched the fresh layer of gray scruff on his chin. "Sounds like a heck of a story."

And one he'd enjoy knowing... and telling.

"Thanks." I needed to be better prepared for this conversation, I realized. There was no avoiding this kind of news in a small town. But for right now, my best plan was to deflect. "Something happened with my brakes. I'm going to give Decker a call."

I dialed the mechanic and family friend. If anyone could explain what just happened, it would be him. When he answered, I gave him a brief rundown of what had just happened.

"I'm getting in my truck now to come tow it, but that doesn't sound right, Ranger. I just changed everything for your brakes and checked the brake line fluid. Everything was fine."

At that moment, Sydney chose to get out of the car. I couldn't tell her to get back in… just like I couldn't stop myself from asking the next question. I had to know. I had to have answers. *I had to protect her.*

"Then what are you thinking?"

"Without looking at it, I can't say for sure…" His voice trailed off into silence.

"What is it?" There was something more.

"I saw the papers about you and the romance novelist," he began, and I tensed. Now wasn't the time to discuss my marriage.

"I don't think that—"

"Ranger, your brother told me it's all fake and that Sydney is your client, so I only bring it up because I have to ask if it's possible that someone tampered with your car?" he asked, and I flinched.

I turned so Sydney wouldn't see or hear. "Tampered?"

My stomach opened up with a hollow sensation at the thought.

"The only other thing I can think of is that someone cut the brake lines, but you keep your car in the garage, so that would be pretty difficult—"

"I haven't been," I blurted out and straightened, seeing Sydney standing on the other side of the car, looking at me with a worried gaze. "I've been parking it on the street to throw off the paparazzi."

"Shit," Decker muttered. "I'll be there in five. I'll know more when I get it back to the shop and can take a look."

Tampered.

Someone had threatened Sydney. Then, the paparazzi figured out where she was. And now, the brakes on my car had suddenly failed. *What were the chances…*

I ran the calculations in my head, coming up with a statistically insignificant number. *There was no chance that it was all coincidence.*

"Hey there, lovebirds."

I turned just as a Subaru came to a stop beside mine, Cindy's smiling voice extending through the window.

"You two need a ride?"

"That would be great, Cindy." I motioned for Sydney to get in the car while I waited on the road.

I didn't say much when Decker arrived. The mechanic was Hunter's age but had been friends with all of us ever since he'd moved to Wisdom almost a decade ago.

He hitched my car, pulled it onto the tow truck bed, and secured it.

"I'll call you as soon as I get this up on my lift," he said, giving my shoulder a squeeze before heading to the cab of the truck.

I slid into the back seat next to Sydney, noticing how tightly she held her arms to her chest.

"Hi there, sweetheart," Cindy greeted me.

"Hi, Cindy."

"What a mess this snow is," she huffed. "What happened? Did you catch some ice?"

I kept my stare focused on the road. "No. Something with the brakes on my car."

"Oh, dear." She shook her head in dismay. "What a time for this to happen, right before Christmas." She sighed. "Well, if you need a ride to trivia night next week, you just give me a holler, okay?"

I felt myself tensing. I wasn't going to mention that I probably wouldn't make it to the New Year's Eve trivia night next week. I had other things to think about... *I had Sydney.*

CHAPTER 17

Sydney

"What is it?" I asked as soon as Ranger got off the phone with Decker.

I knew something was wrong from the second my feet hit the slush outside the car door. If we'd just been sliding on the snow, Ranger wouldn't be calling his mechanic.

Something happened to his brakes that caused us to almost crash, and he clearly was blaming himself for it. Ranger was the most cautious and careful man I knew; his car had been at the shop when I'd first arrived in town. He was probably upset and frustrated that he'd done everything right… and still, something bad happened.

"Ranger…" I walked over to him; he stood almost paralyzed in the living room, staring out the window. "It's okay. It's not your fault."

His head whipped to me. "I know that." He glanced to his phone, tension creasing his handsome features. "Sydney…" His throat bobbed as he took a second to swallow. "The brake lines on my car were cut."

I took a half step back, suddenly feeling like I was in the car again, whipping around out of control. Ranger's hands on my shoulders made it stop.

"Cut?" I choked out the question, my heart pounding a mile a minute. "Like on purpose?"

His mouth tightened. "Yeah."

Someone had tried to kill us—or, at the very least, harm us. And they'd almost succeeded. Less snow. More traffic.

We could be in a hospital right now. Or the morgue.

I swayed and his arms came around me.

"I'm okay." I tried to step out of his hold, but he wouldn't let go. My head tipped up, and I felt my brow crease. "Ranger?"

"You're not okay." His clear green eyes searched mine. "Let me help you."

For him to know that… to say that… But I couldn't. I couldn't let myself keep relying on him. Ranger might be my husband, but he wasn't permanent, and I needed to do a better job remembering that.

"No, you can't. I just… need to be alone," I told him firmly. "I need to shower." I pushed out of his hold and darted for the bathroom, refusing to break down again. Refusing to need to hold on to him again.

He was already doing enough—too much. *He'd married me, for crying out loud.*

Once the shower was running, I felt the tears start to fall. This was the only place I'd allow them. I gripped the edge of the sink, holding on to it as though I were holding myself together.

Cut.

Someone had cut the brakes in Ranger's car. *On purpose.* To slow us down? To catch us? *To hurt me?* The possibilities felt like fingers latching around my throat, tightening with each breath.

Tears dripped into the sink, but I forced my breaths to come out even.

I shouldn't have snapped at him. He was doing everything he could to help me and all I did was try to push him away. My hands slid from the sink and my shoulders dropped.

I need to apologize.

Keeping the water running, I opened the door but stopped

short when I heard Ranger's voice from the front of the apartment. *He was on the phone.* I lingered in the doorframe for a second to listen.

"I said I'm fine." Pause. "Why would I call you when you can't tow my car? I was fully capable of handling the situation, Archer." Ranger's voice was calm but ended with an edge.

I'd written countless protective siblings, but even without that framework in the back of my mind, it was clear from the very first interaction that the older Reynolds siblings took special care in protecting their youngest brother. And it was just as clear that Ranger was working to break from their perception of him.

No, he wasn't like them, neither in physical strength nor stature. But that didn't make him less capable.

"This is all I need from you right now," he declared firmly and I heard his footsteps stop. "That's fine. Thanks, Hunter." There was another pause. "No, I don't want to talk about it."

Before I could hear anything else, his footsteps picked up again and sent me back into the bathroom. I didn't want to get caught eavesdropping; I'd just apologize when I was done.

I stepped into the stream of hot water and let it soak through my hair. Whatever escape I thought I'd find in the shower was short-lived. I had too many questions—too many thoughts that I couldn't handle on my own and that had never happened before.

My life had also never been threatened before.

I'd always been on my own—handled things on my own. After Mom died, I juggled school and work. Then I balanced working and writing until writing became my full-time job. And writing… it was a lonely business. I had friends in the romance community. Peripheral friends because they worked like I did.

The only people close to me were Gina and Vince. And Vince… well… his betrayal only reinforced my reliance on my independence. In hindsight, I'd never gone to him for help. I never told him about my problems or fears, especially when it came to anything book-related. I always attributed it to him not being fully supportive of my career, but I realized it went far deeper than that; some part of me must've always known I couldn't trust him because I never gave him all of me.

But with Ranger… not only did I not have a choice. I didn't want one.

"Shit," I chided myself when I got out for hurrying into the bathroom without a change of clothes. Toweling my hair dry, I wrapped the fabric around me and cinched it over my chest.

Barbecue.

The scent was the first thing to hit me when I opened the door. I walked into the kitchen, and it wasn't until Ranger did a double take from the stove that I realized I'd skipped the part where I should've gotten dressed first.

"I spoke to my brothers." He shuffled his feet—and his gaze. "I made sure to park my car near businesses or houses that I knew had security cameras, so they are going to go through the footage from the last two nights and figure out who tampered with the brakes."

I nodded slowly, knowing I should excuse myself and get dressed, but it smelled so good in there, and I just… I didn't want to be alone anymore.

"Do you think it was him?" I probed. "My stalker?"

"Most likely. This would be a huge risk for the paparazzi to take, and all for what? So they'd have a better chance of getting a few photos?" He frowned. "After thinking about it, I've come to the conclusion that I was the target, not you."

I bit into my cheek, feeling even worse for how I'd blown him off earlier.

The oven beeped. Ranger turned and carefully placed the baking dish inside it.

"What are you making?" I wanted a moment that wasn't clouded by circumstance.

"A barbecue chicken bake. It'll just be about another forty-five minutes until it's done." He set the oven mitts on the counter.

"You didn't have to do that," I murmured and folded my arms just as my stomach chose to speak up and gurgle its gratitude.

Ranger's eyes flicked to my chest for a second before his head dipped.

"I'm sorry about earlier—"

"I'm going back over to the house for tonight—"

We spoke at the same time, but I was the first to break off when I heard what he was suggesting. "What?"

Ranger shifted his weight. "You said you wanted to be alone." He made it sound like a simple fact, but the crease in his brow implied there was more running through his mind. "After dinner, Hunter, Archer, and I are going to take turns monitoring the garage tonight."

"Ranger…" My throat burned with the truth—burned with the fear of admitting out loud that I needed a man I'd hardly met.

"I'll head over once it's dark, so whoever is sitting out there won't see—won't know that I'm not up here—"

"No, Ranger—" This wasn't what I wanted at all.

"Please, Sydney." He reached up and drove a hand through his hair, frustration breaking the pristine angles of his face. "You're right. I can't help you. I don't… I don't know what I'm doing." His brow scrunched. "This has never… I've never not known what I was doing before."

His jaw clenched and released rapid fire like this was the first thing he'd ever failed at.

I stepped toward him, guilt twisting inside my stomach that those few simple words could've inflicted such self-doubt. But for every strength, there was an Achilles' heel. A spot that, when pushed, would send even the strongest or smartest of us toppling.

"Ranger, wait." I bit my lip to stop it from quivering. "I'm sorry for what I said. I was overwhelmed. I didn't mean to make you think I didn't… need you."

"This is my fault," Ranger declared roughly, his expression

tortured. "I thought this story—our marriage—would keep you safe by making me a target, but after today, what if I'm wrong?"

"No—"

"What if you're in more danger because of me?" he insisted, with the same intensity and surety as gravity. Unalterable. Unstoppable. Unshakable. And it knocked the breath right out of me.

"I'm not, Ranger, and I don't want you to go," I whispered, my heart pounding with dread.

It was more than that. *I wanted him here.* I wanted his midnight baking sessions and the encyclopedic entertainment of his conversations. And I wanted him. His kisses. His touch. And the thought of being without that after all these weeks...

"I want you here, Ranger." I slid my tongue along my bottom lip. "I want my husband."

It was the first time I'd referred to him as that. *My husband.* We'd snuck into the courthouse, got married, and then went back to the way things were. Of course, it made complete sense because it was fake. Most of his family didn't even know the truth. But calling him my husband... didn't feel wrong either.

"I'm not doing a good enough job. I'm too... distracted." The word came out like it left a bad taste in his mouth.

"By what?"

"By you." His eyes flickered with something so deep and hungry it felt like my entire body went up in flames. "You're in danger, and all I can think about—" he broke off and seamed his lips shut. "I'm sorry."

He started to step to the side and without thinking, I reached out and splayed my hand over his chest to stop him.

"Tell me."

His heart thumped wildly under my palm as his gaze snapped back to mine.

"Sydney, someone tried to hurt me—you—us today." He tensed violently and then continued. "And all I can think about is kissing you."

"Ranger..." I swayed closer to him, ready to admit it was all I could think about, too.

"Things are very complicated without adding... that into the mix." His voice took on a distinct crackle that made my nipples pebble even harder against the terrycloth towel.

"More complicated? My career is on the brink of ruin. I have a stalker threatening me. The press hounding me to the point where I had to get married to stop them from tearing what's left of my life apart." A pained laugh bubbled up. "*Complicated* could be a welcome vacation from where my life is currently at. But you... this..." I tried to swallow, but I couldn't. My pulse felt like it consumed my entire throat. "This is the only thing that makes sense."

"Sydney..."

I reached up and cupped my hand to his cheek. "Unless you don't want to be here anymore." That was the most painful thought of all. "Unless you really don't want me—"

I didn't know Ranger was capable of a growl until I heard it. Until his hands latched on the sides of my face and pulled me to him.

His mouth came for mine with unabashed hunger, his lips slanting and his tongue pressing between my lips without hesitation. He didn't kiss me like I was his last meal—like I was something to draw out and savor; he kissed me like I was his first meal. Like I was his first taste of something so delicious, he couldn't stop himself from gorging.

Our tongues tangled together in a cycle of wet heat. Of course, he remembered the strokes that made me whimper and how it made me shudder when he sucked on my lip. He remembered every moan and every sigh that gave away my pleasure. He remembered and repeated them until his kiss became a weapon. One that weakened me with want. One that would destroy me with desire.

It wasn't experience that made a man a good kisser, it was attention. Attention to the detail and nuance of a woman's pleasure. Attention to the way she responded over the focus of your own desire. And knowing that I had all of Ranger's attention—every ounce of his brilliant focus—was what made my mind spin. That was what made my core clench and squeeze and want to come. Beg to come.

"Ranger..." Heat licked over every inch of my skin as his hands slid from my waist to my ass, gripping the cloth and my flesh in his palms.

When he pulled me tight, the thick ridge of him pressed against my stomach.

I locked my arms around my neck just as his weight began to propel me backward, my legs shaking as I backpedaled all the way from the kitchen to the bed. After a few steps, I couldn't tell who was trying to move us faster—him or me.

The air around us became infused with heavy breaths and soft moans. I only had a vague sense of the surroundings through the haze of want, and I didn't realize how close we were to the bed before my legs hit the edge of it.

"Ranger!" I toppled back with a small cry.

I hit the mattress first, and Ranger's arm shot out just in time to catch himself from falling completely on top of me, but that was about all he'd stopped. He hadn't stopped us from landing on the bed, and he hadn't stopped my towel from giving way to the tussle, the white fabric loosening and sliding off to my sides.

"Sydney," Ranger croaked, his nostrils flaring.

His gaze raked over my naked body with open hunger—unfiltered lust, from the aching tips of my breasts down to where his knee pressed between my thighs. It was a feat to feel worshipped with just a single look, but that was how I felt—worshipped by the heat and hunger of his stare.

"You're..." His throat bobbed. "Perfect."

Perfect could have so many definitions for this man, yet I was it.

"Please," I begged, my core clenching painfully.

For one more moment, he stayed frozen. His only movement was the inhale and exhale of tension through his jaw.

"I want to taste you," he murmured against my neck. "Please."

"Yes." *God, yes.* I couldn't get the word out fast enough. All I wanted was those lips on my breasts—on my core—lips that had almost made me come from a kiss instead tangling with the most sensitive part of me.

His hand slid from its resting spot at my side to the jut of my hip bone. I shuddered at the first contact of his fingertips to my skin, like the prick of a pin in the fragile shell of a balloon filled with ache. My stomach quivered as his hand forged a path to the base of my ribs, tracing the rigid arc until his knuckles brushed the underside of my breast.

Every time I turned, fresh disaster whipped around me like a tornado, but being here with Ranger was being in the eye of the storm. Safe. Calm. Protected.

I heard the rough catch of his breath, barely processing it before his big palm cupped my breast.

His deep groan was just as pleasurable as his tentative touch, and I couldn't tear my eyes away from his face, from his ravenous attention to my body.

I knew he'd never touched a woman this way before. I knew that my body was making that very first footprint on his mind, and I'd never felt more powerful or more vulnerable before.

"So soft," he muttered, watching himself pleasure me. "Like warm velvet."

He tested and weighed. Stroked and kneaded. Just like the first time we kissed, he explored every inch—learned every peak and crevice and marked every response, mapping it to his perfect memory. *His erotic eidetic memory.* Before long, my head tipped back, and I had to bite my lip to stop the obnoxious moans of want that threatened to spill free.

I wasn't prepared for the warm clamp of his fingers on my nipple. My eyes flung wide and I gasped, my body bowing up toward his touch. Ranger didn't even flinch—didn't break his focus from my chest even though I could clearly see his erection straining against the front of his pants.

His head drifted toward his hand.

"Did you know that sensation from your nipples activates the same area of the brain as the genitals?" he rasped, the heat of his breath landing over my aching flesh in warm warning before his lips closed over the peak.

My back bowed up from the bed, pleasure arcing through my system. I didn't know about what area because it felt like my entire brain was on fire from his touch. The pull of his lips, the roll of his tongue. He worshipped me into oblivion.

"More," I begged, my hands sliding to his shoulders and fisting the back of his vest. "More, Ranger."

"I need... I need to taste you," he blurted out like his ability for rational thought had broken down and then he shuddered. "Can I taste you?"

A moan and a tug in the right direction were all I could muster, my core clenching painfully.

"You write about this in almost all of your books," he murmured, his breath rushing over my stomach. "All except the Broken series."

Writing about women's pleasure—a woman's confidence in her eroticism and sexuality was one of my favorite parts of my job. But if I was being honest, I couldn't remember the last time I'd had a man's mouth on my sex. Giving oral wasn't Vince's thing, and sexual preferences weren't meant to be shamed no matter who they came from. I didn't push it because it wasn't like he was constantly demanding blow jobs from me. If anything, he didn't seem to prefer oral sex at all. *Or maybe he was just getting plenty of head from all his casual hookups that he didn't need to risk any kind of fair play by wanting it from me.*

I never realized until now that the only books I hadn't written oral into were the ones he'd inspired.

"I've never done this before," he confessed straight to my core, and I shivered, feeling warmth rush from my center.

"I want your mouth on me, Ranger." I wanted those full, sculpted lips. I want the knowledge etched into that tongue.

Whenever that mouth worked, it was in perfect sync with his genius, and right now, I wanted that genius devouring me.

He settled between my legs, his shoulders pressing my knees wider as his fingers crafted a hesitant path from my hip bone to the folds of my pussy.

God, he was so gorgeous.

My heart hammered like a runaway drum in my chest as he licked over his lips, feeling his fingers gently trace over the outside edges and then along my folds.

"Ranger," I choked out.

Fear wasn't the only thing building in our bubble. The way I wanted him gnawed a deeper and deeper ache inside me with each day we tried to keep our distance.

My teeth clamped into my bottom lip, moans bombarding the barrier as he used both thumbs and spread me open to his gaze as though he were peeling open the pages of a book.

"Beautiful," he murmured, his gaze roving over my most intimate parts, seeing how they responded to him. "Just one taste."

His head dipped forward, anticipation tipping the world on its axis for a second before the flat of his tongue slid over my sex.

"Oh god…" My eyes shut and my head fell back, pleasure oozing like lava into my veins.

He licked from my entrance all the way to my clit, the tight bundle of nerves rejoicing at the firm velvet pressure he flicked it with at the end.

I must've let a soft moan escape because he looked up at me and rasped, "That's where it feels good."

"So good," I murmured though it probably wasn't a question but a fact.

Ranger probably had anatomical drawings of a woman's body and all its erogenous zones brought up with perfect recall in his head.

"Don't stop." My hips wiggled, the ache in my core so intense it was becoming painful.

Air dumped into my lungs as his mouth returned. Determined

and explorative. This time, it wasn't just his tongue. It was teeth and lips—nipping on my clit, sucking the firm bud into his mouth, flicking it with his tongue. It was one sensation after another. A dissection by desire.

"Honey," he murmured, taking another lick along my seam and groaning as he swallowed. "You always say honey in your books."

I was being tortured... by my own instruction. This man had read almost all of my romance novels, cataloged them in his mind like an erotic encyclopedia, and now unleashed all that knowledge on me—on my body with fervent hunger.

My mouth opened and shut, and if it was possible for my face to feel any hotter, it did. "Am I wrong?"

He moaned. "Not honey. Forbidden fruit."

My gasp turned into a strangled cry when his lips set around my clit once more and sucked hard, milking my body for more juice.

"Ranger," I cried out, driving my fingers into the thick waves of his hair and holding him tight to me, afraid I might shatter.

"So good," he murmured, repeating the torture over and over again until my body felt like it was mush.

Waves of electric heat rolled through me like a typhoon, and I just wanted to let myself go under. My muscles tensed. My core clamped and squeezed. I was so close to the best orgasm of my life it was hard to breathe, but then his mouth drew back, and it felt like my body was stumbling backward down the steep slope.

"Don't stop," I begged, my hand tugging on his hair with a mind of its own.

"I want to find your G-spot." His gaze flicked up my body, crashing into mine.

My jaw dropped. Another wave of want rolled through me, seeing the intense desire crackling in his green stare. I'd never get over his intensity. The way he looked at me like I was his own personal Rubik's cube, and he was determined to unlock every square of my pleasure.

He slid the tip of his index finger along the center of my folds so gently it was painful. "Please."

"Yes," I panted—begged—breathlessly.

The finger tracing along my seam slipped inside me.

"Please, yes," I moaned loudly, trembling as he began to rub and press along my front wall, searching for that elusive knot of nerves.

"*Ranger!*" I cried out when the first burst of pleasure hit.

Ranger stopped, his eyes snapping to mine, and then he stroked again. "Here?"

I jerked, pleasure lashing through me. "*Yes.*"

My eyes rolled back in my head as he mapped out every boundary of that sweet spot inside my sex. When he'd found the borders, his finger returned directly to the center. Whimpers peeled from my lips as he pushed and rubbed. Different directions. Different pressures. Experimenting over every inch of my G-spot until I was panting and my whole body quaked.

"It's making you so wet when I rub it like this," he muttered hoarsely, his fingers doing something indescribable that made my core gush.

"Yes..." My vocabulary was reduced to a single word that came out more like a moan.

"In your books, the heroes always add a second finger."

I made a garbled sound, wanting to tell him he was sufficiently destroying me with one, but I wasn't fast enough. I felt the stretch of my inner muscles as he pushed two fingers inside. I grabbed for the sheets—anything to hold on to before he found that spot again.

"Ernst Grafenberg," he said hoarsely, his focus screwing tight to the push of his fingers.

"W-what?" I choked.

"Ernst Grafenberg was the Berlin gynecologist who discovered this," he said, his two fingers finding a new way to torture me as they twisted against my sweet spot.

"Oh god." I cried out, white-hot pleasure ripping through me. My body clawed at the edge of an orgasm that was just out of reach.

"Not god. The G-spot is named after Grafenberg."

"Ranger." Our eyes locked over my trembling stomach, and I panted. "Are you finger fucking or fact fucking me?"

"Both." His eyes glittered. "Do you want me to stop?"

Dirty talking. So many of my heroes were dirty talkers. Vince was a dirty talker. But a filthy mouth was nothing compared to fact fucking. To watch this man coax pleasure from every hidden and untouched corner of my body over and over again while having enough composure to tell me facts about orgasms and female pleasure… it was like a sun shower or snow on a beach. Unexpected. Incredible.

"No," I pleaded. "Don't stop."

His chest rumbled low and my jaw dropped as I felt a third finger spread my pussy.

"It's more than a spot," he ground out, stroking that *more than a spot* over and over again. "Roughly two inches that swell when… stimulated."

I lost a little bit of my mind the way he said that last word. *Stimulated.* My body drenched his fingers, and he growled in appreciation.

"And with enough stimulation…" he drawled slowly, and I shuddered, hardly getting over the repeat of the word before the hot clamp of his lips tugged on my clit once more.

My body tensed and bowed, a sound escaping from my mouth I didn't even realize I could make.

Oh my genius.

I knew sex could be good. I'd had good sex before… but this… on the surface, I never would've thought or expected it would be like this. I didn't care how *well* I thought I wrote about men going down on their women, reading wasn't the same as doing—and Ranger had never done this.

But Ranger was also Ranger.

I'd never underestimate how quickly and expertly and *differently* this man could learn how to do something.

And right now, he was learning how to do me.

"Ranger," I panted his name, spearing my fingers along his scalp.

Pleasure swirled through me like two different storms that were tied together, both waiting to destroy me. The only thing that was in focus was him. The rhythmic thrust of his fingers crescendoed in time with the hungry snarl of his mouth. Every time his fingers pressed to my front wall, his tongue speared into my clit, and my response to it all spurred him on.

More.

Faster.

Harder.

Ranger was consuming me—giving me everything. *And he was getting off on it.*

His groans of pleasure matched my own. Distantly, I felt even the bed move as his hips rocked against it. But that was all he gave himself. Crumbs of carnal satisfaction compared to everything he worshipped me with.

"You're incredible," he murmured against my sex, his mouth moving like he couldn't get enough. "Perfect. Delicious." Facts became praise. Praise became pleasure. "I just want to make you squirt. I know female ejaculation is possible… I feel how swollen you are. How wet and responsive. I know you can, Sydney," he encouraged me almost without even realizing it. "I just want to taste it—to taste all of you."

Never in my life had I imagined, let alone met, a man who was so intent on a woman's pleasure. *And now, I was married to him.*

His free hand tightened on my thigh. "Please."

It would always be the "please" that got me. Before I saw them coming, those two storms broke over me, one after another. Like an earthquake followed by a tsunami. My orgasm quaked from my clit just before the second one crashed from deep inside me, tearing me apart at the seams.

I screamed, my body convulsing so hard I didn't even realize what was happening until I heard his strangled groan of appreciation as his mouth covered my pussy, drinking down every drop of desire my core drenched him with.

"God, yes," he groaned, laving his tongue through my slick folds until he'd consumed every trace of my release.

It felt like my body would need hours to recover from what just happened. But I didn't have hours. I didn't want hours. I still wanted him.

My hand curled into his hair and tipped his head so our eyes could meet.

"I want you," I murmured, my eyes lingering on his lips, full and glistening with the proof of their erotic excellence.

Fact fucking.

It was a very real, erotic phenomenon. A danger, really. The logical combined with the lustful. It was everything—*everything I never knew I needed.*

The world should really be warned.

Ranger stood, and I pushed up on my palms, my eyes sliding to his waist. He didn't try to hide his arousal, the long length distending the front of his pants.

Ranger tugged his shirt from his waistband while my hands went to his belt, undoing the clasp. We worked in frantic sync to free his cock. He hissed as the weight bobbed free of his boxer briefs.

It was so swollen and red, the angry tip leaking drop after drop of precum. I wasn't sure how he could stand it—how he'd made it so long without even a thought for himself or his own pleasure.

It had all been for me.

I wrapped my fingers around his engorged shaft as I bent forward and swiped my tongue over the tip, catching the salty essence.

"Shit, Sydney." It was more than a groan—more than a warning.

I tipped my head back just as Ranger's hand covered my own, his fist pumping mine up and down his length in complete abandon.

"I can't—I have to—" He grunted like he was in pain, his hand holding mine so tight.

Underneath my fingers, I felt his cock swell even thicker. He was too far gone to stop—to think—to do anything else except move my hand furiously over him.

"Sydney…" It was all he could muster to warn me.

But I didn't want to move out of the way. I'd tasted his release before, and now I wanted to see it. I wanted to watch that beautiful brain of his allow his body to lose control.

I let my head tip back, finding his eyes. His face strained, his mouth parting with the slow, choked gasps of release.

"*Fuck…*" He didn't curse often. Only when something else diminished his ability to find another word. And right now, that was the weight of his orgasm coming over him.

A second later, hot spurts of cum landed on my neck and breasts. Gasping—groaning, he continued to yank my hand along his shaft, drawing thick ropes of release out to paint my skin.

"That was…" His shoulders caved as he sucked in air, and it felt like I'd been holding my breath with him, too. Slowly, his eyes lifted back to mine. "Inconceivable—inconceivably incredible."

My breath caught, and I murmured, "I agree."

The oven timer beeped obnoxiously.

"Shoot," Ranger murmured, releasing his hold so I could let go of him. "I should—I need to get that. And then I'll clean… just stay here."

I bit my lip, wanting to smile as he tucked himself back into his pants quickly, his eyes never leaving the mess he'd made all over my chest.

He'd stopped the timer when there was a loud rap on the door.

"Ranger?"

This time, it was my turn to panic. I recognized Hunter's voice with wide eyes. Shoving myself off the bed, I rushed back into the bathroom. I closed the door but didn't shut it all the way. As long as Hunter didn't come in, he wouldn't see me peeking through the crack in the door.

"One minute," I heard Ranger call with a distinct husk to his voice as he strode from the kitchen toward the apartment door.

"Change of plans," Ranger told his brother. "I'll be fine here on my own."

"Are you sure?" Hunter definitely didn't sound convinced.

"Yes, I'm good."

There was a pause. "You look a little flushed, Ranger. Sweating, even."

"I was just… cooking," Ranger replied, and I grimaced. He was the worst white liar. "Cooking and then very hungry. Did you know eating a large meal can make you hot? It's called gustatory sweating."

I covered my mouth, stifling a laugh.

"What?" Ranger probed.

"Nothing," finally came the other man's reply. "Not a thing." I could hear the smile in his voice. "Alright, well I guess I'll get back to reviewing the footage from around your car."

"Okay, thanks. Talk to you later," Ranger blurted out and shut the door.

His footsteps ate up the seconds until the bathroom door swung open.

"Gustatory sweating?" I arched an eyebrow.

"It's a real thing."

I nodded with a low hum.

Ranger frowned. "Hunter didn't seem like he believed me either." He shook his head, moving by me to grab a washcloth and start the warm water in the sink.

I bit back a smile, my eyes sliding to Ranger's dinner sitting on top of the oven.

"Maybe because he saw your dinner sitting on the stove," I murmured with a smile as he pressed the warm cloth to my skin. "And it hasn't been touched."

CHAPTER 18

Ranger

"When will you be here?" I looked up from my computer, my phone to my ear, as Sydney padded into the living room, her bare feet soft as they hit the rug, her towel wrapped around her.

Her brows creased as Hunter replied on the other end of the line, *"Five minutes."*

"Who was that?" She came and stood in front of me, my face eye level with her waist.

Instantly, my mouth watered.

There weren't many metrics I could find that recorded the average number of times a man thought about sex. There was a study from Ohio that estimated, on average, nineteen times a day. So far, I was at twenty, and it was only two o'clock.

Should I have more because I statistically had more thoughts in general than the average person? Maybe.

Should I have less because I couldn't recall ever thinking about sex this much? Possibly.

To be fair, I'd spent the better part of the morning with my head between Sydney's thighs, exploring the concept of multiple orgasms, so there had been a lot of thoughts then, but I lumped those together and counted them as one.

Tomorrow, I was going to attempt to stack her orgasms. To build one off of another into a continuous orgasm. She was going to love it.

I was going to love it.

For the last six days, I'd been fixated on pleasuring her. *My wife.* Fixated on learning every inch of her body like a scientist who'd discovered a brand-new element on the periodic table. On learning which spots made her tremble, which ones made her moan... and always, which ones made her come.

There was something about bringing her pleasure that made me feel like both the smartest man on the planet and yet like I had so much left to learn. So much to explore. *So many ways to please.*

I tried to assess and pinpoint what it was—how I could do the same things and get such varied responses. But there was one right answer—there were multiple. A woman's pleasure was a beautiful, ever-changing phenomenon. One I would happily discover with Sydney every day for the rest of our lives... if our marriage was real.

One I was going to continue to explore for as long as she was mine.

I shifted my laptop off my groin, my cock hard enough to be uncomfortable.

"Hunter." I cleared my throat. "He'll be here in five minutes."

"Did they find something?"

I rose and adjusted myself. "He didn't say, but I doubt he would come here if they hadn't."

After I'd called off their reinforcements, Hunter and Archer had focused their efforts on the video footage of my car to figure out who had cut the brake lines. It would've been an easy task if the days and days of snow dumping over Wisdom hadn't shut down practically every business and road until yesterday. Of course, the footage from that particular street wasn't digital, so there was no way to view or copy it until my brothers could physically get to the locations.

In the meantime, the snow provided a shelter—a haven. The paparazzi disappeared from the sidewalk, Mother Nature keeping everyone inside. Our internet went out, cutting off our access to the stories they made up until something new garnered their attention; the stories ran the gamut from a fairy tale where a romance author had fallen for her landlord to a revenge relationship. No one called. No one probed. No one photographed. For days, everything stilled until it became easier and easier to pretend it would stay like this forever.

And it was because of that that I didn't want to have sex with her.

No, I did very much want to have sex with my wife. But it would be very stupid of me to let it happen.

Gunner always warned sex could complicate things if you weren't careful. The irony of his advice was not lost on anyone when he'd accidentally gotten Della pregnant.

But I wasn't studied in one-night stands. All I had was the history of facts—feelings—and from that first kiss to making her come on my tongue, every intimacy had only made me crave more in a very addictive way.

Morning. Noon. Night.

The bed. The couch. The shower. The floor.

Being cooped up in the apartment made it easier, but I was constantly searching for a fix of her pleasure on my fingers. A taste of her desire on my tongue.

This must be what having a prescription drug addiction felt like. At first, the intimacy filled a need, then it created its own.

The more I was with her... the more I simply needed her.

And at some point, she was leaving. Wisdom. Me. Our marriage.

I had no experience with sex, but I was smart enough to know that having sex with Sydney was the kind of thing I wouldn't be able to come back from—the kind of thing that would permanently attach the emotion growing in my chest.

She was becoming my addiction, and there was no Narcan for falling for my fake wife.

Sydney took a step toward the window, careful not to get too close but close enough to see the familiar handful of chairs camped on the sidewalk. Right now, there were four of them, all enjoying a thermos of coffee, bundled up in their folding chairs.

There was always someone there watching—waiting, and strangely enough, as soon as there was an indication of us leaving the apartment, they all came out of the woodwork, like one alerted the rest.

"I can't believe they're still here," she murmured, folding her arms tight to her front. She looked over her shoulder. "Gina called while you were doing laundry. She said they're running with a story now that I got married because I learned Vince is dating some supermodel." She let out a bitter laugh. "Like I'm following Kanye West's playbook or something."

I frowned. "You're running for president?"

Whatever it was I didn't understand made her smile, and that was most important. I'd happily be a pop culture Neanderthal as long as it kept her smiling.

"Never mind," she murmured as I put my arm around her shoulder and she turned into my chest.

Just like they always did, her arms wound around my waist and her head nestled on my shoulder, fitting perfectly underneath my chin.

Our bodies fit each other. It wasn't an emotional statement, simply a fact. The emotional, confusing part was that even though I knew there were other women of similar stature and build, I also knew none of them would ever fit me like Sydney.

With her, I didn't feel like the puzzle piece with five sides, having so much to give but nowhere to go.

"I'll never understand why people love to exploit other people's pain," she murmured quietly. "Or how someone could claim so much fiction as fact."

"People respond stronger to negative news stories. It's called the negativity bias," I offered the only thing I could—a rationale for her observation, but before I could stop it, another thought erupted from my mouth, one that had no statistical or factual basis, one that simply came from me. "But I think it's because it lets people ignore their own hurt when they focus on others."

She sighed deeply.

"They'll move on," I assured her.

"Oh yeah?" Her head tipped up. "How long does a big story stay in the news?"

Crap.

"It can vary—"

"The average, Ranger." She knew I had the answer.

"Seven days," I muttered, knowing the cycle of this story didn't seem to be ending anytime soon. "But that's only an average."

She hummed, and my arms tightened when she curled back into me; I didn't want to let her go.

I hated the situation she was in. I hated that I didn't know the answers to her problems. But I couldn't resent this... I couldn't resent what I had with her in this apartment when everyone and no one was watching.

"You should probably get dressed." I let my arms slacken. "Hunter will be here soon."

Hunter had an inkling that I was romantically involved with Sydney, and I got the sense he was happy for me, but I still wasn't comfortable telling him that we'd made the marriage official.

Sydney grabbed a pair of jeans from the laundry basket I'd brought up earlier, a long-sleeve tee, and disappeared into the bathroom. She returned fully clothed, toweling her hair dry, just as a strong knock rapped on the door.

I greeted Hunter. "Hi—what's on your shirt?" I stared at the dark stain down his chest.

"Baby puke," he grumbled and entered. "Or what's left of it."

"Oh." I closed the door behind him. "Everything okay?"

"Yeah, I just made Charlie laugh too hard too soon after eating," he explained over his shoulder as he walked toward the table. "Trust me, puke is better than shit." He grinned over his shoulder. "Gunner said that Skye shit all over him this morning when he went to change her diaper."

Sydney and I both cringed.

"How are you holding up?" Hunter greeted her with a half hug.

"I'm good." Her eyes flicked to mine. "I mean, as good as I can be, I guess. Did you find something on the video?"

"We did." Hunter turned to me as I joined them. "The Mountain Motel had the best footage on the car, though it took the longest to get. How the hell they were still using a VCR to record the feeds is beyond me." He huffed and handed me his iPad with the video paused on the screen. "Early that morning, there was a guy who stopped at your car and looked underneath it."

"That hat." I recognized the cap instantly from the security footage from the driveway. *The same man who left the note.*

"Yeah—"

I zoomed in, but the video was too grainy for a clear picture of the man's face. *Shit.* The best we had was generalities—white male, thirties, dark hair, mustache—but that could still be enough.

"Did you canvas the area? See if anyone recognized him or—"

"Alex Beekman," Hunter said before I could finish. "Diehl and I talked to the clerk at the motel yesterday since we were already there for the video footage, and we lucked out. Beekman is a licensed paparazzo staying at the motel."

"Yesterday?" And they hadn't told me?

"A paparazzo?" Sydney balked.

We'd talked ourselves into circles about who her stalker was, both of us agreeing that it was unlikely that he was a paparazzo. *I guess we were both wrong.*

Hunter's jaw tensed. "Your job is to safeguard Sydney, not to track down answers."

I opened my mouth to argue because that wasn't how all our

cases were handled. Yes, I normally did the tracking down of answers while they were in the field, but I never would've kept something like this from them, even if I didn't have all the answers yet.

But they had from me.

Because I was different.

It got harder to swallow—their brand of protection—something uncomfortable made my chest feel tight.

"Did you find him?" I asked, trying to stay focused, though I could feel Sydney's eyes on me.

Again, Hunter nodded. "He wasn't in his room yesterday when we were there, so Diehl and I went back over this morning. Caught him as he was leaving to get coffee and brought him in for questioning."

"What?" I took a step back, reeling.

Not only had they found him, they'd already questioned him.

"So he's been arrested?" Sydney asked.

"Not exactly." Hunter shifted his weight.

"What do you mean?" I asked forcefully, watching Hunter's eyebrow draw up at my tone.

There were a lot of thoughts fighting for the first ticket out of my mouth, but all of them that focused on my feelings over Sydney's safety were going to have to take a back seat.

"Play the footage." He nodded to the iPad.

I tapped the screen, letting the video advance. The quality of the camera and distance from my car was lacking, but it was enough to watch Beekman go over to my car, crouch and look under it, and then stand up a couple seconds later and walk back to the motel.

Not what I would estimate as enough time to cut brake lines.

"According to Beekman, he saw *another* man coming out from underneath your car that morning on his way back from picking up coffee. He said he went up to his room, dropped off his coffee, waited and watched the car for an hour to make sure whoever it was wasn't coming back, and then investigated. He claims he was just looking for another story."

"Okay, well you should have the video footage of the car before he got to it—"

"It's covered in snow," Hunter interrupted, rewinding through the video until Beekman disappeared from the shot and a second later, the whole frame was covered up in white. "The camera is old and the shield broke off. With the temperatures and the storm, it collected on the glass for two days until it warmed enough to fall off."

"Which was when Beekman went to the car..." *Damn.* "Could he describe the other guy?"

"No. Too far away."

Double fucking damn.

I jerked at the violence of my thoughts. We'd had countless frustrating and dangerous cases before, but none of them made me feel like this.

None of them made me feel.

"Did you ask about the note?"

"Said he didn't know anything about a note, but he was in town that night."

"And he's wearing the same hat."

"He says he was talking to another pap outside the house, and when he complimented the guy on his hat, he gave it to him." Hunter flipped the cover on his iPad closed. "Didn't get a name, and Beekman said he hasn't seen him since."

"What if Beekman cut the lines earlier and then went back to check to make sure it was enough to fail?" My jaw tightened.

His version of what happened was possible but not as probable, in my opinion.

"I think that's what he's hiding," Hunter said flatly. "He was cagey as fuck when we talked to him, even said he was going to call his lawyer if we approached him again. I think he did this and he knows we don't have proof."

"So, he's just... out there..." Sydney said hollowly.

I folded my arms, hiding my balled fists at my sides. "How do we get proof? Can Diehl pull prints from my car? I can ask Decker—"

"The bank down the road has security cameras—newer ones. They are farther away, but it should be enough to confirm the presence of a second person or if it was Beekman at the car earlier."

"And if you can't?" Sydney asked, and only I noticed the slight quiver at the end of her question.

"We will." Hunter leveled her with a steady, reassuring look. "Bank manager is a friend of Mom's; he's going to get us the footage first thing tomorrow, and we're going to get to the bottom of this."

Tomorrow. New Year's Day.

I moved through the next couple of minutes in a daze, thanking my brother and walking him to the door. This was a good thing. We would finally have answers. An impending resolution for Sydney.

An approaching end.

I walked to the kitchen and filled a glass with water, chugging down the entire thing to try and stop the burning in my chest. There was no reason for my chest to burn. To feel tight. It had been hours since I'd eaten—since we'd made pancakes and bacon for brunch.

"Ranger."

I turned when she said my name. Our eyes caught and whatever turmoil I felt in my chest was reflected in her stare.

"They'll get answers," I assured her, rubbing the bridge of my nose. "If he's responsible, Sydney, then this will all be over soon. You'll be safe." I paused and forced the last words out. "You'll be able to go home."

I swore I saw her wince, but I had to be imagining it. There was no reason for it. No reason for her to want to stay here. She was thousands of miles from her home. Her friends. Her life. And as for us…

There was no us. There was friendship and orgasms and an arrangement; the orgasms might be real, but our marriage was fake. Temporary.

"Yeah," she said, nodding her head quickly and walking to the window.

She was probably afraid to hope; she'd been let down so many times in the past.

My jaw ground tighter. I wouldn't let her down. Temporary or not, I was her husband. I would do anything to protect her. Even if it was only so she could safely walk away from me in the end.

My phone rang. "Hello?"

"Hey, I have your car all fixed up." Decker spoke loud enough that even without being on speakerphone, Sydney could hear every word he said. "Are you coming to trivia tonight? I can drive it there and then get a ride back with Dennis after."

Dennis Nelson owned a ranch near Decker's house; they were both staples at Wisdom's senior trivia night.

"Oh, hold on." I muted the call and my eyes flicked to Sydney. "Do you want to go to trivia night?"

It would get us out of here—out of the confined space where my lips would always find hers and where we'd end up tangled in the sheets all night long. It was one thing when her leaving was an eventuality I could forget. Now, it was an inevitability I couldn't ignore.

She turned, a tendril of hair sliding over her shoulder and brushing against her cheek. My fingers itched to right it. To stroke her cheek and land under her chin. Her eyelids fluttered, her eyes glistening underneath her lashes.

I saw that now, too. The glistening. The glittering. Eyes had been nothing more than colorful irises and dark pupils before her. Now, they grew hazy when she was afraid. They glimmered when she smiled. *They deepened when she wanted.*

Before Sydney, facts poured into my mind like water into a cup, filling and filling until it overflowed. Still, I kept adding more. Then she appeared and the filling stopped. She became a part of my life, and I emptied part of the cup to make room for something new— something more. And soon, she'd be leaving it.

"Trivia night?"

I cleared my throat. "It's New Year's Eve trivia night at the senior center." *Something away from here—from this bubble that had just burst.* "If you want to get out of the apartment for a few hours, we can sneak out around the back of the house, and I'll have Cindy pick us up—"

"Yeah, that sounds great," she said with a relieved smile. "Let's go."

I tapped to unmute Decker. "I'll be there."

"Great. I'll bring the Volvo."

"Thanks."

Sydney had her headphones on by the time I ended the call. She'd been steadily working on her manuscript for a few hours every afternoon, the escape into her book giving her another break from the stress.

Usually, I would set her up on the couch with a cup of coffee and some baked snacks. She'd put her headphones on and I'd work on my own computer next to her. When she'd get stuck or frustrated, I'd take her hand and rub her fingers until the grip of inspiration took hold of her again. The intimacy of those quiet moments was another thing I would come to miss.

But the silence had never felt like this—like there was this giant void that opened up between us with no bridge to cross it.

If I felt anything for Sydney Ward, I had to put an end to it right now. *Tonight*. And most importantly, I had to keep my hands off my gorgeous wife. I'd done it before, and I could do it again. My brain still had control over my body. *Of course, it did.*

I filled my glass with more water and chugged it down. We were so close to finding answers—close to figuring out who was behind all of this. *So why did it feel like even with the answers, I was still going to lose?*

CHAPTER 19

Sydney

"Told you I'd get us here in a jiffy." Cindy spun the wheel and turned into the parking lot of the senior center. The Beehive sat back off Main Street near the edge of Wisdom in what used to be an old fire station. The windowless, unassuming building had only a handful of cars parked in the half-lit lot, the full moon providing the rest of the light. In the distance, a pack of wolves howled.

I'd been silent on the drive from the apartment, Cindy consuming the conversational bandwidth in the car. They were close to finding the person responsible for this, and I should be relieved. Instead, the pressure on my chest grew by the weight of six words: *you'll be able to go home.*

What was home? New York?

I thought of my apartment. My office. The gym I went to. The restaurants I liked. The memories were nice and familiar… but they weren't home.

Was Wisdom?

Was Ranger?

I didn't know. I didn't know anything except that as the minutes ticked by earlier, I found it harder and harder to write. The words weren't adding up; instead, they were counting down. Down to "The End." *Of the book and this marriage.*

I couldn't be falling for him—*my husband*. Not his selflessness. Not his awkwardness. Not his dimples. *And definitely not his orgasms.* No, it wasn't possible to be brainwashed by Ranger. Fact fucked, yes. Brainwashed, no.

"Technically, a jiffy is one-hundredth of a second, so it took us longer than a jiffy to get here—"

"Oh, hush. Save that brainpower for the game, pretty boy," Cindy tutted as we exited the car and trod through the snow-dusted ground to the door. We passed by Ranger's car; Decker had arrived before us. When we reached the building, Ranger held the door for us with a smile, those dimples disappearing as soon as his gaze connected with mine.

"Thank you." My murmur of gratitude was drowned out by the noise.

The parking lot was a poor indicator of the crowd inside. Where it was silent—peaceful under the night sky, inside the hall was brightly lit and bustling with seniors wearing plastic top hats and those cheap New Year's Eve glasses that had the year suspended above the frame.

Though I'd seen him briefly at the scene of the accident, I picked out Decker in an instant because he was the only other person besides Ranger and me who was at least three decades younger than the average of the room.

"Estelle! Donna!" Cindy greeted everyone in the crowd like she was a queen, making her way over to her friends.

My eyes traveled around the room. Wood-paneled and wall-papered, the space hadn't been updated in several decades, but there was still a pulse here. Not something new and energetic and trendy, but something tried and stable and true. Streamers and balloons dangled from every corner and ledge, signs for the new year interspersed between them. And though I wasn't up on my old-school country, I was pretty sure Johnny Cash played through the speakers.

In the corner of my eye, I caught Ranger nodding and waving to Decker, leading us over to his friend.

Without the adrenaline coursing through my veins, it was easier to absorb the details of the other man. Warm-brown hair and matching eyes. A mechanic's physique and the forever-stained fingernails to match. His smile was warm and easy as he greeted people on his way over to us.

"Sydney, this is Decker Connolly. Decker, Sydney," Ranger introduced us.

"Nice to meet you. Glad everyone's okay after what happened the other day." Decker extended his hand, and I shook it, noting there was no ring on his ring finger. Of course, I couldn't help but want… Handsome. Helpful. Kind. *Where was his heroine?*

Before he got a chance to talk to Ranger, two elderly women approached and captured Ranger's attention. Both had to be in their seventies, and one's hair was dyed bright purple. I heard the beginnings of them making their case to bring Ranger onto their trivia team for the night before Decker spoke low to me.

"They always fight over him."

"I'm sure." I smiled. Ranger knew everything. Or at least it felt like it. Having him on your team at trivia night was like having a card counter on your blackjack team in Vegas. Ranger glanced at me, catching my stare, and I quickly resumed my conversation with Decker. "So, how did you get roped into senior trivia night?"

Decker chuckled, his easy smile welcoming. "Accidentally… but also on purpose."

"Oh?" I laughed at his answer.

"I work on cars and farm equipment for most of the people in this room. Last year, I got a call from Brenda—she goes by BB. She'd rear-ended someone trying to avoid a bison—don't ask— and needed a tow. Anyway, there was a misunderstanding, and she accidentally texted me this address when she meant to send it to a friend. I thought she needed a ride right away because she was stranded somewhere, so I rushed over there. And yeah… accidentally ended up at trivia night."

"And on purpose?"

His grin quirked on one side. "I decided to stay and play. Didn't hurt that I was on the winning team that night. And then I just kept coming back." He shrugged, looking around the room. "Nothing beats good, honest company and simple pleasures."

My chin dipped, and I heard the low sound I made in agreement. I couldn't argue with him there. Once again, the stark difference between New York and Wisdom grated me like the word *moist* on a page.

What if I didn't go back?

I flinched. I shouldn't be having that thought.

"And how did you end up here? And from what I've seen in the news, married to Ranger?" Even though he asked, he didn't sound skeptical.

I gulped and let my eyes flutter to the ground for a moment. "Accidentally… but on purpose."

Decker gave me a smile that said *fair*, but before he could probe deeper, Ranger returned to our conversation.

"Sorry about that," he murmured. "Thanks for taking care of the car, Decker."

"Of course, man. Any idea what happened?"

Ranger folded his arms. "Hunter and Diehl think they know who the culprit is. They just need proof to arrest him."

"Oh, good." He shook his head. "Fucking unbelievable."

"Yeah—"

"Ranger!" Cindy strode over, her hands on her hips. "What's this I hear about you joining Estelle's team tonight?"

Ranger blinked. "Well, I was on your team last month—"

"Are you sure?"

He gave her a boyish, one-dimpled smile. "You know I'd never forget."

Cindy huffed. "Dang. Alright, alright." She waved her hands

in defeat. "Well, you two lovebirds better take your seats. We're serious about trivia time here, Miss Sydney." She tapped the face of her watch, winked, and then sauntered off to the table in the center of the room.

"Every month, she tries to tell you that you're on her team." Decker chuckled and handed Ranger his car keys.

"She forgets."

"I think you're missing just how much of a hot commodity you are," Decker returned and then looked over his shoulder. "I should probably get to my table. Darla's been staring at my ass for the last five minutes. If I don't sit, she's going to insist on spanking me for tardiness again."

We all laughed, saying goodbye as Decker joined his team.

"We're over here." Ranger stepped to the side, motioning to table three in the corner.

His hand pressed gently to the small of my back as we walked, and I purposely let my gait slow so I could absorb the warmth for longer.

What was happening to me?

After the last week, my body felt like an instrument tuned precisely to his touch. Wound taut to where even the slightest brush made my heartbeat quicken and my cells hum with heat.

I'd started to feel the kinds of things I described in my books— things I didn't think happened in real life, and it was all because of him. Ranger had turned my fiction into fact. *And all I could think was, what would happen if I stayed?*

We reached our seats and Ranger's touch disappeared. He introduced me to the other senior members of our team: Estelle, her husband, George, and Miriam. Estelle and Miriam were fans of my books and, for a few minutes, were much more excited I was at their table than the genius sitting next to me.

"You have to tell us what you have in store for Jenny," Miriam begged. "I never liked Vance from the start."

"We promise we won't tell."

"Oh, leave the girl alone, Estelle," George grumbled.

She swatted his arm. "Sixty years and you think you can tell me what to do?" She scoffed. "Just give us a clue. I'll make you my famous rice pudding—all my friends love it—"

"And then they all die," George chimed in.

"George!" Estelle gasped while Ranger and I tried to contain our laughter.

"Alright, ladies and gentlemen," a jovial voice boomed from the mic at the front of the room, putting an end to our conversation. "Let's get these games started."

The MC introduced himself as Winston. He had on a three-piece suit, a pink paisley handkerchief blooming from his pocket. I smiled, recalling Ranger's.

After welcoming everyone to the New Year's Eve trivia night, he quickly outlined the layout of the game. Six rounds. Three questions. Answers were to be written on the individual answer sheets and turned in to him before time was up. At the end, there was one bonus round where teams could wager any amount of points in one last shot to win.

Ranger grabbed the small answer sheets, a large piece of paper for scoring and reference, and a small pencil—the kind that grandfathers used to do the Sunday crossword puzzle—from the center of the table.

"Do you want to write our answers? I usually do it, but your handwriting is better." He passed everything to me.

"When have you seen my handwriting?" My head tipped. *My signed books.* I grimaced. *Duh, Sydney.*

"When you write notes for your book on the back of old receipts and then leave them on the kitchen table," he said simply, like it was common for everyone to notice those kinds of things rather than just pick up the pieces of paper and throw them away.

"Drinks will be coming around as we begin our first round." Several people in the crowd hooted. Meanwhile, I noticed that George grumbled and pulled out a flask from his pocket. Winston continued, "Round one. New Year's Eve history. First question, In what year was the first ball drop on New Year's Eve?" He paused. "Second question, What time that year did the ball start its descent? And last question, What maritime tradition did this idea come from?"

The volume in the room dimmed to a hum below the sound of Johnny Cash's voice in the background.

"The answer to the first is 1904," Miriam tossed out, tapping her manicured finger on the table. "My grandfather grew up in New York and would tell me stories about Times Square."

"The first ball drop was 1907," Ranger corrected and then cleared his throat. "The first celebration was in 1904 but with fireworks."

Miriam's eyes narrowed.

"You know he's going to be right, Miriam," Estelle chided.

"Alright, 1907." She nodded and waved for me to write down Ranger's answer. "But only because you're pretty."

My eyes flicked to Ranger, watching the color deepen his cheeks as I wrote down the year.

"For the second question, the ball always starts to drop at eleven fifty-nine," I thought out loud. "But the way the question was phrased makes me think that's wrong."

Ranger nodded, confirming my suspicions. "That year, the ball dropped at midnight, not counting down to it."

I wrote *midnight* on the paper. "Why?"

"It's called a time ball," George said roughly, resting his elbows on the table and scratching his chin. "That's the answer to the last one. It's a maritime time signal that occurred at a specific moment when ships could see to set their clocks accurately. So, when they dropped the ball at midnight, it marked the start of the time, not the end of it."

"Exactly," Ranger confirmed. "It switched to a countdown in 1938."

"So, I write a time ball?"

They both nodded, and I jotted down the phrase on the answer sheet. When I was finished, Ranger extended his hand, offering to take the paper to the front. I shivered as our fingers brushed, the hum momentarily returning.

"Alright, ladies and gentlemen. Here are the answers to round one…" Winston revealed the correct responses like he was a game show host, Estelle and Miriam clapping as soon as they heard we'd gotten all three correct.

Did they really think there was any other option with Ranger on their team?

"Round two." Winston plucked the curl of his mustache. "Question one, What happened on New Year's Eve in 1945? Question two, How much does the ball used for the Times Square drop weigh? And question three, What was the first year that Dick Clark's Rockin' Eve special aired on TV?"

"The end of World War II!" George exclaimed, slapping his hand on the table.

"George!" Estelle hissed. "Do you want the other teams to have our answers?" She shook her head and muttered in the loudest whisper I'd ever heard, "I can't take him anywhere."

While George apologized, Ranger gave me the nod to write down his answer.

"Alright, out with it, pretty boy. How much does the ball weigh?" Miriam tapped her finger.

"Roughly twelve thousand pounds," Ranger answered, adding with a cheeky grin, "And it's covered in twenty-five hundred Waterford crystals."

"The answer to the last question is 1985," George chimed in, lifting his flask. "I'll never forget it."

"He loves the New Year's special," Estelle offered.

The game continued through the final round, where we missed two pop culture references. Winston then announced an intermission while they tallied scores and got the TV set up to watch the ball drop.

"I'll be right back," Ranger said and rose before I could ask where he was going. A moment later, he met up with Decker at the front of the room; the two of them clearly the resident tech crew in charge of hooking up the decade-old television and making sure the ball drop was ready to be viewed.

Meanwhile, Miriam topped off everyone's champagne glass at the table except Ranger's; he hadn't touched his.

"So, how did you end up at trivia night?" I asked when he returned.

"I brought Cindy after she had her hip replaced. She invited me to stay, so I did."

"And you liked it enough to come back?"

His tongue slid through his lips and he nodded. "There have only been very few times where I've been"—he wrinkled his nose—"picked first, so to speak."

He said a few, but I knew there was an exact amount he wasn't telling me.

"But here you're a hot commodity," I murmured, trying to push past the way my chest squeezed.

He flushed. "I wouldn't say that."

"I know." I smiled and it drew his dimples out, heating my lower parts for a moment before they disappeared. "What is it?"

He blinked, his gaze dropping for a second. "I'm just angry that Archer and Hunter didn't tell me about the video—about Beekman."

My brows lifted. "But you were with me."

"It doesn't matter. We always share information—*I* always share information as soon as I have it," he corrected, his jaw tightening as he reached for our reference sheet, scanning down our answers like he didn't already have them committed to memory.

"Then why did they wait?"

"Because they worry... because they care." Another tic of his jaw. "It's how they've always been."

It wasn't the first time I'd seen his brothers underestimate him, and though I certainly felt the love and respect they all had for this brilliant man, it was obvious to anyone who knew them for even a short amount of time that they were overprotective of Ranger in ways he didn't need.

"That doesn't mean it's how they should be. If they care enough to protect you, they should care when it goes too far," I told him and reached for his hand. "Have you told them how you feel?"

His eyes widened. "I don't know how to do that."

"You told them how you felt when they wanted someone else to protect me." I gave him a shy smile.

"That was different."

"What? Why?"

Our gazes locked. "Because no one would ever protect you like I would."

My breath caught, his certainty jolting my chest. "Ranger..." I didn't get the chance to say anything else because Winston returned to the mic.

"The points have been tallied, and we're ready for the bonus round," he announced.

Our table was tied for first place, and this final question was our only opportunity to win.

"One question. Write your answer and how many of your points you want to wager on your sheet. You'll have one minute to get your sheet to me." Winston cleared his throat. "Ready?"

The room hooted and hollered.

"When did the tradition of kissing at midnight on New Year's Eve begin and what was the reason?"

A collective gasp rippled through the room, followed by the frantic murmur of conversation.

"Probably the French. They would come up with something like that," Estelle suggested.

"It was the Romans," I said, shocked that I knew the answer to the question. "They thought it would bring love and prosperity into the following year."

"Are you sure?" Estelle asked, not waiting for my answer before querying Ranger, "Is she right?"

"I think so." His eyes met mine, and suddenly, it felt like it was only the two of us at the table—in the room.

"Think so? We need better than a 'think so' to win this," Miriam harrumphed.

"I don't see you with any better answers," Estelle shot over. "She writes romance. I'd trust her on the origins of a kiss over any of you."

I bit into my lip and smiled, watching them bicker.

"Fair point. I'll agree on that," Miriam conceded and leaned forward. "So, then it's up to you, pretty boy. What are you willing to wager on your wife?" She arched an eyebrow.

My throat clamped shut. *His wife.* Every time someone else said it, it made my stomach flutter.

"Everything," Ranger murmured, his voice catching as his eyes connected with mine. Intense. Unquestionable. "I'm willing to risk everything on her."

This time, he didn't need to touch me for my body to hum. For my heart to trip and my breath to stall. *For me to want this man even more than I thought possible.*

"*Fifteen seconds,*" Winston warned, breaking our trance.

I jerked my head down and scribbled down the answer and our total points, and Ranger took the paper to the front.

The whole way back to the table, he stared at me.

It could've taken Winston another minute or another hour to look through all the answers, for all I knew, because all I could focus on was Ranger. The heat of his eyes. The color in his cheeks. The slide of his tongue through his lips like always when he had more to say.

The way he took my hand and the bubble closed around us. "Sydney…" He swallowed

The table jostled, bursting the warmth cocooned around us.

Miriam and Estelle had jumped up, clapping and yelling and knocking the table in their exuberance. It was only then I realized that we'd won the game. Everyone crowded around us, hugging and celebrating, drinking their champagne.

Meanwhile, want… longing… stretched between Ranger and me like a hot rubber band. Pulling tight when other people claimed our attention and then loosening as we drew back to each other.

"Ladies and gentlemen! We're at the minute mark!"

The attention of everyone in the room shifted to the TV. Everyone except Ranger.

"How did you know that about the kiss?"

I swallowed over the lump in my throat. "My mom told me… every year before she kissed whichever boyfriend she thought was going to be her happy ending."

New Year's Eve was Mom's favorite holiday for this reason— *hope*. More than Valentine's Day, it disappointed her to be single on New Year's with no one to kiss.

Ranger stepped closer, the countdown ticking. "Do you believe it's true?"

"I don't know." My lips parted, and I confessed. "I've been too afraid to kiss any of my boyfriends on New Year's."

His prominent brows pulled together and heat rose to my cheeks.

There were various reasons I'd never had a New Year's Eve kiss over the years. Being single. Being home alone. Being up late working. Vince being away. But there were also years when I had no excuse… except this.

Every man Mom had kissed had ended in heartbreak. It was the reason I wanted to write happy endings… and the reason I was so afraid to trust in my own.

Ranger cupped my cheek, his head drifting closer until our breaths tangled.

"*Ten. Nine. Eight,*" the crowd chanted along with the TV. "*Seven. Six. Five.*"

His gaze lowered to my mouth. "And what about your husband?" he rumbled. "Are you afraid to kiss him?"

My inhale sliced into my lungs.

"Four. Three."

There was no question because there was no doubt. At every turn, Ranger had proved I could count on him. To help me. To protect me. To take care of me. And now, to promise a happy ending.

I slid my arms around his neck. "*No.*"

"Two. One."

His mouth lowered, mine lifted, and for the first time, I crossed into the new year with a kiss. *With my husband.*

"I'll move it tomorrow," Ranger murmured, pulling up to the curb at the end of the street.

He hadn't parked this close to the house since he'd stopped parking in the garage, but tonight, the temperatures were flirting with freezing, and it was past midnight. If there was one thing the paparazzi weren't doing, it was camping on the sidewalk, hoping I would sleepwalk out of the apartment and into a PR nightmare; they left their posts late and returned early. The nights I'd worked into the early hours of the morning, I'd counted them disappearing like some people count sheep.

We got out of the car, and Ranger put his arm over my shoulder as we trudged down the snowy sidewalk. The lights in the apartment were on, left that way on purpose to make the reporters think we were still there.

I snuggled closer to his side, breathing in his scent more than anything else. I didn't want that kiss to end. I didn't want any of this to end. There was something here that existed before the paparazzi… before my stalker. And I had to tell him I wanted it to continue, no matter what happened with Beekman.

"Ranger—" I started to speak just as a dark figure appeared from behind a tree not even ten feet in front of us. The lack of lighting and the thick trunk had obscured where he'd been waiting on the other side of it.

"I knew you'd gone out," the man's voice drawled low, his slight slur more of a dead giveaway to what he'd been doing than the flask that glinted from the moonlight.

Ranger immediately removed his arm from my shoulders and stepped in front of me, shielding me from the man's stare.

"And now we'd like to go home."

The man laughed for a second, the sound fracturing into a snarl just before he whipped his flask onto the ground. "You think you can just accuse someone of a crime they didn't commit and get away with it?" he snarled and took a threatening step.

I gasped, making the connection just as Ranger spoke.

"You must be Mr. Beekman," he said calmly. "I didn't accuse you of anything. The cameras showed you tampering—"

"Shut the fuck up, you fucking liar!" He took a threatening step, low light catching on his face. "I didn't cut your fucking brakes."

Spit flew from his lips with the forcefulness of his words, catching on his beard, which made him look older than he probably was. His pupils were completely dilated, but I had a feeling that was due to the alcohol and not the time of night because he still had a ball cap on, even though there was no sun in sight.

"I'm not saying that you did." Ranger lifted his hands, trying to keep the situation calm. "And I'm sure the police will find what they need to confirm your story—"

"Fuck the police." Beekman came closer and Ranger pushed me backward with one hand, putting some distance between us. "The police took orders from your brothers, and your brothers came for me because of you." He looked Ranger up and down and scoffed. "No wonder."

"No, they didn't!" I protested. "You tried to hurt me—"

"Sydney!" Ranger ordered with a tone I'd never heard before. Protective and on edge.

Beekman cackled. "You still can't even stand up for yourself.

Pathetic piece of shit. First your brothers, now you need this stupid, trash-writing bitch—"

"Enough!" Ranger shouted and stepped right in Beekman's path. "Sydney, go to the house and call Archer."

My jaw went slack. I wanted to listen to him—should've listened to him, but I couldn't move. I was afraid to leave him. Ranger had a thousand strengths, but taking on an angry drunk who was twice his size only had to do with the physical kind.

"Sydney," Ranger hissed, looking over his shoulder.

It jolted me into action, and I took two stumbling steps into the road, my hand fumbling my phone from my pocket. My eyes never left Ranger's until Beekman's voice sliced through the air.

"Oh, hell no. She's the one I'm here for. The one I haven't been paid enough to deal with this bullshit."

"You're not here for anyone, and certainly not my wife," Ranger rasped low, but it was the way his eyes shifted, the absolute truth in them, that made my breath catch.

My wife.

Two small words caused me just enough of a distraction that I didn't see Beekman's torso shift until it was too late.

"Ranger!" My warning wasn't quick enough.

Ranger turned, but because he'd been looking at me—looking out for me—he wasn't prepared for the fist that was already flying in his direction. I screamed when the sound of flesh and bone connected in the silence of the street.

Ranger toppled to the side, hitting another car parked on the street before sliding to the ground.

"Ranger!" A strangled cry tore from my lips.

Adrenaline, rather than intellect, sent me straight toward them, but before I hardly got a step closer, Ranger moved with the swiftness and precision of a machine.

He grabbed for Beekman's wrist, yanking on it at the same time as his leg swung out and knocked Beekman's feet out from under him. The larger man crashed face-first onto the ground. In another second, Ranger was on top of him, subduing Beekman with his arm wrenched behind his back to the point where the pinned man was crying out in pain, screaming that he had given up.

Blood ran down from Ranger's nose, and even though the lighting was dim, I knew it was broken; there was too much blood. A choked cry escaped my mouth.

"Call Archer, Sydney," Ranger ordered, no trace of pain evident in his tone.

I scrambled to make the call, giving Archer enough buzzwords to get the situation across. *Beekman. Fight. Police.* Within minutes, Archer and Chief Diehl were at the house, the policeman taking Beekman back into custody while Archer immediately rushed over to us.

"Jesus, Ranger. Are you alright?" He grabbed Ranger's shoulder, shining his cell phone flashlight over Ranger's face. "Is your nose—"

"Fine." Ranger pushed the light away and used his handkerchief to wipe the blood oozing from his nose. "It's fine."

"Good, or Mom would've killed me." Archer shook his head, looking at Ranger's injury and then back at the patrol car. "You did good subduing him after a hit like that."

"Just because you don't let me doesn't mean I don't know how to defend myself, Archer," Ranger replied succinctly but without resentment, refolding his handkerchief and replacing it under his nose.

Archer winced and dipped his head. "Right."

Ranger might not be able to see it, but I did. The remorse his brother felt. And the agony—torn between wanting to protect the youngest of them and needing to accept that Ranger didn't need his protection.

"Beekman claimed he was hired to watch Sydney," Ranger continued. "He didn't say by whom, but that's obviously a part of this that we're missing."

"Okay, well, he's already asked for his lawyer, so nothing's going to happen until the lawyer gets here tomorrow. I'll interrogate him first thing. He's not going to get away—"

"No, I want to speak to him."

"What?" Archer balked. "Ranger, your nose is broken. Let me handle Beekman. You worry about seeing a doctor—"

"Dammit, Archer, I am a doctor," Ranger declared harshly, wiping more blood on his sleeve. "I can handle this"—he then pointed his finger at Beekman—"and I will handle him."

My jaw went slack. This wasn't the first time Ranger had stood up to his brother's protectiveness for me, but this time was different, and Archer felt it, too. I wasn't sure I'd ever seen such a large man look so stunned before.

After a beat, Archer nodded jerkily. "I'll meet you at the station tomorrow morning."

That wasn't exactly what Ranger said, but it was good enough. "Alright."

CHAPTER 20

Ranger

"I can't believe that just happened." Sydney's hollow voice bounced off the tile walls in the small bathroom.

I'd given a brief statement to Chief Diehl even though he told me it could wait until tomorrow. I didn't want to wait. My brothers wouldn't wait. And Sydney wouldn't wait either. Her brief recount built on my own. By the time we were finished, the blood from my nose had finally slowed, but my handkerchief was soaked.

By the time I'd got my shirtsleeve out from my coat, a trail of blood dotted the crusty snow all the way to the door to the apartment.

Sydney had ushered me in here and gave me a towel for my nose.

"Let's get these clothes off," she murmured and proceeded to undress me. Everything I had on was either bloody from the hit or dirty and wet from the snowy scuffle. Or all three.

"He was drunk. We'll get better answers tomorrow." If the flask hadn't given it away, the stench on Beekman's breath did.

She nodded slowly. "Thank you." Her eyes flicked up to mine as she unzipped my jacket and maneuvered me to remove it.

"I can protect you," I said with more force than expected. Of all people, it hurt the most to think that Sydney thought I was incapable.

"You *did* protect me, Ranger." She pushed my sweater-vest from my shoulders; thankfully, I'd worn one that buttoned today rather than a pullover. She lifted her eyes to mine and added, "But you shouldn't have to."

Her gaze took on that look—that color and depth it always did when we kissed—and when that kiss spiraled into more.

I cleared my throat and tipped my head up to the ceiling. Of course, that helped to control the bleeding and it gave her access to the collar buttons of my shirt, but that wasn't why I did it. My body responded to her undressing me, and I needed it to stop. I squeezed my eyes shut as her fingers undid the buttons on my shirt, willing the blood to rush to my head—to rush to my nose—anywhere but the places it was going.

This was fake. *We* were fake.

Fake. *Adjective. Verb. Noun.* We were every definition of the word. But by some inexplicable fault or phenomenon, though I could remember literally everything I'd ever learned, I struggled to remember the simple fact that we weren't real.

"Sydney..."

She ignored me, pushing the fabric over my shoulders until it snagged on my bent arm. I wanted the torture to end, so I moved quickly. Too quickly. My head snapped straight and I lowered my arm, the movement enough to allow a single drop of blood to land on my previously spared undershirt.

Our eyes connected, and an unspoken, "*It has to come off, too,*" as her hands went to my waist.

Sydney tugged the fabric free and slowly peeled it up my torso. I didn't flinch or falter under the heat of her fingers dragging along my bare skin because I'd been tense from the moment she'd shut us in the small bathroom and dragged my coat from my shoulders.

I didn't know wanting someone could be like this. I understood the mechanics of attraction and desire, the logistics of pleasure and sex, but I hadn't understood the reality of wanting her: *an evolutionarily necessary form of insanity.*

"I'll be fine," I assured her, covering my face with the towel again even though the bleeding had stopped—*only once I was partially naked. Funny how that worked.*

"Are you sure?"

No, I wasn't sure. Not when we were standing so close—not when I wanted her so much.

Her brow creased and she placed her hand on my cheek, the other resting on top of mine that held the towel. "If it's broken, doesn't it have to be... put back?"

My eyes fled to the mirror, and I lowered the towel. Carefully, I pressed along my nose, ignoring the pain in order to assess the damage.

"Unless the nasal bones are visibly or palpably misaligned, there's no need for me to see a doctor right now." I traced my fingers along the bruised ridge of my right cheek to the edge of my nose, where it had begun to swell. "He caught my cheek before he hit my nose, so there wasn't enough force to completely break the bones."

I'd never been hit like this before—never been in a fight before. Even in the fight simulations I'd done at the Armorous Tactical training course, no one had hit me even close to this, but again, I knew Hazard's team had gone easy at my brother's instruction.

Because being too smart must mean I wasn't strong enough.

There hadn't really been pain initially, just shock and stars and adrenaline and the sole objective to protect Sydney. Now, I felt the discomfort of the swelling starting to set in.

"It will heal okay." I lowered my hand just as she lifted hers. "I'll just need to ice it for the first couple days to help bring down the swelling."

My inhale caught as she traced the same path from my nose to my cheek, only she didn't stop there. Her fingers blazed their own trail from my injuries down to my mouth.

"Ranger..." She chewed on her bottom lip, but this time, I

didn't want her thoughts to stay inside. I wanted to know—I needed to know what she was thinking.

"What is it?"

She looked up at me in awe. "Is there anything you don't know everything about?"

Yes. Plenty of things. Countless things. But for the first time, I didn't answer her with a fact. I answered her with the truth, and there was only one thing I wanted to know everything about.

"Yes." I blinked and swallowed. "*You.*"

Her mouth parted, her sharp inhale a kind of invitation I'd never experienced before.

There was no way to determine who moved first, whether it was my mouth that lowered or hers that rose up, but our lips met in the middle. Collided with heat and hunger.

In an instant, I was back in that moment when I was on the ground. I felt the cold of the snow under my legs, the wetness of it on my fingertips. The air was fresh compared to Beekman's breath. I recalled the sounds of Sydney's scream and the two puffs of warm air, heavy with exertion, that burst from Beekman's mouth. But most of all, I remembered the two deep-cut lines between his brows, the creased, angry curl of his lips, and the anger in his gaze as his focus—his rage aimed at Sydney.

My wife.

I clasped her face and deepened the kiss, my tongue testing hers before delving into the corners of her hot mouth—the spots I'd found that turned her on. Her body was like an undiscovered world—uncharted and unmarked and left completely for me to explore. Like everything else I encountered, I craved to learn all of it—to know all of it. But there was something different—something powerful to learn, something that no one else knew.

Like discovering a chemical reaction no one had witnessed before.

It was… humbling.

That was why I couldn't get enough of her—because she

humbled me. Because being with her made me feel like I had so much to learn—so much more to grow. To experience. *Being with her made me feel like I had so much more to live.*

Her arms twined around my neck as the kiss deepened. Maybe we were careful of my nose. Maybe the way I wanted her blocked out the pain. All that was certain was that one minute we were in the bathroom, and the next, we were sinking onto the bed, the trail of her jacket, shirt, and then bra, the only indication that we'd walked and not teleported from one spot to the other.

"Ranger." She moaned when I cupped her breast, my lips finding the spot right behind her earlobe that drove her wild.

"God, I love your breasts," I groaned into her neck, kneading the full flesh until she bowed into my grasp.

"Please."

My teeth locked together, feeling the sensitive bud of her nipple roll and then pinch between my fingers. Conversation became a dialogue of touches and gasps, strokes and shudders. My cock strained painfully against my pants, feeling the heat of her through the layers of clothing.

I knew how wet she would be, I could practically taste it. I wanted to taste it. I wanted to drown in pleasuring her. I had to, or I would lose it. My dick was so hard it was ready to burst, and that was what happened every time I touched her. That was why I always started with her—*finished her first*—because as soon as she touched me, it was over.

She made me lose my mind. Not figuratively. Literally. My mind was always with me, an ever-present shadow cast over life. But with Sydney... she cleared the shadow and doused everything in a warm, blinding feeling. And I just wanted to stay there in that warmth for as long as I could.

My lips started to drag down her neck when her hand skated between us and pressed to my cock.

"Sydney." I hissed, unable to stop myself from grinding into her palm. "Let me taste you."

The alternative was a reaction I couldn't predict. One I was afraid was powerful enough to destroy reality to the point where I might believe this was never fake at all.

And that was dangerous.

"I want more." Her hold on my groin tightened, my cock swelling for her, and I gasped for air, dark pleasure eating at the fringes of my vision.

Focus, Ranger. Use your brain.

"The genitals only account for ten percent of the body's erogenous zones," I rambled as she stroked my cock. "Your entire body is capable of arousal and pleasure beyond the simple mechanics of sex." To make my point, I gently tweaked her nipple, making her arch and gasp.

Two days ago, I'd made her come just from teasing the sensitive buds.

"Are you fact fucking me again?" she moaned.

I kissed along her jawline until I reached her mouth. "I thought you liked that." *I knew she did.*

"And if I want you to really fuck me?"

I sucked in a breath. "Sydney..." I drew back. "Should we?" My voice croaked. "I mean, we're married, but we don't have to—I don't want you to think we have to—" I huffed, trying to pick up my thoughts like they were jacks spilled on the floor, but every time I grabbed some, she rubbed my dick, and I dropped them all over again.

"Ranger." Her finger pressed to my lips and stopped me, allowing her eyes to find mine. "Do you want to have sex?"

God, yes. There were some moments where it was the only thing I wanted—more than air, more than breath. There were some moments when I wanted to have sex with her more than I wanted to live, but even then, I didn't want sex more than I wanted to make sure she didn't end up hurt or regretful in the end.

Because there was an end. An expiration. There was the reality that Wisdom wasn't her home, and at some point, she was going to leave.

But then why couldn't I answer her? My mouth opened, but nothing came out.

I wasn't nervous. *Was I nervous?* I knew I could pleasure her. I'd spent the week doing just that. Even if I sucked at sex, I'd make sure to give her enough orgasms that she wouldn't remember.

My chin lowered slightly, breaking her gaze as a lock of hair slid free onto my forehead.

"I want you," she murmured, spearing her fingers through my hair and pushing it back, tipping my head to find my eyes once more.

My jaw clenched.

I was trying to protect her, but I was also protecting myself, protecting the part that cared about her and would only care about her more if we had sex. The part that didn't want to end up hurt or regretful either.

"Don't you think it will make things complicated?" I rasped.

"Do you?" she countered, releasing her hold on my cock and moving her hand to cup my cheek.

Before this—before her—I never would've considered this question. Sex was an act of nature. It was mating. Every other species on the planet managed to engage in it without making it out to be more.

"I've never had sex before." I swallowed. "So probably."

The corner of her mouth twitched, and then her tongue slid over her lips. "This is already complicated, Ranger." Her thumb traced gently over my injured flesh, highlighting the truth of her words. "But I want to be complicated with you."

The primal part of my brain that had a direct line down to my cock exploded with want—with a feral kind of need not to take but to know. To know what it was like to be with her. To know what it felt like to have my body buried in the depths of hers. To know the most intimate part of her body with the most animalistic part of mine. A kind of erotic intellect.

I lifted my head and claimed her mouth.

I didn't want her to ask again if I wanted to have sex. I never wanted her to question how much I wanted her ever again. She was everything I'd ever wanted.

Sydney whimpered, the sweetest sound as it landed on the sweep of my tongue.

There were so many uncertainties right now—so many questions, but this kiss was the only answer.

My free hand roamed over her body, drowning her senses and my own. I couldn't think. The imprints of her books in my memory—instructions I'd relied on—faded. I was thoughtless. Powerless. Consumed.

Her fingers worked at my belt and then the waist of my jeans, but I pulled back so quickly I lost my balance and crashed back on my ass.

"If you touch me, I'm going to come," I told her bluntly.

There were probably more eloquent words, but I couldn't find them.

Slowly, I rose up on my knees and returned to the edge of the bed, my gaze never leaving hers. My hands went to the waist of her leggings, stripping them along with her underwear and leaving her in nothing but her socks.

"Socks?"

"They stay." I swallowed hard, my voice hoarse as I continued, "Cold feet can affect your ability to fully relax and thereby affect your ability to orgasm."

She smiled and pressed her sock-clad foot to my thigh, sliding it toward my groin until I stopped her, grabbing her ankle.

"Take your pants off."

I stood, my gaze holding to hers until she let her legs drift apart, baring her pussy. I groaned and grabbed for the waist of my boxer briefs, yanking the fabric off my dick like it was plastic over my mouth, suffocating me.

My teeth ground together, watching the way she watched me

strip, the hunger in her eyes when my cock bobbed heavily in front of me, a bead of moisture dripping from the tip.

I straightened and gripped my dick, the red tip bulging from my fist, but I couldn't let go. Just the way she was looking at me, dragging her tongue over her lips, made me want to come. My cock pulsed into my fist.

It was nothing more than blood rushing into the arteries in my shaft, the veins closing, pressure building. But god, it felt like a noose around my neck, needing release on pain of death.

Precum leaked onto my fingers, and I choked out. "I don't have a condom."

It was more than that; I didn't own them. Never had purchased them. *Because I never did this.*

"I'm on birth control."

I swallowed and nodded. *Bare.* And it was more than my dick—it was all of me that was unprotected when it came to Sydney. But still, I was drawn to her. Drawn to danger like a moth to a flame.

Still holding my cock, I knelt—crashed really, hardly feeling the hard floor as it collided with my knees. My free hand grabbed her thigh, sliding along the silken skin to the core of her.

"Ranger—" She inhaled sharply as I squeezed her clit and then released.

"I'm not going to last long," I said through tight teeth, sliding two fingers through the seam of her puffy folds. As soon as they hit her entrance, I pushed them inside, searching for her pleasure—and my confidence.

I was ready to come at just the thought of being inside her—of having sex with her. I felt... dumb. Naive. Like I was a decade younger than I was. *Like I'd been waiting for this moment for an entire lifetime.*

She grabbed at the covers, fisting them as my fingers curled in that "come hither" motion right into her G-spot.

"That's it," I praised as her desire drenched my fingers.

"God, Ranger." Her head thrashed as I stroked my fingers again. "How... How are you so good?"

Because I paid attention. Because I forgot the whole of myself in order to memorize every nuance of her.

And it wasn't hard. The way she moaned. The way she trembled. The way her breath caught and her hips lifted. She was so responsive, telling me a thousand different ways what felt good.

I stroked my fingers again, another warm rush leaking onto my palm. I couldn't not taste her. I needed to taste her. I needed her right there, on the brink of orgasm, just like I was.

I covered her clit with my lips, her cry piercing the room. Instantly, one hand was in my hair, her legs tight on my shoulders. I sucked and lapped until her inner muscles rippled along my fingers.

"Yes, Ranger. Yes, *yes*—" she gasped as I pulled away, my lips covered with her juices.

"I needed you there." Her breath released and she watched me rise. "Because I can't think."

It was the truth. My mind was blank. There was only my cock in my hand, throbbing to be inside her.

"That's because the urge to ejaculate comes from your spine, not your brain," she murmured as I rose over her.

My eyes whipped to hers, and I blinked in a daze. "Are you... fact fucking me?"

Her small smile made my chest tighten. "Turnabout is fair play."

Oxygen knotted in my lungs as her legs drifted apart, her sex spread before me.

I reached for the nightstand, grabbing her vibrator from the bag in the drawer. Her eyes widened. I wasn't taking any chances. My grip on my cock was the pin in the grenade. As soon as I let it go, there'd be no way to stop the explosion that would follow, and I was going to make damn sure she broke with me.

Dropping the toy onto the mattress beside her, I lined my cock up to her entrance, a low hiss of steam leaving my mouth when my tip brushed her slick slit.

"Please, Ranger," Sydney murmured, wiggling her hips. "I need you."

A deep groan spilled from my chest as I pressed into her heat.

"Oh god…" I choked as her body clutched me—squeezed me—the strangle on my cock as tight as a noose on my neck.

"You're so big, Ranger," she breathed. "You feel so good."

I wished I could say I went slow so she could adjust, but it was all because of me. It was all so I could adjust to the hot clutch of her pussy gripping my shaft. There was no describing how good it felt or how hard it made me.

"This is… I can't…" My head dropped, my forehead resting on her shoulder.

I was losing my mind. Or maybe I'd already lost it. No wonder people thought about sex so much. No wonder they craved it like a drug. Now I understood. She felt so amazing. Perfect. Indescribable.

My wife.

Her hands slid to my shoulders and then along my back, stroking. Encouraging. A sheen of sweat broke out on my skin as I pushed deeper, unable to stop even if I tried.

Propping one hand on the bed, I grabbed for her knee, pushing it back so I could sink all the way in.

"More, Ranger." She fisted her hand in my hair and tipped my head back, forcing my eyes to her. "More," she repeated and then squirmed, the sensation making my cock swell so thick I swore I could split her.

"Fuck, Sydney." My whole body tightened. "Don't… Don't do that. I'm so close to coming."

"Me too," she moaned and then slid her leg around my waist, drawing me that final inch inside her where my cock bottomed out against her womb. "Please, Ranger. Please fuck me."

"Oh god…" My jaw locked and my hips began to move.

It wasn't something I could learn or prepare for. The way I moved was instinctual—a primal retreat and thrust of my cock through her tight heat. One thrust and I felt my release grip my spine.

But I couldn't stop.

I drove into her again and again. Harder and harder. My release spiraling

I recognized her breathless gasps, each one telling me she was getting closer to what we both needed. But I couldn't risk it—not when every thrust through the hot clutch of her muscles threatened to end me.

I fumbled for her vibrator, dark pleasure eating away at the corners of my vision. The toy woke with a low hum, and I shoved it between us.

"Ranger!" As soon as the vibration hit her clit, her body clamped around me, and I saw stars.

She clung to me, her hand clawing at my back as I pinned the toy mercilessly to her clit as I fucked her.

"Yes. Oh god. Yes." Her cries turned frantic. Her nails dug deeper into my back. And I felt the walls of her pussy lock tighter and tighter around me.

I couldn't think. Couldn't see straight. Not when she clenched like this around me. My hips slammed forward, and Sydney screamed as she came. It was the most beautiful sound I'd ever heard, and it destroyed me.

"*Fuck.*" I drove into her, burying my swollen, aching length as the pressure in my spine finally released. I shouted as I came, my hips jerking as my cock pumped into her.

"Wow," Sydney murmured a few minutes later after we'd both floated down from the high.

"Yeah," I croaked, happy to be at a loss of words with this as the cause.

I pressed my lips to her shoulder, savoring the way she shivered.

"You didn't need the vibrator," she murmured, her fingers toying with a strand of my hair.

My head tipped up, finding her eyes. "I wanted to make sure,"

I rasped, my voice finding a new tenor it had never reached before. "The average female orgasm lasts twenty seconds while a male's only lasts about seven… I needed my seven to be in your twenty."

She moaned and pulled my face to hers, our mouths colliding in a fervor that made it clear once wasn't enough to put out the flame. *Not even close.*

"Is your nose okay?" she murmured.

"It's perfect." Honestly, I couldn't even feel it. I couldn't feel anything except what was left of my orgasm ravaging my body and the urge to fuck her again.

I drew my lips down her neck and then over her breasts. I slid out of her so my mouth could travel lower, my cock making a mess I'd worry about later. When I reached the edge of the bed, I sank to my knees rather than standing straight.

"What are you doing?" Sydney pushed up on her elbows, eyes widening.

"We're going to do that again," I declared matter-of-factly, meeting her gaze as I pushed two fingers back inside her quivering muscles, massaging them with her cum and mine. "But until I'm capable"—I glanced down at my heavy, hanging cock that was already pulsing back to life—"we're going to see how many orgasms I can give you in the next twenty minutes."

"Twenty minutes?" Her eyes bulged, her hips jerking when I brushed over her G-spot.

"The average refractory period for a man." I thumbed her clit and stroked her inner wall again.

"Oh god." She fell back on the bed and shuddered. "Twenty minutes…" She whimpered. "I won't survive twenty minutes."

My lips curled. "Good thing I'm usually above average."

CHAPTER 21

Ranger

"I'm coming with you." Sydney stood in front of the bed, dressed in jeans and determination.

God, she was beautiful.

My cock stirred like we hadn't had sex four times between last night and this morning. Twice before falling asleep. Once in the middle of the night, when I came back to bed after icing my nose for twenty minutes. And then once more this morning when I woke up with her ass cradling my dick. It was too soon to call it an addiction, but I couldn't stop wanting her.

Her hair was draped in a long braid over her shoulder. She had on a T-shirt and a familiar flannel button-down left undone—

"Is that my shirt?" My head tipped to the side.

"Do you mind?" She wrapped her arms over her.

"Never." My throat bobbed.

She looked just as good in my shirt as she felt a part of my life. And if that wasn't a complication to worry about, I didn't know what was.

Meanwhile, my face looked the part of a punching bag this morning. My nose had swelled and discolored, the bruise spreading to my cheek and the lower portion of my orbital rim, but that wasn't going to stop me. Not from getting answers.

"I don't think his lawyer is there yet, but I want to be waiting when he is," I told her, returning my attention to the buttons on my vest. When I looked up again, she was in front of me.

"How's your nose?" Her fingertips touched my cheek and my breath released in a low stream.

I couldn't care less about my nose when she was touching me. "It's alright." I firmed my lips for a second. "How are you?"

"I'm good." Her eyes dropped to my mouth with a look that made my cock start to harden.

We made it to the police station without incident. The small building was steeped in the scent of freshly brewed coffee and stale cologne. Inside, there were two desks in the main room, a small table for coffee and a mini-fridge along the side wall, and a holding cell and conference room in the back.

"That looks like it hurts," Chief Diehl remarked after greeting us. "You sure you don't want to let Archer handle this?"

I stiffened, but only Sydney noticed. "It's only a minor fracture of the nasal bone and cartilage. Thankfully, it left my mental capacity intact."

The chief winced and his expression changed. "Sorry, Ranger. Still hard to picture you as anything other than the little boy I knew when your dad held this job."

In his defense, he wasn't the only one.

"Can I get you some coffee?" He led us over to his desk, the station not big enough for the chief to have his own office.

"No, thank you," Sydney replied, and I shook my head.

"Okay, well you can wait here. I'll bring Beekman to the conference room to wait for his lawyer."

I pushed up from the chair. "Can I talk to him?"

Chief Diehl sighed. "You know I can't let you—"

"But I'm not a lawyer or the police. I'm the man he assaulted"—I swallowed and steeled my spine—"and I'm prepared to not press charges for this or my car if he's willing to tell me the truth."

It was physically impossible for the chief's eyes to go any wider, but it was Sydney who spoke first.

"Ranger, you can't do that." She reached for my hand and squeezed.

This was why I hesitated when she said she wanted to come with me, but it was the best solution. *And I'd gone through the calculations for all of them.*

"I can, and I want to—I have to."

I needed to know why he was here—what he meant when he said he wasn't getting paid enough for this. And I was prepared to waive my shot at justice if it meant getting those answers for Sydney.

"Son, I don't think—"

"I'm not asking you to think, Chief Diehl. I'm asking you to tell Mr. Beekman that he can walk out of this precinct this morning with his reputation intact if he'll simply have an honest conversation with me," I said firmly, holding my ground.

I was sure I'd sounded rude, but it wasn't my intent. I simply needed him to understand that this was my decision to make. Not his. Not my brothers. Mine. And my mind was made up.

"Alright," he acquiesced with a sigh. "Give me a minute to talk to him, and I'll be right back."

He wasn't gone from the room for a second before Sydney rose and claimed my attention.

"Ranger, you don't have to do this," she insisted. "He's going to have to talk anyway. He obviously attacked you, which only makes him look that much guiltier for tampering with your brakes. There's no reason for you to give up your right to justice."

"If I don't, it could be days—weeks before we get any answers, and I'm not willing to wait that long. I want you to have answers. I want you to have your life back."

Her breath caught.

Her response made it seem like I'd said something wrong, but for the life of me, I couldn't figure out what. I was doing this for her—because I'd promised to protect her, even at my own expense.

But before I could ask what was wrong, Chief Diehl's voice rang through the silence, "He's ready to talk."

"You're really not going to press charges?" Beekman looked at me suspiciously from across the table, his posture aloof, his handcuffed hands resting in his lap.

He looked worse for the wear. Red-rimmed, bloodshot eyes. Hair matted to one side like he'd slept with his head against a wall. Shirt wrinkled and stained. I had a feeling some of those brown marks were blood from my nose.

But I wasn't one to talk with my nose swollen and purple.

For Wisdom PD, their conference room also doubled as their interrogation room. It was nothing like what you'd see on TV. No cameras. No two-way mirror. Just a bare table, three chairs, faded wallpaper, and a small shelf in the corner that had a tripod sitting on top of it where a camera *could* attach if necessary.

"I'm not a liar, Mr. Beekman." I firmed my lips and stared at him. "Last night, you gave me the impression that there was more to this situation than I thought, so either you're here to take advantage of my desire for answers, or we can wait for your lawyer to arrive."

The other man remained unmoving in his chair, still uncertain.

Fine.

I sat forward and rested my hands on the table. "Have you seen the show *Suits*?"

The subject change jarred him.

"Of course," he scoffed. "How else was I going to write something on Meghan Markle when she married Prince Harry?"

"Great, then it will suffice for me to say that my brain works similarly to Mr. Ross's." The college dropout never went to law school but successfully pretended to be a lawyer because he had a photographic memory.

Beekman raised his eyebrows. "Similar?"

"Similar because Mike Ross has a photographic memory. I have three PhDs, an eidetic memory, and an IQ of one-eighty-five. So, I guess you could say I'm like Mike Ross on steroids, and I will have no problem advocating for myself in court." I pointed to my nose. "This is second-degree aggravated assault. The felony charge of causing serious bodily injury without a deadly weapon can result in up to a ten-year prison sentence and a fine of up to five thousand dollars."

The red orbs of his eyes widened.

"But first-degree attempted murder? That is a life sentence without parole—"

"Now wait, I said I never—" he tried to interject, but I spoke over him.

"Considering this attack happened immediately after you were caught on video and questioned about tampering with my brakes, the statistical probability of convincing a jury that you didn't mean to hurt me the first time but did mean to hurt me the second is somewhere between five and seven percent—"

"Alright," he shouted, his hands and the cuffs banging on the table in frustration. "Christ, I'll tell you the truth."

"Smart decision." I smiled. "Now, what did you mean when you said you weren't paid enough for this? Do you mean for the story?"

Beekman sat forward, his mouth downturned like a man who had been beaten.

"First things first," he declared and drilled his finger onto the top of the table. "I didn't cut your damn brakes."

"Okay," I accepted it as fact. I'd promised not to press charges, so what reason would he have to continue to lie? "Now answer my question."

"No, I didn't mean for the story. I mean, yes, I was getting paid for the story, but that's not why I'm here." He sagged back in the chair again, shaking his head. "I wasn't hired to write a story. I was hired to create one. Paid to create bad press and keep the media focused on Sydney Ward."

I hoped my face didn't betray my shock, but I hadn't seen that answer coming. Not in the slightest.

"By whom?" My stomach felt tight, like my insides were being twisted and turned into lead knots.

He took a deep inhale. "Vince Bauer."

The tightness in my gut erupted into flame.

If I hadn't shocked Chief Diehl by showing up without my brothers and then waiving my right to prosecute Beekman for assaulting me, I definitely shocked him when I stormed out of the interrogation room fifteen minutes after entering it, grabbed Sydney's hand, and pulled her out to the car.

"Ranger," she gasped. "What's going on?"

I shuffled her into the car, holding my rage by a tight leash until I'd pulled out from the police parking lot.

"What did he say?"

I stared at my hands on the wheel. I always drove with two hands. *Ten and two.* It was the safest way to drive, and I always did what was safest.

Until now.

Until now, when the most dangerous thing I could do was not hold on to her.

I peeled my right hand from the wheel, using my left to steer as I took her hand in mine. Her fingers were cold, so I squeezed them tight.

"Beekman didn't come out here just to write a story on you. He said he was paid to come here and create bad press—to keep feeding the negative media frenzy around you. To do whatever it took to continue destroying your reputation. Make up stories. Fudge facts. Create drama. It was because of him that everyone knew where you were."

Her stricken look hurt worse than my broken nose.

"What? Why?" Her eyes glazed. "Who hired him?"

"Vince hired him, Sydney," I said hoarsely. "Beekman swore he was hired to do whatever it took—write whatever it took to ruin the rest of your career."

CHAPTER 22

Sydney

"Can we just keep driving?" I murmured when I heard the blinker start to click.

I didn't want to go back to the apartment. I didn't want to stop moving. As soon as I stopped moving, it felt like the last shambles of my life would finally crumble down on top of me.

"Whatever you need."

Ranger continued to hold my hand as he drove past the turn-off to Main Street that would take us back to the apartment, instead continuing straight on the road as it headed out of Wisdom.

Vince.

I hated the tears that pricked in the corners of my eyes. Once again, my ex-fiancé made me feel like a fool—like a puppet in my own life. I watched the mountains move by the window, the peaks and valleys tracing the very heartbeat of the land.

"Sydney—"

I sniffled and wiped my cheeks and then my nose. "Tell me what he said."

"He claimed he was hired to come out here and 'fan the flames'—his words—of your last interview. To draw out more reporters and paparazzi."

My head moved in slow motion. That sounded like Vince. Bitter. Spiteful. Vindictive. He always wanted to be the center of attention, and he couldn't believe it when I walked away from our engagement because he'd been unfaithful. I couldn't believe how I could've missed all the signs and fallen for someone who was so narcissistic and untrustworthy.

"I can't believe he would do this. I mean, I can, but..." I pressed my hand to my forehead and sagged into the seat. "So, this whole time... all of this was because of him."

"According to Beekman."

The car slowed and Ranger turned off into the parking lot of an auto shop. *ALT Automotive.*

"This is Decker's garage," he said and started to spin the wheel. "I'm just turning around."

I nodded, watching the scenery spin.

"Did he confess to cutting the brakes then, too?"

"He insists he didn't." Ranger drove us back toward Wisdom. "Said he saw someone crouching underneath it and thought they were planting a tracking device."

"Tracking device?" I almost choked. *Seriously?* And to think there were still readers out there who refused to believe that reality was stranger than fiction.

"Apparently, Vince was enraged over the whole... married story. I guess it was another reporter who took that photo of us in the street and broke the narrative. Beekman promised he was going to fix it—spin it into a negative rather than a happy ending."

"But he couldn't prove that our marriage was fake," I murmured, sliding a glance across the console.

My husband. At least that part of our plan—making sure the marriage was legitimate—was now justified.

"Vince told Beekman there was no way you were married and that he had to find proof that the marriage was faked, that it was all a show to save your reputation," Ranger continued, driving slowly back through Wisdom. "Beekman said when he couldn't prove it,

Vince was furious, so when he saw someone by my car, he thought Vince had hired someone else to do the job. He thought he wasn't going to get paid, and then when the police brought him in for questioning…"

"He panicked."

"Yeah."

I pulled my lip between my teeth just as the building faded into our rearview. Out the window, my eyes traveled over the bike path that was now covered in snow. To think I'd been riding along it not that long ago. Now, the trail was nowhere to be found.

Just like my life.

A few weeks ago, it had been this clear, outlined path. And then I'd come out here and that path was covered—piled over in something I couldn't change or stop. It was still there, but only if I wanted to dig through everything to find it.

My head tipped and I looked at Ranger.

I wasn't sure how much I wanted to dig anymore.

Ranger turned, and I looked just in time to see that he was taking us back to Reynolds Protective.

The drive had been cleared, but again, the landscape looked so different, covered in white. Strange how something could seem so different yet familiar at the same time.

"You don't have to go in," he said, parking the car out front. "But I have to talk to my brothers."

I nodded slowly, still trying to process all of this.

"Is this… all because of the book?" Ranger asked hesitantly.

My throat tightened. I'd expected backlash from readers that I'd killed Vince's fictional counterpart, but from Vince himself? He'd never even read the books. Of course, there were scores of readers who hated him for what he did to me, but since when did he care about them? Plus, I'd ended the engagement months ago. Why retaliate now?

"I don't know," I confessed. "But I know who might."

I fished my phone from my pocket, opened it and searched for Gina's number. She picked up after the second ring.

"Hey, Syd. How are you? How's everything with Mr. Fine—"

"You're on speakerphone," I blurted out quickly, not that I really cared if Ranger heard her now; I was pretty sure that my wearing his shirt this morning cemented just how far and how fast I'd fallen for my fake husband.

"Oh, wonderful. Hi, Ranger."

I loved the hint of color that had already risen to his cheeks.

"Hello, Gina."

"Gina." I brought the phone directly in front of me. "What have you heard about Vince recently? Not the stuff about him bashing me, but about his actual life."

"Why?"

My mouth opened, but nothing came out.

"We have good reason to believe Vince is behind what's been happening with the press and the threats out here," Ranger said with his characteristic quiet firmness.

"That motherfucking piece of shit. I'm going to kill him. Screw killing his character. I'm going to wring his pathetic, narcissistic neck—"

"Gina—"

"Right, sorry." She let out a sound of frustration and then spoke. "Yeah, I heard some things recently, and then I sort of… well…"

The fog of the morning cleared in a second. "Gina, what did you do?"

She sighed. "You know that gig Vince told you about right before you ended things?"

"Yeah, the TV show or something."

"Yeah, well, right before your book was released, I caught wind through a friend of a friend that Vince had actually landed the male lead in an upcoming Netflix series based on a popular fantasy book series. All the bells and whistles. He wasn't lying; it was going to be big for his career."

My throat tightened. "Was?"

"Your book came out, and you started getting all this backlash like no one remembered what he'd done to you," she went on. "Anyway, I was watching TV while making dinner one night, and of course, it just so happened that they were interviewing the director of this upcoming series, and I realized I knew her."

"Gina..." A pit opened up in my stomach.

"You know fantasy isn't my preference, and especially with Vince involved, I didn't even look into the series because I knew I wasn't going to watch it. But then, when I realized the director was in my sorority in college—that I knew her. I couldn't just let it go."

My heart pounded louder.

"So, I contacted her and the original author of the books—also a female—just to make them aware of the character they were casting."

"Oh god." I groaned and covered my mouth with my hand, feeling sick.

My hand shook, and Ranger grabbed my phone before it fell.

"Syd, this is how the industry works. When you mess up, your career pays for it. Just look at what happened to Johnny Depp and Amber Heard. Or even Liam Hemsworth after 'Flowers,'" she protested. "I didn't tell them they couldn't work with him. I just made them aware of the press and backlash they might face by casting a serial cheater as the face of their hero."

"So, they didn't," I choked out.

Her silence was all the confirmation I needed.

"About a week before your interview, I saw an article that the show was going in a different direction for casting the male lead, and later that day, the director emailed me and thanked me."

That was it. A hot tear traveled down my cheek, but not for Vince. He didn't deserve to be a hero in anyone's story... but neither did I deserve to become the villain.

"Syd, I'm so sorry. I just... I couldn't do nothing," Gina said, her voice shaking.

I didn't even know what to say. I appreciated her loyalty and compassion. I appreciated her desire to protect me—to get justice for me. But I wished I could've told her it wasn't worth it—that he wasn't worth the trouble.

"I know."

"Are you sure... how do you know it was him?"

I swiped the tears from my cheeks, but suddenly all of the emotions gnawing at my insides all morning started to unleash.

"A paparazzo attacked us last night outside the apartment—" Ranger spoke up when he realized I couldn't.

"Oh my god, are you okay?"

"We're both fine," he assured her. "But he confessed that Vince hired him to come out here and fabricate negative press about Sydney."

It was all coming together. Why all those reporters and paparazzi had appeared out of nowhere. Why they stayed in spite of the weather and the holidays. It wasn't just for a good story—it was because they were being paid to ruin my life.

"Did he send the note? Was he responsible for everything?" She gasped. "What about all those emails from the bogus accounts you couldn't trace? I bet you he hired some bot farm to fabricate them."

Ranger cleared his throat. "He claims he wasn't responsible for the note, but he said Vince's instructions were clear to do whatever it took to ruin Sydney, and he's pretty confident that he wasn't the only one Vince hired for this job."

"So, someone cut your brakes because they wanted a good, *bad* story? Or was the bad press not enough, so he decided that ruin meant kill—"

"We're going to handle Vince," Ranger broke in, but her thought already took hold.

Was that where this was at? He couldn't do enough to tank my career, so he was going to have someone kill me?

Gina huffed, "I hate him. I'm sorry, Syd, but I do, and I don't regret speaking out about his character, but I regret not realizing just how shitty and sleazy he was and just how far the depths of his vindictiveness would go."

"I know," I murmured.

From there, Ranger told her we would keep her updated and brought the conversation to a close.

"I should probably call my lawyer—" I broke off with a gasp "What is it?"

"That's how he found me," I realized. This whole time, every piece fit except how he'd known I'd come to Wyoming.

"Through your lawyer?"

"Yes—but no." I grimaced. "As soon as I left New York, Vince started talking to the press every chance he had. When Gina told me about it, I contacted Don—my lawyer, to send a letter warning him to stop defaming me. Don asked for my address here in case he needed to send me anything while I was away."

"You need a new lawyer," Ranger growled, sounding like Don was going to be next on the chopping block.

"No." I shook my head. "Vince probably flirted with Don's assistant for the information after he got the letter; she was always hitting on him whenever he came with me to review book contracts."

"Sydney…"

"We should go in," I declared and reached for the door handle. If I stayed in the car any longer, I was going to fall apart.

This time, he held my hand as we walked inside the building. We followed the same path up the stairs but went directly to Archer's office rather than the conference room.

The second time through, the conversation went quicker than the first. Ranger recounted the details he'd learned from Beekman, though I couldn't tell what surprised Archer more: the truth or that Ranger had gone without him this morning. And then he conveyed what we'd learned from Gina regarding his motive.

"So, you think it was one of the other paparazzi who cut your brakes?"

"Beekman is confident that Vince hired others for the

job—confident that he probably hired them to do more to ruin Sydney." I could hear the hard pull of anger in Ranger's voice. "He wanted Sydney to be afraid. Alone and afraid and vulnerable."

Except I hadn't been because I'd had him.

"Wouldn't be the first time the paparazzi were responsible for a dangerous accident," Archer grumbled.

Now that we knew what was happening—and why—the next steps were pretty straightforward. Archer was going to pay a visit to the rest of the paparazzi this afternoon, informing them that anyone who stayed would be subject to harassment charges. Meanwhile, Ranger and I were going to call Don and have him draft a cease and desist letter to be sent to Vince, revealing that we knew what he'd done, and if he didn't leave me alone, not only would I press charges, but we would release Beekman's statement to the press and ensure that he'd never get another job in the entertainment industry.

As large as the dangers and stressors surrounding me had been, that quickly did they all seem to crumble.

When we were finished, Archer walked us to the door, his kind smile comforting right up until he added, "I'm glad we have some answers—some closure on this because I bet you're ready to go home."

My own smile faltered. *Home.*

"Thank you," was all I could manage. I couldn't even look at Ranger, afraid of what I'd see.

The danger was gone. The situation that had kept me here was over.

And the only thing left was a marriage that was supposed to be anything but real.

"Can we stop for coffee?"

Archer suggested steering clear of the apartment until he and

Chief Diehl were done speaking with the rest of the paparazzi, but that wasn't why I didn't want to go back.

Going back meant accepting that everything I felt… everything Ranger and I had built together over the last two months had to come to an end. Going back meant facing all of the things—all of the touches and the looks and the moments—that made me fall for my fake husband. And out of all the lies I'd fallen for in my life, believing I knew better than to fall in love with Ranger was the biggest of them all.

It was the arrangement—the agreement. Yes, technically, we'd said that the marriage would stay in place until we were certain the threat was gone and the stories died down… but that was only a matter of time now.

"Sure."

We crossed back into town, and it was only another two blocks before Ranger pulled into a spot in front of the Worth Hotel. Brilliant Brews was at the other end of the block.

My boots crunched into the snow just outside the door. As soon as I shut it, Ranger was there, offering me his elbow to hold on to, and I couldn't hold back my small smile.

What kind of man offered a woman his elbow anymore? Or a handkerchief?

My husband.

We walked in silence to the coffee shop, and I wondered if I wasn't the only one mourning the end of the life we'd been living. No, that was foolish. This was Ranger's idea from the start—his plan. And if anyone could keep emotions out of a situation, it was him. Sure, desire had snuck through the cracks, but he was the one who'd worried about complications.

He was the one concerned about this becoming more than what it was.

I balled my hand into a fist, my nails digging into my palm while I fought back tears. Once again, I felt like an idiot—a romance author so deep in her own head that I believed my own fairy tale.

Ranger held the door, and I took the opportunity to wipe the icy tear that snuck onto my cheek. The bell dinged, and every eye in the place turned to us, but the only thing I felt was the warm slide of his fingers as they laced with mine.

My breath caught, hope latching like a burr inside my chest.

"Ranger!" The barista at the espresso machine squealed. "Congratulations!"

The word twisted the knife already staked to my heart, but I didn't have time to think about it before the place descended around us. The baristas. Trish and Lydia were also here. And the few other faces I didn't recognize, but the way they looked at me and murmured made it clear they realized I was Wisdom's resident celebrity.

Good or bad, Ranger's broken nose took up most of the conversations. He chalked it up to a fall which wasn't the whole truth though neither was it a lie.

I remembered Jess from the grocery store, and she introduced me to her business partner, Tara. They heaped free pastries onto a plate for us, including some of their famous vanilla chai muffins, and whipped up my usual latte even though I hadn't been in for one in weeks.

"Look at you two." Trish's wide smile was the next to greet us right before she pulled me in for a hug. Behind her was Lydia, who took a good look at Ranger's nose before shaking her head and pulling him in for a big hug.

We didn't see her last night, but Archer had brought her up to speed on what happened after we'd gone up to the apartment.

As soon as she let Ranger go, her warm arms and welcoming smile came for me. "Sydney." *The only other person who knew our marriage was really real.*

"Oh, Ranger. Jerry wanted me to ask you a couple of things about your apartment." Trish linked her arm with Ranger's and pulled him to the side, leaving Lydia and me alone for a moment.

"Everything okay?" Ranger's mom asked.

My head bobbed quickly. "Yeah."

What else could I say? We'd figured out why this was all happening and who was the culprit. *How could everything be anything but okay?*

"You might be a good storyteller, Sydney, but you're a poor liar. Just like my son." Her gaze slid lovingly to her second-youngest child.

"We figured out why all of this happened and who was behind it," I told her.

Her eyes widened as she looked at me. "Well, that's wonderful news."

I nodded. "The paparazzi should be gone within the hour."

I folded my arms, trying to hold my emotions back from her penetrating stare. Instead, I only managed to draw her attention to the fact that I was wearing her son's shirt.

"You don't want to leave," she declared with a triumphant smile.

My jaw slackened for a second before I clamped it shut and said, "Once they're gone, it'll be safe for me to go home."

She didn't respond right away, and I knew it was because I hadn't really addressed her claim. *How could I when she was right?*

I stared at Ranger, watching him the way I had when I first came out here. Absorbing every nuance of his expressions. The shy warmth of his smile, those dimples pinned at either end. The slight dip of his head. Giving Trish all of his attention.

Or most of it. His eyes flicked to mine.

"You know you don't have to go, Sydney," Lydia said quietly, placing her hand on my shoulder. "You can stay."

Could I?

"That wasn't the plan," I clung to the facts because that was what Ranger would do.

"My son tries to be what everyone wants him to be before he thinks about what he wants for himself. The perfect storm of being so smart and so caring; he knows what everyone needs from him and he can't stop himself from giving it."

My head lowered. It was one of the first things I'd noticed about him—how he went out of his way to be what everyone else needed.

It wasn't a bad thing. It made him a loving son, a caring brother, a loyal friend. *A dedicated fake husband.* But it also left him with little room to shape himself because he didn't want to disappoint someone else.

"If you want him to be okay with you leaving, he will be." Her strained stare found mine. "But I think you and I both know that's not what he really wants."

My breath caught, but before I could respond, Tara called Lydia's name and set her drink down on the bar.

I immediately searched for Ranger, but my view of him was blocked by two women and a man who'd been in the coffee shop when we arrived, though I hadn't met them before.

"Sydney Ward? We're such huge fans." The women immediately introduced themselves as Nina and Jane, a schoolteacher and a nurse from the area. We chatted for just long enough for them to offer their support and congratulations before Jess called out their names at the counter.

"I'm Darren." The man with them stepped forward and extended his hand with a hesitant smile. "I've been a fan—following you since the beginning."

It felt clammy when I shook it, but I'd met plenty of nervous fans before. "Thank you so much."

He took the opportunity to tip his head forward ever so slightly and assure me, "I just want you to know I don't believe—never believed the lies they wrote about you." His sincerity gave me chills.

"Thank you." I smiled quickly and pulled my hand away just as Ranger came to my side.

"Hi, I'm Ranger." He stared frankly at the man.

"Darren." There was no handshake offered with this introduction. Probably for the best since Ranger didn't shake hands.

"Darren Smalls?"

The other man drew back, uncertainty clouding his face. "Do I know you?"

I looked at Ranger. *Did he know this guy?*

Ranger blinked and then smiled. "I read your emails of support to Sydney. You said some very kind things."

Of course, he remembered everything.

Darren huffed. "Well, of course I did. She's incredible."

I brought the travel cup to my lips and took a careful sip of the hot latte.

Ranger met my eyes over the lid and smiled. "I think so, too," he declared. "It's why I married her."

I barely stopped myself from spitting my coffee all over the man in front of me and settled on choking on it instead. Ranger took my cup and scrambled to get me a napkin. By the time the coughing fit subsided, Darren, Nina, and Jane had all left. Lydia and Trish came over and walked with us out of Brilliant Brews.

We hugged goodbye, but before we parted ways, Lydia wagged a finger at the two of us. "Don't forget, Christmas is next Friday. I'll see you both at the house."

She was referring to their make-up Christmas dinner, but still, she expected me to be there—expected me to stay.

For the first time in weeks, there was no one waiting at the end of the driveway to the house. No paparazzi. No cameras. No campout chairs and coolers of food.

There was no one to pretend for.

Ranger pulled up to the garage. I'd miss the way he waited for the door to completely rise before driving inside. I'd miss the way he held the door for me and followed me up the staircase. I'd miss everything I'd come to know about this man.

It was crazy. This was crazy. I should be jumping for joy—relieved that I was safe. That all of this was because of Vince and now it was ending.

"Do you want tacos for dinner?"

Tacos was his way of telling me he knew something was wrong without me having to say it. God, I was really going to miss the little ways he cared for me.

"Sure." One word was all I could manage before I sank onto the couch and buried my face in my hands, the exhaustion and emotion of the day catching up to me.

Tears leaked free, trapped between my palms and my cheeks. *Could I really just tell him I wanted to stay?*

Lydia's words came back to me, but instead of encouraging me, all they managed to do was feed my doubts. If Ranger's singular fault was that he tried too hard to be what everyone wanted—needed him to be—how could I expect this to be any different? If I said I wanted to stay, he'd agree because it was what I wanted. He'd agree, and this would be the complication he'd worried about. He'd agree, and I'd never know if he felt the same.

Plus, it was more than staying. We were married. Officially, legally married. This wasn't, well, let me stay and see where this goes. We were already at the finish line. There was no going back to rerun the race.

"Sydney..." The couch dipped under his weight, and I couldn't help but sag into his warm embrace when it circled me.

I'd miss the way he held me.

"It will just be a couple more days to make sure they're gone and make sure Vince doesn't try anything like this again."

My chest burned with the strength it took to hold back my cries, knowing he was trying to comfort me, but it was only making this worse.

"It's just a few days and then you can go home. I'll sort out everything..." he said softly, pressing his lips to my hair. "A few days, and it'll be over."

A small cry broke from my lips. *It was over.* And that was the straw that broke the camel's back. A strangled sob burst free before tears flooded down my cheeks.

"I'm here. I've got you." His hold tightened, steadying me as I shook.

I bit into my cheek, but it wasn't enough to stop my sobs. They tore from my chest like they were taking the beating organ inside it with them.

"Just let it out." Ranger's fingers traced my back. My arms. "Let it go."

I couldn't hold it back even if I tried. Not when he held me like he did—not when I wasn't sure when he'd hold me again. Tears streamed down my face, my chest heaving with each sob. I cried for everything. I cried for what Vince's betrayal had done to me. I cried for how much Ranger had stepped in to help me—and how much he'd sacrificed to make sure I was safe. I cried for Gina and what she thought she had to do to defend me.

"I'm sorry," I blubbered.

"Don't be sorry." He produced another handkerchief from the pocket of his vest.

"How many of these do you have?" I murmured, my voice watery as I took the cloth from his fingers and pressed it to my face, inhaling deep the soft citrus scent.

"A dozen. Mom got the embroidered ones for me for Christmas three years ago."

I balled the fabric square in my fist, refusing to let it go. Maybe he wouldn't notice if I took one back to New York with me.

Who was I kidding? Of course he would.

I wiped my nose once more, offering weakly, "Well, I'm sure my nose is now about as red and swollen as yours."

"You're beautiful."

My breath caught.

Compliments hit differently when the man giving them made them sound like fact rather than flattery. *Like the sky is blue. The earth is round. And you are beautiful.*

Fact.

I shivered, brought back to the moment by the stroke of his thumb on my cheek.

"What is it?"

The ball in my throat inflated. All the answers were there, crashing against the barrier to tell him that even though this was over, I wasn't ready to leave.

In the end, I chickened out and said nothing.

His thumb brushed back and forth over my skin, each stroke so tender it made my chest ache. He tipped my head up, forcing my gaze to his. "What can I do?"

Our breaths collided. My heart picked up its pace as my gaze drifted down to his mouth, a different kind of ache knotting between my thighs.

"Kiss me," I whispered. And let me pretend for a little while longer.

I drowned in that perfectly clear and cloudless gaze as his hand slid to the back of my neck. Without question or worry, his mouth crushed mine. Our tongues tangled in greedy strokes, desire igniting my body to life. The moan that escaped my lips reminded me that no one ever had or probably ever would learn me the way Ranger had.

The thought made me angry and hungry, so I locked my arms around his neck and held on tight. Our kiss turned frantic and sloppy, tongues dueling and demanding more. If I was living on borrowed time with him, then I was going to dig myself into as deep a debt as possible before leaving.

He groaned and pulled me onto his lap, my knees sinking into the couch on either side of him.

"Sydney." His palms framed my face, pushing my hair back and searching my eyes.

His gaze was tormented—the kind of torment that only a genius felt when he understood everything else in the world except what was hurting me.

"Please, Ranger, don't stop kissing me."

Ever. But I'd settle for tonight.

He pulled my mouth back to his. I tried to be careful of his nose, but it was hard when he didn't pay it any mind as he devoured me.

My clothes came off in swift movements, my gaze never leaving his. When he went to unbutton his vest, I stopped him.

"Leave it," I panted, straddling his lap once more.

I reached for his waist, flipping open his belt and freeing his heavy cock into my hands. Placing my hand on his shoulder, I rose up and dragged the tip along my slit, coating him with my desire.

"Sydney..." he trailed off with a long groan as I impaled myself on him, gasping at the sudden tenderness of muscles that had been well used last night. But as quickly as I felt it, the sensation was gone, replaced by a familiar hunger.

Borrowed time meant there was no time to fool around. No time for fact fucking or foreplay. I just wanted to be consumed.

I sank all the way down, burying him to the root with a gasp. In this position, his cock rubbed along my G-spot at the same time as his happy trail teased my clit. Heat clawed through my body, gnawing so deep I felt it in my bones.

I searched out his mouth, dueling my tongue with his and desperately trying to remember the fact.

No matter how many ways this felt right, it didn't make it real. But, God, did it feel real...

My body moved in rough motions, riding him in search of release.

"Fuck," Ranger choked out and grabbed hold of my hips, pumping me up and down along the length of his cock. His head tipped back, and I could follow the ripple of his jaw muscles all the way down his throat.

And there was nothing that turned me on as much as a genius losing his mind—losing the strongest part of him because of me.

The slick sounds of our bodies coming together echoed in the room, my whimpers detonating each time the tip of his cock jammed into my G-spot. We were sloppy and wild and desperate. And I didn't let up when he ground out my name, trying to slow my movements so he wouldn't come first.

"Don't stop," I begged, sinking my teeth into his bottom lip.

With a deep groan, his hips drove into me. He buried himself against my womb, where I felt the hot rush of his release as he came, his strangled grunts like music to my ears.

How many times had I written the reverse scenario for a hero in one of my books? Countless. How many times had I considered it could be the same for a woman? Few? None? Ranger told me a woman's orgasm had a neurological component; he proved it with all his erotic facts. And now, feeling his body lose control—feeling his desire consume him—I proved it to myself.

I ground up and down on his cock, clawing for the tip of that peak.

"You're incredible." His hoarse words tipped me over the edge, and I cried out as my release swept over me.

My heart slammed against the front of my chest, my hips bucking with violent pleasure as my body wrung him dry.

Our hot breaths crashed and swirled between us, filling the space of long minutes until they were no longer ragged. Then Ranger's arms locked around me and lifted us from the couch.

My legs circled his waist, holding him tight—keeping him inside me as he carried me to the bed. The whole time, I kept my face buried in the crook of his neck.

Distantly, I heard the booming thunder of the storm that had finally reached us. Rain clattered on the window as though even nature tried to shelter us from reality with her storm.

"Don't let go," I murmured, even though he'd already positioned me on top of his chest.

The tips of his fingers brushed along my skin, soothing me until my consciousness finally started to relax and drift off.

"I won't."

I fell asleep pretending like he meant forever.

CHAPTER 23

Ranger

Almost two weeks had passed since we'd learned the truth about Beekman, the paparazzi, and Vince. During that time, word spread quickly through the remaining paparazzi that there was no more story there. Within forty-eight hours, they'd all cleared out of Wisdom. Meanwhile, Sydney's lawyer threatened Vince with a legal suit and career suicide if he didn't back off; he did. There'd been no stories in the news about her for four straight days.

She'd also mentioned another matter to him she'd need his help with once she was back.

Our divorce.

But that was the only remark about our arrangement or her leaving that she'd made all week. She made no attempt to pack. She booked no flight. And I couldn't... understand. *Was this supposed to be a clean break? A slow transition?* I didn't know how this was supposed to end; I couldn't even explain how it had begun. It had just happened, and now it was. *We were.*

I tried to take a deep breath but couldn't. For days, my chest felt like there was a permanent growing weight affixed to it. I checked my blood pressure and pulse and every reading came back normal, but the weight remained.

My gaze drifted up from the screen on Mom's oven and out the window. First, it went to the windows above the garage, looking for Sydney. Always looking for her. I didn't want her to leave, but I couldn't ask her to stay. So we kept living like the charade was real.

I rationalized that she needed more time to feel comfortable. Maybe she wanted more time out here to work on her manuscript that, for obvious reasons, had shifted to the back burner. But there was something that made me wonder if it was more. Like a remainder on a long division problem or an unstable byproduct in a chemical equation that still needed to react, *there was something left over that still needed an answer.*

My head turned, and I scanned the empty street in front of the house.

Now there were no cameras waiting for us every time we left the apartment together. No one followed us to the grocery store or over to Brews for a morning coffee. No one searching for a story when we visited Gunner and Della and my new niece, Skye. There were still people in town—fans who recognized and approached Sydney, asking for a picture or an autograph, but it was nothing like before.

Nothing was like before.

We'd even stopped over at the Betty, and Sydney signed Jerry's entire collection of her books. When we left, she said she planned on sending him a signed copy of every future release of hers. A future I wouldn't be a part of. Which was all according to the plan, but somewhere along the way, my brilliant idea turned into a bad one.

The oven beeped that it was heated, and I carefully placed the two foil-covered trays of lasagna inside.

Things would go back to the way they were before, and that was nothing to complain about. I had a good home, a great family, a good life. I was growing my investments and my role in our business. I had other good things in my life and the capacity to learn more and fill the hole that would open up once Sydney left.

I would be fine. It wasn't anatomically possible for a heart to break; therefore, there was nothing to worry about.

"Thanks for all your help, honey." Mom pressed a hand to my shoulder.

I hadn't even heard her come in.

"Of course."

"Oh, you got sauce on your vest." The dark-red spot stood out on the light gray.

She went to the sink, wetting a paper towel, while I set the oven timer. Mom had made her famous lasagna ala vodka for our belated Christmas dinner. My brothers and their families were due over in less than an hour.

"What's Sydney up to? Writing?" Mom dabbed at the spot on the fabric.

"It's fine. It'll come out in the wash." I took the towel from her, swallowing hard. "And Sydney's been trying to get back to a normal routine after what happened."

She'd been in front of her computer, furiously tapping away at the keys, when I got out of the shower. One look was all it took to stoke what seemed like an inextinguishable flame—and what prompted her to declare that I had to give her a couple hours alone or she'd never get any work done.

It was a fair assessment. We'd spent more time than not having sex. In the bed. On the couch. In the kitchen. In the shower. I finally understood how previous guests had broken the bed frame in the apartment.

I couldn't get enough of her, and it wasn't because our time was running out; it was simply because it was her, and all I wanted was more.

"Normal after what happened or normal now that she has you?"

My head snapped to her. "This... we aren't going to continue," I said, ignoring the giant lump in my throat. "She's already spoken to her lawyer about the divorce." At least, it was mentioned.

"Ranger..."

"Mom, you knew this was the plan all along."

She huffed and folded her arms. "Plans change."

"Not this one," I declared.

"Why not?" She wouldn't back down. Moms never did. "I see the way the two of you are. I saw it from the day I met her. From the day I took you both to the courthouse to get married. Your plan might've been for the press—for Sydney's reputation. But your feelings weren't. You can drag as many clouds as you want in front of the sun, honey, but that doesn't stop it from shining."

I gripped the edge of the counter, wanting to believe her but needing not to. I couldn't keep Sydney—keep this. And it wasn't clouds that prevented it. It was complications.

"This can't change, Mom. I'm not that guy." She had an entire life that was thousands of miles away. What could I possibly ask her to stay for?

"What do you mean you're not that guy?" She looked more insulted than I was.

"I mean that I'm... weird. Smart, but weird. I carry a handkerchief. My social life consists of senior trivia nights. My vests are always flour stained. Or sauce stained." I motioned to the spot she'd pointed out earlier. "And I live in my mom's basement. I'm not the kind of guy who gets to ask the girl to stay."

Mom glared at me. Of course, she would disagree, but I was her child; her perception was skewed.

She patted my chest, her lips pulling in a tight smile. "I always wondered..."

"Wondered what?"

"If you were capable of being dumb, but now I know," she quipped, her palm turning into a single finger that drilled into my chest. "Because that was not only the dumbest—but the only dumb thing I've ever heard come out of your mouth, Ranger Reynolds."

My cheeks heated. *Dumb.* I wasn't dumb. I was realistic. Thoughtful. Practical.

"Even if I was, her whole life is back in New York. It's not...

logical… for her to stay," I mumbled at the end, trying not to get hung up on the inconceivable idea that I was being an idiot.

"And since when has love ever been shown to be logical?" She pinned me with a stare I'd only ever seen her give my brothers—the one she levied on them when they'd done something wrong and she knew it and she was just waiting for them to accept it.

But I couldn't accept this.

I couldn't accept that what I felt was love because if it was, then falling for my fake wife would single-handedly be the most foolish, idiotic, thoughtless thing I'd ever done. And I was a lot of things, but I wasn't an idiot.

I was the one who always made the right decision because I always knew beyond a doubt what the right decision was. I never… I could never…

"It's not love, Mom; it's not real. If it were, I wouldn't have kept it from my brothers," I choked out and then stepped around her, the savory smell of the lasagna oozing into the room. "I should go change. I'll be back over soon."

"You're zero for two in this conversation, honey," Mom called out when I reached the door. "The reason you didn't tell your brothers about the marriage isn't because it was never real; it's because you've been afraid to admit that it always was."

She walked over to me, and I saw the tears cling to the tips of her lashes.

"I wouldn't be afraid to admit it. Why would I be afraid?" The weight on my chest was unbearable.

"Because you remember—I know you remember, honey," she said so quietly I almost couldn't hear her. She reached up and pulled the chain of her necklace out from her shirt, her fingers finding Dad's wedding band at the end of it and holding tight. "But you only remember the end."

The day Dad died was the day my memory began. Every speck of a detail. Every word or look or smell. I didn't remember him, only everything after him.

"You don't remember what came before," she said and came closer. "Of course, we talk about him. Share stories. But you don't have the happy ingrained in you in the same way you do the sad. And I know that's not my fault, that there's nothing I can do to bring him back and change that. There's also nothing I can do to erase your memories of my grief."

Her chin dropped, and for the first time, I had the sense that she recalled those first few weeks with the exact same clarity that I did. The times she threw up because she sobbed so hard. The moments I heard her tell Trish she wished she'd died with him. Just because I hadn't fully understood those things at that time didn't mean I hadn't carried them with me until I could.

The love and relationship I'd once confided to Gunner that I wanted was also something I feared. An unknown that was as powerful as it was unpredictable, so much so that it had almost destroyed my mother.

It was easier to believe I was hard to love than it was to accept that it was hard to love. It was hard to choose vulnerability and uncertainty and irrationality over everything else. And if I asked Sydney to stay, that was what I'd be doing.

My heart pounded like it was going to break right through my ribs.

"I can't change what you know, honey." Tears streaked down her face now. "Which is why I need to tell you something that you don't, and that is that I'd do it all again—I'd love your father all over again, even knowing how it ends. Every single time."

There were a few things in the universe that I had no explanation for at present, and one of them would always be how Lydia Reynolds managed to know more about me than I did.

What she was saying didn't make sense. *Who would pick a future they knew they would lose? Who would pick a future knowing the pain and sorrow it would bring?*

"Don't spend the rest of your life trying to forget what could've been," she added because she knew—she knew I'd *never* be able to forget.

Not for a single second of my future would I ever be able to forget how I'd fallen for Sydney.

I dragged my hand through my hair, my thoughts spinning at speeds even I couldn't decipher. I had to get out of here.

"I'll see you in a little," I said and bolted out the door, heaving the cool January air into my lungs.

One cold breath was all I got before letting myself through the door to the apartment. When I didn't see her right away, panic was injected into my veins. She wasn't the only one who looked over her shoulder all week, and she wasn't the one who went down and checked the brake lines each morning even though my car had been securely kept in the garage.

"Sydney?" I coughed, hoping to disguise the hoarseness of my voice.

The bathroom door swung open. "You're back." Her voice was muffled by the array of bobby pins stuck between her lips.

I stopped short when I saw her. She had on a red velvet dress I'd never seen before. It clung to her chest and waist and then flared out over her hips. She'd dressed it down with black cowboy boots and was in the middle of pulling her hair back into a half ponytail.

"Della loaned me the dress," she said, plucking the last two bobby pins from her lips.

My gaze popped up. "You look beautiful."

What if I did love her? What if that was the reason she could steal my breath along with all my thoughts? What if that was why I was willing to do anything for her—for her happiness—even if it meant letting her go?

"What's wrong?" She read me like a book.

"Nothing." My tongue pushed through my lips and pulled them back tight for a second. "Can we talk about New York?"

I didn't want the uncertainty any longer. I wanted to know how many minutes—how many moments I had left with her in my life.

I wanted to be prepared so that what happened to Mom wouldn't happen to me.

Her eyes widened, and I swore I saw her wince, but then the timer in the kitchen went off and she darted to the oven.

"Maybe later? Or tomorrow?" She shoved on the oven mitts and pulled out the tray of Nutella brownies from the oven, switching all the dials off. "I don't want to be late."

Tomorrow. One more night.

"Okay." My throat bobbed and I nodded.

I was an idiot.

The next twenty minutes passed in a blur. I changed out of my sauce-stained vest while Sydney cut up the brownies and arranged them on a plate, preparing for a dinner that felt more like the Last Supper than it did a first Christmas.

"Are you sure this is okay?" she asked just before we walked out. "I don't want to be overdressed, but Della insisted I take the dress…"

"You look perfect."

She let out a long breath. "Okay." She licked her lips. "I just… I haven't spent holidays with family—any family—since my mom died. Vince wasn't close with his parents, plus half the time he was working…"

"You're perfect." I reached out and took her hand. "And they're all excited you're going to be there."

My throat closed.

It wasn't a lie. My whole family was thrilled that Sydney was staying for Christmas dinner. After what she'd gone through, they were happy to have her celebrate with us. And I knew she would fit in perfectly, just like she did every other part of my life. Book club. Trivia night. Quiet moments. Midnight baking. Phenomenal sex.

And now, family dinners.

Tonight would be one more memory I'd never be able to forget. *What a genius I was to be able to recall perfectly all the moments that hurt me the most.*

"That was… delicious." Gunner sat back in his seat, his hands on his stomach.

Dinner had been a community event, everyone taking turns holding babies and entertaining infants until we all had a chance to eat. I'd been right; from the moment she'd walked through the door, Sydney had blended in with my family even better than I did.

It wasn't surprising, but for once, I wished I'd been wrong.

She talked and laughed, empathized and joked. She fit like a piece I knew I was missing, and as the minutes churned by, I grew more reserved, wondering how I was going to let her go.

Now, only Della and Zoey were absent from the table because they'd gone into the living room to breastfeed.

"Your brother did most of the work." Mom pointed to me. "I just made the sauce."

"Well, it was top-notch. Kudos to you and Baby Brains."

"Wait until you taste the brownies," Sydney chimed in.

"God, I shouldn't even think about more food right now." Gunner chuckled and tipped forward, reaching for the Old Fashioned that Keira had made for him and Archer. He took a long swig, and I realized the second I was in trouble when he grinned at me and then looked back at Sydney. "I have to say, Sydney. I'm surprised you didn't hightail it out of here as soon as the press cleared out. Is Wyoming growing on you?"

Archer and Hunter suspected—more than suspected what was going on between Sydney and me, but Gunner had been too busy moving and relearning life with a newborn to know we were involved.

His eyes twinkled at me, and my entire body tensed. He was trying to be playful—to set me up with the woman I was already married to.

"It is, but I also just have some... things I have to finish before I can leave."

"Well, I think Ranger would be happy if you stuck around for a little longer."

"Gunner..." Archer's familiar warning rumbled from the head of the table.

At the opposite end, I felt Mom's eyes trained on me, the words she'd said earlier replaying in my mind with perfect clarity. *You haven't told them because you're afraid it's real.*

She was wrong. She had to be wrong. I was going to prove that she was wrong.

My fork clattered onto my empty plate, and I blurted out, "We're married."

Gunner stared at me, blinked, and then smiled. "Funny, Baby Brains. God, I still can't believe the stories they wrote. What a racket." His head shook.

"Gunner, it wasn't fake," I interrupted him, catching Mom's wide eyes for a second before I glanced at Sydney.

"Ranger..." She breathed my name, but I couldn't determine if it was in relief or dread.

"Sydney and I got married. Four weeks ago—the day the story ran," I said, focusing on the only thing that felt comfortable. *The facts.* "When I asked Archer and Hunter to come manage the paparazzi so I could get Sydney out of the apartment, it was so Mom could take us to the courthouse."

Now I had everyone's attention. And disbelief.

Gunner gave his head a quick shake and laughed. "You're getting better at fooling me, Baby Brains—"

"He's not lying, Gunner," Mom's voice carried through the room, not because it was loud but because hers always carried the most weight.

My pulse thudded loudly in my ears, a wild drumbeat hammered by adrenaline. I'd never seen any of my brothers so silent... so shocked before. Then again, I'd never done anything shocking in my life. I was predictably predictable. And, like always, Gunner's fuse was the first one to ignite.

"Are you fucking kidding me?" Gunner shouted out angrily, his chair rattling underneath him.

His outburst drew Zoey and Della in from the living room. Della immediately went to his side and placed her hand on his shoulder, her expression worried as she bounced with Skye on her shoulder.

"No. I just told you we actually got married—"

"Dammit, Baby Brains, I know you're serious. What I don't fucking understand—"

"Gunner," Archer clipped, but as always, Gunner didn't listen.

"No," he barked and then reached up to grip Della's hand, holding on to it like it was the only thing keeping him barely civil. "I want to know why the hell you got married? Why you didn't tell us—didn't talk to us—"

"Well, I think that's obvious," Kiera murmured.

"Probably because he wasn't marrying you, sweetheart," Mom chimed in over Kiera.

Gunner's head whipped in her direction. "And you were okay with this? How could you be okay with this for him?"

"It wasn't her choice, Gunner," I broke in, offering Mom a tight smile; this wasn't her battle to fight. "It was my decision to do this. To help Sydney."

"Wanting to help someone isn't a reason to marry them. Jesus, Baby Brains." His hand slapped down on the table. "I know you're fucking smarter than that—"

"Why don't you let him talk for a second, Gunner?" Hunter growled, succeeding only in making himself Gunner's next target.

I knew what was going to happen next. I'd watched it happen a thousand times over the years. They would argue while I waited on the sidelines. The only difference now was that the battle they were fighting was mine, but I was the only one not allowed to take a stance.

"Why don't you give a little more of a shit that our little brother just fucking married a stranger—"

"She's not a stranger, Gun—"

"Don't start with me, Archie." Gunner pointed his finger at me, though his attention was locked on Archer. "This is fucked up, and you know it. He should've come to us—told us what was going on before he just went and married someone without thinking—"

"Please, stop."

I tensed when Sydney spoke, her tender voice cracking under the weight. I knew to just let Gunner get it all out. That was how his reactions worked: big explosion, rapid fizzle. I reached for Sydney's hand and squeezed, about to tell her it was okay—that I knew how my brothers worked and that I expected nothing less in this moment. But I didn't get a chance.

"I'm sorry, Sydney," Gunner bit out, his jaw flexing rapidly. "But this conversation is between me and my brother—"

"No, it's not," she clipped, her eyes flashing angrily. "You're not having a conversation *with* your brother. You're having an argument *about my husband,* who is sitting right here in front of you."

Her husband. *Hers.*

My jaw went slack and air burrowed deep in my lungs. Her words didn't hit me like a freight train. They spun me out of control like that afternoon my brakes had been cut. I'd gone into this conversation heading in one direction, prepared for a familiar outcome, and then those two little words derailed me. Sent my mind spinning off track and through the walls I'd created for myself all those years ago.

Archer sat back in his chair, folding his arms with a look of surprise on his face. Hunter remained unmoving—waiting to see what played out next. But Gunner… the furious scowl on his face melted and he looked at Sydney with… recognition.

Gunner was always the first to come to my defense—and he'd come to it with an irrational level of protectiveness. And now, he sat and stared at my wife, recognizing her as someone who would do the same.

"Sydney." My grip tightened too late; her fingers slid out of mine as she folded her arms.

"I'm sorry," she looked at me, the flush in her cheeks brought on by anger disappeared as quickly as it came. "I'm just... I need to go."

"Sydney—" I rose and reached for her, but she was already out of the room.

I'd always thought she was brave. Brave for leaving Vince. Brave for writing a book that was hard for her even when she knew she'd face backlash. Brave for marrying—for trusting me and allowing me in when she'd been let down so many times before. But hearing her stand up to my brothers shocked me but didn't surprise me at the same time.

She was a fighter, and she wasn't just fighting for her own happy ending. She was fighting for mine.

And maybe she wasn't the only one... had I really told them to prove Mom wrong? Or had I revealed the truth about our marriage because I didn't want to be afraid anymore?

"Shit," Gunner muttered, his shoulders slumping with regret.

"Yeah, shit," Hunter chided.

I inhaled slowly, tempted to walk away. Tempted to go after Sydney and forget about my family, but the way she'd stood up for me, it gave me the strength to stay. *Because how could I tell Sydney I was in love with her if I was afraid to admit it to myself?*

And to them.

There was a reason my brothers treated me the way that they did and a reason I let them. *Love.* Now, it was for the same reason that they deserved the truth.

"Ranger, I'm sorry," Gunner muttered, his voice cracking with true regret. And he'd called me Ranger. He never called me anything but Baby Brains.

But sympathy wasn't the same as understanding, and I'd spared them the understanding for too long.

"Tom and Jerry."

"What?"

"Tom and Jerry," I repeated, resting my hands on the table. "It was what we were watching the day the police came to the house the day Dad died."

An indescribable stillness settled over the table.

"Archer was in the kitchen doing homework while Mom unpacked her new Crock-Pot. Hunter was avoiding his homework and bugging Mom about going for ice cream with Dad when he got home."

"Ranger..."

I went through the details of that day. The smell of the house. Which of my toys were out on the floor. What Mom was wearing. The exact point in the episode when the doorbell rang. I listed the foods people brought. The flowers people left. I remembered the string of friends who came to check on us—stay with us until Mom was okay on her own.

"I remember all the times we hid in the closet, pretending to play a game of pirates so we wouldn't hear Mom screaming. Crying." I drew a shuddered breath. "I remember each time Mom sobbed and begged that she'd died, too."

With each fact, their eyes went wider. Like most incredible things, they'd always focused on the abilities and the power of my memory... never the other side of the coin.

"You see, the brain does this incredible thing when it experiences trauma. It isolates the details—the memories. It hides them—buries them under scar tissue until, with time, all that's left is a fossil of the pain that once existed. At least, for you." I let my eyes move between theirs. "But all this time, I've remembered it all. Carried it all. Every detail. Every look, every tear, every sob, every scream. I've carried it all."

Once again, my mind worked, engraving every molecule of this moment. The low lights over the table. The lingering aroma of lasagna in the air. The flicker of the twinkle lights wrapped around

Mom's tree that I could see in the living room. It etched the scene and carved into it the emotions. Della's hand pressed to her mouth, her chin quivering. Zoey, with the sleeve of her sweater pressed to her cheek to catch the tears that wouldn't stop falling. Keira grabbed for Archer's hand, not bothering to hide the way my mention of Dad's death brought up memories of her own.

I heard the soft sound of Mom's muffled cries from her end of the table, clutching Dad's ring on her necklace like her life depended on it.

"For the last twenty-six years since that day, I've accepted your sheltering and appreciated your protection. I know that I'm different, and I know without you, certain parts of my life would've been more challenging—more painful. Without you… I wouldn't be here. I wouldn't be the man that I am." I lifted my hands from their support on the table and straightened my spine. "But to be the man I want to be… to be her husband… you need to know that for the last twenty-six years, I've protected you, too.

"I might not be as strong or as physically fit, but all this time, I've carried the weight of the grief you've been able to forget. A weight that hasn't changed for me from the moment it was placed on my shoulders. Every breath, every step. Every minute, every day." I grappled for one more breath. "I'm not asking for recognition. I'm not claiming that knowledge is the heaviest burden a person can bear. But I am demanding your respect."

Archer's chair creaked as he shifted his weight. I could count on both hands the collective number of times I'd seen my brothers cry, but that was exactly what I was witnessing. All three of the strongest men I'd ever known, their eyes glistening with tears waiting to fall.

It wasn't my intent; this was just the truth. Inconvenient. Emotional. And necessary.

"I knew exactly what I was doing and what I was thinking when I told Sydney we should get married. It wasn't careless or irrational, and she wasn't a stranger. Not to me," I declared. "There was a purpose—a plan to help her. The only thing I never accounted for was the way I would feel." My chest caved with a heavy exhale. "And I think I would be the dumbest man in the world if I told you how I felt about her before telling her."

There were more apologies and another conversation headed my way, but not tonight. I'd made it clear to everyone in the room how I felt about my wife. Now it was time to make it clear to her.

I'd reached the side door when a hand landed on my arm.

"Ranger." Mom hugged me before I could stop her.

"I'm going to ask her to stay," I rasped low.

When she drew back, her eyes flooded with more tears.

"I know." She tried to blink them back, but it didn't work. "I just had to tell you that your dad would be proud of you."

CHAPTER 24

Sydney

I jumped when the door swung open, balling a damp tissue in my fist.

It only took him a moment to find me—my clothes strewn all over the bed, my suitcase open on the floor. For two weeks, I'd shoved every thought of leaving to the furthest corner of my mind. I'd ignored the parts of my lawyer's emails that kept requesting more information on the divorce, only responding to the parts about Vince. I went through the week pretending like this was my life here. Coffee. Writing. Baking. All with him.

Neither of us wanted to face reality—like a reader savoring the final pages of a story, unwilling to let it end. Only the best fantasies make us want to live in them forever, and Ranger... he was the very best.

But when I stood at their dining table to defend him, I couldn't hide in that fiction any longer. There was no reason for me to be here... except to be with him. And that wasn't part of the plan.

"Sydney."

"Don't, Ranger." I stood from the bed, wiping the fresh set of tears from my face and dragged my gaze to his. My breath stuck in my chest like it was nailed to the walls of my lungs. He was so handsome.

His unruly hair. His full lips. His generous heart. I gasped at the fresh rush of pain and declared, "I'm so sorry for what I said... I never..."

I never should've intervened with his family. He'd made the decision to tell them about our plan, and I'd stirred up something that was only my business if he were actually my husband.

"What are you doing?"

"I need to pack." My lip quivered.

And book a flight. And call a car. *And figure out how I was going to forget him.*

My head dropped. A second later, the warmth of his body surrounded me—embracing me at the same time as his knuckles brushed my cheek. I shivered at the heat of the touch. His fingers caught a single tear before they lowered to nudge my chin, lifting my eyes back to his.

"Will you stay?"

Another sob broke free. Three little words that I'd uttered to him so many times—so many nights over the course of our relationship. And now, he'd turned them on me.

"Don't ask that," I begged, my voice cracking just like the pieces of my heart.

The knuckles catching my tears turned into his whole hand cupping my cheek, his other hand lifting to create a frame for my face. It was so warm and familiar and comforting I didn't have the strength to break from his embrace, not when every ounce of it was channeled into walking away from him.

"Why not?" Ranger tipped my head higher, confusion creasing his brow.

I'd written countless endings before... I could write this one, too, even if it was the first time the heroine didn't get her hero.

"Because that wasn't the plan. The plan was that when the stories ended, so would we."

He inched closer, his body crowding mine. "But I don't want this to end, Sydney."

Another sob overtook me. And then another. I couldn't stop

the cries that racked my body. I didn't want this to end either, but Ranger couldn't mean that. There was too much baggage attached to the thought of staying. Hope was clouding reality. Fantasy deluding the facts. My heart was overwriting the truth with everything I wanted.

"Sydney, look at me." His warm touch erased the tears from my face until they finally slowed, and I could focus on him. "Do you know what the observer effect is?"

I blinked and tried to think, but my brain was too muddy to think about anything, let alone some obscure science fact.

My head shook in his hands, not trusting myself to speak.

"The observer effect is the phenomenon where an object changes—is altered simply because something or someone is watching it," he murmured rapidly. "From the moment you got here… the moment you first looked at me, Sydney, you changed me simply because you saw me. Not just who I was but who I wanted to be. Every molecule of every cell. Every thought and fact. Every feeling. And I don't want to go back. The person I'm meant to be is the person I am when I'm with you."

"Ranger…"

Tears slipped like silk trails down my cheeks. *Was he really saying this? Was he even real?* Now I was starting to really question everything. Had he even come back to the apartment, or was the man in front of me just a figment of my fantasy?

"It hasn't been long. You hardly know me." It wasn't my words I was saying. They were everyone else's doubts that crashed over me like waves.

"According to Einstein, time is relative—a measurement affected by gravity. And in the eleven weeks, six days, nineteen hours and thirty-six minutes since I met you, I've never fallen so hard, yet my feet haven't left the ground. The only conclusion is that gravity has changed because you're around, and therefore time has, too."

It was too much. Facts and feelings made a mess of my mind. *Only Ranger would be able to use science—to use the theory of relativity to prove how he felt about me.* A rush of overwhelming joy hit me hard. I grabbed for his shirt, clutching it and burying my head into his chest as I sobbed. *He loved me.* And who could doubt it? Who could doubt him?

It took a minute before my tears slowed to a trickle and my cries ebbed into hiccups. The whole time, he held me like I was the most precious thing he'd ever known. Inhaling deeply, I peeled my cheek from the solid heat of his chest.

"Are you sure?"

"Having a life I can't forget isn't the same as having a life worth remembering. And the only life worth remembering, Sydney, is the one that has you in it. You're my snow angel, the part of all of this worth savoring… you're my magic." His warm breath fused to my lips. "Say you'll stay tonight… and the rest of your life?"

Relief pushed the air from my lungs, and I clutched his shirt, holding on to it like I was holding on to him.

"Stay, Sydney." This time it wasn't a question. "As my wife."

"Yes."

He smiled. *God, those dimples.* "Say it again."

"Yes!" I cried out again, winding my arms around his neck.

A second passed, short yet stretched the way his gaze roamed my face, both of us savoring each other and this moment. And then his mouth slanted over mine, his tongue sliding along my bottom lip to tease me before delving deep into my mouth.

His kiss rewrote every line—every word of my story's ending until it was only about him.

Time bent and dipped, swirled and stopped. It wrapped us in something that had no beginning and no end, and the urge to tell him how I felt became too strong.

I drew back, panting heavily with a smile pressing my cheeks wide.

"Ranger, I—"

My eyes snagged on a flicker of something in the window a second before the glass shattered with a loud crash.

"Sydney, get down!" A second later, my back was on the bed and Ranger was on top of me, shielding me with his own body.

Our chests collided in frantic breaths, the violent sound dissipating as quickly as it came.

"Stay on the floor and out of sight from the window," he ordered.

I nodded, feeling his weight start to lift. As soon as I was free, I slid to the ground on the side of the bed, pushing back until I almost hit the wall. I clutched my arms over me, cold air barreling into the apartment and dragging my attention to the broken window.

My jaw went slack when I saw the brick that lay in the middle of the glass.

A brick.

Someone had thrown a brick through the window.

Just as Ranger reached for it, voices from outside echoed into the apartment. *His brothers.* It was easy to hear them with the hole in the window. Footsteps pounded up the stairwell., deep voices calling for Ranger and me.

But all I could focus on was the brick.

Ranger picked it up, but when he stood, his back was to me.

"Ranger!" Archer was the first to burst through the door, his head whipping around the room, matching all the pieces together of what just happened. "Everyone alright?"

I nodded as Hunter and Gunner filtered in behind their older brother. Both of them glanced at me first. Gunner's gaze flickered deeply with remorse before they assessed the room like Archer had done. All three of them had come in with weapons drawn, and when they tucked them away, I felt safe enough to stand.

"Someone threw this through the window." Ranger examined the brick. I caught a glimpse of something white on it before Archer came to stand beside him and blocked my view.

"I'm going to go check on Mom and the girls," Hunter declared, disappearing back into the stairwell.

"I'll check the street." Gunner followed right after him.

My heart pummeled against the front of my chest, adrenaline quickly eliminating the cold from my bones. Archer and Ranger shared a look—one that spoke volumes.

"What is it?"

Ranger passed the brick to his brother and faced me, his expression both grim and angry. "Sydney—"

"What?" I demanded, my bare feet slapping on the floor as I went to them and extended my hand. "Let me see it."

Ranger's jaw flexed and then he nodded to Archer, who proceeded to show me what they'd been looking at.

My heart plummeted into my stomach. The streaks of white I'd seen hadn't been dust or scuffs; it was writing.

Whore was slashed in angry lines on the flat of the brick.

"Oh god."

In an instant, every ounce of safety and security I'd regained over the last five days crumbled like snow under the blazing sun. Fear poured like lava into my veins.

"Sydney."

I breathed deep as Ranger's arms locked around me, clutching me to his chest where there was nothing for me to feel or breathe or see except him.

"Get her out of here." Archer's low voice filtered through my husband's shield, and I felt Ranger's chin dip against the side of my head in agreement.

CHAPTER 25

Sydney

For the second time in the space of an hour, the concepts of time and gravity and relativity came into play. Fifteen minutes passed in what seemed like the space of a blink under the weight of the attack.

Whatever angry skepticism I'd felt from Ranger's siblings at the dinner table vanished completely as, without hesitation, they helped us gather our things from the apartment so we could leave.

Keira and Zoey helped fill my suitcase with my clothes. Della stayed with Lydia in the house, the two of them looking after all the kids, while Ranger's brothers scouted the streets and interviewed the neighbors, searching for any information on the person who'd done this.

Whore.

My stomach churned. It didn't make sense why someone would write that about me—why they would throw a brick through my window to get the message across. The press—the paparazzi who'd been following me were financially driven. And Vince... yes, I'd threatened to press charges if he didn't leave me alone, but would that really drive him to this? There were plenty of other insults than *whore*; he was the cheater in our relationship after all.

"Time to go." Ranger looped his arm around my shoulder, holding me to his side as we descended the stairwell.

"Where are we going?" My brain was foggy, searching for answers that I didn't have.

"The Worth." Gunner stood at the bottom of the stairs, holding open the door, a large SUV parked right outside it, the door open and the engine running.

I looked up to Ranger. "Just for a couple nights until we know who did this." He pressed a kiss to my forehead.

"We upgraded all of the security since Della and I moved in," Gunner assured firmly, stepping aside so that I could climb into the back seat of the SUV next to the car seat holding his sleeping daughter.

Ranger kept a hand on me as I climbed in. I scooted to the center, expecting him to follow me inside.

But he didn't.

"Ranger?" I choked out, fear paralyzing me.

"I need to review the security footage with Archer, then I'll grab my things and I'll be there."

I started to shake my head. I didn't want to go anywhere without him.

"Please, Sydney." The hoarseness in his voice stopped me. "I have to protect you. I..." he stopped himself, pursing his lips tight. "I have to do this. You'll stay with Gunner and Della until I get there. I won't be long."

Being separated from him was the last thing I wanted, but I also wanted answers. We both did. And everyone knew that Ranger was going to process that footage faster than anyone else, and if there was a chance of catching who'd done this, they had to act quickly.

I reached out and pushed a wild strand of hair back from his forehead. "Okay." My chin bobbed, feeling like the weight of an anchor was attached to it. "Ranger." I stopped him before he could close the door.

Our eyes locked, the words burning on the tip of my tongue to tell him I loved him.

"I know," he murmured softly before I could utter them and then shut me inside, patting the window to indicate to Gunner he was clear to drive.

Of course, he knew. He knew everything.

"I'm sorry, Sydney," Gunner's voice carried to the back seat, his eyes flicking to mine in the rearview. "What I said… how I behaved earlier was unacceptable."

Della's hand snuck across the console and took hold of Gunner's with wordless encouragement.

"I don't know that I'm the one you need to apologize to," I told him honestly, my gaze skating to the sleeping baby in the car seat next to me.

I reached out and tucked my finger into Skye's tiny fist. She didn't even stir, and I wished I could be as calm and oblivious to everything going on as her.

"I need to apologize to Ranger, I know," Gunner rasped with a deep sigh, the subtle slump of his shoulders drawing my attention back to him. "But you deserve an apology, too. I have a bad habit of underestimating my little brother because I've always…"

"Protected him."

"Yeah," he croaked with a nod. "I guess it was always easier to believe he needed it because he wasn't like the rest of us, but it wasn't the truth. Turns out, he might've been the strongest, not just the smartest of us all."

I swallowed over the lump in my throat, always knowing Gunner had a good heart, just a misplaced temper.

The streetlights flickered by the window, their warm orbs of light coming into focus as we slowed in front of the hotel. There was a slew of cars parked at the curb and in the street, most still running with their flashers on as guests loaded and unloaded their belongings. It was a Friday night, but could this all be people checking in for the weekend?

"There's a wedding reception at the hotel tonight," Della explained, the crush of well-dressed people making more sense.

"I'll drop you three off and then park around back so the guys can help me with your things. It'll be a mess if I try to stay parked out here," Gunner said and brought the SUV to a stop out front, doubling up next to another car. "I'll bring the carrier with me, Dell."

"Thanks." Della peered over her shoulder at the car seat. "Sydney, do you mind…"

"Not at all." I unclipped Skye from her seat, carefully lifting her tiny form into my arms. I couldn't help but take a deep inhale of her soft, newborn scent.

Della opened the back door for me, taking her daughter and cocooning her to her chest from the cold. A car honked and I jumped, my nerves as fragile as eggshells. Then the unmistakable rapid-fire clicks made my head whip to the side, engulfed by a fresh wave of paranoia about photographers. *What if some had stayed? What if they'd staged this attack?*

Then I saw the bride and groom decked out in their wedding garb, with the bride sporting a thick white fur wrap as they strolled down the sidewalk, their wedding party staged behind them as the photographer captured the gorgeous shots.

Not photographing me. My warm breath exhaled in a giant puff of relief into the frigid air.

I followed Della as she wove through the cars and the crowd to the entrance to the hotel.

"Good evening, Ms. Bolden, Ms. Skye." The bellman held open the door.

"Hi, Albert. Thank you so much," Della greeted him with a kind smile. "Make sure you're staying under the heaters!"

I glanced up, noting the electric heaters that had been installed underneath the awning.

"Yes, ma'am." Albert tipped his head and smiled.

Even if Della wanted to, it was impossible to talk to him any longer because there were so many people, and it wasn't any less crowded in the lobby. Finely dressed guests milled about during the cocktail hour before the reception.

The Worth was Wisdom's stately legacy hotel, and it showed. The rich finish on the wood floors. The ornate design on the beige carpet. The landscape paintings of the Tetons on the walls. The musky scent pervaded every crevice, its notes heavy on history and luxury. Fear scratched them with painful precision to my memory.

I kept my arms crossed and my focus on the back of Della's head as we made our way to the elevators. I could hear my heartbeat over the crush of wedding guests, and it only heightened my anxiety. With every shoulder I bumped and the rising sound of the crowd, it felt like the walls around me were closing in.

Even once we made it through the guests and reached the elevator bay, the cold grip of dread wouldn't release my throat.

"It's going to be okay, Sydney." Della took my hand and squeezed. "They'll figure this out."

I could only nod and then give away how on edge I was when the ding from the elevator made me flinch.

The doors opened, and we stepped inside. Della swiped her card and hit the button for the top floor. I didn't even realize my gaze had fallen to the floor until the doors jostled in protest as someone's hand prevented them from closing.

As soon as they were wide enough, a man wearing a dark winter jacket and ball cap stepped inside. He kept his head down as he turned and punched the *door close* button.

"Sorry," he muttered.

His voice made me tense. Something didn't feel right. *He* didn't feel right. But before I could say something—do something—-the doors shut him in with us.

My throat tightened, time stretching as we climbed each floor. There was something about him, and it wasn't the fact that he hadn't selected another button on the elevator tree. There was something else. Something my brain wanted to remember, but the stress of the night put it out of reach.

I didn't dare look at Della because I didn't want to worry her. I was probably overreacting. Looking for danger in every direction because I had no idea where it was coming from.

When the elevator stopped at the top floor, my breath rushed out in relief.

The doors opened, and the man stepped to the side to allow us out before him. *Yup, I'd been overthinking it.*

I was right behind Della, about to step through the doors, when the big winter jacket and the man wearing it blocked my path.

"Not you," the man's low voice growled as his head lifted, letting me see under his hat.

I gasped. "Darren."

The man from the coffee shop.

"You're staying with me." He grabbed my arm, and I immediately tried to wrench free, his fingers biting like bullets into my skin.

"Hey! What do you think—" Della broke off with a cry when Darren shoved me.

I whimpered in pain as my back hit the back wall of the elevator, but that was nothing compared to the panic that stabbed my gut when I watched Darren turn and pull a gun from inside his jacket, aiming it at my friend and her newborn baby.

"Della!" I cried out.

The new mother half turned to shield Skye from the weapon but made no other sudden moves to provoke him.

"Sydney's coming with me," Darren warned.

"Okay, I'm going with you, Darren. Wherever you want—whatever you want," I blurted out, trying to regain his attention and willing to do anything to get him to aim the gun anywhere other than the baby.

He stepped back and punched the mezzanine button. My breath exploded from my lungs when he finally pointed the gun at me; I never thought I'd feel relief at being the target of a firearm, but when the choice was either me or an innocent child, there was no question.

"Call for help—try to stop me, and I'll kill her," he snarled at Della.

Kill me.

A week ago, he'd been praising me to my face at the coffee shop, and today, he was prepared to take my life.

"Sydney," Della's broken murmur pierced my heart as the doors began to shut, but there was nothing she could do—not without putting her child in grave danger.

I held her eyes and nodded slowly. She had to let me go. It was the only way. I managed to keep a stoic face until the doors closed. *At least Della and Skye were safe.*

"Why?" I choked out as he crowded me and pressed the barrel of his gun to my side.

I bit my cheek, trying to focus on the pain rather than panic.

"You were mine," he snarled, drops of spittle landing on my cheek. "You told me how much I meant to you. How important I was. You loved me and we were supposed to be together."

My jaw went slack. Unlike Beekman, who was drunk and angry, there was no trace of alcohol on Darren's breath. No trace of anything except potent delusion spewing from his mouth.

He wasn't just a fan or a celebrity stalker. He was stalking me—*Sydney*—because he was in love with me.

We reached the mezzanine and Darren shuffled to my side, keeping the gun wedged against me in warning but concealing it by the position of our bodies.

"Move."

There were too many people who'd had too many drinks and too much else to focus on for anyone to spare a second glance at the man and the woman weaving in silence through the lobby. No one looked at our faces, let alone where Darren had his gun wedged against my side.

Everything started to blur as my heart beat in my throat.

The crowd was every bit to his advantage, concealing what was really going on and making it impossible for me to cry for help without putting dozens of lives in danger.

I searched for Albert—the bellman. Maybe Della had gotten word to him—maybe he could help me. My far-fetched hope dissolved when Darren veered us behind another couple so that we exited as one giant group.

This time, I didn't even feel the bite of the cold because it was nothing compared to the ice in my veins.

"Say one word, and I'll shoot the bride."

My throat tightened, watching the happy couple look at each other and kiss as their photographer captured a few more photos. They had no idea that while their lives were just starting, mine was being threatened.

Darren walked me toward the street, a million cars doubled up out front, camouflaging crime with chaos. I looked up at the face of the hotel. Della had to have called Gunner by now—Ranger had to know what was happening. He'd know what to do—how to find me.

Maybe even once we were away from the crowd—the other people, I could talk him down. I could escape.

"It didn't have to be like this," Darren muttered, dragging me toward a car with its flashers on at the end of the row. "You were mine. You. Were. *Mine.*"

"Darren, please—"

"No!" He rammed the gun into my side, and I choked on panic, light-headedness making my vision dim for an instant.

When it filtered back in, we were approaching a car I recognized. *Oh god. No.*

Please, no.

"You escaped Vince and we were supposed to be together. It was our turn," he rambled on as he stopped next to Cindy's car.

She had no idea.

My friend had no idea she was about to help the man kidnapping me.

"I tried to get rid of them—tried to get rid of… him. You were never supposed to be in that car. He was supposed to crash. *He was supposed to die,*" he spat, and my knees buckled; *he'd tried to kill Ranger.* "But you still stayed. You still picked him. A nobody."

"Please," I begged, my lip quivering.

Seething eyes met mine. "You ruined our happy ending, you *whore.*"

Red-hot fear lashed at my stomach. He was insane, but I couldn't confront him with that. Not now. Not in front of Cindy. He'd just admitted trying to kill Ranger; I wouldn't risk that he'd harm Cindy.

"Don't make a scene," he ordered under his breath and opened the back door to the car.

I clung to Cindy's bubbling voice and held on to it like a life raft.

I had to play along—I had to make her think everything was normal and that Darren was a friend, so I could buy time. If she suspected anything else, I didn't know what she'd say or do—what danger she'd put herself in to help me.

Ranger would figure out what happened. He'd figure out how to find us. Not because he was the smartest man I'd ever known but because I could count on him. *He'd promised.*

CHAPTER 26

Ranger

"Here." My fingers slammed on the keyboard to stop the footage as the shrouded figure approached the garage.

The man was wearing a dark winter coat, a ball cap with the Brilliant Brews logo on it, and was clearly holding a brick in his right hand.

I switched the playback to normal speed as Archer bent over one shoulder and Hunter over the other, the three of us waiting to get a good look at his face.

He kept his head down, weaving through my brothers' cars parked in the drive until he was close enough. My fist flexed, a kind of anger I'd never felt before poised to unleash as soon as I could see—as soon as I could know who this man was.

Archer gripped my shoulder, squeezing tight as the seconds ticked, the man clearly thinking about—debating what to do. And then his head snapped up like a sound had triggered him.

Sydney's happy cry when she'd yelled "Yes."

The moment that started this was also the one that would end it. My fingers moved with lightning reflex to pause the video at the split second when the man's face was clearly visible.

"Who the hell—"

"Darren Ross," I answered in an instant. "He's a fan of Sydney's. We saw him at Brilliant Brews two weeks ago."

"A fan? Why the hell would he chuck a brick—"

"Oh god." My hands came to either side of my head, pulling my hair back painfully. "It was him this whole time. The note. The brakes. The brick."

The events ticked off like dominos toppling over.

"I thought we were sure it was the paps Vince hired—"

"No," I cut Hunter off and shoved back from the desk so forcefully the chair toppled. "It was him from the start. The note... we said it had to be someone stalking her. Then the press arrived and it was easy to think it was them—easy for Darren to hide behind them. But he's been stalking her this whole time, waiting for the paparazzi to leave her alone just as much as we were."

Fact after fact. Piece after piece. It all came together.

"I have to call her—let her—" I grabbed for my phone. My hands shook so badly I fumbled and dropped it on the floor. It landed faceup just as a call from Gunner lit the screen.

"Gunner, it's Darren," I said into the mic as I tapped to put him on speaker. "Not me, I mean the man who threw the brick—the man who's after—"

"He has her."

The world stopped. I knew it wasn't possible, but it did. Time, space, the whole of it halted on those three words.

"What?"

Archer grabbed my wrist, both of us holding my phone so I wouldn't drop it.

"He was here—at the hotel. He must've followed us when I left the house—"

"How?" Archer growled.

"Where were you?"

"I dropped the girls off out front. There's a wedding tonight, so the hotel is packed. I was just going to park the car and grab the bags.

I had no fucking idea this guy was brave enough to stick around the scene of his crime and then fucking follow us—"

"How did he take her?" My mind was spiraling. I needed more facts. Facts led to answers. Facts led to finding Sydney.

"Della said he got on the elevator with them. Waited until they reached our floor and Della got off before abducting Sydney—"

"Why didn't she do something? Why didn't Sydney fight back?" My questions were hard. Curt. But I didn't have the wherewithal to decipher any other emotion other than anger.

"He had a gun, Baby—Ranger." Gunner's voice cracked. "He pointed a gun at my wife and daughter."

"Fucking Christ," Archer muttered while a shudder racked my body.

"They left the hotel. There's no way he would've kept her here," Gunner continued. "I'm pulling up the front feeds now to see if they caught the direction they went."

"Where is he taking her?" I muttered over and over again, balling my fists against my temples like I could drag the knowledge from my brain. "Where, Ranger? Where?"

Archer grabbed my wrists, stopping me from banging them into my head.

"Ranger, you're going to figure it out. You're the smartest man in the room—"

"No," I barked and speared my fingers through my hair, my breaths coming in rough chops. "I can't focus on anything for more than three seconds at a time right now, which makes me unequivocally the dumbest person in the room."

Archer growled and grabbed my arm. "Gunner, we're coming to you."

He hauled me through the house with Hunter right behind us. My body followed like a marionette on strings, capable of moving but only at his direction because my thoughts—my mind was somewhere else.

Sydney had sacrificed herself to protect them. *My wife.* But now he had her. The man who threatened her. The man who'd tried to kill... me.

I stumbled in the snow just as we reached Archer's SUV.

"I found them leaving the hotel," Gunner revealed as soon as the last door shut. "Looks like he took her into the street, probably to a car."

Archer pulled out of the drive and floored it toward the hotel.

"What do you mean probably? The cars pull up to the curb. The field of view from that camera should capture the entire vehicle—"

"Not when the cars are stopped a couple rows deep out front because of the wedding."

No. I tipped forward in the seat, feeling as though my entire stomach was trying to claw its way up my throat.

Archer planted his hand on my chest and pushed me back into the seat. "We'll be there in two. Call me if something else comes up." He took my phone and ended the call.

My fingers locked into fists on my knees.

"I can't think, Archer. I can't... breathe," I admitted hoarsely.

"I know, Ranger, but we're going to find them. We're going to find her," he assured me in the way only he could—the way he had for the majority of my life, not as my older brother, but as the closest father figure I had.

The rest of them remembered Dad. All I had was Archer. From four years old on, he was the one I went to when I had problems. He was the one I looked up to and admired. He was the one that stepped in and shouldered responsibilities that never should've been placed on him in the first place.

My phone buzzed in the cup holder, and I lunged for it.

Jerry.

I ignored the call. Whatever he wanted would have to wait.

A second later, Hunter's phone in the back buzzed, and he answered right away. "Jerry, now's not—"

"Dammit, Hunter, are you with your brother? I think Cindy's

in trouble," he yelled so loud he didn't need to be on speaker for Archer and me to hear him.

"What?" Hunter barked and put Jerry on speakerphone. "Why do you think something happened to Cindy?"

"I was just locking up the shop when I heard beeping at the intersection. I looked over and recognized Cindy's car stopped at the light behind another car. The thing was, she wasn't honking normally. Short beep, then long, then short. Dot, dash, dot."

"SOS."

"Why would Cindy honk—"

"Because Sydney is in the car," I blurted out, facts spewing out so fast I prayed they made sense. "He doesn't have a car out here, so he called one, not realizing Cindy knows Sydney."

"Fucking bold," Archer grunted. "He's banking on Sydney being unwilling to put anyone else in harm's way."

"Cindy must've realized Sydney was in danger—being held against her will, so she honked the SOS."

"Wait, Sydney's been abducted? Jesus." Jerry started huffing like he was running, and then I heard a car door open and shut right before his truck rumbled to life.

"How the hell would Cindy think to honk an SOS—"

"Because it's in Sydney's book." My finger pounded on the dash in front of me, flipping through the storyline as I pulled it from memory. "In *Concealed Danger,* Maya beeps SOS as she's driving past Mac's place, hoping he'll realize she's in danger—"

"Dammit, I knew there was a reason she replicated the scene. Knew as soon as I tried to call her and she didn't answer that she wasn't just pulling my chain." Jerry's tires screeched.

I grabbed Hunter's phone. "She must've seen you, Jerry. She knew you'd get the reference. Knew you'd call us."

My mind was a monster inside my head, needing to consume more information before it devoured itself in fear.

"Which way were they headed?" Archer demanded.

"Toward Jackson. I'm in pursuit—"

"Christ, Jerry. The man who took Sydney isn't stable. He's been stalking her—he's the one who cut Ranger's brakes. You shouldn't—"

"Goddammit, man!" Jerry hollered. "We can all be heroes when we need to be." And then he ended the call.

"Shit," Archer swore. "Hunter, call Diehl. Have him get with Jackson PD. I want everyone coming for this guy from every direction."

Hunter immediately sank back into the back seat, firing off calls to every friend we had in law enforcement. Meanwhile, I stared numbly at the road in front of us, the dotted line not moving fast enough to catch up with my racing heart.

"We know where they're headed, Ranger. It's only a matter of time until one of us catches up."

"That's not what I'm worried about."

His gaze flicked to me. "What is it?"

I tried to swallow, but I couldn't. I'd wanted facts, but now they were drowning me.

"Darren was a fan of Sydney's books," I said hollowly. "If Jerry recognized the call for help, there's a good chance he did, too."

CHAPTER 27

Sydney

"Pull over." His voice was like nails along a chalkboard.

"I'm sorry, dear. What did you say?" Cindy asked, the chipperness in her voice catching at the very end.

No matter how hard I'd tried, she'd known something was wrong from the moment I slid into the seat with the stranger who'd stayed all but silent aside from directing her to take us to the bus station in Jackson.

Whether it was his mistake for assuming that Cindy didn't know me—didn't know better than most that Ranger and I were together—or the arrogance of his delusion, Darren had given himself away as a threat within moments of us being in the car.

I'd smiled and caught Cindy's gaze in the rearview, playing along with his charade and willing her to do the same. And she had.

Right up until she'd honked an SOS as we passed Jerry's hardware store.

It was Darren's mistake assuming I had no connection to the Uber driver he'd hired, but it was Cindy's unknowing error to assume the man abducting me hadn't read my books.

"*Pull. Over,*" he shouted, whipping the gun from my side and pointing it at Cindy's head.

"How rude," she huffed, and if it wasn't for the life-threatening predicament she was in, her brave response would've almost been comical.

"Now!" Darren punched the back of her seat with his hand holding the gun.

I jumped and tried to stop my cry, sure that the gun was going to go off.

I couldn't claim to know him at all. I'd received… millions… of fan emails over the entire course of my career, so it was only because of Ranger that I connected those dots and vaguely remembered his emails praising my books—praising me. But even recalling how he'd been in the coffee shop compared to this, I could only think that he'd gone through some sort of mental break or complete deterioration of his sanity.

One minute, he was telling me how much he loved me and that we were going to be together. The next, he hated me and threatened my life.

Cindy slowed the car, coasting to a stop on the side of the highway. We weren't that far out of town. Maybe only a couple of miles, but if we were stopping, that would buy us some time… or cost us our lives.

"This is all your fault, you know," he snapped at me and then barked at Cindy, "Get out!"

"Please—"

"Her blood is on your hands," he swore and shoved her out of the car.

My stomach plummeted, and I scrambled to get out of the car. "Please, Darren, you don't have to do this," I begged, rounding the hood. "It was just a horn. No one else will realize—no one will know my books like you do."

Except the man who could recite them all by memory.

I shoved Cindy behind me. "Please, just leave her here, and I'll go with you—"

"Leave me here? I'm not letting you get back in my car with this wackadoodle—"

"Enough!" Darren fired, and I pulled Cindy to the ground with me.

My heart pounded just as loud as the gun going off. It took a second to realize he'd fired the shot high. I didn't think I was crying, but there were tears on my cheeks.

"Then this is where it ends," he said somberly.

The way he shifted between rage and desperation and despondency wasn't normal. In any other scenario, I would've pitied the man who was so obviously mentally ill.

"This whole time, I loved you like no one else. Supported you. Waited for you."

Air rushed in and out of my lungs. I couldn't focus on what he was saying because it wasn't real. What was real was Cindy clutching at my shoulders. What was real was the cold snow underneath my fingertips and the gun aimed at my chest. What was real was the burn of fear exploding in my chest.

"The love you wrote about, the happy endings you wrote about... we could've had that, Sydney. We could've—" He sucked in a harsh breath, one personality overtaking another. "But you had to marry him."

Headlights appeared in the distance, approaching fast. My breath caught. I swore there was the faint sound of sirens on the breeze, but I wouldn't get my hopes up, not when Darren could end this all in an instant.

"Darren..."

He cocked the gun, betrayal turning his eyes to the darkest obsidian.

And then the vehicle began honking. Obnoxiously honking.

"It's Jerry," Cindy whispered behind me and gave me a little shake.

Everything happened so fast. Darren turned as the truck

approached, the lights glinting off the lines of wild rage creasing his face.

"What the fuck—" His snarl deepened as Jerry's truck headed straight toward him.

Oh my god. Was Jerry going to run him over?

Another second and Darren swung the gun toward the oncoming vehicle, firing off a round.

"Jerry!" I screamed.

Darren fired again. *Twice.* I grabbed Cindy's arm and pulled her back, propelling her away from the car as Jerry headed straight for the car.

Another second and there was a loud crash. An accident we knew was coming.

Cindy and I both stopped and turned. Smoke plumed from the crushed hood of Jerry's truck. The airbag had deployed. Metal and glass and debris scattered onto the road. He'd crashed into the side of Cindy's car—right between Darren and us.

Had he hit… had he killed…

"She's mine!"

A cry escaped my throat.

Jerry hadn't killed him, just put a barrier between us. *And put himself in danger.*

"Stay back here," I ordered Cindy and rushed toward the mangled truck.

If Jerry was still in there, he was a sitting duck.

I caught Darren's eyes over the wreckage; he'd dove out of the way at the last second, blood smearing his face. His lip curled and he began to round the back of Cindy's car.

"All your fault," he repeated, but before he got far, another SUV screeched to a stop.

Ranger.

My chest heaved with relief a second before the sirens I thought I'd been imagining became real, their loud warning getting closer.

"Put the gun down, Mr. Ross," Archer's voice boomed over the scene. "Sydney, you okay?"

"We're okay," I called back.

"You can't have her. I won't let you have her," he swore over and over again, trapped in his own delusion. He leveled the gun at the SUV.

A shadow caught the corner of my eye. *Hunter.* I pressed a hand to my chest, my exhale whooshing out as Hunter snuck around the back of Jerry's truck.

"You good?" he whispered.

I nodded and glanced over my shoulder as Cindy joined us.

"Stay behind me," he ordered, moving carefully in front of us.

Their plan clicked. Distract Darren while Hunter flanked him from behind.

"It's over," Archer growled.

Darren was outnumbered; he had to see that. But there was no recognizing it—not for a man in his state.

"She's mine. *She's. Mine!*" His gun held firm in front of him.

"No, she's not." *Ranger.* I'd know his voice anywhere. In the middle of any storm. From my first moment to my last. I'd always know that voice that was always so sure. So calm. *So loyal.* "She's my wife."

I sucked in a breath. Three words. One moment. Everything changed.

Darren roared.

Hunter straightened from behind the truck and shouted, "Drop it!"

But not before Darren fired off a single shot.

One shot.

And then three more.

It took a second to realize the others had come from Hunter, Archer, and Ranger—all of them hitting their target as he dropped to the ground.

Sirens arrived.

People shouted.

Chaos.

I felt hands on my arm—Hunter's hold to steady me, but I pulled away and ran for the other side of Jerry's truck.

"Ranger!" I collided with him and locked my arms around his neck, sagging against the heat of his body.

He grunted and held me tight.

Around us, activity swirled. The police. An ambulance. Footsteps and sirens. Conversation and commotion. It all swirled around us, but none of it could reach me. Not here. Not in his arms.

"I love you," he murmured against my hair, kissing the side of my head.

I whimpered into his neck, tears soaking my cheeks.

"I love you, too," I sobbed, my entire body shaking to get rid of the tension it had held at bay for the last hour.

I didn't know how long we stood like that, whether it was seconds or minutes before Archer's voice broke the bubble.

"Two shots, center mass. Pretty impressive, Ranger."

I turned my head, letting my hand slide to the front of his chest. Behind Archer, Darren's body lay sprawled on the ground. Lifeless. His weapon hanging from his fingertips.

There was a cop photographing the scene, another bagging the firearm for evidence, and two other men unrolling a body bag to take him away.

"Thank you," Ranger murmured, and I caught his tight smile. "I guess I do my best work under extreme terror."

A watery chuckle broke from between my lips. It was quickly drowned out by Archer's low laugh.

I tipped back to look at Ranger when I felt something wet seep under my fingers.

"Ranger." I drew my hand up in horror. It was so dark out, it was impossible to see the stain on his shirt, but on my fingers? His blood darkened the flats of my fingers and palms. "He shot you."

"*What?*" Archer roared. "Ranger, why did you—Christ." He yelled for the paramedics.

"I'm fine."

"No, you've been shot. The wound needs pressure—" he broke off as one of the EMTs came over. "My brother's been shot in the shoulder."

"It was a clean shot," Ranger informed the other man as he grabbed for a gauze pack.

"Archer!" Chief Diehl called out from over by the body.

Archer looked at me. "Sydney—"

"Go. We're good," I told Archer so he could go speak to the police.

My hand never left Ranger's as we went to the ambulance. The whole time, Ranger explained to them exactly where the bullet had gone, which important structures it had missed, and why it was really nothing more than a flesh wound.

In the mix of it all, I saw Jerry being wheeled to the second ambulance on a stretcher, Cindy walking next to his head. A cry bubbled loose, and I rushed over to them.

"Jerry!"

"I'm fine, I'm fine."

"Fine?" I choked out. "You're on a stretcher and your head is wrapped like a mummy."

"He has a concussion," Cindy translated. "They just want to take him to the hospital, do a few scans, and be sure everything is okay."

Jerry huffed and replied, "Trish is always saying I need some sense knocked into me, so I figure at least now I have proof that it was."

Somehow, I laughed even though I was still crying.

"Well, you certainly knocked some something into my car," Cindy grumbled.

I looked at the scene of the crash. Both cars were probably totaled, and it felt like a miracle that a concussion was all he'd managed to walk away with.

It felt like a miracle we were here at all… and it was because of them.

"Thank you," I murmured, wiping my face with my sleeve.

"Yes, thank you both." Ranger's smooth voice injected into the conversation as he came to stand beside me. His shoulder was bandaged and one arm was in a sling to keep everything stable, but his other arm he slid around my waist, cinching me to his side.

"Oh, don't thank us," Cindy tutted, her eyes twinkling. "That was invigorating. The moment I knew you were in trouble... seeing Jerry come out of the store... I knew he'd get my message!"

"And then I rammed your car to keep psycho man away from you two."

"You made a great team," I praised them hesitantly.

"Chief Diehl should hire us," Jerry declared.

"He should!" Cindy exclaimed gleefully. "We're practically professionals."

I looked between them in disbelief, scrambling for something to say to deter them, but the EMTs beat me to it, lifting Jerry into the ambulance.

"I'll ride with him," Cindy patted my arm. "Trish is meeting us at the hospital."

"Okay, but are you sure?" I squeaked.

"Sydney." Ranger distracted me as they closed the doors to the ambulance, not leaving me with any other choice. He reached up and brushed his fingertips along my cheek, threading them back through my hair.

I exhaled slowly, welcoming the goose bumps that covered my skin with warmth. My eyelids fluttered closed, feeling the pull of his lips as they dipped toward mine like two magnets ready to collide.

A soft moan melted off my tongue at his soft kiss. His tenderness brought a fresh well of tears to my eyes as he kissed me slowly. Deeply. Until I gladly let go of every other thought except for him.

"Let's go home," he murmured, and I felt myself nod.

As he guided us back to Archer's SUV, my eyes snagged on the ambulance that had treated him as it pulled out onto the road.

"Don't you have to go to the hospital, too?" I wondered. They'd taken Jerry for a suspected concussion but left the man with the gunshot wound? That didn't make sense. "You were shot—"

Ranger shook his head, a lock of hair spilling onto his forehead. "I told them I was fine."

My chest squeezed. He didn't know that, but I knew that argument wouldn't hold up. He most likely did know that he was fine, which was both annoying and relieving at the same time.

"And they don't want a doctor to take a look at you?" I probed.

Even in the dim emergency lighting, I could see color lift to his cheeks. "I told them I'm a doctor."

My jaw dropped. "What?"

"I am a doctor, so technically, it wasn't a lie."

"Oh no? Then what was it?" I choked out.

One dimple punctuated his grin. "A second opinion."

I groaned, unsure if I wanted to laugh or cry, as I tipped forward against the uninjured side of his chest.

"I'll get it looked at tomorrow," he promised. "Right now, I just want to be with you."

After everything, I couldn't argue with that.

CHAPTER 28

Ranger

"Ready?" I stood with my shoulder propping open the door to our hotel room, watching as Sydney did one more lap through the suite to make sure we hadn't forgotten anything.

We didn't, and it wasn't like the Worth wasn't three point seven miles from the apartment in case we needed to come back.

"Think of this as your honeymoon." Gunner had said when he'd ushered us into the biggest room at the Worth Hotel three weeks ago.

It was convenient that my brother and Della had just moved out of the suite and into their own home just after Christmas. They were preparing to start renting the room to hotel guests but generously told us to stay there for as long as we needed.

We'd taken three weeks.

Three weeks for me to recuperate. Three weeks for the window at the apartment to be repaired. Three weeks for the buzz in town to settle and the investigation to close.

Three weeks for just Sydney and me.

Not really. Between Mom and my brothers, Cindy and Jerry and Trish, we'd had a revolving door of guests. Even Gina flew out last weekend to visit. I'd never heard a person screech so loudly as when Sydney told her that she was staying out here permanently.

"Ready." Sydney stepped in front of me and smiled.

I tried to take her bag from her hand, but she tugged it back. "I can carry it. You were shot, and the doctor said to take it easy for four weeks."

"He was being overly cautious."

"And you are not that kind of doctor."

I harrumphed. "You weren't complaining about my knowledge of anatomy last night when my tongue was—"

"Ranger!" She scolded but couldn't keep the smile off her face as she clutched her bag and led the way down the hall.

The doctor said I could resume light activity after fourteen days. I'd tried to convince Sydney that sex wasn't just light activity but also benefited wound healing because it released oxytocin, but she wasn't having it. Our compromise had been oral sex until the full four weeks were up.

In the elevator, her hand slid into mine the way it always did.

"I love you." I couldn't stop saying it. I'd told her I loved her one-hundred-and-twenty-six times in the last two weeks, and the way it made me... feel... never changed.

Her smile widened.

"What is it?"

"I love the way you say it."

My head cocked to one side and I blinked. "How do I say it?"

She gave a little shrug. "Like it's a fact."

"It is a fact." I stared at her, confused.

I'd always perceived love as this amorphous emotion, something I wanted, but I was never sure how I'd be able to understand it enough to hold on to it. But it wasn't. It was concrete. It was as strong as gravity. As swift as lightning. As warm as the sun and as enduring as time. It was an equation made of variables of touch and taste, conversation and connection, but it was one that wasn't meant to be solved; it was meant to be lived.

Sydney laughed. "Exactly."

She pushed up on her tiptoes to press her lips to mine just before the doors opened.

By now, we were familiar with the morning staff at the hotel. Even though she was still supposed to be on maternity leave, more often than not, we ran into Della at one point or another in the lobby, usually with Skye swaddled to her chest.

A few days after the kidnapping and shoot-out, Archer and Hunter met us in one of the small conference rooms on the mezzanine. They informed us that the police had concluded their investigation into Darren Ross and confirmed what I'd suspected.

They'd also uncovered more details that were harder to stomach.

Darren had stalked Sydney from New York to Wyoming. Apparently, the search of his motel room revealed binders of photos and articles about Sydney. It was consistent with an erotomanic stalker but no less disturbing to hear. They'd also found his journal indicating he believed she'd come out here to begin a new life with him.

They reinterviewed everyone involved with every incident. Armed with a photo of Darren, the flower shop confirmed he was the one who placed the cash order. He'd then followed the delivery to the house, wanting to see Sydney's reaction. Instead, he'd watched me take the bouquet up to her apartment and stay late into the night.

It was the turning point.

The moment his love turned to hate.

He'd left the note stuck in the door for her to find the next morning. Whatever his plan was after that, he couldn't have accounted for Vince's attempt to terrorize and tank Sydney's reputation. Because of the press and the cameras and the security, Darren had been forced to keep his distance. The separation, combined with the published news that Sydney and I were married, sent him spiraling.

He'd cut my brakes, knowing I'd been leaving the apartment alone because Sydney wanted to avoid the cameras.

When we arrested Beekman, Darren had bided his time, watching as we pinned all his crimes on the paparazzi. He'd waited for them to clear... waited for things to settle. Ironically, he was so obsessed with Sydney he refused to believe the stories that we were actually married. But the night of our family dinner, the security cameras caught him lurking at the edge of the fence. He'd overheard Mom and me talking—realized that he'd lost Sydney to me, and that prompted the brick.

A final desperate attempt to take her for himself.

He'd overheard my brothers talking in the driveway about us going to the hotel. He'd called a car—Cindy—to take him there, where he waited for them to arrive.

The fact that he'd managed to get Sydney alone and back to a hired ride without a hiccup was quite a feat in itself, but that was where his luck ended. He'd been pronounced dead at the scene, his body returned to distant family members in New York to be buried.

"You lovebirds ready?" Cindy rubbed her hands together, waiting for us on the sidewalk alongside my Volvo.

Since her car had been totaled in the accident, I'd offered Cindy mine to drive until she got a new one.

"Ready to go home," Sydney said and hugged her.

Home.

Husband.

There were several words that played a much bigger part in my vocabulary nowadays, and I wasn't complaining.

Cindy gave us the latest update on her car hunt as well as Jerry's recovery, assuring us that book club was still happening this weekend because Jerry would have to be "brain dead" to postpone book club.

"Wait, where are we going?" Sydney asked as Cindy pulled a U-turn and headed in the opposite direction of the apartment.

"A short detour."

"A surprise," Cindy giggled from the front seat.

Sydney looked at me, but I forced myself to only smile. There was a lot I could say, but I wanted to wait until we got there.

A few minutes later, we turned down the drive to Reynolds Protective.

"Ranger..."

"I want to show you something." I squeezed her hand.

Cindy parked out front, waiting in the car as I led Sydney away from the building.

It wasn't the best day for this. There were inches of snow on the ground and the bite in the air was sharp, but I had to bring her here. Before we went back to the apartment, I had to know...

I wrapped my arm around her shoulder, guiding us behind the building.

"You see those trees over there?" I pointed to my right. "Beyond them is where Hunter and Zoey live. And farther beyond that, Archer and Keira." I took a step and angled us to the other side. "And right there is where Gunner and Della live now."

Their new construction home on the left was the most visible from where we stood.

"I didn't realize all your brothers lived here."

"We could, too."

Her head snapped up to mine.

"When we bought the land for the business, we each took equal portions of the remaining acreage." I lifted my hand again and pointed straight out. Fields led to a forest that led to mountains. "My parcel runs along the back of the property, closest to the park."

"Ranger..."

"I picked it because I thought it would be the easiest to donate to the park for conservation. I never planned on building on it because..." I trailed off and my lips pulled tight. "Well, I guess because I never planned on you."

Sydney faced me, locking her arms around my waist and searching my eyes.

"What about your mom?"

"Mom…" My mouth tipped in a smile. "Mom will be just fine without me living there."

I'd known it for a long time, but it was easier to believe I was staying there for her than accept that I'd been protecting Mom like my brothers had protected me—out of love, but unnecessarily.

As we'd spent the last couple of weeks at the hotel, I'd realized my error. I'd realized Mom was more than fine on her own. She was happy because I had Sydney. And that was when I started thinking about this land. It had always been a piece that didn't fit into the jigsaw puzzle of my life. A piece to a future that wasn't possible without Sydney.

"I'd like to build a home here. With you." My throat grew tight. "I want to build… my future with you."

My wife.

Her mouth parted, her eyes glistening.

"If you want," I added hoarsely.

A wide smile broke over her face. She rose up on her tiptoes, her answer coming a second before her lips touched mine.

"I do."

Those were my second-favorite set of words she'd ever spoken to me; the first came not long after.

"I love you, Ranger."

"I love you, too." I held her close. "And it's a fact."

EPILOGUE

Sydney
Six months later

"It's done." My cheeks hurt my smile was so wide.

"Really?" Ranger rose immediately from his desk.

We had adjoining offices in our new home, and I'd been buried deep in the editing cave of mine for the last three weeks.

After everything that happened with Darren, I'd taken a break from writing. A real break. One that gave me time and space to think about what I was doing and what I wanted to do. And during that time, I'd come to the conclusion that I was meant to be a writer. No matter what had happened, the good, the bad, *the stalker*, this was who I was meant to be.

So, I'd delved back into the final book of the Broken series and buried myself in the manuscript until I gave Jenny the happy ending she deserved—*the one I'd finally found for myself.*

Not only that but the idea had been thrown around (there was still dissent over whose initial idea it was) to open a romance bookstore in Wisdom. It was more than thrown around, actually. Zoey, Jerry, Trish, and I had met several times to discuss a business plan, location, and time line.

By next year, the Ever After bookstore would be the newest small business to grace Wisdom's Main Street.

"I just sent it off to Gina."

He let out a whoop and rushed over to me, lifting me up in his arms.

"Ranger!" I held on and laughed as he spun me in circles.

My toes touched the floor and that was when it hit me. Nausea. Like a tsunami.

I grunted, covered my mouth, and then bolted for the bathroom, my knees barely crashing in front of the toilet before I unloaded the oatmeal Ranger had made me for breakfast into the bowl.

When I looked up, there was a handful of paper towels waiting for me.

"Thank you," I mumbled, wiping my mouth.

Next came a small cup of mouthwash and a hand to help me stand.

"I don't know what's wrong—"

"You're pregnant," Ranger declared, and it was a good thing the mouthwash wasn't already in my mouth, or I would've showered him with it.

"What?" I balked and shook my head. "You can't know that. It's just nausea. I need to take a test—"

"You've been sick in the morning for the last month. Your breasts have been larger. Your sex drive more voracious—"

"Okay." I lifted my hands in surrender and then slowly met his gaze. "Am I… are we really…"

"Yes."

My hands went to my stomach. A baby. *Our baby.*

I could never doubt him. *How* it happened, I could only guess that in the mess of trying to finish this book and building and then moving into a new house, I'd forgotten to take my birth control.

I snapped my head up. "How long have you known?" I asked and then swished the Listerine in my mouth while he answered.

"I've suspected for the two weeks."

"And you didn't say anything?" I balked.

"Well, statistically, I still had a greater chance of being wrong then, whereas waiting until this week, the likelihood that you're not pregnant is very slim, considering how much sex we had when we first moved in."

Heat flooded my cheeks… and between my legs.

We'd had sex in every room of our new home to see if it was different depending on the room. It wasn't. It was mind-blowing whether it was on the bed or the bathroom floor. But we'd repeated the experiments several times just to be sure.

"Is it… are you…" The words balled in my throat. We'd ended up married under pressurized circumstances, and though we'd talked about kids—it was impossible not to when my ovaries basically exploded every time I saw Ranger with his nieces—talking about having them and actually having one were two very different things.

"The thought of you having my baby actually makes me really horny."

I coughed and then choked and then laughed.

His hands framed my face, making sure he found my gaze before adding, "And really happy."

"Me too." A sudden rush of tears filled my eyes.

"I love you, Sydney."

"Fact?" I always asked now; it was our own little joke.

His dimples pressed into his cheeks. "Fact."

"I love you, too." And I wasn't sure I could get any happier.

I brought my lips to his and kissed him until we were stumbling backward to the bedroom, that appetite he'd mentioned kicking in.

Clothes came off. Bodies came together. And within minutes, he had my body coming apart with pleasure as he released into me.

"Was this the ending you'd write for yourself?" he murmured, pulling my body close to his.

"Not even close."

"No?" he asked, worried.

I smiled. "This isn't an ending, Ranger. Just another beginning."

One day, I'd explain that happy endings were only for books. In real life, love was only ever the start of happy beginnings.

BONUS EPILOGUE

Ranger

Five years later...

"What do you think would happen if I went up there and told them I changed my mind?"

My head snapped from the growing crowd to where Mom peeked out of the window beside me. Almost all of Wisdom was waiting for her. The street closed off and packed with people outside the Worth Hotel.

"Well, I should let Archer know before you do that so we can prepare—"

"I'm not changing my mind, honey." Mom reached for my arm and squeezed, smiling at me tenderly.

"Oh."

She sighed. "I'm excited for a new adventure, but it's bittersweet to see this one end."

Today was Mom's last day on the job. Her last day leading this town as the mayor of Wisdom, and everyone had come out to honor her.

"You could stay."

Three terms. Twelve years. That was how long Mom had been mayor. The longest serving in the town's history. And no one was forcing her to go. If Lydia Reynolds said she was running for mayor again, she'd win the election by a landslide, and that wasn't a supposition; I'd run the various statistics and probabilities against current population data and voting trends, and every time she came out on top.

Mom hummed. "I think it's time for me to start a new chapter."

There was a twinkle in her eyes that only appeared when she was thinking about, talking about, or doing anything with her grandchildren. Which was what she was going to be spending almost all of her time doing from now on.

In five years, the four of us had produced a lot of grandchildren. Nine currently, with two more on the way. And Mom couldn't get enough.

So, she'd decided not to run again. And we'd built her a small cabin on the Reynolds Protective property so she'd be close to all of us.

"Da-da!"

I spun at my daughter's voice. "Jane." I scooped her up, holding her warmth to me. "Why aren't you with your sisters and Uncle Gunner?"

"Because she's too quick for me," Gunner replied, striding into the room with his son, Drake, in one arm and my other toddler daughter, Betty, in the other.

Behind him followed his daughter, Skye, and Hunter's daughter, Charlie, who laughed and giggled to themselves, the two of them so inseparable that a large majority of the town thought they were sisters.

"Where's Keira?" I asked.

Gunner and Keira were on kid patrol with slight assistance from Zoey and Sydney, though not much because the two of them were currently pregnant.

"She's lecturing Theo not to chase Naomi around the hotel."

"He's only four. It's unlikely that he'll comprehend what she's—"

"Do you want to tell her that?" Gunner charged with an arched brow. "Because I sure as sh— Because I don't."

I swallowed. "No."

"Didn't think so."

Theo was Archer and Keira's oldest son and Naomi Hunter's younger daughter.

"Where's Lucy?" Mom asked as she went around, doling out kisses to every child in sight.

Lucy was my youngest daughter at eleven months old, but in another couple months, she'd be ousted when Sydney gave birth again.

"I think Sydney is feeding her?" Gunner's face scrunched. "There are too many of them. It's an army of children. A zoo. Ranger is the only one smart enough to keep track of them all, which is probably why he's on his fourth one."

I shifted Jane to my other arm. "Being able to count isn't how I ended up with four children. I don't think I need to explain to you the mechanics of how babies are made."

"Well you certainly have it down to a science."

Four babies. A new home. Sydney's bookstore. A lot of snow-angel moments had happened in five years. More than I thought would ever happen in my lifetime.

"I should head out there before your brothers think I skipped town." Mom shuffled by us and slipped out of the hotel's dining room and into the lobby.

A second later, Sydney burst through the door, holding Lucy to her shoulder while burping her.

"Jane." She sighed. "There you are."

Jane curled into my shoulder, giving her mother a playful smile.

"Alright, I think that's my cue to go drag Della from the kitchen," Gunner excused himself.

After Mom's short farewell ceremony, we were hosting a small luncheon here at the Worth, and of course, Della was coordinating everything.

"You are such a daddy's girl, Miss Jane Reynolds." Sydney gently rubbed Jane's back and then looked at me and smiled. "And I don't blame her."

The way she looked at me lit a fire in my blood, and I dropped my head down to kiss her, almost stealing one before she pulled back.

"If you start that, we'll never make it outside, and your sister just got here."

Gwen, her husband Chevy, and their twin boys had flown in from California to celebrate Mom's retirement. They were supposed to arrive yesterday, but their flight had been canceled.

"Well, if Gwen just got here, then we have at least another seven minutes while she hugs and talks to Mom and my brothers. And seven minutes is plenty of time for us—"

"Ranger!" Sydney playfully swatted my arm, her eyes glittering with want.

Pregnancy had only added a layer of intensity to our intimacy, but I guess with baby number four on the way, that was obvious.

"Rain check?" I pressed a kiss to the side of her head and led her to the door.

"For your seven minutes in heaven?" she teased.

I dipped my head to her ear and murmured, "I prefer seven minutes in Sydney."

Outside, we greeted Gwen and her family, the five of us collecting on the stairs and sidewalk outside the Worth. The line of Mom's grandchildren almost spanned the whole block.

I threaded my hand with Sydney's, our eyes connecting as we shared a secret smile. After five years and three kids, the germs passed between hands were nothing in the grand scheme of it all… except a reminder of where we started. *And how much cleaner it would be to be kissing her right now.*

Our attention shifted then to the podium, Mom taking a stand at the mic as the crowd settled into a reverent silence.

"I've never been one for words or long speeches. After twelve years, I think you all know that it's been my actions and my dedication to this town that have spoken the most," Mom began, pausing to smile and keep herself collected. "But I do want to say thank you. It has been my honor and pleasure to serve as mayor to the town… to the people… who held me up when I wasn't sure I'd ever stand again."

Sydney curled into my side, lifting her hand and wiping a tear from her cheek. In the corner of my eye, I saw Gwen blinking rapidly before Zoey handed her a tissue.

"But now, I must accept my promotion from mayor to Mee-Maw, which, at this rate, might turn into another town all on its own." The crowd chuckled as she motioned to all of us—all of her grandchildren.

"So, before I go and we get to the good part of all this—the food—I want to remind you the heart of wisdom is kindness." She paused. "The heart of this town is kindness. And that's not the legacy I leave behind, it's the legacy I've merely guarded for the last twelve years. A legacy that remains even when I go. A legacy that will be carried forward by Ms. Nelson."

Mom motioned to the younger woman who was succeeding her, Janine Nelson, whose family had been ranchers in Wisdom for as long as I could remember. And then, taking her hand, she lifted both their arms and cheered, "To Wisdom."

"*To Wisdom.*"

Like the burst of a damn, the shouts and claps and festivities began.

A day full of celebrations culminated in family taco night back at Archer's house. There was also cake and more champagne. The kids played until they tired themselves out. And finally, we all ended up gathered in the living room around the fireplace, a warm weight hanging in the air.

It was the end of an era. For all of us.

The thought felt like a weighted blanket: heavy yet soothing.

We'd come through so much together *as a family*.

"Did you see this coming, Baby Brains?" Gunner met my gaze and nodded to the sleepy scene.

Archer sat with Keira in his lap, the woman he'd thought had died all those years ago; their two sons asleep on pillows on the floor next to Hunter's two daughters, the four of them sporting fake tattoos that Keira drew on their arms.

Hunter sat in front of Zoey, who was on the couch, her one leg draped over his shoulder as he rubbed her foot, the woman who'd fled to Wisdom to escape a stalker. Gunner sat on the love seat with Della, with Skye and Drake sleeping on their laps. Gwen and Chevy were also sitting on the floor, their sons tucked in bed in Archer's guest room. And finally, Mom, who stood by the fireplace, gently swaying Lucy in her arms.

I dipped my chin down, looking at my immediate family. Jane curled to one of my sides, Betty stretched over my lap, and Sydney tucked under my other arm.

I'd never been surrounded by such love before.

And even if I had... without Sydney... I wouldn't have recognized it.

"It was statistically unlikely," I admitted. The four of us finding love? Having families? Mom retiring from her run as mayor?

A statistical improbability.

But here we were.

"So we beat the odds?" Gunner smirked, pleased.

I started to reply when Gwen chimed in, "I always knew we were going to end up here."

She had the attention of the whole room, her smile lighting it up just like Mom's did.

"No, you didn't. None of us were looking for love—"

"Because love isn't something you look for," Mom corrected, both of them halting to let the matriarch speak. "Love finds you whether you're ready for it or not." Her eyes glistened as she looked over the room. "And it's the best thing to ever happen to all of you. And to me, to be able to witness it." Her lip quivered, her attention stuck on me for a moment as she added, "Your dad would be so happy."

She was blinking back tears as Gwen went up and hugged her.

After a few moments of silence, Gunner chimed back in, "All I'm saying, Gwen, is if Ranger didn't know—"

"Yes, I did," she cut him off decidedly. "And Sydney knew, too."

I looked down at my wife, watching her brows lift slightly. "I did?" she said, her voice taking on a sleepy drawl.

"Of course, you did." Gwen rested her head on Chevy's shoulder. "Your books would never end any other way."

"True." Sydney hummed, tipping her head up to look at me with a coy smile.

"It's a eucatastrophe," I declared, watching ten sets of eyes stare at me blankly.

"A ukulele?" Gunner cocked his head, trying to hold back a smile.

I shook my head. "Eucatastrophe. A sudden and favorable resolution of events."

"Seriously? Now I think you're just making this shit up," he teased.

"It's a real word. You can look it up—"

"Or you could just call it a happy ending like the rest of us." Gunner winked at me.

"It's a eucatastrophe," I muttered under my breath.

"How about"—Sydney broke in, her hand searching for mine as she smiled up at me—"we just agree that in the end, love wins."

It did.

Statistically speaking, it always did.

The End.

OTHER WORKS BY
DR. REBECCA SHARP

Covington Security
Betrayed
Bribed
Beguiled
Burned
Branded
Broken
Believed
Bargained
Braved

The Vigilantes
The Vendetta

Reynolds Protective
Archer
Hunter
Gunner
Ranger

Carmel Cove
Beholden
Bespoken
Besotted
Befallen
Beloved
Betrothed

The Kinkades
The Woodsman
The Lightkeeper

The Odyssey Duet
The Fall of Troy
The Judgment of Paris

The Sacred Duet
The Gargoyle and the Gypsy
The Heartbreak of Notre Dame (TBA)

Country Love Collection
Tequila
Ready to Run
Fastest Girl in Town
Last Name
I'll Be Your Santa Tonight
Michigan for the Winter
Remember Arizona
Ex To See
A Cowboy for Christmas
Meant to Be

The Winter Games
Up in the Air
On the Edge
Enjoy the Ride
In Too Deep
Over the Top

The Gentlemen's Guild
The Artist's Touch
The Sculptor's Seduction
The Painter's Passion

Passion & Perseverance Trilogy
(A Pride and Prejudice Retelling)
First Impressions
Second Chances
Third Time is the Charm

Standalones
Reputation
Redemption
Revolution: A Driven World Novel
Hypothetically

Want to #staysharp with everything that's coming?
Join my newsletter!

ABOUT THE AUTHOR

Rebecca Sharp is a contemporary romance author of over thirty published novels and dentist living in PA with her amazing husband, affectionately referred to as Mr. GQ.

She writes a wide variety of contemporary romance. From new adult to extreme sports romance, forbidden romance to romantic comedies, her books will always give you strong heroines, hot alphas, unique love stories, and always a happily ever after. When she's not writing or seeing patients, she loves to travel with her husband, snowboard, and cook.

She loves to hear from readers. You can find her on Facebook, Instagram, and Goodreads. And, of course, you can email her directly at author@drrebeccasharp.com.

If you want to be emailed with exclusive cover reveals, upcoming book news, etc. you can sign up for her mailing list on her website: www.drrebeccasharp.com

Happy reading!
xx
Rebecca

Printed in Great Britain
by Amazon

ea9cac49-04c1-4b71-9802-227bd1264416R01